The
STUDIO
GIRLS

Also by Lisa Ireland

The One and Only Dolly Jamieson
The Secret Life of Shirley Sullivan
The Art of Friendship
The Shape of Us
Honey Hill House
Feels Like Home
Breaking the Drought

The STUDIO GIRLS

LISA IRELAND

MICHAEL JOSEPH
an imprint of
PENGUIN BOOKS

MICHAEL JOSEPH

UK | USA | Canada | Ireland | Australia
India | New Zealand | South Africa | China

Michael Joseph is part of the Penguin Random House group of companies
whose addresses can be found at global.penguinrandomhouse.com

Penguin
Random House
Australia

First published by Michael Joseph in 2024

Cover design by Debra Billson © Penguin Random House Australia Pty Ltd
Cover photography by Inga Borska/Arcangel, everettovrk/Adobe Stock
Author photograph by Nikita Cherry
Typeset in 11.5/16 pt Adobe Caslon Pro/Mrs Eaves San OT by Midland Typesetters, Australia

Printed and bound in Australia by Griffin Press, an accredited
ISO AS/NZS 14001 Environmental Management Systems printer

A catalogue record for this
book is available from the
National Library of Australia

ISBN 978 1 76134 544 9

penguin.com.au

MIX
Paper | Supporting
responsible forestry
FSC® C018684

We at Penguin Random House Australia acknowledge that Aboriginal and Torres Strait Islander
peoples are the Traditional Custodians and the first storytellers of the lands on which we live and
work. We honour Aboriginal and Torres Strait Islander peoples' continuous connection to Country,
waters, skies and communities. We celebrate Aboriginal and Torres Strait Islander stories, traditions
and living cultures, and we pay our respects to Elders past and present.

For Wendy

3 October 1955

I can't get the sound of the camera shutter out of my mind.

Have I done the right thing?

Think about the rent.

It started innocently enough, with me in my swimsuit by the pool. Danny has always been a gentleman in the past, so I wasn't worried. Besides, the money was too good to turn down.

The first few shots were of me lounging in my bathing suit, dangling my feet in the pool. But then he moved on to the real reason I was there.

'That's lovely, honey.' Click. 'Drop the beachball.' Click. 'Turn to face the pool and look back at me.' Click, click. 'Good! Stay like that, but unfasten the top of your bathing suit.' Click, click, click. 'Attagirl. Now let it fall.' Click, click, click, click. 'Turn to face me.' Click, click . . . CLICK!

Think about the dress.

'Do I have to show my face?'

He shrugged. 'Men don't just want tits and ass. They want a pretty face. But you could wear a wig if you like. And we could play around with sunglasses for some of the shots. Besides, my client is in Europe. No one here will ever see the pictures.'

1

What other choice did I have?

I hope Danny's true to his word. The movie studios are quite uptight about their stars. I don't want to lose a part once I'm famous because of these silly photos.

And I WILL be famous! Mark my words.

27 December 1999

Breakfast at Sal's Diner on a Monday feels odd. It's not our regular day, but with Christmas falling on Saturday this year, we've had to reschedule.

Julia had suggested giving the whole thing a miss this week and I'd agreed. 'Fine by me. We'll see each other at the Studio Club reunion on Tuesday anyway.'

But Peggy wouldn't hear of it. 'We won't get a chance to talk properly at the reunion. Besides, I'm sure we'll all need to debrief after Christmas.' So here we are.

Peggy waves as I wend my way to our regular table, and I make an exaggerated 'O' with my mouth to demonstrate my shock at her punctuality. Peggy used to be the most reliable of us all, but these days she has a lot on her plate – too much, if you ask me. Between shooting her long-running TV show *At Home with Peggy Carmichael*, her church commitments, the charities she runs and her ever-demanding daughter, it's a miracle she finds time to squeeze in a weekly catch-up with her two oldest friends.

She rolls her eyes at my expression and stands so she can greet me with a kiss. 'Don't look at me like that, Sadie.'

Even dressed casually, Peggy is the epitome of style. Her thick blonde hair is smoothed back into a low ponytail, and she's wearing designer jeans and a white T-shirt topped with a fashionable (and no doubt expensive) coral linen blazer. Personally, I favour comfort over fashion, but today's outfit – a mustard-coloured velour tracksuit with sneakers – is a particularly poor effort. The fleeting look of distaste on Peggy's face confirms this ensemble is one that should be reserved for early-morning dog walks only.

'I can't believe you're the first to arrive,' I say, as Peggy sits and I slide into the opposite side of the booth.

'I couldn't wait to get out of the house. Harmony and the kids are still at my place. She arrived on Christmas Eve and announced that she and Jett had split. She's moving back home.'

'Again?' I fish in my handbag for my glasses so I can read the specials menu.

'Yes, again.' Peggy sighs as she watches me perch the specs on the end of my nose. 'I don't know why you bother with those. You don't need to read the menu. You always order the same thing.'

'The specials change weekly, and I like to make an informed choice.'

Peggy's expression reveals her scepticism at my explanation, but she doesn't argue. 'Right. Anything good on there?'

'You'd be able to see for yourself if you put on your reading glasses.'

'Touché. But they make me look like an old granny.'

'You are a granny.'

She pokes out her tongue and we both laugh.

'So how long do you think you'll have Harmony for?'

'Who knows? I honestly don't want to think about it. Let's talk about you instead. How did you survive the holidays?'

'Fine,' I say, not wanting to go into detail about my sister's visit from New York. 'Hannah was the same as ever.' I have had a turbulent relationship with my only sibling since our teens, but age has mellowed us and for the past ten years – since my Gianni died – Hannah has insisted that we spend Christmas Day together.

Peggy knows what I mean without me having to explain. She's heard it all before. 'You saw Angela and her family, though?'

4

I smile. 'Yes, on Christmas Eve. That was wonderful, as always.'

Every year Gianni's sister, Angela, and her husband, Gabe, open their home to a seemingly endless stream of relatives and friends, who arrive carrying trays of lasagne and cannelloni. Gabe, beer in hand, tends to the pork spit roast in the yard while Angela brings out platter after platter of appetisers. The abundance of good food and wine and effervescent company is always bittersweet. I'm glad to be counted as family by these beautiful people, but being with them always makes Gianni's absence palpable. It breaks my heart that his nieces and nephew call me Zia, but the youngest of them can't remember their Zio Gianni.

Peggy nods and, perhaps sensing my melancholy, changes the topic. 'I hope Julia won't be too much longer. I have news I'm dying to tell you.'

Before I can ask her what sort of news, Joe appears with a pot of coffee and pours us both a cup. 'Would you like to order yet, ladies, or are you waiting for Miss Newman to join you?'

'We'll wait, Joe, thanks. Julia will be along any minute,' Peggy says, and then, as if summoned by the mention of her name, Julia sweeps into the diner, breathlessly spouting her apologies as she makes her way to the table.

'Darlings, I'm so sorry,' she says. 'Tony called just as I was about to leave and I simply couldn't get away. You know what he's like.'

'Coffee, Miss Newman?' Joe asks.

Julia bestows her most charming smile on him. 'Goodness, Joe, am I ever going to convince you to call me Julia? "Miss Newman" makes me feel so old.'

Joe blushes. He has had a crush on Julia from the day he started working here, and she can't seem to stop herself from fanning the flames. The fact that Julia is old enough to be his mother doesn't seem to bother either of them. To be fair, Julia looks damn fine for sixty-five.

Obviously she has good genes, because while Peggy spends a fortune on maintaining her looks – having her hair coloured and styled and booking herself in for 'spa treatments' (otherwise known as cosmetic surgery) – Julia is ageing naturally. Her shoulder-length hair is a glossy grey, a colour not that far removed from the ash-blonde she sported in her youth. The crinkly laugh lines around her eyes and a somewhat crepey neck are the only real signs that she's entered her senior years. In a turtleneck and sunglasses she could easily pass for forty-five or younger. Even now, years after she filmed her last movie, she still deports herself like the star she used to be.

Once upon a time, Julia Newman was one of the most recognisable faces in Hollywood, but her onscreen career was short lived. After making ten movies in under a decade she gave it all up to start her own production company in the 1960s, which has now grown to be one of the biggest studios in America. Her face might not be gracing our screens anymore, but as one of the richest and most powerful women in Hollywood, she's as much of a public figure as she ever was.

Peggy shuffles over and Julia takes a seat beside her. 'Coffee would be great,' she says. 'Thank you, Joe.' She looks at him with doe eyes and he scurries off to the kitchen.

'Didn't you just spend Christmas with Tony?' Peggy asks. 'Haven't you had enough of each other? More to the point, isn't his wife sick of you?'

Julia laughs. 'She doesn't mind. She knows there's nothing romantic between us. Besides, he was calling to talk business.'

As far as ex-husbands go, I'm willing to bet that there's not a nicer one than Tony. He and Julia have been divorced for many years now, but they spend nearly every holiday together and talk on the phone most days. To the outside world this probably seems strange, but it's not that surprising, really. Their marriage was never a traditional one. It was a union based on mutual need rather than love. Julia used to say that was the secret to their success. Her vision combined with his business acumen – and a timely injection of funds courtesy of Tony's wealthy family – were the building blocks that took Jeweltone from a niche production company back in the 1960s to the behemoth it is today. Although they have long been divorced, the business keeps them intimately connected, and they're still the best of friends.

I cock an eyebrow. 'What business were you discussing? Anything exciting?'

'Unfortunately not. Can you believe I've been offered a role in a sitcom? As a grandmother, for heaven's sake!' Julia screws up her nose.

I look at her incredulously. 'How on earth did that come about?'

'Tony, god love him. I was complaining about missing the more creative side of filmmaking. I was talking about directing, of course, but Tony misinterpreted my words and put out feelers for acting roles.' Her cheeks flush pink and she takes a sip of water.

'Doesn't matter how you got the role, it's still exciting to be cast,' Peggy says. 'Congratulations!'

'Good grief, I'm not going to take the job.'

'Why not?' Peggy's tone is defensive. After all these years and all her success, Peggy is still sensitive about the fact that Julia was a bona fide movie star, whereas her fame came through roles on the small screen.

'It's humiliating enough that Tony went about begging people to cast me, but this being the only role on offer is downright mortifying.'

Peggy opens her mouth to argue but I nudge her under the table with my foot and she has the good sense to close it again.

Julia throws up her hands in frustration. 'It's insulting, that's what it is. I mean, not that I was looking for an acting gig, but if I was, I wouldn't want to play someone's grandmother. Why is it that women our age are never the main character? We're always an add-on – someone's mother or wife, never someone's lover. And god forbid an old crone like me be cast as the lead. There are no major roles for women in their sixties.'

'You're the head of a studio,' I say. 'Can't you do something about that?'

'Believe me, I'm trying, but I'm only one voice at Jeweltone. And, to be honest with you, there's a lack of great scripts – at least great commercial scripts. It's hard to get a project over the line if the team can't see how we'd make money out of it.' She looks at me. 'You should write something for us, Sadie. I could produce and direct. We could cast Peggy as the lead.'

'That would be great,' Peggy says. Her eyes flash with excitement. 'Wouldn't it be a blast to all work together again? Just imagine the fun we could have.'

7

Julia claps her hands and beams, clearly pleased with herself for coming up with this suggestion, but it's not something I can get on board with, even hypothetically. Best to be up-front about it. 'I'm sorry, but I can't do that.'

Peggy frowns. 'But—'

I raise my hand and motion for her to stop. 'No. Let's not go there. I'm not a writer anymore. Can we please change the subject?'

Peggy looks like she wants to argue the point, but eventually she says, 'Okay, okay. I think it's a shame, that's all.'

Always the peacemaker, Julia redirects the conversation. 'What's your gossip, Peg? I'm dying to know.'

Peggy leans forward, resting her elbows on the table, beckoning Julia and me to come closer. 'Oh, girls,' she says, her voice almost a whisper. 'I can't believe this. I have news about tomorrow night's reunion.'

Before she can elaborate further, Joe arrives with Julia's coffee and asks if we're ready to order. We're creatures of habit. Peggy has waffles, Julia has an egg-white omelette and I order two eggs, sunny side up, bacon, toast and a hashbrown. Just as she does every week, Julia comments that I am so lucky to be able to eat what I want without gaining weight.

'Good grief, Julia, you've been saying that since we were girls sharing meals together at the club, and for decades I've been telling you the same thing: stop worrying about your weight. You are gorgeous. A few extra pounds won't change that. At our age, we need to embrace who we are.'

Julia looks embarrassed. 'I know you're right. It's habit, I guess, after all those years of being forced to diet by the studio.'

'Jules, seriously, eat a donut every now and then, would you? It's not a crime, and besides, they're delicious.'

She laughs. 'So I hear.'

Peggy seems keen to move on. 'Do you remember Babs, from the club?'

Julia nods. 'Of course. She's one of the reunion organisers, isn't she?'

'She's on the committee,' Peggy says. 'And she's also on the board of my Books for Kids charity. We had a book drive before Christmas and Babs called me this morning to give me the final figures.'

'Right,' Julia says, glancing towards the kitchen. 'I hope our food won't be long. I'm starving.'

'Julia, listen!' Peggy snaps. 'Babs said she'd just looked at the RSVPs for tomorrow night and that the turnout was excellent. And then she told me something I could hardly believe. Girls, you'll never guess who's coming to the reunion.'

Goosebumps rise on my skin despite the warmth of the room. I suddenly know what Peggy is about to say.

Peggy pauses, her eyes darting from me to Julia and back again before she finally announces, 'Vivienne Lockhart!'

I let out an involuntary gasp but say nothing. I have no words to express the mix of emotions I'm experiencing.

Julia's mouth tightens. 'Are you sure?'

'Who knows if she'll actually go through with it, but she's replied to say she's coming. Frankly, I'm shocked that the committee was able to find her. No one has heard from her for years.' She turns to me. 'You haven't been in touch with her, have you, Sadie? I mean, if she was going to contact anyone it would be you.'

I shake my head. All four of us were close back in our Studio Club days. Vivienne and I were roommates, and she was more like a sister than a friend to me. I tried my best to stay in touch with her after she left Hollywood. Not that Julia and Peggy know that. At the time of her departure, Vivienne was persona non grata as far as they were concerned. We exchanged letters and even spoke on the phone occasionally at first, but after a while Vivienne stopped writing and I lost track of where she was. It's been decades since we communicated.

She was on the cusp of being a star back in the 1950s, so none of us could believe it when she suddenly left Hollywood. She'd worked so hard to be taken seriously as an actress, and I thought – we all thought – she would let nothing stand in the way of her success. Being her roommate, I knew her better than the others and maybe that's why I still have a place in my heart for Vivienne.

'I don't think I can be in the same room as that woman,' Julia says. 'Maybe I won't go.'

9

'Oh, Jules.' I reach across the table and take her hand. 'There will be more than a hundred people at the function. Even if she does come, you don't have to talk to her. In a crowd like that, she'll be easy to avoid. You've been looking forward to tomorrow night for ages. And with the old place up for sale, this might be the last chance we get to spend time there. Don't let this news stop you from coming.'

There's a look of grim determination on Peggy's face. 'That woman's caused enough heartache. Vivienne Lockhart can't be allowed to spoil our reunion too.'

1955

Chapter 1

Sadie

Sadie Shore had been dreaming about her arrival at the Hollywood Studio Club for months. In her mind, it would be a triumphant moment. She would stride gracefully across the lobby, impressing her fellow residents with her poise and style. The other girls would look at her approvingly and she would smile in return, knowing she had finally found the place she belonged.

Dressing in the latest fashion wasn't usually high on her list of priorities. In fact, she'd spent most of her university days dressed in pants and button-down shirts or old sweaters stolen from Papa's closet – a fact that caused her mother great disappointment. When Mother had finally relented and agreed to let her move to California, her one stipulation had been that Sadie update her wardrobe. Much to everyone's surprise, Sadie had agreed. She and her mother had quite different objectives – Mother hoped she'd find a suitable husband, whereas Sadie craved the freedom of her own career – but at least they could both agree that in Hollywood, image was everything.

Her mother had spared no expense, filling Sadie's suitcase with outfits from New York's finest fashion houses. The belted grey wool dress and jacket Sadie had chosen for her arrival at the club was considered the height of fashion, and Sadie had surmised it would create the perfect first impression. There was just one tiny factor she had neglected to consider: the Californian heat.

Her grey suit was damp under the arms and crumpled from the various modes of transport she'd endured. The combination of heat and perspiration had turned her carefully styled brunette curls into a mop of frizz. Her journey, which had begun three days earlier at Penn Station and ended with a taxi ride from the bus terminal in downtown Los Angeles this afternoon, had left her frazzled and frumpy. As she dragged her oversized suitcase up the steps and through the entrance of the Hollywood Studio Club, she felt like an ungainly giraffe.

To make matters worse, the (smaller than she'd imagined) foyer was buzzing with activity. Peppy cheerleader types sporting ponytails and poodle skirts cast pitying glances at her as she wobbled her way to reception in her yet-to-be-broken-in heels.

A glamorous blonde dressed in a pale pink short-sleeved sweater and a tight black pencil skirt stood in front of her at the reception desk, gleefully counting out twenty-dollar bills. 'There!' she said, jubilantly. 'That's everything I owe, plus two months in advance.'

'Vivienne, dear,' said the worried-looking woman behind the desk, 'where did you get so much money? I know we've been asking you to pay up, but I didn't expect . . .' The woman glanced at Sadie and lowered her voice slightly, but not enough to make herself inaudible. 'I told you we could put a payment plan in place. Tell me you haven't gone and done something—'

'Don't you worry, my darling Miss McGovern. I promise I haven't done anything illegal. This money is all mine. Well, all *yours* now!'

With that, the blonde sashayed away from the desk and up a set of stairs, leaving the woman behind the desk with an exasperated expression on her face. She peered over her cat-eye glasses at Sadie. 'Yes?'

Sadie placed her suitcase on the floor and spoke as confidently as her tired and nervous disposition would allow. 'Hello. I'm Sadie Shore.'

The frown remained unchanged. 'Miss Florence McGovern, Studio Club director. How may I help you?'

'I'm checking in today.'

Florence McGovern looked her up and down, and then opened a binder on the counter, sighing as she did so. 'I'm afraid I don't have any Shores registered for check-in. Or any Sadies, for that matter. Perhaps you have the wrong establishment. This is *the* Hollywood Studio Club.' Her emphasis made it clear that Sadie was most definitely out of her league.

Sadie's stomach squirmed, and not solely because she'd hardly managed to eat anything since boarding the train in New York. To her dismay she felt tears pricking the backs of her eyes. 'Are you sure?'

'Quite sure.' Miss McGovern snapped the binder shut.

Not having accommodation wasn't on the long list of things Sadie had been nervous about. When she'd confided that she was planning to escape to Hollywood, Aunt Sarah – her confidante and co-conspirator – had made inquiries on her behalf and subsequently taken care of all the arrangements. Sadie had worried a little about travelling across the country alone, but she assumed all would be well once she arrived at the Studio Club. It wasn't like Aunt Sarah to make a mistake.

This was a disaster. Her aunt had paid two months' rent in advance. Sadie had some cash in her purse for living expenses, but that wouldn't last long. Maybe she'd have enough for a night or two in a hotel, but she really had no idea of what that would cost, let alone whether it would be safe to stay in a Hollywood hotel on her own. Her mother would have conniptions at the very idea.

'Please, Miss McGovern, could you have another look? My aunt assured me she had made a firm booking.' Despite her best efforts to remain calm, there was a distinct waver in her voice.

The expression on Miss McGovern's face softened. 'Do you have somewhere to go? Relatives or friends who could take you for the night?'

'All of my family and friends are in New York. That's why Aunt Sarah chose this place for me. She wanted me to be somewhere safe.'

'Sarah, you say?' Miss McGovern's forehead creased again as she flipped open the binder once more. She ran her finger down a list of names and looked up at Sadie. 'What is your aunt's surname?'

'Freeman.'

Florence McGovern smiled, and Sadie realised the studio director wasn't so old after all. 'Mystery solved! I'm not sure how this happened, but there's been a clerical error. One of the girls who helps out in the office has accidently recorded your aunt as the person checking in. I'm happy to tell you there is a room for you here after all.'

Relief flooded through Sadie's body and – to her horror – the tears she'd been holding back began to fall.

Miss McGovern reached beneath the desk and produced a freshly pressed handkerchief, which she handed to Sadie. 'I'm sorry for the mix-up.' She was frowning again. 'Are you all right?'

Sadie dabbed her eyes and pulled herself together. This wasn't the first impression she'd hoped to make. 'Quite. I'm sorry. It's been a long journey.'

'Indeed.' Miss McGovern produced a typewritten sheet titled *House Rules*. 'We like to think we are quite progressive here at the Studio Club; however, there are some non-negotiable rules, which we enforce for everyone's safety and comfort.'

'Of course.'

'Your rent is paid on the first of the month. It includes use of the rehearsal areas and all other club facilities. There are sign-up sheets to book the rehearsal areas, and we also have music, acting and dance classes onsite that you can participate in if you choose. You'll get two meals a day. Most girls have breakfast and dinner here, unless they have a date, of course.' She pointed to a ledger on the left-hand side of the counter. 'This is the sign-in book. You must sign out when you leave the building and sign back in on return.'

'I understand.'

'Curfew is midnight – you'll need a special exemption to be out later, and those are only granted for work purposes. If you abuse this privilege, you will be evicted. Your dates may wait in the lounge area, but no men are allowed above the first floor.' Miss McGovern cleared her throat. 'And this should go without saying, but nevertheless: no hanky-panky of any sort in the bedrooms. I know pretty much anything goes in New York, Miss Shore, and we're not too uptight here either, but every girl has a right to feel safe in her own bedroom.'

Sadie stifled the urge to tell her that romantic entanglements were the last thing on her mind. In fact, quite the opposite. She was here to escape the notion that marriage was mandatory for a happy and successful life.

Thankfully, one of the ponytailed residents bounded up to the reception desk and introduced herself, putting an end to Miss McGovern's lecture. 'Hello,' she said, flashing a set of dazzlingly white teeth. 'I'm Peggy Carmichael. You must be new.'

Before Sadie could answer, Miss McGovern spoke. 'Peggy. You'll do nicely. Would you help Sadie here find her room and give her the tour? I have some important jobs I need to take care of ahead of a new arrival we have booked in for later this week.'

'I'd be happy to. Which room is she in?'

The housemistress handed Sadie a key. 'Room 212. She's sharing with Vivienne.'

Peggy pulled a face. Miss McGovern pursed her lips and rebuked the young woman with a sharp look before directing her next comment to Sadie. 'I'm sure you and Vivienne will get along famously. Now, dinner is at six but if you are famished before then, Peggy will show you where you can make yourself a cup of coffee.'

'Come on.' Peggy said. 'Let's get you settled and then we'll sort out a hot drink and a snack.'

Sadie murmured her thanks to Miss McGovern and followed Peggy up to the second floor, puffing with the exertion of carrying her gigantic case. As they walked along the corridor, Peggy gave a running commentary of each room's occupants and their various skills. 'Babette and Trudie are in 202. They're inseparable – a bit cliquey, if you ask me, but friendly enough. Babs is a magician with hair. Handy if you have a big audition coming up.'

'Oh,' said Sadie. 'I'm not an actress. I'm a writer, or at least hoping to be one, so no auditions for me.'

Peggy, who was a couple of strides ahead of her, turned and laughed, her gaze shifting from Sadie's head to her toes. 'Well, that explains it. You don't seem like the Hollywood type. Not that you're not gorgeous – you are, of course – but you just don't have the air of an actress. With your height you could easily be a catwalk model, I'd say, but you don't carry yourself like one.'

Heat rushed to Sadie's cheeks and Peggy immediately looked mortified.

'I've insulted you. I'm so sorry! I have penchant for putting my foot in my mouth.'

'I'm not offended. It's just, well, I'm a bit nervous about whether I'll fit in here.'

'No need to worry about that! Being a bit different will be an asset. That you're a writer means you won't be in competition with the other girls for parts.' She lowered her voice to a stage whisper. 'There can sometimes be a bit of jealousy over that sort of thing.'

'I hadn't thought about it like that.'

'Well, no need for you to think about it at all because it won't be a problem for you. And we can always use a good writer to help us write skits to perform. Honestly, by the end of dinner you'll have made more friends than you can count.

'Now, here we are.' Peggy stopped outside room 212 and gave a sharp rap on the door.

'It's open,' a breathy voice answered.

Peggy opened the door and gasped. 'Vivienne! For Pete's sake!'

Sadie's new roommate was propped up on her bed reading *Anna Karenina*. She wore a pair of black-rimmed reading glasses, lace panties, a huge smile . . . and nothing else.

Chapter 2

Peggy

The moment Sadie smiled, Peggy knew she was redundant.

Sadie was looking at Vivienne as if she was the most fascinating creature on Earth. 'I'm Sadie Shore,' she said. 'Your new roommate.'

Vivienne stood and, seemingly undaunted by being caught out naked, offered Sadie her hand. 'Vivienne Lockhart. Pleased to meet you.'

Sadie either had impeccable manners or she was used to such goings-on, because she didn't bat an eyelid. 'Likewise.'

Exasperated, Peggy shook her head. 'Vivienne, put some clothes on, please.'

Vivienne rolled her eyes and replied in her slow, milky voice, 'You can run along now, Peggy. Sadie and I need some time to get acquainted.'

Peggy averted her gaze from Vivienne's shapely body and addressed Sadie. 'But I promised Miss McGovern I'd give you the tour.'

'Thanks, Peggy.' Sadie gave her a conciliatory smile. 'But honestly, all I want right now is to unpack and freshen up a little. I'm sure Vivienne can point me in the direction of the bathroom.'

19

'Fine,' Peggy snapped, unable keep the disappointment out of her voice.

Sadie had the good grace to look a little embarrassed. 'I'll see you at dinner, then?'

Peggy huffed off. She knew when she wasn't wanted. It was a darn shame that Sadie had been placed with Vivienne, a vixen who had no idea about how to behave in polite society, a woman who thumbed her nose at good manners and who didn't care what anyone thought. Who in their right mind sat around reading *naked*, for heaven's sake?

It really wasn't fair. Sadie seemed nice and Peggy had hopes of making her a friend. Didn't she have a spare bed in her room, now the only vacant one in the whole club? Why couldn't Sadie have been placed with her? She'd always thought of herself as one of Miss McGovern's favourites. She went out of her way to follow the rules and be helpful, and as a reward Miss McGovern often chose her for special tasks – like organising the Christmas play last year, and speaking to the newspaper reporter who'd recently done a story on the club. Perhaps she'd overestimated Miss McGovern's affection for her? Because surely she would have been a better choice as roommate for a new resident.

In any case, she hoped Sadie wasn't the type who would be easily led astray. Vivienne was nothing but trouble. Nobody liked her.

Sadly, that was the one thing they had in common.

Oh, the other girls were friendly enough. They occasionally let Peggy borrow their clothes for an audition or a date. They smiled politely when she started a conversation and always responded appropriately to her cheery 'hello' when she passed them in the hall. No one was mean or awful. But no one was especially chummy either. No one called out across the dining room for her to come sit with them. No one asked if she wanted to go dancing, or how her date had gone. Not that she dated often – she was choosy – but still.

It had always been this way for her. At school she'd been seen as rigid and pious – certainly not fun – but at church, and even in her own family, she was labelled 'rebellious'. She'd hoped that the Studio Club would be the place where she was finally accepted for herself, but once again she'd been disappointed. This was just another place she didn't belong.

Peggy didn't understand it. She'd done everything she could to fit in. Admittedly, she'd been something of a misfit when she arrived. For starters, her wardrobe had been sadly lacking, but she soon made use of the club's sewing machines to assemble new garments and remodel her old ones into more fashionable pieces. Table manners were another issue. At first she was confused by all the different pieces of cutlery, but she'd quietly observed the other girls and copied their actions. Now, no one would ever guess she'd been raised in a house where eating multiple courses was considered gluttonous.

She was unfailingly cheerful and friendly, and always happy to share what she'd learnt from her many auditions. She might not be a star yet, but she'd had a few small parts and currently had a contract with a major studio, which was more than most of the girls could say. But it seemed the other residents of the Hollywood Studio Club did not take kindly to her well-intentioned suggestions for improvement.

Vivienne, she had to admit, was not lacking in drive or resilience. Like Peggy, she understood that if you wanted to make it in this business, you had to put yourself out there, and get back up after you'd been knocked down. Vivienne auditioned a lot and, consequently, she'd had a few parts. She seemed to be in a dry spell lately, but Peggy knew that wouldn't last forever. Vivienne had too much ambition to just give up. She'd make something happen one way or another. The problem was, Vivienne had no scruples, so if she wasn't cast on her talent, she'd find other ways to get what she wanted.

Peggy pursed her lips. No joy could come from that approach. Vivienne would see soon enough.

Chapter 3

Sadie

Once Peggy left, Vivienne grabbed a robe from the messy pile of clothes on the chair at the end of her bed. She turned her back and slipped into the robe, facing Sadie once again as she tied it at the waist.

Despite her feigned nonchalance, Sadie was relieved. Not that she judged Vivienne for being comfortable in her own skin – that sort of confidence was to be admired – but her nudity *was* a tad distracting. Sadie had begun to wonder how she would carry on a conversation without her eyes drifting to Vivienne's (frankly enormous) breasts.

Thankfully, with her roommate's decency now restored, she didn't have to worry.

'So sorry about that,' Vivienne said. 'I wasn't expecting company and I was just relaxing. I wouldn't usually invite anyone in when I'm naked – well, not unless it was Marlon Brando himself.' She winked at Sadie. 'But when I heard Peggy's voice I just couldn't help myself. I thought it would be a bit of a lark. Old Peggy can be a little . . . uptight. I hope you don't think me too wicked.'

'Not at all. I like a good joke.'

Vivienne's eyes twinkled. 'I think you and I are going to get along just fine. And I promise I won't be lolling around naked now I have a roommate.'

As Vivienne went on to show Sadie where she could put her things, pulling her own clothes off hangers to make space, Sadie took in her new surroundings. The room was larger than she'd expected and had lots of natural light, thanks to the substantial window on Vivienne's side of the room, and it had its own washbasin, which was a pleasant surprise. There were two single beds covered in pretty floral bedspreads, not that you could see much of Vivienne's now that it was strewn with clothes. Beside each bed was a nightstand with a lamp; the one on Vivienne's side was piled high with books. There was an armchair at the foot of each bed, and beside that each girl had her own set of drawers. The shared closet was on Vivienne's side of the room and next to it was a small desk, which doubled as a dressing table. The desk housed a telephone and a large oval mirror, and was littered with half-empty bottles of nail polish, an assortment of eyeshadows and lipsticks, pens, tissues and a pile of magazines.

It was a mess, but Sadie didn't care. She instinctively knew that she was in the right place.

Vivienne's manner was warm and inviting. She waved away Sadie's protests about not needing too much space. 'You'll be needing it soon enough if you are about to start auditioning. Say, why don't you and I hit the shops tomorrow? I can show you the best places to find a bargain.'

'I would love to have a look around, but I'm afraid I'll need a job before I can spend any money.'

'Ah.' Vivienne screwed up her nose. 'I know that tune only too well. Luckily for me I had a well-paying modelling job this week, so I can splash a bit of cash. But now that we're roomies, what's mine is yours. Feel free to raid my wardrobe if you need anything for an audition.' She held up a violet dress against her body. 'Well, perhaps not this beauty. I haven't worn her yet and I have a feeling she's going to bring me luck. But, honestly, anything else I have is fair game. Help yourself.'

Sadie doubted she would look good in any of her roommate's clothes. Vivienne was average height, with an hourglass figure, whereas Sadie was as skinny as a beanpole. Nevertheless, she appreciated the offer. 'Goodness, that's so kind of you, but I won't be auditioning for parts. I'm a writer. I'm hoping to find work in the script department at one of the studios.'

Vivienne dropped the violet dress onto the bed and placed a hand over her heart. 'A writer? Oh, how wonderful! I can't believe I get to share my room with a writer. I just *love* to read, but I could never write, not properly. I scribble away in a journal, but it's just my own silly thoughts, not a proper story. You must be awfully clever, and brave too.'

'Oh, I don't think I'm especially clever.' Though Sadie found herself beaming at the compliment. 'It's just what I like to do. I could never dream of acting. I'm in awe of anyone with that talent.'

'Well, look at us.' A wide smile settled on Vivienne's face. 'We're a mutual admiration society. I think you and I are going to have a lot of fun together, Sadie Shore.'

Chapter 4

Peggy

The dining room was more crowded than usual and it hummed with excited chatter. No doubt there was some sort of gossip afoot, but Peggy would be the last to know, as usual.

As she scanned the room for an empty seat, she saw Sadie beckoning to her. Well, that was a turn-up for the books – Sadie had saved her a place! Peggy found herself smiling as she sat herself next to her potential friend. Unfortunately, Vivienne was seated on Sadie's other side. It was bad luck, really. Vivienne hardly ever ate in the dining room at dinnertime; she was frequently out on a date. Never mind. Peggy wasn't going to let her presence spoil the opportunity to get to know Sadie.

'How are you settling in?' she asked as Sadie passed her the bread-basket.

'Fine, thank you. Although I'm finding things quite different to home. I'm not used to such an electric atmosphere at dinner. Meal-times are quite sedate in the Shore house.'

'To be fair, it's not often this crowded. You seem to have struck us on an unusually busy day.' She looked at Vivienne. 'It's not like you to grace us with your presence at dinner.'

'I've had a long day, so no date tonight. Besides, I didn't want Sadie left to her own devices,' Vivienne replied.

Peggy narrowed her eyes. 'How kind, but there was no need to trouble yourself. I'd already told Sadie I'd see her at dinner.'

Sadie lowered her gaze and busied herself with buttering her roll.

Darn it! In her race to put Vivienne in her place, Peggy had made herself seem churlish. She didn't want Sadie thinking she was one of those mean girls who didn't include others. She forced herself to smile. 'In any case, it was lovely of the two of you to save me a seat. I appreciate the gesture.'

Sadie glanced up and smiled while Vivienne looked like she'd sucked on a lemon. Babs and Trudie scampered over to their table, both wide-eyed and giggling.

'Are these seats taken?' Trudie asked.

Peggy shook her head. 'They're all yours.'

Babs dragged out a chair and planted her curvaceous backside on it. 'Thanks. We were supposed to be going on a double date, but pulled the pin when we heard about the announcement.'

'What announcement?' Vivienne asked.

Babs was momentarily distracted by Sadie's presence. 'Hello. I don't think we've met. I'm Babs, and this is Trudie.'

'Sadie. I arrived today.'

'So, what's this about an announcement?' Peggy interrupted. Of course she was curious, but equally she didn't want Babs and Trudie encroaching on her fledgling friendship.

Babs leant in conspiratorially. 'There's a rumour going around that Julia Newman is moving into the club. Janet is in the typing pool in Harry Gold's office at Goldstar. She's seen Julia's new contract and part of it states she has to live here for the next three years!'

Vivienne slammed her hand on the table excitedly. 'No way! That can't possibly be true. They're saying Julia's the next big thing – the new Grace Kelly. She'll be raking in the pay cheques soon. Why would she want to live here?'

Babs was adamant. 'Janet swears it's the truth, doesn't she, Trude?'

Trudie nodded so vigorously she reminded Peggy of one of those little bobble-headed dogs people placed in the rear window of their cars.

'Looks like we're about to find out,' Babs said, inclining her head towards the room's entrance.

Peggy followed her nod to see Miss McGovern coming through the door. The club's director strode to the front of the room, stopping by the service counter. She clapped her hands to gain their attention.

'Ladies, please!' Miss McGovern waited for the chatter to die down. 'I had not anticipated sharing this news with you until all the details had been finalised, but I see that some of you are already discussing the matter at hand, so you leave me no choice.

'The rumour is true. From Friday, Julia Newman will be calling the Hollywood Studio Club her home.'

A cheer went around the room, followed by an excited hum of chatter. Once again, Miss McGovern waited until the noise died down before she continued. 'It is, as you know, unusual for a young woman who is already a rising star to be housed among us. In Miss Newman's case, she is far from home and because of her heavy filming schedule, she hasn't had a chance to meet many other women her own age. The studio thinks it will be beneficial for her to live among other like-minded girls who can help her settle into her new life.

'We at the club take pride in welcoming newcomers to Hollywood. I would like to take this opportunity to welcome Miss Sadie Shore, an aspiring writer from New York, to our home. I hope you will all make Sadie very welcome.' She paused then to allow a brief round of applause for Sadie, but most of the girls were so focused on the news about Julia that they barely bothered to look in her direction.

'Obviously having an up-and-coming star among us means we will have to make some extra accommodations. I'm sure I don't need to tell you that Miss Newman's privacy must be respected. Gossip will not be tolerated and, heaven forbid, should any of you take it upon yourself to speak to reporters about her, your tenancy at the club will be terminated immediately. I'm expecting you to treat Miss Newman with courtesy and make her feel at home. Are there any questions?'

Allison put up her hand. 'Which room will Julia be housed in? I thought we were at capacity.'

'It's true that all our single rooms are occupied, but we do have one spare bed.' Miss McGovern smiled in Peggy's direction. 'Miss Newman wouldn't hear of any of our girls giving up their rooms for her and has graciously agreed to share until a single room becomes available. For the time being, at least, she will be roommates with Peggy Carmichael.'

❧

Peggy couldn't sleep.

She was in her normal sleeping position: on her back, covers pulled tight, eye mask on. She'd put on her hand crème and said her prayers as usual. Everything was as it should be. But nothing was the same.

Julia Newman, a woman who Peggy had admired from afar, was about to become her roommate. Not that Julia would know this, but Peggy had played a small role in Julia's upcoming film, *One Starry Night*. It was Peggy's biggest role in a movie yet, and Julia played the lead opposite Cal Brooks. Unfortunately, the two of them hadn't had any scenes together, so the closest she'd got to Julia was catching the odd glimpse. But now they were to share living quarters!

It was news so delicious that nothing she did could quieten her mind.

Peggy hugged herself and let out a little squeal of glee. It really was too good to be true. Being roommates invited an intimacy that no one else could share. She just *knew* that Julia was the friend she'd been praying for all this time.

Although, there was the slight worry that Julia might *not* be a dream roommate. What if she wanted to move all Peggy's things around? Even worse, what if she thought she was above the rules and expected Peggy to cover for her? A flutter of unease rippled through her stomach.

After Miss McGovern had left the dining room the other girls had plenty to say. It seemed everyone knew someone who knew Julia; however, the reports on her personality were wildly conflicting. There were tales of her being a complete diva on set and bossing everyone around. Some girls said she'd argued with Grace Kelly when they'd worked together on a movie, and that poor Grace had left the set in tears! Other girls refuted this, saying they'd heard she was a doll, and that the rumours were started by jealous wannabes who Julia had beaten for the role. Peggy felt sure that if Julia had been a diva to work with, she would have heard it about it from the other actors or extras on *One Starry Night*.

She sat up in bed, removed her eye mask and switched on her lamp so she could find the copy of *Modern Screen* she had stored in her nightstand drawer. It featured an article about Hollywood actresses on the rise and although Peggy had already read the magazine cover to cover, she wanted to revisit the section on her roommate-to-be.

Julia Newman grew up on a dairy farm in Nebraska. An only child, she was raised by her father from the age of three after the tragic death of her mother.

In the summer of 1953, Julia got a job at the local drugstore and was still employed there when she entered a statewide beauty pageant. After winning the pageant she was offered a modelling job as the face of a brand-new, all-automatic washing machine.

Julia toured the country to promote the washer and eventually found herself in Hollywood, where she and a friend decided to answer a casting call for extras at Goldstar Studio. When studio head Harry Gold spotted Julia in the crowd of hopefuls, he singled her out for an audition.

This led to a supporting role in Goldstar's The Lost Jewels *alongside Grace Kelly. The director evidently liked her work, because she scored a major role in his next movie,* Small Town Serenade, *which also starred Montgomery Clift.*

In mid-1954 she filmed the iconic role that would cement her as an up-and-coming star. When Secrets of the Heart *debuted earlier this year, audiences lapped up her performance as Margot, an icy heiress who yearns* to be loved for herself. Julia has since gone on to film the yet-to-be-released One Starry Night, *which will premiere on 4 July next year.*

She is currently working on a new movie called A Gentleman's Proposal *– her second movie with heart-throb Cal Brooks. Modern Screen caught up with Julia on set to ask her how she was feeling about her rise to stardom.*

'I'm terribly lucky!' the blonde beauty said, in between takes. 'I know many girls would kill for this role, starring opposite Cal Brooks, so I'm not taking anything for granted. I'm so fortunate to have been given this opportunity and I'm not going to waste it. I know that it takes hard work to get to the top in this business and I'm not afraid of that.'

Peggy flipped the magazine shut. Those weren't the words of a diva. In fact, Julia sounded a lot like her. Like Peggy, she knew that being a star required hard work and she was prepared to do whatever it took. Yes, she'd had some luck, but she seemed grateful for it.

For now, it was safe to assume that Julia would be a good roommate. Peggy would reserve her judgement until she'd had the chance to get to know Julia, of course, but there was one thing she knew for sure: being Julia Newman's roommate would shine a light on her in a way that hadn't happened before. And Peggy wasn't one to pass up an opportunity.

Chapter 5

Julia

'Daddy, I don't think you understand. This is a big deal. I'm signing on with a studio as a star. It will give me guaranteed work for years.'

'Batting your eyelids at a camera for money isn't something to be proud of, Julia. For heaven's sake, come home before this goes any further. Dear god, your mother . . .' He trailed off, leaving it to Julia's imagination to decide what her mother would think if she were alive to hear her news. Nothing good, if her father's tone was anything to go by.

Julia swallowed down the hurt. Clearly her father didn't understand the significance of the contract she'd just signed. Daddy did not approve of 'showbiz', as he called it, and had made it clear that he thought she was making a laughing-stock of herself with this 'damned fool acting caper'.

Her duty was clear in his mind. She needed to be back home, taking care of him and looking for a husband. The end goal was to provide a grandson who would inherit the farm, so that Daddy could die safe in the knowledge that his blood still worked the land.

But Julia had other ideas. For years, she'd fantasised about leaving. She hadn't exactly dreamt of being on the silver screen; her imagination hadn't been that specific. All she'd ever wanted was to be free from the constraints of home. Free of the drudgery, the endless toil, but most of all, she longed to be free of her father's blatant disappointment in her.

As a child she had all the material things she needed – a warm bed, plenty of food and decent clothes – but her father kept her at arm's length, his affection rarely on display. She'd tried her best to be the perfect daughter in the hope that if she pleased him, she'd see his softer side more often. Then, at sixteen, she'd discovered the truth: she'd contracted scarlet fever as a toddler and her mother had caught it from her. Aunt Betty said that her shattered father was simply trying to guard his heart from being broken again, but Julia wondered if the real reason he couldn't love her was because he blamed her for her mother's death. Either way, it seemed there was nothing she could do to change the way he felt about her. Still, she couldn't help but live in hope.

Now, not only was she working and earning good money, she was on her way to being *the next big thing*. If nothing else, stardom would mean she'd be able to pay for modern farm machinery and to employ farmhands to help work the land.

'The studio has shown a lot of faith in me by offering an ongoing contract. My agent says the new movie is going to be a huge hit and that's why they are taking care of me so well.'

Julia's father gave a grunt of disbelief. 'If you're such a big deal, why are they putting you up in a dormitory?'

'It's not a dormitory, it's an exclusive club for young women who work in the movie industry. I will be sharing with another actress to begin with, but that's only because the place is so popular they don't have a spare single room right now. Lester, my new agent, says I should be flattered that they care so much about my wellbeing. It was Mr Gold's idea. Lester says the studio boss only gets involved in things like this when he has big plans for an actress. According to him, the studio is investing heavily in me and they want to protect me, which is why they are insisting I live at the club. And anyway, I think it will be fun.

It'll give me a chance to make some friends. I haven't really met anyone my age out here. It's hard when you are working all the time.'

'Julia, what's gotten into you? Playacting is not *work*. This has gone too far. I should have put my foot down months ago, but I thought you'd come to your senses on your own. You've got a pretty enough face, I'll grant you, but that town is no place for a farm girl like you. You might have fooled those movie bosses for a moment, but you'll get found out soon enough and then where will you be? No decent man will want a wife who's flaunted herself for all the world to see. Stop wasting your time and come home, before it's too late.'

The pain she'd been pushing down bubbled up into anger. 'I will do no such thing. Even if I wanted to, I couldn't. I have a legally binding contract. But the thing is, Daddy, I don't *want* to come home. I'm an adult now. It's my life and I'm choosing to live it here in Hollywood.' She put the receiver down without waiting to hear her father's response.

Later that morning, as she stood on the steps outside the Mediterranean-style building that housed the Hollywood Studio Club, Julia's bravado disappeared. What if her father was right? What if she didn't fit in here?

It was too late to be contemplating that now. She had a contract, and living here was part of the deal. She forced herself to take a steadying breath as she walked through the arches and pushed open the large timber-and-glass entry door.

The light-filled foyer was buzzing with activity. There were girls dotted around the place in armchairs and leaning up against the reception desk. Others lounged on the stairs, peeking down at her through the wrought-iron balustrading and whispering behind their hands. It was clear her arrival had caused a bit of a sensation. Maybe this wasn't going to turn out the way she'd hoped.

She'd been in Hollywood for more than two years now and hadn't managed to make any friends. At first, she'd had Lena, another beauty pageant winner who'd modelled alongside her for the washing-machine company. They'd gone to the casting call together, just for a bit of fun. When Julia had been singled out for special attention by the studio boss, Lena had been happy for her. She'd figured that it wouldn't be long before she got her break too. But as the months went by without Lena being offered a role, Julia started to detect bitterness in her friend's voice every time they talked about Julia's burgeoning career. They'd been sharing a little apartment, but last month Lena had given up and gone back to Kansas.

It was then that Julia realised she had no other friends out here in California. Acquaintances, yes, but not true friends she could really talk to. When the studio had raised the possibility of her moving into the Studio Club, she'd thought it might just be the answer to all her problems. Now she wasn't so sure. Instead of one jealous roommate, she faced the possibility of dozens.

A slightly older woman scurried across the tiled foyer towards her. 'Miss Newman . . . Julia – may I call you Julia? – let me introduce myself. I'm Miss McGovern, Florence McGovern, director of the club. I'm here to make sure you have everything you need.' She took both of Julia's hands into her own and squeezed them. 'We are so very happy to have you here.'

Julia put on her movie-star smile. 'Please do call me Julia, Miss McGovern. I'm delighted to be here.'

Beaming, Miss McGovern released her hands and stepped back. 'I'm so sorry we were unable to accommodate you in a single room, but we are quite full at the moment. As soon as a single becomes available it'll be all yours. In the meantime, you'll be sharing with a lovely young woman. I'm sure the two of you will get along famously.' She paused to beckon over a peppy blonde, who was wearing an almost maniacal grin. 'Miss Julia Newman, may I present your new roommate, Miss Peggy Carmichael.'

'I'm so pleased to meet you, Miss Newman. I'm a huge fan,' Peggy gushed.

'Please, call me Julia.'

'Peggy, dear,' Miss McGovern interrupted, 'would you mind taking Miss Newman's suitcase up to your room while I give her the tour?'

'Of course. I'd be happy—'

'Oh, there's no need for that.' Julia didn't want to get off on the wrong foot with her roommate. Having her act as a personal porter was out of the question. 'Miss McGovern, I am so very thrilled that you have personally welcomed me. I imagine you are an extremely busy woman, and I am reluctant to take up any more of your precious time than is necessary. Peggy can show me the ropes, and if I have any questions I'll make sure to seek you out.'

Miss McGovern frowned and looked as if she might protest, but her gaze flitted to Peggy's excited face and her expression softened. 'How very thoughtful of you. Thank you. I'm sure Peggy will do an excellent job of showing you around. If I don't see you beforehand, I will see you at dinnertime. You can let me know how you're getting on then. I'll leave you girls to it.' With that, she turned and headed off towards the reception desk.

Julia picked up her case. 'I'm all yours. Where to first?'

'We'll head upstairs so you can put down your things and then I'll show you around upstairs – it's mainly bedrooms, but there are few other things like bathrooms and utility rooms that you'll want to see. Then I'll show you all the good bits: the library, rehearsal rooms, the living and dining areas, and the courtyard.'

'Fabulous.' Julia followed Peggy up the sweeping staircase to the second floor. The whispering girls quickly dispersed, suddenly appearing very busy. Some greeted her by name as they passed on the stairs, but a few pointedly looked away as if to say, 'You're no better than any of the rest of us', which, of course, she wasn't. Success might have its perks, but there were definitely drawbacks as well. She'd have to work hard at showing these women that she didn't have tickets on herself if she hoped to make any friends.

'Here we are.' Peggy held open the door to an impeccably neat bedroom. It wasn't huge, but it was bright and cheerful. 'This one's yours,' Peggy said, pointing to the single bed on the right. 'Unless you'd prefer . . .'

Julia threw her suitcase up onto the bed. 'No, this one's fine.' She slid off her lightweight camel-coloured coat and removed her gloves.

'Phew, that's better. I've lived here for more than two years and I'm still not used to the weather. I can't believe it's so warm at this time of year. Back home we'd be starting to dust off our winter coats by now.'

Peggy opened the small closet, took out an empty hanger and handed it to Julia for her coat. 'Your family's from Nebraska, right?'

'Yeah, I grew up on a farm there, but there's not much family to speak of. Just me and my dad. How about you?'

'Wow. Just you and your dad. I'm jealous – I'm one of eight kids.'

Julia's mouth dropped open. 'Really? I envy *you*. I always wanted sisters, or even a brother.'

'Let me assure you, they are not all they're cracked up to be. Eight kids – six of them girls – growing up in a tiny three-bedroom, *one-*bathroom house in Wisconsin wasn't always fun.'

'Still, at least you would never be lonely.' She opened her suitcase and pulled out a dress.

'I was never alone, that's for sure.' Peggy handed her another hanger.

'You must miss them.'

Peggy frowned. 'It's sort of hard to explain. I love my family and I do miss their company – especially my little sister Joanie. We used to brush each other's hair every night. But I was the odd one out in my family. It's possible to be surrounded by people and still feel lonely.'

'What do you mean?'

'Ever since I was little, I've been singing and dancing. Everyone else in my family is very serious. My eldest brother, Michael, is a priest. John trained as a dentist, and he works in the family practice with my dad. Two of my sisters are nurses, one has just entered the convent and Mary, the oldest, is married with three kids already. Even little Joanie wants to be a teacher.'

'But surely they don't mind that you have different aspirations?' Julia asked as she continued to unpack.

A sad, hollow laugh sprang from Peggy's lips. 'My ambitions are considered sinful,' she said. 'My father thinks acting is the devil's work and my mom constantly talks about my vanity and greed.'

'It must have taken courage to leave.'

'I guess. But I feel as if this is my calling. I mean, why would God give me these talents if He didn't want me to use them? Entertaining people brings them happiness. I can't see the sin in that.'

'Me either.' Julia put her folded nightgown under her pillow and turned to face Peggy again. 'My dad doesn't think acting's a sin, but he thinks it's a waste of time. He thinks I should be back in Nebraska, taking care of him and looking for a husband. So, Peggy, you're not alone anymore, or at least you don't have to be. I'm hoping you and I will become great friends.'

'Oh, Julia, I'd like that very much.'

Julia sat on the edge of the bed – *her* bed – and kicked off her shoes. She'd filled the empty drawers with her undergarments, pants, tops and sweaters. Now it was a matter of squeezing the dresses, skirts and jackets into that tiny closet. Goodness only knew what she would do with the rest of her things. The studio was sending more boxes over tomorrow. She'd have to have a word with Miss McGovern about what could be done, because she was already taking up more than her fair share of wardrobe space. To think, when she'd first arrived in Hollywood she'd had just a handful of dresses that were suitable for auditions, and not much else to speak of. So many times she'd wished she had a fairy godmother to provide her with just one perfect outfit. Now she had more clothes than she knew what to do with.

That was it! *She* could be the fairy godmother now.

'Peggy, do you think you could show me where Miss McGovern's office is? I have something I want to chat to her about before we do our grand tour.'

❧

The day passed pleasantly enough. Peggy had shown her around the club and Julia had to admit the facilities were first-rate. Every bedroom was equipped with a telephone, there was a laundry room for washing and ironing, and utility rooms furnished with sewing machines for the residents' use. The building itself was gorgeous. The interiors were various shades of pink, green and tan. Spectacular arched windows allowed light to fill the living areas, and decorative iron was used throughout the building. The furnished outdoor patios and sun-drenched courtyard were lovely, but Julia was most enamoured of the spacious rehearsal rooms and performance areas. The rooms were empty when they'd visited but Peggy told her about the classes on offer and about the shows the girls put on from time to time.

'Sometimes we are asked to entertain business groups or the club's benefactors,' she explained. 'But other times we write and perform acts purely for our own amusement.'

'Sounds fun!' Julia said, and she meant it. She was really looking forward to being part of this sorority-like community.

The guided tour of the building took longer than Julia had imagined it would – the building was large and there were lots of people who wanted to stop and chat as they made their way through each floor. It was almost dinnertime when they made it back to their room. After a quick freshen up, Julia followed Peggy to the dining room.

'Julia, Peggy, over here.' Sadie – a writer Peggy had introduced her to as they'd inspected the library – beckoned for them to join her at a table on the far side of the room. 'We saved you some seats,' Sadie said as they approached the table.

'We?' Peggy asked.

'Vivienne and me.' Sadie nodded towards the empty bentwood chair beside her. 'She's just collecting a breadbasket for us. She'll be back in a moment.'

Julia took a seat beside Sadie, her nerves slightly soothed by Sadie's reassuring smile. The room was crowded. Chatter and high-pitched laughter combined with the clink of cutlery and the sounds of chairs being dragged across the tiled floor made for a noisy, and somewhat overwhelming, atmosphere.

'Gosh, Sadie, thanks for saving us a place.'

A curvaceous blonde – Vivienne, she presumed – placed a bread-basket in the middle of the table and took a seat opposite Julia. 'The rabble are out in force tonight to check you out. Some of them would have been at work or at auditions this morning when you arrived. No one wants to miss out on the chance to clap eyes on the famous Julia Newman in the flesh.'

God, this was the last thing she needed – people paying her unnecessary attention. What if Peggy or her friends got jealous, the way Lena had? She tried to laugh off the idea. 'Me? I doubt it.'

'Oh, honey, you are kidding, aren't you? These girls all want what you have. Every single one of them wishes they could be you.'

'Oh.' Julia lowered her eyes and stared at the placemat in front of her. She hated being the centre of attention. Oddly enough, it was her chronic shyness that had led to her acting career. Her father, greatly concerned about her lack of confidence, had enrolled her in a modelling and deportment course. He'd hoped the course would improve her chances of catching a husband. The course had led to the beauty pageant, and then the modelling job, which had eventually landed her here in Hollywood. Right now, Julia was wishing she'd taken tennis lessons instead.

Peggy shot Vivienne a withering glance. 'Vivienne! Don't say that.'

'Why not? It's the truth.'

'You're making Julia uncomfortable,' Peggy replied.

'Better that she knows what she's up against,' Vivienne replied. 'Forewarned is forearmed, I say.'

'Perhaps you should *say* less,' Peggy quipped.

'I'll say whatever I damned well like. I'm not trying to make anyone uncomfortable. If anything, I'm trying to help.' Vivienne fixed her gaze on Julia. 'I'm Vivienne, by the way. Vivienne Lockhart.'

'Pleased to meet you, Vivienne.'

'As someone who is often the subject of chatter among this crowd myself,' Vivienne continued, 'my advice is not to pander to them. Just be yourself. Do whatever makes *you* happy. The gossip will die down either way. And you can't please everyone.'

'Vivienne's right,' Sadie said, surprising not only Julia but also everyone else at the table, if their expressions were anything to go by. 'Look: unlike all of you, I don't know what it's like to be even slightly famous. I certainly don't know what it's like to have women jealous of me.' She turned to Vivienne. 'Or men lusting after me. I *do* know what it's like not to fit in, though.'

'Really?' Peggy asked. 'I can't imagine that. You seem so sure of yourself.'

Sadie laughed. 'I've had years of practice. I was definitely the odd one out at university.'

'How so?' Julia asked, genuinely interested, but also relieved that she was no longer the sole focus of the conversation.

'I've always known I was a bit different. I was that kid at school who always had her head in a book. I preferred to read than play tag. I was never really interested in playing with dolls or skipping games. I guess you could say I was a bit of a loner. Don't get me wrong – I wanted friends, just not enough to feign interest in things I didn't care about.'

Vivienne leant in, seemingly fascinated by this information. Peggy had stopped frowning and was listening intently too.

'Go on,' Julia said.

'I managed to get through school well enough. My grades were fine – not outstanding, but passable – and I made a few like-minded friends. But when school finished I was lost. My father was making noises about marriage. He kept inviting the sons of his friends over for dinner. It was highly embarrassing.'

Julia nodded in solidarity. She knew exactly what Sadie was talking about.

'I wasn't ready to be married. I could see my life disappearing into servitude, so I begged my parents to let me go to university.'

'And your father agreed?' asked Peggy.

Sadie nodded. 'My mother convinced him that a university education would enhance my chances of marrying well.'

'How'd she figure that?' Vivienne chuckled.

'Something about girls from educated families having high-achieving brothers, I think. Anyway, off I went to university, where once again I was the odd one out. The girls there were either great scholars,

40

aiming for careers as doctors or academics, or they were biding time until their rich husband arrived. I didn't fit into either group. I wasn't – and I'm still not – interested in marriage. I'm not a great scholar either. All I want to do is tell stories.'

'You *don't* want to get married?' Peggy seemed incredulous.

'Nope. I see nothing appealing about birthing snotty-nosed brats, who I have to look after as well as running a household, while my husband gets to go off into the world to pursue his dreams. No thanks.'

Peggy looked aghast at this statement, but Vivienne was studying Sadie with admiration in her eyes.

'So, Julia,' Sadie continued, 'I think Vivienne hit the nail on the head when she said just be yourself. I've found that it's easier if you don't explain. Simply do what you want and don't make excuses. People will respect that . . . eventually.'

Julia wrinkled her nose. 'The thing is, girls – and I'm kind of embarrassed to admit this after what you just said, Sadie – but the thing I want most in life is to belong. To be loved for myself. I'm not even talking about romantic love, necessarily. I'm not ready to walk down the aisle, although it might be nice one day. Right now, what I hunger for is friendship. I have no family to speak of. No sisters or brothers, and the one friend I had out here in California has abandoned me. It was hard for her to watch me getting roles when she was struggling to find work. I tried not to rub her face in it, but in the end she resented me anyway.'

'No point being loved for something that you're not,' said Sadie.

Julia nodded silently, not trusting herself to speak. If only they knew what a fraud she was. Her name was basically the only thing left of the girl who had left the farm two years ago. Everything else about her had changed – her hairstyle, her weight, the way she spoke, the clothes she wore, even the way she walked. The studio seemed hell-bent on moulding her into someone else. Their perfect star.

The worst thing was, she couldn't even act. She was starring in Goldstar's next big movie and yet she had no talent whatsoever. It was only a matter of time before everyone found her out.

Peggy offered her the breadbasket, but she shook her head. When she'd signed on to do her first movie with Goldstar she'd been told to lose ten pounds and been given a prescription for diet pills. 'These make life easy,' the studio's doctor explained. 'You'll never feel hungry again.' It was true the pills took her appetite, but they also made her heart pound and caused her to feel so anxious she found it hard to concentrate on learning her lines. Once the ten pounds were gone, she ditched the pills. Of course, she then had to stay on a strict diet to maintain her slim figure. No bread, no dessert and only small portions. 'Never finish what's on your plate,' the studio's dietitian had advised.

'Shall we go up to get our meals?' Sadie asked.

Vivienne and Peggy stood, but Julia hesitated. The thought of all those eyes fixed on her as she crossed the room made her nauseated. 'I'm not very hungry,' she said.

'Come on,' said Peggy. 'We'll be with you all the way.'

'Don't let the hyenas win,' Vivienne said. 'Or at least give them something to talk about. We can stage a fight over the last chicken drumstick if you like?' She winked and Julia began to laugh.

'Okay. I'll come. Maybe let's save the fight for a slow news day, though.'

The other three laughed, and Julia basked in the glow of their approval.

Later, as they ate their desserts – black coffee for Julia, fruit compote and ice cream for everyone else – Miss McGovern entered the dining room and clapped her hands to get their attention. 'Girls,' she said. 'I have an announcement.'

It took a moment but eventually the room quietened. 'Here at the Hollywood Studio Club, we want the best for all of you. Many of you are aspiring dancers and actresses, and we understand how important it is for you to head off to auditions looking your very best. That's why we provide you with the facilities we do. I'm pleased to announce that due to the generosity of our newest resident, we have an exciting addition to make. Beginning tomorrow there will be a garment library operating out of the utility room adjacent to the laundry.'

A curious murmur circled the room and Miss McGovern held up a hand to quieten the noise. 'The library will be filled with items for your use – dresses, skirts, blouses and coats. Shoes, belts and handbags too. If you need an outfit for a big audition – or even a date – you are welcome to borrow whatever you like. This new service was the brain-child of Julia Newman, and she has graciously donated many outfits to get us started. I encourage you all to follow her lead. If you have a dress or coat that is rarely worn, consider putting it in the library for your friends to borrow. Any resident may take advantage of the library, which will work on an honour system. All we ask is that you return the items in the same condition they came to you. Please launder and iron them, and repair any damage before popping them back. Knowing you all as I do, I'm trusting that won't be an issue.'

A spontaneous round of applause started up and Miss McGovern smiled before concluding, 'That's all for now, girls. Enjoy your dinner.'

There was an excited buzz in the room and several girls came over to thank Julia or congratulate her on the idea. She knew the gesture wouldn't be enough to win everyone over, but it seemed as if she was off to a good start. She finished the last drop of her coffee and placed the cup on its saucer. 'Girls, I know it's early, but I'm going to head upstairs for a shower and then hit the sack. I have to be on set at the crack of dawn tomorrow, and besides, I'm afraid if I stay here much longer I'll be tempted to eat dessert and then I'll be in trouble with the wardrobe ladies.'

'Do you remember where the shower room is?' Peggy asked.

'Yes, yes. I'll be fine. You stay here and finish your meal. I'll see you later.'

Upstairs, under the hot running water, Julia finally relaxed. It might not have been her decision to move into the club, but it looked like Mr Gold had been right. This *was* the best place for her. Peggy was a lovely roommate who'd gone out of her way to make her feel welcome. Sadie was wonderful too. Vivienne, well . . . she was an interesting one. Julia still wasn't sure what to make of her. The garment library seemed to be a hit with the other girls, though. All in all, she'd call her first day a success.

As she turned off the water and began to towel herself dry, she heard two other voices enter the communal bathroom.

'*La di da,*' said one voice. 'Who the hell does she think she is?'

'Full of herself, that's for sure,' replied the second voice.

'Did she really think we'd be *grateful* to receive her old cast-offs? They're not even hers to give, not really. I heard they belong to the studio.'

Julia clasped her hand over her mouth. They were talking about her!

'What's she even doing living here? I don't get it. Her star is on the rise, she must be able to afford a place of her own.'

'Janet told me the studio insisted. Apparently Little Miss Diva can't be trusted to keep herself out of trouble. They don't want another Ingrid Bergman on their hands.'

'Makes sense. Still, I don't see why we have to suffer. I don't want my dates craning their necks for a glimpse of *her* when they're supposed to be waiting for *me*.'

'And she's already old Florence's favourite. No doubt she'll be getting privileges the rest of us don't get.'

Hot tears pricked Julia's eyes.

'Although, she does have to share – at least for the moment – with Pious Peggy.'

The first voice cackled. 'Yes, I almost feel sorry for her.'

'Are you two done?' A third voice – this one familiar sounding – joined the conversation. Was that Vivienne?

'The basin will be free in a moment,' the first voice replied.

'That's not what I meant, and you know it.' It was definitely Vivienne.

'I beg your pardon?' said voice number two.

'Have you even bothered to speak to Julia? To get to know her a fraction before casting judgement on her?'

The question was met with silence.

'I thought as much. Because if you'd given her the time of day, you'd know that she is warm and generous. And, more to the point, just like

44

the rest of us, she's doing her best to make it in a world where men rule and women count for nothing. You should be thrilled for her success, not jealous of it!'

The sounds of beauty cases being clicked shut filled the room. Julia heard the bathroom door creak open and assumed the first two were making an exit.

But Vivienne wasn't done with them yet. 'And by the way, Peggy might be pious but at least she's not a bitch!'

Still in the shower stall, Julia stifled a laugh. Maybe living at the Studio Club wasn't going to be a bed of roses. Maybe she would never be universally liked or admired. But maybe she had something better than that, something she'd longed for her whole life – true friendship. She'd only known Peggy, Sadie and Vivienne for a day, but somehow she knew they were destined to be part of her life forever.

Chapter 6

Sadie

'Shore, telephone for you!' Sadie's boss, Ivan, scowled at her from behind the diner's counter.

'For me?' She tore table seven's order from her pad and pushed it onto the incoming spike before ducking behind the counter and taking the receiver.

'Make it quick,' Ivan said, 'or you'll find your pay docked.'

Who on earth would be calling her here? Dear god, had something happened to her dad?

'Hello?'

'Sade, it's me, Julia. I'm sorry to call you at work, but this can't wait. What time do you finish?'

'What? Why?'

'Just answer. What time?'

'Six o'clock, unless Ivan asks me to do overtime. We're so busy right now. People are coming in after doing their Christmas shopping.'

'You can't work back. I need you to come straight home—'

Sadie's stomach clenched. 'Why? What's wrong?'

'Nothing's wrong. Quite the opposite. I've got us a table at Musso and Frank's tonight. You need to look your best.'

'Are you seriously calling me at work to discuss our dinner plans? And this better not be a set-up. I've told you before – I'm not blind dating.'

'It's not a date. Listen to me, Sadie, this is a big opportunity. Harry Gold's personal secretary has quit. It'd be the perfect job for you. Harry likes his secretary to be pretty *and* educated. He prefers college graduates. I'd recommend you for the position, but I know Harry and he's more likely to take you on if he "discovers" you himself. He always dines at Musso and Frank's of a Thursday evening. I pulled a few strings and got the four of us a table near his. I'll introduce you and let him know you're looking for work at the studio. He's sure to take the bait. But the booking is for seven-thirty and you have to look a million bucks, so you need to get home in time for us to do your hair and make-up, okay?'

'What if I have to work overtime?'

'Just tell Ivan you can't. Look, Sadie, I know it's not a writing job, but it's a foot in the door. This could be your big break. Don't let me, or more importantly yourself, down.'

Julia hung up just as Ivan bellowed, 'Shore, service on table nine, *now*!'

Heads turned when the waiter showed them to their table. Of course they did. That's what happened when one stepped out with Julia Newman. Peggy and Vivienne were beauties in their own right, obviously, but Sadie wasn't used to being the centre of attention.

It wasn't that she was plain, more that she didn't fuss too much over her appearance. What was the point when she spent most of her spare time holed up in the writers' room off the club's library, banging away on a typewriter? It seemed to her that most women dressed to please men rather than for their own purposes, and she really couldn't be bothered with that. Besides, on those occasions when she did make an effort, she didn't seem able to pull off quite the right look. She preferred to dress for comfort rather than style.

Not tonight, though. The girls had given her the full makeover. Vivienne had done her make-up and Julia tamed her wild curls into an elegant updo. She was wearing a sophisticated emerald-green dress. It was a Pierre Cardin, one of the gowns her mother had purchased as part of her new wardrobe. Julia had insisted on lending her a fur stole, and she'd borrowed a pair of heels from Vivienne. The black satin purse was her own.

She'd felt awkward coming downstairs dressed to the nines, but Julia had insisted, and now she was at the restaurant she understood why. Her normal attire would have made her stand out for all the wrong reasons here.

The waiter led them to a private booth. As Sadie sank onto the maroon leather seat she was reminded of dinners in New York with her parents. There were so many things she didn't miss about her life back home, but she did occasionally miss the city itself – the stores, the restaurants, the accents. Every now and then she even missed the weather. There was something to be said for curling up in front of a fire on a cold winter's day. Out here, winter was barely noticeable.

The truth was, she was wondering if her father had been right after all. Maybe it had been ridiculous to think she could make it in LA by herself. She'd been here almost three months and she wasn't any closer to getting a job as a scriptwriter. She'd tried each of the studios and they'd politely taken her resume, promising they'd be in touch if a suitable position became available. As yet, no one had called.

Her friends assured her that it would happen in time. 'Hollywood is all about relationships,' Peggy told her. 'You have to get out and meet people. Every party, every date, every audition is an opportunity.'

'But there aren't auditions for scriptwriters. I've applied to every studio without luck. I'm not sure there's anything more I can do,' she'd replied, and Peggy hadn't had an answer for that.

She wasn't sure about Julia's grand plan for her to work in Harry Gold's office. Typing letters and making coffee wasn't what she'd envisaged when she'd dreamt of a studio job. And honestly? This idea of somehow bumping into Harry Gold and him miraculously offering her a job seemed ludicrous. But Julia had been adamant. 'What's the worst thing that could happen?' she'd asked. 'We all have a nice dinner? How terrible! It's my treat, by the way.'

Julia had a point there. If nothing else, it would be fun for the four of them to share a lovely dinner, away from the club and unencumbered by dates. Sadie resolved to enjoy the night for its own pleasures and not think too hard about what might come of it.

'Shall we have champagne?' Julia asked in response to the waiter's question about aperitifs. 'My treat, remember.'

'Oh, that seems a bit extravagant,' Peggy said.

'Live a little, Peg,' Vivienne replied. 'It's not as if you have to be up early tomorrow.'

'Don't remind me. But I guess you're right. One drink probably won't hurt.'

Julia ordered a bottle and, once the waiter was gone, lowered her voice. 'He's here already and he's seen us.'

'Where?' asked Sadie, slightly panicked. 'And how do you know he's seen us?'

'He nodded at me as I walked to the table. Everything is going to plan.'

'Aren't you worried you'll get in trouble for being out on a school night, Julia?' Vivienne said.

'Not at all. I'm not allowed to *date* during the week, but no one said anything about having dinner with my friends. A girl has to eat, doesn't she?'

Vivienne wrinkled her nose as she took a bread stick from the basket at the centre of the table. 'I'd hate to have to answer to the studio the way you do.'

'I wouldn't care,' Peggy jumped in, before Julia could answer. 'I'd give anything to have what Julia has.'

'Oh, Peg,' Julia said, 'your turn will come, just you wait and see. With your talent, it's only a matter of time before you get a major role.'

Peggy's eyes flashed with irritation. 'If only that were true!'

'If *One Starry Night* is the hit everyone thinks it will be, you might get some attention. It certainly won't hurt to have it on your resume when you're auditioning,' Julia said. 'Goldstar will be sorry they let you get away when you get snapped up by one of the other studios.'

'Maybe.'

It was unlike Peggy to be anything other than cheerful and optimistic, but last month her option with Goldstar had expired and the studio had declined to sign a new contract. She'd been auditioning without luck and had recently started working as an extra. It was good, honest work, but not what Peggy yearned for. Sadie understood her frustration.

To date, Julia was the only one of their quartet to taste success. Vivienne had secured some supporting roles but nothing major. She was a survivor, though. Sadie had no doubt she'd make something happen for herself, because what other choice was there? Vivienne didn't talk about it much, but Sadie knew that there was no safety net for her friend. Unlike the rest of them, Vivienne didn't have a family to go home to. Sadie's parents might not understand her, or even approve of the life she was leading, but Sadie knew they'd be there if she chose to go back home. Peggy and Julia had similarly fraught relationships with their families, but at least they had families. Vivienne seemed to have no one else in the world other than the three of them.

Once the waiter poured their champagne, Sadie was jolted from her thoughts by Julia's toast.

'To new friends. May our bond continue to grow.'

Peggy smiled, her mood sunny once more. 'To friendship,' she said.

'To friendship!' Vivienne and Sadie echoed.

Another waiter arrived soon after with their menus. They all listened intently while he rattled off the day's specials. For a while their attention was focused on what to order. Sadie was debating the merits of a pasta dish with Julia, who seemed to think it would be delicious but

50

prohibitively fattening, when a man stopped by their table. Assuming he was one of the waiters, Sadie looked up at him to ask his opinion and was startled to find Harry Gold himself smiling down at her.

'Good evening, ladies.'

'Harry,' Julia said, in a sultry voice. 'How lovely to see you.' She held out her hand to him and he kissed it. 'May I introduce you to my dearest friends in the world?'

'I'd be delighted if you would.'

'Harry Gold, I'd like you to meet Miss Vivienne Lockhart, Miss Peggy Carmichael and Miss Sadie Shore. Ladies: Harry, as I'm sure you know, is the illustrious head of Goldstar Studios.'

Sadie's throat went dry as Harry Gold nodded and smiled at each one of them in turn. 'Are you girls all residents of the Hollywood Studio Club?'

'We are,' said Vivienne, expertly fluttering her lashes in his direction.

Sadie felt sick as she watched the studio head's gaze move from Vivienne's face to her chest. Julia must be crazy if she thought he was going to take any notice of a plain Jane like her when she was sitting opposite a sexpot like Vivienne, who seemed to light up from within every time a powerful man paid her attention. Even Peggy, who was a natural beauty, faded into insignificance beside Vivienne's luminosity.

Harry Gold nodded towards the champagne glasses. 'And what are we celebrating? A successful audition, perhaps?' His gaze returned to Vivienne.

'No, no, nothing like that,' Julia said. 'Sadie here is just a little homesick, that's all. We thought we'd treat her to an Italian meal to remind her of home.'

Mr Gold turned to look at Sadie properly. 'You're from Italy?'

'New York.'

He laughed. 'So, Miss Shore, you don't like California?'

'Oh no, I like it very much, but every now and then a girl needs a little taste of home, especially seeing as I won't be there for Christmas this year. Julia assured me that Musso and Frank's would fit the bill.'

'Ah, now I hear the accent,' Harry said. 'I'll be sure to keep you in mind, Miss Shore, if we're casting a movie that calls for a gal from New York.'

'Oh, I'm not an actress, Mr Gold.'

'No? What brings you to Hollywood, then?'

'I'm a writer.'

His eyes sparkled with curiosity. 'And what have you written?'

Sadie's courage faltered. 'Well, I haven't had anything published yet. I was hoping to get a job in the script department of one of the studios, but I haven't had any luck.'

'I'm sorry to hear that.' Harry's gaze drifted back to Vivienne.

'Sadie's being modest,' Julia said. 'She's writing a screenplay.'

Harry smiled benignly, his attention still focused on Vivienne. 'How wonderful.'

'It will be,' Julia assured him. 'Sadie's not just a pretty face. She's a college graduate and the smartest person I know.'

Heat rushed to Sadie's cheeks at her friend's praise. 'Oh, I wouldn't—'

'Is that so?' Harry turned to look at her once more. 'Where did you attend college?'

'Sarah Lawrence.'

He looked impressed. 'Are you working at the moment, Miss Shore?'

Sadie nodded. 'I have a job waitressing.'

'I'm sure a smart girl like you can do better than that. Listen, I don't know that we have any vacancies in the script department right now, but I do have an opening in my office and I think you'd be perfect. Why don't you swing by the studio tomorrow morning, say around ten, and we can have a little chat about it? I'm keen to put someone on before the start of the new year.'

'Oh!' Sadie couldn't keep the excitement from her voice. She could hardly believe Julia's plan had actually worked. 'That would be wonderful, Mr Gold. Thank you so much.'

'Any friend of Julia's is a friend of mine.' He smiled briefly at Sadie and then turned his attention back to Vivienne. 'Delighted to have met you all, ladies. I'll leave you to enjoy your champagne.'

28 December 1999

I'm standing in front of my wardrobe trying to pick an outfit for tonight's reunion. Peggy has told me to 'dress up' but I'm not sure how far to take that advice. She and Julia are wearing proper evening gowns, but I'm wondering if that's overkill. Besides, no matter what the two of them wear they'll look perfect – they always do – whereas I always seem to be just shy of the mark. I look at the pile of discarded garments on my bed and, no closer to a decision than I was an hour ago, decide a break is in order. Perhaps a coffee will bring me the clarity I need to decide.

My dachshund, Weenie, follows me out of the bedroom into the kitchen, her paws pattering on the terracotta floors as she tries to keep up. As I grind beans to be added into Gianni's beloved *caffettiera*, Weenie turns donuts at my feet, clearly expecting a treat for herself. When the coffee's done, I take two pieces of biscotti from the cookie jar – one for me, one for Weenie – and head out to drink my espresso on the terrace.

Looking out over the garden always brings me peace. It's hard to believe now, but I used to have no interest in gardening. This glorious backyard was Gianni's domain, but once he was gone I couldn't bear to see it wither and die, so I had no choice but to learn how to care for it. In the early days after his death, tending this garden was the only thing that kept me going. Over time, as I watered, pruned, planted and weeded, I realised that putting my bare hands into the soil Gianni had toiled kept him close. Now, every time I pick a lemon or a tomato, or I smell the sweet scent of lavender wafting in through the terrace doors, I feel as if a little piece of my darling is still with me.

When I lost him, the well of words inside me ran dry. No matter how hard I tried, I couldn't for the life of me think of anything worthwhile to write. What would be the point without Gianni to read it for me? How could I finish a script without talking to him about my draft, without his insightful suggestions and constant encouragement? It simply wasn't possible. Instead, I poured all that pent-up creativity into his garden.

I like to think that Gianni is guiding me from beyond the grave, although I'm not sure he'd completely approve of all my choices. He was mainly concerned with building a productive garden, whereas my gift is creating beauty. In any case, whether it's divine intervention or simply an ability I didn't know I possessed, gardening has been my saviour. It's taken some time but as well as tending Gianni's patch, I've built a new career making beautiful outdoor spaces for others.

'Vivienne's back,' I say, in the general direction of the lemon tree. 'What do you make of that?' My eyes scan the yard, looking for a sign – sometimes I fancy Gianni talks to me through the garden – but today he's silent. I sigh heavily. This is a situation I will have to face alone.

Ever since breakfast with the girls yesterday morning, my brain has been in overdrive.

Girls. How ridiculous that we still call each other that when we are, of course, fully grown women. But we met in our youth and to each other we are perpetually young, even though the signs of ageing are now visible in us all.

Well, maybe not *all*. Vivienne has not aged a day in my imagination. The last time I saw her in the flesh she was in her twenties. Back then her skin was unlined and dewy, her hair thick and lustrous, and she had a figure that stopped men in their tracks. Have those luscious curves now morphed into fat? Will age have thinned her once plump lips? Is her skin now saggy and wrinkled like mine? It's hard to picture her as anything but the sex kitten she was. There were a couple of photos snapped of her in Northern California in the months after she left Los Angeles, but since then, nothing. I always thought she could have been the greatest actress of all time, but I guess the press saw her as just another failed Hollywood wannabe.

The thought of seeing her again makes my stomach fizz with excitement and nerves. Once, she was my closest friend. Maybe it was foolish of me, but I loved her. The others do not feel the same way about Vivienne's sudden reappearance, though. Julia still carries the scars of her betrayal. Time has passed but the wound is yet to heal, and I think it's safe to say that's not likely to change. Peggy . . . I'm not sure how she's feeling about facing Vivienne again.

Whatever happens, I am the one who will be caught in the middle. Torn between the girl I once knew and loved, and the women who've been by my side through the best and worst times of my life.

I'm not sure there's an outfit for that.

All the dithering about what to wear to this reunion has made me late. I hadn't counted on the traffic being jammed in the streets around the Studio Club. There's a line of cars headed towards Lodi Place, which my driver joins, but it takes us ten minutes to get anywhere near the club's entrance.

It seems there's been a bumper turnout to this reunion, probably spurred by the fact that now the latest tenants have left, the building is up for sale and there are whispers that a developer wants to buy and demolish it. This might be our final chance to bid the old girl farewell.

After an afternoon of trying on different ensembles, I settled on the outfit I bought to wear to the Emmys the last time Peggy had been nominated. It's a floor-length black dress, and more fitted than I'd usually wear. I've paired it with silver strappy heels, which are not in the slightest bit comfortable. I had worried this outfit was excessive for the alumni reunion, but now that I'm here, I'm glad I didn't settle for slacks and a silk blouse.

There's an actual red carpet, flanked by reporters and fans, which stretches from the kerb to the entrance, and when my driver pulls up in front of it I regret the decision to come alone. Peggy and Julia are coming together but I declined Julia's offer of a ride, agreeing to travel home with them instead. I figured that would give me the best of both worlds – peace and a clear mind on the way to the event and the opportunity for the three of us to debrief on the way home. Now I'm desperately missing my friends as I step onto the red carpet alone.

Fortunately, neither the reporters nor the crowd are interested in me. I'm not a movie star and I never have been. They crane their necks to look past me to whoever is in the car behind. Maybe they'll get lucky with the next arrival. I make my way along the carpet and up the stairs to the entrance as fast as my too-high heels will allow. Just inside the door I'm greeted by one of the committee members – a much younger woman than me who I don't recognise. She hands me a name tag and tells me to make my way through to the area on my right, where drinks and hors d'oeuvres are being served.

I haven't been inside this building since the late 1950s. Although the decor is different, the building itself hasn't changed much. My head moves from side to side as I attempt to take it all in. The reception area with its wall of pigeonholes looks the same, except a big desktop computer has replaced the leather-bound ledger that once held pride of place on the desk. The sweeping staircase off to my left still has the wrought-iron and timber balustrade I remember, and the huge arched windows that give the building its distinctive character also remain unchanged.

I follow the crowd into the living area and am momentarily swamped with memories of this room: Peggy sitting in the armchair under the window, filing her nails; Julia, cross-legged on the floor, entertaining us all with behind-the-scenes gossip from the set of her latest movie; Vivienne curled up on the sofa, reading. All the old furniture is gone, though. The rooms are empty except for some mass-produced pieces that have been hired for tonight's party. Bar tables adorned with white tablecloths and silver helium-balloon centrepieces are dotted around the room. Chairs line the perimeter, in an obvious concession to the many older guests, and the walls are hung with large photo boards. I drift over to the one nearest me and spy a photo of Vivienne doing Peggy's make-up. My eyes mist with tears, but before I can get too carried away with emotion, Peggy's voice comes from behind me. 'I can't believe we got here before you!'

I turn to face her. Both she and Julia are laughing.

'Neither can I! But I couldn't decide what to wear, which held me up a little, and then the driver insisted on letting me out at the red carpet, so we were stuck in that line of cars.'

Julia tilts an almost-empty champagne glass at me. 'You look gorgeous, darling.'

'Thank you. You're looking very lovely yourself. And you too, Peg. As always.'

Peggy eyes the room and then nods her approval. 'Everyone seems to have made an effort, although I have to say, ladies, we are the pick of the bunch.'

Julia laughs as she flags down a passing waiter. She swaps her now-empty glass for a full one and takes another, which she hands to me. Peggy's glass is still half-full, which indicates that Julia has downed hers faster than usual. She's not much of a drinker these days, especially at events like this, because she likes to keep a clear head. Perhaps she is steeling herself for a possible meeting with Vivienne. I'm not sure that adding alcohol into the mix will yield desirable results, but with Julia already tense, I'm reluctant to raise the issue, even gently.

Is Vivienne even here? Perhaps we are getting ourselves worked up for no reason.

As Peggy and Julia talk fashion choices, I surreptitiously scan the room. There's no sign of her but that doesn't mean she isn't lurking somewhere. There must be at least fifty women in this room alone, and there are more in the old dining room. I'm not even sure that I would recognise her these days. I could be looking right at her and not even realise.

I dare not ask the others if they've spied her. Julia seems to be calm enough – her overly enthusiastic consumption of alcohol notwithstanding – and I don't want to say anything that might upset her equilibrium. Peggy, it seems, has no such qualms, because she answers my unasked question.

'She's not here yet, but they're expecting her.'

I glance at Julia, who takes another swig of champagne, and then turn my attention back to Peggy. 'How do you know?'

'The lovely alumni member who greeted you at the door – Connie – happens to be a fan of mine. I asked her to give me a nod when Vivienne arrives but not to tell Vivienne I'm here. I said I wanted to surprise her.'

'How will Connie know it's her?' I ask. Vivienne hasn't been sighted for years, and I'm not sure anyone younger than us would remember her from her film career.

'She probably won't recognise her, but Vivienne will have to register and pick up a name tag, just like the rest of us,' Peggy says, with a hint of irritation in her voice.

'Of course,' I say, feeling foolish. I turn my attention back to Julia. 'Jules, you know you don't have to talk to her, right? In this crowd it will be easy to avoid her. There's no reason to get worked up.'

'I'm not "worked up". I'm totally fine,' she responds tersely. 'However, I will not be speaking to that woman. Just so we're clear.' Her eyes bore into mine, making it plain that she sees me as the weakest link where Vivienne is concerned.

We're interrupted then by a woman I don't recognise who wants a photo with Peggy and Julia. I offer to take it, which is why I am the one who notices Connie waving in our direction. Once the photo is taken, I hand the camera back to the woman, who is gushing about how much she loves watching *At Home with Peggy Carmichael*. I try to catch Peggy's eye, but she's too busy basking in compliments to notice.

And then it's too late.

Vivienne Lockhart is standing at the room's entrance.

1956

Chapter 7

Peggy

Peggy checked her appearance in the full-length mirror one last time. The pale pink floor-length sheath she'd made herself was an almost perfect copy of a Dior dress she'd seen Doris Day wear. The material had cost a bomb, but it was worth every penny. To make it unique she'd added an organza train, which she'd attached at the shoulders, and she'd sewn a row of tiny fabric rosebuds along the neckline. Matching elbow-length gloves and pink kitten heels completed her look. The result was stunning, even if she did say so herself.

It seemed the whole of the Studio Club was excited about the premiere of *One Starry Night*, even though most of them wouldn't be attending – at least not as invited guests. Quite a few of the girls planned to make their way down to the cinema to watch Julia and the rest of the cast walk the red carpet. The general excitement had translated into a desire to be involved in the preparations in some small way. Julia's gown was provided by the studio, and she was getting her hair and make-up done at the Max Factor Beauty Room, so she wasn't around for the other girls to fuss over. That left Peggy, Sadie and Vivienne in the spotlight.

While the other two seemed bemused by all the attention, Peggy revelled in the moment. Trudie loaned her a pale pink satin purse, Janet painted her nails and Babs had done a lovely job on her hair. Her golden locks were now twisted into an elegant knot on top of her head with a couple of soft curls left loose to frame her face.

Vivienne had insisted on doing her make-up, and Sadie's too, despite Sadie's protests that there was no need for her to be 'all gussied up'.

'It's a big premiere. You never know who we might meet,' Vivienne explained as she applied a layer of blue eyeshadow to Sadie's lids. 'It's important to look our best.'

These were Peggy's thoughts exactly. She was hoping that if she looked the part, perhaps a director would notice her, or the press might interview her. Julia might be the star, but she had a tiny role in the movie too. It was just a few lines, but who knew? It might be enough to catapult her to bigger and better things. She was getting a chance to walk the red carpet and she wasn't going to waste it.

Sadie, however, seemed unconvinced. 'For you, maybe, but I'm not an actress. No one will be looking at me.'

'This is Julia's big night and we are her guests,' Vivienne said. 'We don't want to let her down. Now close your eyes and let me finish.'

As a member of the cast, Peggy was an invited guest in her own right. Theoretically, she could even bring a date, but Sharon from publicity had strongly suggested she go with Brad Tillman, another actor with a minor part, and Peggy – ever eager to please – had gone along with that suggestion.

Julia had been given two tickets for VIP guests and Peggy knew that she'd excitedly offered one of these to her dad. But he'd been unable to make it and so she'd gifted the tickets to her friends instead.

There was a knock on her door. 'Peg, are you dressed?' Sadie called as she opened the door and poked her head around the corner. 'Wow! You look absolutely stunning.'

'Do you think so?'

'I really do. You're going to knock everyone's socks off!'

'We make a pretty pair, then.' For all her protests about dressing up, Sadie looked lovely. Babs had managed to tame her wild dark curls into a French roll and she wore a simple floor-length cornflower-blue gown. 'You look gorgeous, Sade.'

'Thanks. I didn't want to let Julia down by being her frumpy friend.'

'You are never frumpy, but tonight you have outdone yourself. Where's Vivienne? Is she ready?'

'She was just dabbing on some perfume. We'll go down first, to make sure your date is already there, and when we give you the nod you can make your entrance.'

'That's very thoughtful of you.'

'Not at all. I know the focus is on Julia, but it's a big night for you too.' Sadie took one of her hands and squeezed it. 'I'm looking forward to seeing *both* my beautiful friends on the big screen tonight.'

'Thanks, Sadie.'

Vivienne, dressed in a figure-hugging white satin dress with a plunging neckline – way too daring in Peggy's opinion – was waiting for them at the top of the stairs. 'Well, ladies, I think the three of us will turn some heads tonight. Let's get this show on the road!'

Brad was waiting downstairs and seemed suitably impressed with her appearance. 'What a lucky fellow I am to have such a beautiful girl on my arm. I'm honoured to be your date, Peggy,' he gushed.

'Thank you. Now, shall we go? I don't want to be late.'

When they arrived at the Chinese Theatre, Peggy was thrilled to see hundreds – maybe even thousands – of people lined up to catch a glimpse of their favourite stars. There was no time to enjoy the moment, though, as she and Brad were quickly ushered down the red carpet. A few photographers snapped the pair of them, and one reporter asked her name, so that was a start, she supposed.

She had hoped to wait outside until Julia arrived, so she could greet her friend and wish her luck. She figured when the press saw that she was a close friend of the movie's leading lady they would want to know more about her. Unfortunately, they'd arrived well ahead of Julia's car and the ushers insisted they make their way inside immediately.

There wasn't any sign of Vivienne and Sadie, even though their car had left the club at the same time as Peggy's. Never mind. Julia had made sure they would all be seated with her. That fact alone should be enough to make people sit up and take notice.

In the theatre foyer, a waiter approached them with saucers of champagne. 'Here's to a successful premiere,' Brad said, raising his glass.

Peggy tipped her glass slightly but said nothing. Brad really was quite handsome but she'd seen him act – he was never going to be a star. As far as dates went, he was a suitable escort for tonight but she didn't want him getting the wrong idea. She was looking for more than what Brad Tillman had to offer.

'Well, look at us, hobnobbing with all the stars,' he said. 'Isn't that Cary Grant over there? Oh, look, there's Liz Taylor.'

'I'm sure you've seen at least some of these stars on set,' Peggy replied coolly. For heaven's sake – didn't Brad realise that if you wanted to be treated like a star you had to act like one?

'Yeah, of course I have, but I don't know . . . all dressed up like this and all in the one room, it kinda feels different, you know?' He sounded exactly like the smalltown boy he most likely was. Just like all the boys back home she was trying to escape.

Fortunately, she was saved from further small talk with Brad by the arrival of Sadie and Vivienne. 'What happened to you two?'

Sadie smoothed down her frock self-consciously. 'Stuck in traffic. I was worried we would be late. But Julia's car was just pulling up behind us. She's walking the red carpet now.'

'It might take a while,' Vivienne added. 'She can't go two steps without a reporter or a fan stopping her.'

Peggy fought the rush of envy she felt. She was pleased for her friend, truly. Was it so terrible that she wanted the exact same thing for herself?

An announcement came through the PA system, asking those gathered in the foyer to please take their seats. As they made their way to the cinema's entrance, Brad took Peggy's ticket from her to show the ushers. Vivienne and Sadie followed behind.

The entire theatre was decked out in red, white and blue to mark the Independence Day holiday. Miniature American flags adorned each seatback and hung from the front of the stage. A young man in a smart red uniform showed Peggy and Brad to their seats, four rows from the front. Vivienne and Sadie were ushered to the first row.

'Excuse me,' Peggy called to the usher. 'I think there's been some sort of mistake. I'm supposed to be seated with Miss Newman.'

The usher looked irritated but asked to see their tickets. 'I'm sorry, miss. These are your seats. There's nothing I can do about it. The first three rows are for VIPs and they're reserved. These here are some of the best seats in the house, miss.'

'They're fine,' Brad said. 'Thank you so much.'

The usher nodded and took his leave.

Peggy shot him a furious glance. 'Julia promised we'd all be together.'

Brad frowned at her. 'These are much better seats than I imagined we'd have.' He lowered his voice to a whisper. 'Look, there's James Stewart just a few seats over and . . . good grief, that's Ava Gardner in the row *behind* us. You should count yourself lucky. Most of our cast-mates will be way down the back.'

'But,' Peggy said, indignantly, 'I'm Julia's roommate. Her *best* friend. Why should I be all the way back here when Vivienne and Sadie are right up front? They're not even in the movie.'

'For heaven's sake, Peggy, sit down and stop making a scene. Do you want us to end up in the back row? Just relax and focus on enjoying the night.'

If Brad Tillman thought he was getting a goodnight kiss from her later that evening, he was going to be sadly disappointed. She opened her mouth, about to tell him she would not be bossed around by the likes of him, when the theatre lights suddenly went down. A spotlight was trained on a microphone stand at the centre of the stage, in front of the screen. The evening's emcee stepped up to the mic. 'Ladies and gentlemen, welcome to Grauman's Chinese Theatre on this Fourth of July holiday. We are, of course, all here tonight to see the premiere of a dazzling new film, *One Starry Night*.'

Peggy tuned out. She already knew what the movie was about. She wanted to get on with the viewing now, to see herself up there on the screen. It wasn't the first time she'd been in a movie, but she'd never been in such a big-budget film before, one that was destined to be a hit. And it was the largest speaking role she'd ever had. In the past she'd mainly been hired for her dancing skills. Occasionally she'd had a line or two as well. But this time she had a whole scene with the leading man, Cal Brooks. It was an airport scene and she'd got to wear a smart Dior suit that showed off her figure beautifully. The director had told her she'd been great. Even though Goldstar had let her go, surely after this performance she'd get an offer from one of the other studios.

Financially, things were becoming dire. She'd been working as an extra to get by. She kept hoping that would lead to something more, but even after auditioning for practically every part going, she hadn't been successful. Well, there had been *one* offer, but it wasn't a movie. Last week she'd auditioned at Ciro's nightclub for a singing gig. This morning the manager had left a message to say the job was hers if she wanted it. She'd call him first thing in the morning to tell him the bad news. Ciro's might be a famous club, but she hadn't come to Hollywood to be the opening act for anyone. She'd come to be a star!

The spotlight moved from the stage to the entrance at the rear of the theatre, and the emcee's voice boomed from the microphone. 'Ladies and gentlemen, I give you the director and stars of tonight's movie. Please make welcome director James Graydon.' Applause filled the theatre as the director made his way down the aisle and continued as the leading man, Cal Brooks, was welcomed. 'And now,' the master of ceremonies said, 'it is my very great pleasure to introduce our beautiful and talented leading lady, Miss Julia Newman!'

The applause was thunderous as Julia stepped into the spotlight. Peggy gasped when she saw how stunning her friend looked. Julia's frock had a strapless black satin bodice and a full skirt comprised of layers and layers of white organza. She wore black pumps, elbow-length black satin gloves, and carried a matching satin purse. Julia's ash-blonde hair was combed back off her face and set into loose waves.

A single strand of pearls and a white fur stole, which was draped elegantly around her shoulders, completed her outfit.

Julia made her way down the aisle to take her seat, stopping to blow Peggy a kiss on the way. Peggy's heart sang at the gesture. This was going to be a magnificent night.

The movie wasn't hard to enjoy. It had an engaging storyline, and Cal played the part of a bad boy with a good heart perfectly. If Peggy were to be critical – and she *never* would be outside of her own thoughts – she would say that Julia's performance was a trifle restrained. Not terrible, of course, but missing the depth that a truly great performer brought to the screen. Peggy couldn't help but think if she'd been given the role of Lila she would have played the character with more heart.

Suddenly the moment she'd been waiting for was upon her. Cal's character was entering the airport. There she was, walking towards him. She leant forward in her chair eagerly, but seconds later her excitement turned to confusion. Something was wrong. Instead of crashing into her and sending her belongings flying, Cal was now heading up the stairs. Now he was running towards the departure lounge.

Her scene had been cut!

Peggy slumped back in her seat and didn't even attempt to stop the tears from coming. It wasn't fair. She'd done everything right, *everything*.

She worked on her craft as much as possible, taking singing, dancing and acting classes. She auditioned for parts big and small. She was cheerful and optimistic, always listened to feedback and tried her best to respond. No matter what happened, she never, ever complained.

Where had that got her? Precisely nowhere. Instead, her charming but talentless roommate was the hottest star in Hollywood. She loved Julia like a sister and didn't want her to fail, but she couldn't help but feel the injustice of it all. Why Julia? Why not her?

Brad leant over and offered her his handkerchief, which she reluctantly accepted. He picked up her hand from the armrest and squeezed it. 'It's very romantic, isn't it?'

Peggy pulled away and dabbed her eyes before sitting up straight. Tonight might be the worst night of her life, but she would not compound it by allowing Brad to think he had a chance with her. Nor was she going to let this setback derail her. She was tougher than that. Her mama always said God had a plan for each of his children. God loved her, she knew this. He wouldn't let her down. She just needed to be patient. In the meantime, she supposed she wouldn't be disappointing the manager at Ciro's after all.

Chapter 8

Sadie

Sadie closed Mr Gold's office door behind her, leaving her boss to contemplate the list of replacement actors she'd suggested. This time yesterday she'd had to deliver the news that Columbia were refusing to loan out William Holden for Goldstar's next big movie. Her boss's fury at this rejection had caused the atmosphere in their luxurious suite of offices to feel stifling, despite the recently installed air conditioning. Thankfully, he was calmer today, albeit still furious with his counterpart at Columbia.

As she entered her office, she saw Jack Porter had planted his backside on the corner of her desk. He grinned as she approached. 'Have dinner with me tonight?'

Sadie rolled her eyes. Jumping Jack, as the typing pool called him, was the stereotypical Hollywood cad – a tall, dark and handsome devil. He was charming, but as a reporter he was not to be trusted. She'd been working as Harry Gold's personal secretary for almost seven months now and she'd got wise to the press's tricks.

The job had turned out to be more demanding – and more interesting – than Sadie could ever have imagined. She'd envisaged a nine-to-five job where her main duties would be taking dictation and typing letters (neither of which was her forte), but these tasks were often relegated to the junior secretaries. Sadie's role was somewhat more . . . she wasn't sure how to describe it. Intimate, perhaps. And varied.

It had taken her a few months to gain his trust, but now that she had, Harry required her opinion on *everything*. Sadie was consulted on which tie he should wear, which gifts to buy his wife, where he should eat dinner and even which screenplays he should acquire. No one got to speak to Harry without going through Sadie – they literally had to *go through* her office to reach his – which made her the object of much flattery. Jack Porter had been trying it on since the day she'd arrived. He was nothing if not persistent.

'Sorry, Jack. I have plans. Was there something else you needed?'

'Geez, Sadie, you make a fella feel unwanted.' He was holding a rolled-up magazine, which he pointed at her. 'What about a quick drink after work?'

'No. Now, what can I do for you? If you're wanting an appointment with Mr Gold, I'm afraid he's booked up all afternoon. I might be able to squeeze you in for five minutes tomorrow morning if you're prepared to come in early.'

'Nah, that's fine. It was you I wanted to see.'

'Well, you've seen me. Now, if you don't mind . . .'

Jack unrolled the magazine and opened it up on her desk.

'For heaven's sake. I have work to do.'

'Hold on to your hat. I want to show you something.' He flicked to the middle of the magazine and pointed to an article. 'Have you seen this? It just hit newsstands this morning.'

Sadie glanced at the headline. *No Fireworks: July Fourth Fizzle*. Underneath was the promotional photo for Julia's newly released film. Sadie's mouth went dry as she began to read.

There is no doubt Julia Newman is one of the most beautiful women to ever grace our screens. The camera loves her, and audiences can't help but be drawn in by her breathtaking beauty. The question is, can she act?

After first coming to our screens in a supporting role, Miss Newman has recently gone on to star in several of Goldstar's big-budget productions. The studio seems to be positioning her as their number one leading lady, their very own Marilyn Monroe or Grace Kelly. But unlike those ladies, Julia simply doesn't have what it takes.

Princess Grace brought class and authenticity to her roles. Marilyn oozes sex appeal. Sadly, Julia does neither. Audiences have given her the benefit of the doubt so far, but her lacklustre performance in One Starry Night *might have the execs at Goldstar wondering if she is worth their investment.*

Sadie couldn't bear to read more. Poor Julia. Perhaps she wasn't up to Grace Kelly's standard yet, but she had never claimed to be.

She narrowed her eyes as she looked at Jack. 'Why are you showing me this?'

'Well, you're friends, aren't you?'

'Yes, but if you think that means I'll give you any behind-the-scenes gossip, you are very much mistaken.'

Jack's eyes widened in what could only be mock horror. 'As if I would put you in that position. I was merely alerting you to the story in case you hadn't seen it. I imagine Julia will be quite upset by it. Particularly if Harry is thinking about releasing her from her contract.'

'Forget it, Jack. You're not getting a word out of me. Off you go. I'm busy. Go and annoy someone else.'

Jack held up his hands in a show of surrender. 'If you change your mind about dinner . . .'

'I can assure you I won't.' Fortunately, the office phone rang at that precise moment. She picked up the receiver while shooing Jack away with her free hand. 'Mr Gold's office, Sadie Shore speaking.'

'Sadie, it's me, Julia. There's some sort of technical hitch over on sound stage seven, so we're finishing up for the day. I was wondering if you had time for lunch.'

Usually, the answer would be a firm no. Sadie's days started early and ended late. She only got time away from the office to eat when she was required to accompany Mr Gold to a lunchtime meeting. But considering the article she'd just read, she wondered if she might make an exception. If Julia was aware of the article – and given the tone of her voice it seemed likely that she was – she could probably use some company. 'Let me see if Mr Gold can spare me for an hour or so. I'll call you back in five minutes.'

She knocked briefly on her boss's door before entering. He looked up and said, 'What do you think of Montgomery Clift to replace Holden?'

Sadie nodded. 'I can see that. In fact, he might be an even better choice.'

'Okay. Let's put in a call to his agent. See if we can set up a meeting with Clift and the director.'

'I'll get onto it right away. Mr Gold, I was wondering if you would mind terribly if I took an hour or so off for lunch today?'

He looked concerned. 'Is everything all right? Are you unwell?'

'Oh, goodness, no. Nothing like that. It's just that . . .' She glanced at the pile of newspapers and magazines she'd placed on his desk earlier that morning. They looked to be untouched.

'What? What is it?'

She sighed. 'It's Julia. Have you read Freda's piece in *Screen Magic* today?'

'I haven't got to the papers yet. What's that sour old cow saying?'

Sadie retrieved the magazine from his desk and opened it to the relevant page. 'I'm sorry I didn't see this earlier. I was taken up with the Columbia situation.'

Mr Gold grunted and held out his hand for the magazine. He quickly scanned the article, thumping the magazine down on his desk when he was done. 'Goddammit! Vicious old crone. What the hell does she know?' He took off his glasses and pinched the bridge of his nose between his thumb and forefinger. 'It's not *true*, is it? I mean, you've seen the movie. What did you think?'

'Of course it's not true,' Sadie said, rushing to defend her friend. 'It's unfair to compare her to Marilyn or Grace. Julia has different qualities to those women, and besides, both of them have been around for a while. Julia's just getting started. She's still learning.'

'Hmmm.' He didn't sound convinced.

'Look at the box office takings. If she's such a flop, why do audiences love her so much?'

Mr Gold perked up. 'Yes! You're quite right. Her previous movie was a smash hit and there's no reason to believe *One Starry Night* won't be the same. You saw the crowds lined up to attend the premiere. I haven't got the full figures from last week yet, but the early reports were very encouraging. Bloody Freda doesn't know what she's talking about. You know, she's always been particularly close to Ralph over at Columbia. Maybe he put her up to this.'

'Maybe.' It was possible. Although, if Sadie was being perfectly honest, there was a kernel of truth to Freda's story. Julia was an adequate actress, but there was nothing compelling or outstanding about her performances. Julia was aware of this and worried endlessly about her lack of skill. Which was why Sadie was concerned about the impact the article might have on her.

'In any case, what does this'—he tapped the article with his hand—'have to do with taking lunch?'

'Julia just called to ask if I could meet her today. It's out of the ordinary for her and I wondered if she might be upset.'

'Yes, I see. Good thinking. Take lunch. In fact, take the afternoon if you need it. We can't have our star feeling out of sorts. Especially when we're only halfway through shooting her current movie. I can't have her losing confidence before the film's done. Julia needs to be kept happy. Take her to Chasen's and put it on the studio account.'

'Thank you, Mr Gold.'

'Don't mention it. Just make sure you get in touch with Clift's agent before you go. Set up a meeting for first thing tomorrow. Don't take no for an answer.'

'Consider it done.'

Chapter 9

Julia

Julia looked up from the menu she'd been studying. 'Isn't this lovely? I have to say, when I called earlier I didn't think Harry would agree to let you off the lot. I thought a quick bite to eat in the canteen would be the best I could hope for, if anything. Now I find out he's given you the afternoon off *and* he's paying for us to have lunch. What's this all about?'

Sadie smiled at her from across the booth. 'What can I tell you? He's in an unusually generous mood.'

'That doesn't sound like Harry. He never agrees to anything unless there's some benefit to him. Are you blackmailing him, Sade? What do you have on him that I don't know about?'

Sadie turned her palms to the ceiling. 'Nothing, I swear.'

They were briefly interrupted by the waiter taking their order. Sadie went for the ribs with a side of potatoes au gratin. Just where that girl put her food was a mystery. She ate like a horse but never put on an ounce of fat. Julia chose a salad. As always.

'Really, Jules?' Sadie asked after Julia instructed the waiter to leave the dressing on the side. 'Live it up a little, just this once. The ribs here are amazing, and the steak too. Or what about the lobster? The studio's treat, remember.'

'I've got to watch my figure. After all, my looks are all I've got going for me. It's not as if I can act.'

'Oh, Jules.' Sadie's smile faded. 'You've seen Freda's article then?'

Julia sighed. 'It was all anyone could talk about on set. Of course, no one spoke directly to me about it, but I could hear the whispers and see the sideways glances. It wasn't great. I couldn't focus. In fact, if I'm being honest, I'm almost certain that there was no technical difficulty. I think the director could see how rattled I was and shut us down for the day to give me a chance to lick my wounds in private.'

'You know the article's not true, don't you?' Sadie looked at her sympathetically.

That was the thing. People made up stories about her all the time. Julia was becoming used to reading about fabricated love affairs or supposed arguments with her co-stars. She didn't let lies like that get to her. But this story was different because in her heart she knew Freda was right. 'Isn't it? Let's face it, Sadie, I'm no Grace Kelly.'

'You don't need to be Grace Kelly. You just need to be you. Don't let one snippy article get you down. The audience loves you.'

That much was true. For some reason moviegoers were happy to part with their money to see her substandard acting. Perhaps she gave them hope that one day they too might find themselves up on the big screen. After all, if a talentless hack like her could become a star, anyone could. 'Maybe. But they'll wise up eventually.'

'I think you're being far too hard on yourself. Mr Gold says—'

'So Harry's seen it? Oh god.' That was why he had given Sadie the afternoon off. She was there to manage Julia. To smooth things over so the movie could be completed. 'That's why he sent you, isn't it? To butter me up and tell me I'm great so I'll go back to work tomorrow without any drama.'

'No!' Sadie looked indignant for a moment but then her shoulders slumped and she leant back against the red leather booth. 'Well, yes, I suppose. Mr Gold doesn't want you upset, and that's more than likely to do with the fact that you are in the middle of shooting his next big-budget movie. But that's not why I'm here. I came because I'm your friend and because I thought you might need me. I know he's my boss, but you're far more important to me than any job could ever be. I hope you know that.'

Julia looked across at Sadie's earnest expression and knew she was telling the truth. 'Thanks, Sade. I feel the same way. And you can tell Harry to relax. I thought he knew me better than that. I'm not a child who throws tantrums. I take my responsibilities very seriously.'

'If it's any consolation, Mr Gold doesn't believe a word of the article. He thinks Freda was put up to writing it.'

'Really? By whom?'

'Someone at Columbia. Our studio's feuding with them at the moment and Mr Gold thinks this is their way of trying to sabotage the movie.'

Julia sighed. 'It wouldn't matter so much if it weren't true. To be honest, I'm surprised it's taken this long for me to be found out. I'm no actress.'

'What you need is a little break. Let's not talk about Freda's awful article any more. Let's make the most of having the afternoon off.'

Julia raised her glass and smiled. She doubted she would get Freda's words out of her head anytime soon, but that didn't mean Sadie's afternoon should be spoilt. 'Agreed.'

After the waiter delivered their entrees, the conversation turned to Sadie's screenplay.

'How's it coming along?' Julia asked. 'When can I read it?'

Sadie screwed up her nose. 'I'm getting close to the end, but I haven't had time to work on it much these past couple of months. Mr Gold has me in the office at the crack of dawn and, as you know, I'm rarely back at the club in time for dinner. That only leaves week-ends, and even then . . .'

'Yes, I know, even then you're at his beck and call. Harry works you far too hard. We hardly see you anymore. Sometimes I'm sorry I ever pushed you into this job.'

'Oh, goodness, I'm not.' Sadie put down her fork. 'It's not what I came to Hollywood to do, but I love my job. I've learnt so much about the industry – about the world, really. Honestly, I think I've gathered enough material for a dozen screenplays.' She paused. 'Although, they might be a tad controversial. I'm not sure anyone in Hollywood would produce them. I can't see too many producers being happy about having their dirty laundry aired in public.'

'Perhaps a novel, then.'

'Yes. Perhaps. But that's all a long way off. I need to finish the current project first. Harry has promised he'll look at it when I'm done. Vivienne's been reading it and giving me notes.'

'Vivienne?'

'Yes. You see, when I'm stuck, it helps to read the script aloud. Sometimes Viv and I read the parts at night before we go to sleep. I think her acting experience helps. Some of her comments are very insightful.'

'I think Vivienne's a better actress than people give her credit for. A couple of times she's asked me to run lines with her before an audition. She's really very good. Probably better than me, truth be told.'

'Oh, hush. You're a star, and that doesn't happen by accident.'

'Doesn't it? I'm not sure. But let's not go down that path right now. I wish there was something I could do to help Viv get a proper acting role. I know she's getting lots of modelling work, but she deserves so much more. I've suggested her for a few parts, but each time the director either had someone in mind or wanted a bigger name.'

'You're sweet to want to help. I wouldn't worry too much, though. Vivienne's smart, talented and ambitious. More than that, she's tough. That counts for a lot in this business. She'll get there in the end.'

'Maybe you're right.'

'It's Peggy I worry about. She tries so hard, but she just doesn't seem to be getting anywhere. She's acting as if everything is fine, but I don't think she's thrilled about this singing gig she's taken on. Speaking of which, you are coming tonight, aren't you?'

After the morning she'd had, Julia really couldn't think of anything worse than having to go out and put on a happy face, pretending that the whole of Hollywood wasn't talking about her behind her back. 'I'd really rather not, to be honest. Sitting in a smoky nightclub till all hours when I have to be on set early tomorrow is not my idea of fun.'

A look of disappointment settled on Sadie's face.

'Never fear, Sadie, I'll be there to support her, regardless. I wouldn't dare miss Peggy's big night. Things have been a bit strained between us this past week.'

'Really? Why?'

Julia took a moment to sip her champagne before she answered. 'I'm not exactly sure. It started after the premiere. I think she was upset that her scene was cut, but when I raised the issue, she brushed me off, saying it was no big deal.'

'I think it *was* a big deal to her.'

Julia had repeatedly tried to talk to Peggy about it, but each time Peggy had seemed annoyed and changed the subject abruptly. 'Maybe I'm misreading the situation, but she seems kind of mad at me. I can't work out why. She must know I didn't have anything to do with the way the movie was edited?'

'I'm sure she does. She's just hurting, that's all, and . . .' Sadie trailed off, seeming unsure of how to finish the sentence.

'And what?'

'Maybe she's not angry at you, but perhaps she's a teensy bit jealous. I know she loves you, but it must rankle just a little to watch your roommate get everything you've ever wanted.'

'Yes, you're probably right.' Julia chewed her lip and then sighed in resignation. 'In any case, I have no choice but to turn up and show my support for her tonight.'

'I'll book us a table. The manager is always accommodating, and I'm sure once I drop your name we'll have no problem getting a favourable seat. Will you be bringing a date?'

'You know how Harry feels about me dating on weeknights.'

'Let me handle Mr Gold. You could bring Cal. Mr Gold would be delighted to see you with him, weeknight or not. I think he's hoping for an off-screen romance between the two of you.'

'Harry knows very well that Cal's interests are much more centred on the *male* cast members.'

Understanding dawned on Sadie's face. 'Ah . . . I didn't realise. That explains why Mr Gold's so keen for the two of you to be seen together. Should I invite him anyway? Vivienne's bound to have a date.'

'Go ahead. Cal's good company. What about you? Are you bringing anyone? It's been ages since I've seen you go on a date. You're at the studio around all those good-looking actors all day. There must be someone you fancy?'

'Nope. Between my job and my writing, there's just no time.'

'Pfft. Don't give me that. You need to make time, and tonight's the perfect opportunity. I'm sure there's a long line of fellas who'd give anything to date you.'

'There's no shortage of offers, that's for sure. But they all want something – access to Mr Gold or a behind-the-scenes scoop.'

'So what? That's just how this town works. Use it to your advantage. I'm not talking about love and marriage here, just having a little fun.'

'A night out with you, Viv and Peggy *is* my idea of fun. I'd rather not spoil it by having some smarmy chap along for the ride.'

'Suit yourself. Maybe it's for the best. We don't want Peggy thinking tonight is about anyone but her.'

28 December 1999

Four decades have passed since we last saw each other but I recognise her instantly. Soft blonde waves frame her face, just as they did when we were first roommates. Her made-up face is marked by the passage of time – I can see that from here – but her signature red lipstick and her dazzling smile are unchanged. She's wearing a long silver dress, nipped in at the waist but with a full sunray pleated skirt, and carrying a purse in the shape of a fan. The outfit is an exact replica of the one she wore to the premiere of *Agnes Grey*. Or maybe it's the real thing. She's certainly slender enough to be wearing the original.

Julia's voice cuts through the noise of the crowd. 'Well, well, look who's here. Seems like she hasn't changed a bit.' She pushes past me and heads towards the dining room.

Peggy and I glance at each other. 'I'll go,' she says, her face ashen. 'You stay here and head Vivienne off at the pass if she even attempts to look for Julia. Maybe Vivienne's ready to make amends, maybe she isn't. But either way, Jules will never forgive her. It's probably better if we keep them apart – for both their sakes.'

I nod, rendered speechless by the apparition before me, not to mention Peggy's take-charge attitude. Usually I'm the one to step up in a crisis, but I'm rooted to the spot, unable to think clearly.

'Sadie?' Peggy looks at me intently. 'Did you hear me?'

I nod and Peggy scurries away.

Now that Julia and Peggy are safely out of Vivienne's orbit, I can focus my attention completely on her. Her arrival hasn't caused the stir I thought it might. Of course Peggy, Julia and I are curious to see her after all this time, and I suppose there will be others who lived at the club at the same time as us who will have wondered what became of her. But many people in this room probably have no idea who Vivienne Lockhart is, or once was.

Not for the first time, I'm grateful for the advantage my height affords me. Being at least half a head taller than most of the crowd gives me an unimpeded view of Vivienne and her companion, a young woman.

I fix my gaze on her face, hoping to catch her attention, and as if she's reading my mind, within seconds our eyes lock and she bestows that dazzling smile on me.

And then she waves.

My heart leaps and I find myself moving towards her. Her young friend is looking at me now. She coaxes Vivienne away from the crowd and they head in my direction. Vivienne takes slow and tentative steps, but I glide across the floor as if being pulled by a magnet.

Suddenly we are face to face.

'Vivienne,' I say, my voice barely above a whisper. 'It's been so long.'

'Too long, darling.' Her hand reaches for mine. She has the skin of an old lady – loose and papery. This shouldn't shock me, but it does. It seems even in the face of evidence to the contrary, my brain still believes Vivienne is no older than the last time we met.

The young woman, who still has her left arm linked with Vivienne's, extends her free hand for me to shake. 'I'm April,' she says. 'Ms Lockhart's assistant.' Her grip is firm, and I take to her immediately.

'Sadie Shore,' I reply.

April's eyes light with recognition and she smiles. 'I thought it was you.'

I frown for a moment, trying to work out how I would know this young woman. 'I'm sorry, have we met before?'

'Oh no, we haven't. It's just that Ms Lockhart has told me so much about you, and I've seen photos of you when you were all living here.'

Vivienne still has photos of us? I wouldn't have been surprised if she'd burnt the lot of them. 'Well done to you for your detective skills. I've changed quite a bit since then.'

'Maybe not as much as you imagine.' April looks at Vivienne. 'You and Ms Shore – Sadie – were roommates, weren't you?'

'Yes. Sadie.' Vivienne smiles brightly. 'My roommate and my best friend.'

I'm years past menopause but I feel heat building inside of me akin to a hot flush. I fear I may dissolve into a puddle. I desperately want to take Vivienne into my arms and tell her I never blamed her for what happened, or if I did, I forgave her long ago. But although her words are warm, Vivienne seems to be holding herself at distance. It feels as if there's a glass wall between us.

I decide not to rush her. 'How have you been?' I say. 'It's been such a long time since we talked.'

'Very well, thank you.' She smiles politely. 'And you?'

I'm slightly taken aback by her detached answer but return her smile. 'I'm well too. But I want to hear all about you. What have you been up to?'

'Oh, this and that. Keeping very busy. We're very busy, aren't we?'

She looks at April, who nods. 'Yes, indeed.'

'Where are you living these days? Last time we talked you were in Northern California – Monterey, I think. But that was decades ago. Are you still there or back in Hollywood?'

'Hollywood can be a cesspit, darling. You have to know how to play the game.'

It's an odd answer. Perhaps she has a reason for not wanting to disclose where she lives. But it is noisy in here, so maybe she simply hasn't heard me correctly. 'Yes, quite. Are you just here for the reunion or are you back in town permanently?'

She frowns. 'I'm not sure.'

'Ms Lockhart is working on a book,' April cuts in. 'A memoir of her time here, in fact. Which is one of the reasons she decided to come to tonight's reunion – to help with the research.'

The heat that flooded my body just moments earlier is replaced by a chill. The hairs on my forearms stand to attention and goosebumps rise on my skin. I look Vivienne in the eye. 'A memoir? Really?'

'Yes,' she says brightly. 'I like to write. April helps me.'

My stomach churns. She clearly has no remorse. What on earth will she say about why she left? Will she try to justify her actions? Or make something up? A book will dredge the whole thing up again. I open my mouth to ask if that's a good idea but think better of it. What does it matter if she's writing a book? Even if Vivienne does manage to finish it, it's unlikely to get picked up by a publisher. To me and my friends, Vivienne Lockhart is endlessly fascinating. She was a gifted actress, a burgeoning star, and a trusted friend who betrayed us spectacularly before disappearing from our lives. Of course, we are dying to know what became of her. But to the rest of the world she's just another actress who didn't quite make it. I doubt that any publishing house would be interested enough to give her a book deal.

'Are you working on a screenplay or a book right now?' April asks.

It takes a moment to realise that the question is addressed to me. 'No. I haven't written since . . .' I trail off, unable to say it. I have not written a word since Gianni died. 'I haven't written anything for about ten years. I'm a landscape architect now. I design gardens.'

'Oh.' Her disappointment is obvious.

I eye April suspiciously. Perhaps my initial assessment of her was misguided. Why does she care if I'm a writer or not? Vivienne can't seriously think that I would be willing to help with this ridiculous idea. I turn my attention back to my old roommate. 'What made you decide to tell your story now, Vivienne, after all this time?'

She looks confused for a moment. April clasps her hand and gently prompts her. 'Why do you want to write a book, Vivienne?'

'For George,' she says.

'Ms Lockhart's partner, who sadly passed away earlier this year,' April adds.

'Oh.' That explanation takes the wind out of my sails somewhat. 'I'm so sorry for your loss.'

Vivienne smiles. 'Thank you.' She looks past me, her focus on something or someone I can't see.

My pulse quickens slightly. Please don't let it be Julia or Peggy.

Eventually her gaze meets mine again. 'It's been lovely chatting,' she says, 'but I probably should keep moving. I need to work the room. You know how it is.' She takes half a step back and looks around, as if she can't wait to get away from me.

That's it? After forty years all she has to say for herself is, 'Hello, I'm writing a book, goodbye'? Maybe I was wrong to give her the benefit of the doubt. Maybe Julia and Peggy were right all along; maybe she is a monster.

April glances at me and tugs Vivienne's arm. 'There's no rush, Vivienne. We have plenty of time. I'm sure you'd rather be talking to your old friend Sadie than anyone else.'

Vivienne scowls. 'Of course I would, but we can't always have what we want. I need to make the most of this opportunity while I can.' The scowl disappears as suddenly as it arrived as she spies a waiter with a tray of full champagne glasses. She beckons him over and takes a glass.

The waiter extends the tray to me, but I hold up my still almost-full glass and shake my head. April also refuses the waiter's offer of champagne. She looks pointedly at Vivienne. 'Are you sure that's a good idea?'

'Champagne is always a good idea.' She turns away from us abruptly.

April's obvious dismay is illuminating. Vivienne is drunk! That would explain why she seems unsteady on her feet and her odd demeanour. It must have taken enormous courage for her to come here tonight, knowing that she would likely have to face Julia and Peggy. Who could blame her for having a few wines to fortify herself? But April's clear concern makes me think that perhaps tonight's inebriation is not an isolated incident. Maybe she has a problem. Vivienne always was a party girl. I thought she'd put that behind her, but maybe not. As I watch her disappear in the crowd, my fingers find the pendant at the base of my throat and I rub the smooth edges of the heart for comfort. My anger ebbs away and is replaced by pity.

April gives me an apologetic smile. 'Perhaps we can catch up later.'

I nod, unable to summon any words. After forty years of thinking about the moment I would see Vivienne again, it has come – and gone. I'm not sure what I expected, really, but it certainly wasn't this.

Chapter 10

Peggy

Peggy had just finished curling her hair when the stage manager entered the dressing-room. 'Peggy Carmichael?' he called out to the room full of chattering girls.

'Here.'

'Mr Hudson wants to meet you.'

Peggy glanced back at the sequined dress hanging on the rack behind her dressing table. It had dozens of tiny buttons that would take ages to fasten. 'But I'm not dressed.'

'Just come as you are. I'm sure I don't need to remind you what a huge star Charlie Hudson is. Best not keep him waiting.'

Peggy stood and tightened the belt of her robe to make sure it was secure. This was not how she'd hoped to meet the headliner of tonight's show, but who was she to argue? She needed this gig. 'Okay.'

She followed Ernie to Mr Hudson's dressing-room.

'Miss Carmichael for you, Mr Hudson.'

'Send her in.'

Ernie inclined his head towards the door. 'Go on, then. Don't be shy.'

Peggy sucked in a deep breath. Charlie Hudson might be a big star, but he was a man. A Black man. It felt improper for the two of them to be alone together behind closed doors. Miss McGovern would not be pleased at all. Especially if she knew that Peggy wore nothing more than a robe over her underwear. And if her parents knew, they'd likely disown her.

'Hurry up, Carmichael. Mr Hudson's a busy man.'

She nervously pushed open the door.

'Peggy!' Charlie Hudson jumped up from his seat and crossed the room to greet her. He took both her hands in his and squeezed them. 'I'm delighted you've agreed to open my show. Billy tells me you're a real talent.'

Peggy was chuffed to hear that the club's owner thought so highly of her. 'Oh, Mr Hudson, thank *you*. It's truly an honour to be on the same bill as you. I was thrilled when Billy told me who I was opening for.'

He smiled warmly. 'None of this "Mr Hudson" business, now. You call me Charlie, you hear?'

'Okay.' Peggy's hands were trembling. Charlie Hudson was the biggest star she'd ever spoken with – apart from Julia, of course, but she didn't really count. She'd met a few of the big names on the sets of movies – Cal Brooks, Eddie Fisher and Elizabeth Taylor, for instance. But she'd been given strict instructions not to approach these stars between takes, and none of them had ever bothered with her outside of work. Charlie Hudson, on the other hand, had asked to meet her, and now he was *thanking her* for opening his show. Maybe this nightclub gig was going to turn out okay after all.

'You're shaking. Oh! Of course you are. You're probably freezing in that robe. I've clearly interrupted you while you were getting dressed. Please forgive me.'

Charlie really was a sweet man. She was going to enjoy working with him. 'Not at all. I'm practically ready; I just have to slip into my gown before I go on.'

He looked at his wristwatch. 'Still another thirty minutes or so, but I won't keep you. Here's the deal – you come on and do the first, let's say, five numbers, warm the audience up for me, okay? Is that what you were expecting?'

'Yes, Billy said I'd do four or five numbers tonight. I prepared six songs, just in case.'

'You're a true pro, Peggy. So, tonight you take the first five and I'll take it from there. Let's see how that goes. We've got eight weeks together so we might mix it up a bit now and then – keep everyone on their toes, eh? – but we'll just ease ourselves into it tonight. What do you think?'

'Sounds wonderful.'

Charlie moved towards the door and held it open for her. 'All right, then. I'll let you go get ready. See you out there.'

Back in the shared dressing-room, Peggy's fingers fumbled with the buttons on her spangly dress. Marie, one of the dancers, took pity on her. 'Here, let me help you. First-night jitters?'

'Thanks. I'm not sure why I'm so nervous. It's hardly the first time I've been in front of an audience.'

'You'll be fine. Charlie's a generous performer. He might be a big name now, but he's never forgotten where he came from. He got his start here, you know? I worked on his very first show and he was just as nervous as you are now.' She held the dress open for Peggy to step into.

'Really?'

'Sure.' Marie gently turned her around and began to button the dress. 'He was opening for another big performer who shall remain nameless, but let's just say that guy is known in the industry for being a jerk. He was awful to Charlie – even tried to make him miss his opening number by wedging a chair under Charlie's dressing-room door.'

Peggy turned her head to face Marie. 'No!'

'Uh-huh. Luckily one of the dancers broke a heel just before the act was about to start and had to come backstage to change shoes. She noticed the chair and freed him.'

'What a close shave!'

'Yes, but you would never have known. He went on cool as a cucumber. The crowd took to him right away, and that was his start. He's never forgotten what that night was like, though. He's always lovely to us girls and he makes sure that whoever he's performing with feels welcome.' Marie finished doing up the last button and tapped her lightly on the back. 'So don't you worry, sugar. You go out there and knock 'em dead. You've got all us girls and Charlie Hudson rooting for you.'

Chapter 11

Sadie

Upon arrival at the nightclub, Sadie, Julia and Cal were ushered through the crowd to the show room. Sadie never ceased to be impressed by Ciro's. The place oozed opulence with its silk-covered walls and ornately framed stage area, but its most glamorous feature was the clientele. Even though Sadie dealt with huge stars every day as part of her job, seeing them gathered together like this, all dressed up in their finery, reminded her that she was living a most extraordinary life.

The host guided them through the tables covered in crisp white linen cloths and adorned with Ciro's signature tealights, until they reached their seats, right at the edge of the stage. Vivienne and her date had already arrived and were now so deep in conversation that they barely noticed when Sadie and the others approached. Cal pulled out the chair beside Vivienne's date and gestured for Sadie to sit. As she did, Vivienne glanced up.

'Oh, hello darlings! You're here. Sorry, I didn't see you come in.' She moved her chair back so she could get to her feet, and her date, who'd had his back to them until now, stood as well. He turned to greet the rest of the party.

'Jack!' Sadie gasped. Jack Porter was the last person she expected to see Vivienne with.

'Well, hello. Fancy seeing you here.' Jack beamed at her.

'You two know each other?'

'We do,' said Sadie flatly. 'Jack blows in and out of my office quite regularly.'

'Keeping my finger on the pulse,' Jack explained.

'Oh yes, of course.' Vivienne said. 'I should have realised.' She took hold of Jack's hand and pulled him towards the others. 'Have you met our friend Julia?'

While Vivienne was making the introductions, Sadie took a few deep breaths. Why did Vivienne have to bring *him*? Was she serious about dating him? Not likely. Vivienne was probably working some angle. Looking for some free publicity in the hope that it would get her noticed by a studio. Sadie couldn't quite put her finger on why, but seeing the two of them together made her uneasy.

'Shall we order some drinks?' Cal asked. 'Champagne for the table?'

'I have an early start tomorrow,' Julia protested.

'Ah, one drink won't hurt.' Vivienne winked at her. 'Live on the wild side for once.'

'Oh, maybe just one, then. To celebrate Peggy's opening night.'

'How about you, Sadie?' Cal asked.

'What? Oh, yes, champagne is fine. If you'll excuse me for a moment, I'm just going to powder my nose before the show starts.'

'Ooh, good idea,' Vivienne said. 'I'll come with you.'

Irritated, because she really did want a moment to herself, Sadie took off towards the bathroom with Vivienne tottering along behind.

'Wait up, Sade. I can't go too fast when I'm wearing these heels.'

'Hurry up. I want to be back in my seat before Peggy's show starts.'

'Relax. We've got ages yet.'

Reluctantly, Sadie slowed down to allow her friend to catch up.

'This should be a fun night.' Vivienne hooked her arm inside Sadie's elbow. 'I hope Peg's up to the job.'

'Of course she is,' Sadie snapped. 'Peggy's got a beautiful voice and I won't hear anyone say otherwise.'

Vivienne withdrew her arm. 'Geez, steady on. I only meant I hope she's not too nervous. She hasn't been herself the past few days.'

'Oh.' Sadie drew a breath. 'Yeah, I guess I'd noticed that too.'

Once inside the ladies' room, Vivienne disappeared into a stall and Sadie stood at the basin, staring into the mirror as she reapplied her lipstick, even though it still looked perfectly fine.

Vivienne came to stand beside her and turned on the faucet. 'So, what's got your panties all in a twist?'

'Must you be so vulgar?' Sadie whispered and nodded her head towards the closed stall doors.

Vivienne didn't comment. She dried her hands, reached into her purse and pulled out a packet of cigarettes. She offered one to Sadie, but Sadie declined.

'I think we should be getting back. Jack is probably missing you.'

Vivienne struck a match, lit her cigarette and inhaled deeply. As she slowly exhaled, just for a moment, her image in the mirror was obscured by smoke. She turned around and rested her backside against the counter. 'So that's what this is all about?'

'What do you mean?'

'Is it because I brought Jack?'

'Well, yes. I wish you hadn't invited him, that's all.'

'And why's that?'

'Do I need to spell it out? He's a reporter, Vivienne. I spend all day every day dodging him and his ilk, I don't want to spend a rare night off having to watch what I say lest it ends up in the papers tomorrow.'

A slow smile spread over Vivienne's face. 'You like him.'

'I do not!' Sadie's cheeks burned.

'Really? That's a shame, because he sure likes you.'

'What? No, he doesn't. He just wants to keep in my good books because he thinks I'm useful.'

'If you say so, but a few minutes ago when I was introducing him to Julia – one of the hottest stars in Hollywood right now – he could barely drag his eyes away from you long enough to even look at her.'

For some inexplicable reason, Sadie's heart leapt. Could it be true? But even as the thought was forming she dismissed it. 'Don't be ridiculous. Jack is a player and is no more interested in me than in any other woman. Besides, even if he was, I'd never date a man like him.'

'He seems pretty sweet to me.'

'Sweet? Jack? That's not a word I would use to describe him.'

'Well, he's certainly sweet on you.'

'I told you that's not true. What on earth do you two have to talk about, anyway?'

'Books, mainly. He's a writer, you know.'

'He's a reporter. That's not the same thing.'

'I don't know about that. Anyway, he's writing a novel.'

'A novel? Jack? I had no idea . . .' Sadie's shock at this news gave way to embarrassment. Of course she had no idea. She'd never bothered to ask him one thing about himself. Jack had asked her about her screenplay numerous times and she'd waffled on self-importantly without ever reciprocating. What must he think of her?

'If it's not about me dating Jack, then what's wrong? You don't seem yourself tonight.'

Sadie's shoulders sagged. 'I'm sorry. I didn't mean to bite your head off. I think I'm just tired.'

'You're sure that's all it is? Because I never want anything to come between us, Sade.' She slipped her arm around Sadie's waist. 'You, Julia and Peggy are the most important people in the world to me. I hope you know that.'

Chapter 12

Julia

Julia had almost finished her glass of champagne by the time Sadie and Vivienne returned to the table. 'I was beginning think you two had been kidnapped.'

'Nothing so interesting,' said Vivienne. 'Just a bit of girls' talk, that's all.'

'Oh.' Julia pouted. 'Now I'm sorry I didn't come too.'

'Don't worry. You didn't miss anything important.' Sadie picked up her champagne glass and made an informal toast. 'Here's to Peggy's big night, and to the best friends a girl could ever ask for.'

Everyone lifted their glasses and drank. Julia was surprised to find her glass empty after the toast. She wished she didn't have to be on set so early in the morning; she'd rather let her hair down and enjoy this time with her friends. The first glass of champagne had gone down well and she'd love another, but she shouldn't . . .

To heck with it! She was sick of being so damned responsible all the time. Vivienne was right. She needed to walk on the wild side every now and then. Besides, maybe the alcohol would help her sleep. She'd barely slept a wink since the first lukewarm reviews about her performance in *One Starry Night* had started to come in. Sadie had tried to reassure her that Harry wasn't fussed, and she was probably right. The box office takings were all Harry cared about and as far as Julia knew there wasn't anything to worry about in that department. But it wouldn't always be that way. She feared the movie she was filming now would be no better. Once she'd lost her novelty value as a new face, the public would surely notice how wooden she was on screen and then Harry was bound to drop her like a hot potato. It wasn't as if there weren't plenty of talented young actresses just dying to take her place.

Take Vivienne, for example. It was crazy that she wasn't contracted to a studio. She was sex on a stick. That alone should have been enough to make the studios take notice, but Sadie – who knew what she was talking about – was adamant that Vivienne could act too. Julia just hoped that Paramount or MGM snapped her up before Harry Gold realised she would make a much better star than the one he was currently promoting.

She smiled at Cal. 'Be a love and pour me another, would you?'

'With pleasure.' Cal picked up the bottle of Moët.

Vivienne looked at her from across the table and winked. 'That's my girl!'

A wave of guilt enveloped Julia. She liked to think that success hadn't changed her, that she was still down to earth, one of the girls. But here she was worrying about her crown being stolen by Vivienne. Had she really become so caught up in her own success that she was afraid of being usurped by one of her closest friends? Vivienne deserved success as much as she did, if not more. There was room for both of them, wasn't there?

Peggy came on after Julia's shrimp cocktail had been eaten but before her Caesar salad had arrived. While the evening's host was introducing her, the band began to play. Peggy slipped into the spotlight, rather nervously, Julia thought. She glanced at Sadie, who was sitting next to her, to see Sadie biting her bottom lip. Julia slid her hand into Sadie's as Peggy began to sing.

She'd chosen to open with Rosemary Clooney's 'Come On-a My House', which, if she'd asked for an opinion beforehand, Julia would have told her was at best ambitious and at worst a mistake. But Julia would have been wrong. Because Peggy was making that song all her own. Julia had heard Peggy sing before – in the rehearsal room at the club, mainly – but never like this. Out in front of the band, wearing a tight-fitting sequined black gown, Peggy looked every bit the star. She moved with ease and confidence, inviting the audience to sway and tap along with her. And her voice! She had everyone in that room hypnotised; Julia included. Sadie squeezed her hand and whispered, 'That's our girl.'

Julia couldn't have been prouder.

When the song finished there was rapturous applause and Vivienne let out a long, high-pitched whistle. Sadie, who seemed unusually uptight tonight, chastised her roommate. 'Vivienne, please!'

'Leave her be, Sade,' Julia said. 'Peggy deserves our appreciation. I don't think anyone would judge Vivienne for her enthusiasm.'

Vivienne blew her a kiss and Julia laughed, feeling more relaxed than she had in days. This was what mattered. Not reviews, not being famous – just being with friends, with people who she loved and who loved her back.

After her fifth number – each one as wonderful as the first – Peggy handed over to Charlie Hudson and his band. Charlie kissed Peggy's cheek as he took the microphone from her, declaring to the audience, 'How about that, ladies and gentlemen? Miss Peggy Carmichael. Remember that name and remember you saw her here first, at Ciro's nightclub . . .'

Peggy bowed and waved graciously as she made her final exit. Minutes later, she slipped into the spare seat next to Vivienne. While the girls took turns congratulating her, Cal topped up all their glasses and ordered another bottle of champagne.

Vivienne was asking Peggy how it felt to be a singing sensation, and Peggy was replying in excited whispers so as not to interrupt the show. Charlie Hudson's voice now filled the room and Julia, who was too far away from Peggy to hear her responses anyway, leant back in her chair to enjoy his performance.

Charlie's voice was familiar enough. Vivienne had a transistor radio and she often tuned it to the Black radio stations, where Charlie's songs were played on high rotation. Come to think of it, she'd even heard him once or twice on mainstream radio. Julia enjoyed his music as much as the next person, but he wasn't a particular favourite of hers and she'd never seen him perform live. Now that she was seeing him in the flesh she understood what all the fuss was about. The radio didn't do justice to his voice, which was rich and smooth and surprisingly sensual.

It wasn't just his voice that had her mesmerised. He was handsome, although not in the usual way, she supposed. His build was athletic, but wiry – like a runner – and he wasn't the tallest man going around. But there was something in the way he moved that drew her eye. In fact, she couldn't avert her gaze. Every time he smiled in her direction – which was often – her insides squeezed, and she found herself holding her breath, only exhaling when Charlie's attention flitted elsewhere. Several times during the first number, he came close enough to her table for the pair of them to lock eyes, and each time her breath caught in her throat. Charlie Hudson oozed charm and charisma and, if Julia didn't know better, she would swear he was singing just for her.

After a set that lasted almost an hour, Charlie called Peggy up to the stage again. Peggy's momentary startled expression was enough to tell Julia that her friend hadn't expected this recall, but she recovered quickly and was soon back up at the microphone, sporting a wide smile. Charlie whispered in Peggy's ear and she nodded enthusiastically. Charlie gave a signal to the band, and they began to play Cole Porter's 'I Get a Kick Out of You'. Peggy and Charlie sang the song as a duet, much to the audience's delight. The song ended to rapturous applause. Peggy's opening night had been a resounding success.

It wasn't long before Peggy was back at their table, breathless with excitement and arm in arm with Charlie Hudson himself.

'Everyone, I want you to meet Charlie. He insisted on meeting my family, and I told him that you're it! At least, you're the closest thing I have to family here in LA.' Peggy introduced Charlie to each of them, starting with Vivienne and coming to Julia and Cal last.

Charlie took Julia's hand in his and looked right into her eyes. 'Julia Newman. It's such an honour to meet you. I've long admired you from afar.'

Heat bloomed in Julia's chest and then crept up her neck and into her cheeks. What was wrong with her? Men said things like this on a regular basis. What they usually meant was, *I'd like to admire you up close and naked, if possible.* Normally such flattery had no effect on her, but here she was, blushing like a schoolgirl. 'Me? My goodness, I'm flattered.'

Charlie laughed easily and released her hand. 'Let me just say – and I didn't think this was possible – but you are even more beautiful in the flesh than you are on the screen.'

Ridiculously, Julia found herself speechless. Fortunately, she was saved from having to reply when Cal thrust out his hand for Charlie to shake. It seemed Cal and Charlie had met several times before.

'Hey buddy, how're you doing?' Cal asked.

'Just fine, just fine. Happy to be back here in LA, though. My manager's had me playing a lotta shows in Vegas. Man, that place is crazy!'

'Crazier than old Tinseltown?'

'You'd better believe it!'

'Say, Charlie, why don't you join us for dessert? We've ordered more than enough to share. Take my seat and I'll chase down a waiter, see if we can get another chair and another place setting.'

'Why, that'd be great, pal. I appreciate it,' Charlie replied, his gaze never leaving Julia.

Vivienne and Peggy excused themselves to powder their noses and Sadie was deep in conversation with Jack, which left Julia to entertain Charlie alone, at least for the moment. He pulled out the chair for her and, once she was seated, took his place next to her as Cal had suggested.

Charlie wasted no time on small talk. He leant forward and looked into her eyes. 'Tell me all about Julia Newman,' he said. 'I want to know everything – where you're from, what your childhood was like, when you started acting and how you ended up here in Hollywood. I want to get to know you, Julia, and there isn't a moment to waste.'

Inexplicably her pulse thudded in her ears. 'Honestly, Charlie, I'm not that interesting. To answer your questions, I'm a simple farmer's daughter and I ended up in Hollywood accidentally. If you listen to the critics, I haven't started acting yet, at least not well. And I'm afraid they're right. I am a complete and utter fraud.' She paused. 'Gracious, I don't know where that came from. Sorry.'

If Charlie was surprised by her candour he didn't show it. 'I'm intrigued,' he said. 'Tell me more.'

'I don't know how I ended up here. I never wanted to be an actress. It just kind of happened.'

Charlie slapped his knee and laughed. 'Well, aren't you just a breath of fresh air? It's so unusual to hear someone say something honest in this town! Good god, I swear I can go weeks without having a real conversation. These days it's all "Yes, Mr Hudson; no, Mr Hudson" or "Let me tell you how talented I am, Mr Hudson."' His eyes, still gazing into hers, were twinkling with delight. 'So, if you didn't want to be an actress, how did you end up on the screen?'

Julia forced herself to breathe. What was going on here? It felt as if her heart – which was now beating double time – had started to swell inside her ribcage. It was the strangest sensation; not at all comfortable and yet she didn't want it to stop. Nor did she want Charlie to divert his attention elsewhere. Why had she blurted out that stupid thing about being a fraud? She racked her brain for something lighthearted and witty to say but came up blank. With Charlie waiting for her answer, she figured she'd started with the truth and now she might as well keep on with it. 'Like everything else in my life, I guess. I just bumbled along until something happened. Now I'm a star who doesn't deserve to be one.' She was making a fool of herself, but she couldn't seem to stop. The wine had loosened her tongue and Charlie's rapt attention enticed her to unburden herself.

She went on to tell him about her desire to leave Nebraska and winning the beauty pageant. She talked about Harry discovering her at the extras call-up and how it was only a matter of time before the public realised what the critics already knew: she was talentless. She'd soon have no choice but to hightail it back to Nebraska, back to her disapproving father, who, by the way, had never seen any of her movies. How about that?

Charlie took her hand. 'Why is that, do you think?'

She sipped her drink and thought about it. 'He thinks I'm making a fool of myself, I guess.'

'Well, in my opinion he's wrong about that, but if you aren't happy being an actress, I think you could do anything you set your mind to. You're beautiful and charming, and articulate, too. The world is your oyster, so to speak. And forgive me for talking about such a crass topic, but I'm sure you've made a little money by now. There's no need for you to go back home unless you want to.'

Charlie was right! Strangely, she never really thought about the money she was making. Kip, her business manager, took care of all her finances. The studio paid for her to live at the Hollywood Studio Club and she had store credits at all the places she liked to shop, as well as a weekly cash allowance. Kip told her she could always ask for more if she needed it, but she never did. Occasionally Kip called her to a meeting to talk about her finances, but she had no interest in what he was saying. The only question she ever asked was if she was broke. This usually made Kip laugh. He always replied 'Far from it', and that was enough to satisfy her.

Charlie's voice, low and mellow, drew her back to the conversation. 'I hate to think about you up and leaving Hollywood when we've only just met, but you have to do whatever makes you happy.'

'You know, Charlie, I think you are the first person in my life who has ever suggested that my happiness was something that should be taken into consideration. But enough about me. Now it's your turn.'

As Charlie talked lovingly about his family and answered Julia's questions about his rise to fame, she found herself edging towards him. Her knee was tantalisingly close to his and every inch of her skin was electrified at the thought of their bodies touching beneath the table, where no one else could see. She wanted to know Charlie, to really listen to him with the same attention he had just paid to her, but her mind was so filled with her desire to be touched by him, there was no room for anything else. She tried to focus on his mouth, on the words he was forming, but that was a mistake. All she could think about was those lips kissing hers. She forced herself to look away.

At some point Cal must have returned to the table because he was now seated in between Peggy and Vivienne. Julia hadn't noticed his return. In fact, she hadn't given him a single thought since Charlie sat next her. She hoped Jack hadn't noticed her preoccupation with Charlie. Jack seemed like a nice enough guy, but Vivienne had told her earlier that Sadie had some sort of bee in her bonnet about him being here, so maybe he wasn't to be trusted. He was a reporter, after all.

She caught Cal's eye and gave him an apologetic look. He winked. Oh god, was she being that obvious? She needed to put some space between herself and Charlie, before not just Jack but any other reporters or plain old gossips noticed there was something to see.

'Charlie,' she said. 'I'm so sorry; it's been terribly rude of me to monopolise your time like this.'

'Not at all. Right now, there's nowhere else I'd rather be.'

'You're very kind, but there are a lot of other people here tonight who I'm sure would appreciate spending a little time with you.'

Charlie shifted back in his chair. 'I should be the one apologising for taking up your time, but you know what? I'm not sorry. Not one little bit. One should never apologise for following their heart.' He leant closer and, just for a moment, his thigh pressed against hers. 'Goodnight, Julia.' He kissed her cheek gently. 'I hope we'll see each other again soon.'

28 December 1999

By nine o'clock I've had enough of the reunion. My feet hurt, I've made all the small talk I can bear and had more than my fill of nostalgia.

Throughout the night I've caught glimpses of Vivienne, but we haven't spoken again. The anticipation of reuniting with her combined with the anticlimax of our meeting have completely drained me and now I'm longing for the evening's end.

Once the speeches are over and the crowd begins to thin out, I find Peggy and Julia and tell them I think it's time to leave.

Peggy's not having a bar of that. 'We can't leave without checking out our old rooms. Let's sneak upstairs and take a look.'

'They're probably locked,' I say.

But she won't be deterred. 'We won't know unless we look, will we? Come on, if nothing else we can get a photo of ourselves outside our old bedroom doors.'

There's no refusing Peggy when she wants something. I've learnt that it's quicker not to argue. So we drag ourselves up the stairs on a fool's mission, because of course the rooms are inaccessible. Still, we pose for photos, which Peggy takes with her brand-new digital camera, and that seems to satisfy her.

'I don't know about you two, but it's well past my bedtime,' I say. 'I think it's time to call it a night.'

Peggy laughs. 'How did we get so old?'

As we make our way along the corridor towards the stairs, the conversation turns to our nightly routines and how they've changed since we were girls sliding in just ahead of curfew and staying up until the wee hours talking. Before we get to the landing, Julia grabs my arm. 'I wasn't going to ask,' she says, 'but I can't seem to help myself. You talked to her. What did she have to say?'

I hesitate for a moment as I replay the conversation with Vivienne in my head. I'm not sure how much to tell them. 'Nothing much.'

'Come on, Sadie. Don't hold out on us,' Peggy says.

'I'm not. Truly. She was odd. Distant. She made polite small talk and said nothing revealing about herself.' I decide against mentioning the memoir. Why upset the others about a project that might never get off the ground? 'I think she might have been drunk, actually.'

Peggy purses her lips and for a moment I see the prim young woman she once was. 'She always was a lush.'

'Why on earth did she bother to come?' Julia says, her voice rising. 'It doesn't make sense.'

'Beats me. I had hoped that maybe after all these years she wanted to make amends, but I guess I was wrong.' To my horror, my eyes fill with tears.

Julia puts her arm around my shoulders. 'Oh, Sadie, you big softie. You've always been the peacemaker, the fixer, but sometimes things just can't be fixed. Sometimes you just have to let go.'

When we reach the foyer, it's almost empty except for the event staff, who are buzzing around collecting glasses and packing them away. Babs and a couple of the committee members are milling about behind the reception desk, deep in conversation.

Peggy waves to Babs. 'Thanks for a lovely evening, Babs. I'll be in touch!'

Babs looks up and fixes her gaze on me. 'Oh, Sadie, you're still here. Thank goodness.' She scurries out from behind reception and makes her way over to us. 'We have a bit of a problem,' she whispers.

Peggy looks alarmed. 'What's wrong?'

'It's Vivienne,' she says. Julia sighs, and Babs gives her a sideways glance but continues. 'She won't leave.'

Julia folds her arms across her chest. 'I don't see what we can do about that.'

Babs has a desperate expression on her face. 'She seems confused. She insists that she just wants to go up to her room and go to bed.'

'Perhaps she's had too much to drink,' I say.

'Nevertheless, she can't stay here. I was hoping you might be able to talk to her, Sadie. She might listen to you.'

'I'm sure there's no need to worry. Where's her assistant? Surely April can manage this without my intervention.'

Babs isn't budging. 'April's nowhere to be found.'

'For heaven's sake, Babs,' Julia huffs. 'The woman has probably just gone to bring the car around.'

'Well, that's the thing. Nobody has seen her since before the speeches. It looks like she's left Vivienne to fend for herself. Please, Sadie, can you at least try? She won't even speak to me. Connie had to bribe her with a sherry to make her stay down here. She was hellbent on heading upstairs to her room.'

'I suppose I can try.' I look at Peggy and Julia. 'You two go ahead. I'll get a cab on my own when I'm done.'

'Sadie,' says Julia, 'this isn't your problem. Didn't we just talk about letting go?'

'We can't just leave her here.'

'Maybe you can't, but I most definitely can.' She turns to look at Babs. 'Perhaps you should call the police if Miss Lockhart is unable to care for herself.'

Babs looks aghast. 'I don't think there's any need for that.'

'Well, in any case, I am leaving.' Julia looks at Peggy and me. 'Are you two coming?'

I shake my head. 'I'm sorry, but I can't.'

Julia gives me a final despairing look and then marches off towards the exit.

'Don't worry, she'll get over it.' Peggy gives my hand a squeeze. 'I'll talk to her. Will you be okay here?'

'Sure. You go.'

She kisses me on the cheek. 'I'll call you in the morning.'

Babs leads me into the living area, where Vivienne is sitting in an armchair, drinking sherry. 'Vivienne,' she says. 'Here's Sadie to talk to you.'

Vivienne appears perplexed for a moment but then smiles. 'Hello. I like your dress. Where have you been, all dressed up like that?'

Babs raises her eyebrows at me.

I pull up a chair next to Vivienne. 'Where are you staying tonight?'

Her brow knits in confusion. 'Why, here of course. This is where I live.'

'Right. Look, Vivienne, I wanted to talk to your assistant – April, isn't it? I'm wondering if you know where she went?'

'April?' She ponders the question. 'No. Can't say that I know anyone called April. For a moment I thought I did – one of the dancers in *Follow Your Heart* – but now that I think of it, her name is Alice.'

Clearly something isn't right. 'Perhaps I have her name wrong. There was a young girl here earlier who said she was your assistant. Do you know where she is now?'

She laughs. 'Assistant? She must have been pulling your leg. What would I need an assistant for?'

This is getting me nowhere. I try a different tactic. 'Okay. Do you perhaps have a cell phone on you?'

'There's a telephone at reception. Or there's one in my room, if you'd like to come upstairs.' She is definitely not well and needs to be in bed, but with April gone there's no way of knowing where Vivienne is staying. Even if we had the name of her hotel, that would be a start.

I look around for her purse and spy it on the ground beside the armchair. I lean down and pick it up. 'Vivienne, is this yours?'

She doesn't answer. Her eyes are closed now and her head lolls forward.

'Vivienne?'

Her eyelids flutter open for a moment, but still no answer. I hate to do this, but I can't see any other option. I carefully open her purse and look inside. There's not much – a small wallet, which has some cash and an expired driver's licence, a lipstick, a compact and a sealed envelope. I pull out the envelope and find it is addressed to 'The Ladies of the Hollywood Studio Club'.

I hand the envelope to Babs. 'I think this might be for you.'

She reads the front and then tears the envelope open. It contains a two-page letter, which Babs begins to read. After a few moments she clasps her hand over her mouth.

'What? Babs, what is it?'

'The assistant has done a runner and left Vivienne in our care!'

'What do you mean, "our care"? Why does she need to be in the care of anyone?'

'Here. See for yourself.' She hands the letter to me.

I quickly scan the note to see what Babs is on about. One particular line jumps out and slaps me in the face.

As you might have noticed, Vivienne is unwell. She has a progressive form of dementia . . .

1957

Chapter 13

Sadie

Sadie scanned the newspaper through bleary eyes. She'd learnt that it was in her best interests to get to the office early each morning and search the daily papers for news concerning the studio and its stars, or any story that might have an impact on the day-to-day running of Goldstar. That way she could get ahead of any problems before they came to Harry's attention. This morning, though, she'd been fifteen minutes later than usual, and Harry was uncharacteristically early.

She'd been at Ciro's the night before with her friends. Peggy had been working at the club for several months now, sometimes as a backup singer, but usually as the opening act for whatever big name the club had booked. At first, she'd thought that her singing might get her noticed by someone important, which might then lead to a movie role, but as the months had ticked by without such luck, poor Peg had become increasingly despondent.

Recently, Julia had suggested that they needed to show their support for Peggy by attending her shows more regularly. Sadie had agreed, thinking it was a lovely gesture until she saw who the headline act at Ciro's was. Charlie Hudson was back for the month of January.

He was in town again after a long run in Vegas and suddenly Julia was desperate to give Peggy a boost. Last night, when Julia and Charlie talked, seemingly oblivious to all but each other, Sadie had feared she wasn't the only one taking notice.

'Sadie! Come into my office now!' her boss barked through the office intercom.

She jumped up quickly and made her way to Harry's desk. 'Yes, Mr Gold?'

'Explain this!' He shoved a copy of *The Times* across the desk and Sadie immediately saw the problem. A huge photo of Julia and Charlie leapt out at her. They were clearly deep in conversation, and leaning so close to each other their foreheads were almost touching.

'It's nothing, Mr Gold, I swear.'

'I thought Julia was dating Cal Brooks?'

'Er, they're on again, off again. You know how it is.'

Mr Gold looked as if he very much knew how it was.

'But I was there and I swear to you that nothing untoward happened. Charlie Hudson is a friend of ours. Julia and I know him because our friend Peggy works at Ciro's. She opens for Charlie when he plays at the club. He just came over to pay his respects, that's all.'

'Respects? Looks like he was doing more than being courteous. A lot more.'

Sadie thought quickly. 'It's just an opportunistic photo; you know how these reporters are. Charlie talked to all of us. Someone has snapped this photo surreptitiously at an angle that makes it look as if there is something going on. I can assure you that isn't the case.'

'Humph.' Mr Gold did not seem convinced. 'This is why we have her living at the Studio Club. This is why we have rules. We're trying to *protect* her.'

Protect the studio's investment was what he really meant, but Sadie wasn't about to argue. 'I know, I know.'

'You know, but does she?'

'I'm sure—'

110

'Never mind all that.' Mr Gold snatched the paper back. 'What's done is done. Let's set about fixing this mess before it gets out of hand. I can't have people thinking my biggest star is dating a . . . a . . . well, you know. Charlie Hudson's a good guy but he's not the right fit for Julia. Understood?'

Sadie wanted to say no, she didn't understand, and what's more she didn't see how this was her problem. But she needed her job, so she bit her tongue. Besides, she knew what her boss was like. Right now, this was a disaster but by lunchtime he would have forgotten about it and moved on to something else.

'What would you like me to do?'

'Set up a lunch today for Cal and Julia. Call them both and tell them I need them to be there. Square it away with Julia's director. I'm not sure what Cal's doing right now – he's not scheduled to start filming *Big River* until next week – but tell him this lunch is his number one priority. Then I need you to leak the details to the press. Not everyone – I don't want it to look like a set-up. Just one reporter will do. Someone we can trust. We need to get the story out that Julia and Cal are still an item – maybe even hint that a wedding is in the air.'

Sadie's mouth went dry. Neither Julia nor Cal would be happy to find out they were now engaged to be married. They all knew how these things could take on a life of their own.

'Maybe that's overcooking it a little. We don't want to protest too much, so to speak. It might make people suspicious.'

'Hmm, you could be right. But nonetheless, they need to put on a good show. They're actors, for god's sake. Tomorrow morning, I want *this*'—he slammed his hand down on the paper—'to be a distant memory. The only news I want to read about is how Julia Newman and Cal Brooks can't keep their hands off each other.'

'Don't worry, Mr Gold. I'll sort this out, I promise.'

Sadie scampered back to her desk to start making calls and was greeted by Jack, who'd somehow managed to talk his way into her office even though she'd instructed the junior staff that she wasn't to be disturbed before ten o'clock. 'How did you get in here?'

'Nancy from the typing pool thinks I'm your boyfriend. She's convinced all the others that it's true.'

'What? Honestly, Jack, I—'

'Don't be mad. I'm here bearing gifts . . . well, not for you, exactly, but I come in peace.'

'I'm not mad. In fact, you've just saved me a call.'

'You were going to call me? Be still my beating heart.'

'Relax, Romeo, it wasn't a social call. I need a favour. Or, more specifically, Mr Gold does.'

'Anything for you.'

He flopped down in the seat opposite her desk as she rifled through the stack of newspapers she'd left on the sideboard. When she found *The Times*, she flicked it open to the offending page and handed it to Jack.

He let out a low whistle. 'I take it Harry wasn't too pleased to see this over his morning coffee.'

'You guessed right. Now it's my job to fix it.'

He looked up from the paper. 'How are you going to do that?'

'Harry thinks sending Julia and Cal on an intimate lunch date should do the trick. We just need someone to see them and report it.'

'I take it that's where I come in?'

'It'd be an exclusive, Jack. We don't want it to look staged, so we're only leaking the details of this date to one reporter, someone we can trust.'

'You trust me? I'm touched.'

'Don't get ahead of yourself. You're the best of a bad bunch as far as I'm concerned.'

'Aw, come on, Sadie, don't be like that. You know I'm one of the good guys.'

'You'll do. I'm about to make a reservation for one o'clock at Perino's. If you happened to be in the area around that time, you'll have an exclusive for *The Tribune*.'

'Consider it done.'

'Thank you. Now, what can I do for you? If you were wanting to see Mr Gold, he's otherwise engaged.' She lowered her voice. 'And even if he wasn't, he's not in the best mood right now, so whatever it is, I'd leave it until much later in the day.' She glanced down at the open diary on her desk. 'I could probably squeeze you in around four, if you want to try your luck then.'

'That's very kind of you, but I'm actually here to see you.'

'Look, Jack, thanks for helping us out with the . . . situation at hand, but as you can see I'm quite busy. I haven't got time to be chatting with friends.'

'So we're friends now? Glad to hear it. I knew I'd win you over eventually.'

Exasperated by his unwillingness to move on, Sadie picked up the telephone receiver. 'I'm sorry, but I need to get on with making these calls.'

'Hold your horses. As lovely as it is to see you, this isn't strictly a social visit. I'm here to give you something for Vivienne.' He handed over a large manila envelope.

She raised an eyebrow. 'What's this?'

'Open it and you'll see.'

She flipped up the unsealed flap and slid out a fat wad of paper with the title *Agnes Grey: A screenplay*. 'I don't understand.'

'They're casting this movie next week. I'm buddies with the director, Sam Hayden. I went to college with Sam's younger brother. In a way, it's because of Sam that I ended up out here in California.'

So, Jack had gone to college. He was still yet to mention the novel Vivienne had told her about months ago, even though Sadie had given him ample opportunities. She'd begun to wonder if Vivienne had mis-understood, but perhaps not. Maybe underneath that brash reporter's facade there was a deeper mind than Sadie had first imagined. 'Okay, but what does this have to do with Vivienne?'

'Sam's agreed to let Vivienne audition. The studio wanted Elizabeth Taylor but MGM refused to loan her out. They're looking for someone else. I thought Vivienne might fit the bill.'

'Vivienne . . .' Sadie said, not quite understanding. 'For Agnes Grey. I mean . . .'

He creased his brow in confusion. 'What? She's an actress, isn't she? I thought she was quite good in *Follow Your Heart*. I know it wasn't the lead, but she played her part well.'

'Yes, she was very good, but that was a role that was more . . . I'm not sure how to put this . . . suited to her.'

'You mean because she played a vamp?'

'No, not exactly. But you have to admit, Vivienne's very sexy.' Her cheeks flamed with heat. This was not the sort of conversation she wanted to be having with Jack Porter, especially not when the subject was her best friend.

'Absolutely she is.'

So he *did* like Vivienne. Sadie was unsure why this knowledge bothered her. 'Agnes Grey is not a particularly sexy character.'

'Maybe you're underestimating Vivienne. She's smart and observant, two qualities all the best actors have, in my opinion. On our last date we talked a lot about books, and she mentioned being a fan of the Bronte sisters, which is one of the reasons I thought of her for the role.'

On our last date? Was Jack still seeing Vivienne? If so, she'd kept it under her hat. Viv was often secretive about the men she was seeing. Sadie sometimes wondered if that was because they were married or otherwise off-limits, but she couldn't imagine why Viv would keep quiet about a relationship with Jack. A weight settled in Sadie's stomach. She'd never taken Jack's flirtations seriously, but maybe deep down she'd hoped just a little that he really did have a thing for her. Obviously, she'd been a fool.

She swallowed down the lump in her throat. 'Do you really think she has a chance?'

'I wouldn't have put her name forward if I didn't. The fact that she's familiar with the book will put her streets ahead of some of the other actresses vying for the part. I honestly think she has a real shot. I met up with Sam last night and we talked about the movie. When I mentioned Vivienne he said she sounded really promising, so this morning I called past his place to get a copy of the script. Said I'd pass it on. He'll see her next Friday, if she's keen.'

Jack was right. Sadie was ashamed of herself for falling into the trap of seeing Vivienne as one dimensional when she was anything but. 'You don't want to give her the script yourself?'

'No time to chase her. I already have a full day, and apparently now I have a lunch date as well.' He winked at her good naturedly.

'Thank you, Jack. Vivienne will be thrilled, I'm sure.'

'Happy to be of service. Tell her to be at Paramount Studios at eleven o'clock sharp. Sam Hayden will be expecting her.'

Chapter 14

Peggy

For once in her life, Peggy had kept her big mouth shut. It had been so difficult not to tell the other girls about her audition callback, but she didn't want to jinx herself. Especially not when things finally seemed to be going her way.

Early last week, along with dozens of other hopefuls, she'd made her way to Paramount Studios. When her turn came to read, she'd been unable to shake off the feeling that this audition would be just like all the others. She went through the motions but it was probably her weakest performance ever. She was sure she wouldn't get a second audition. But she was wrong! She'd found an envelope on her bed when she got home from the club last Friday.

It'd been hard not to tell Julia about the callback when she'd asked if Peggy had got the message. 'When I got home last night there was an envelope pinned to our door. I put it on your bed. Did you find it?'

'I did. Thanks.'

'Everything okay?'

'Fine, thanks. It was just a message from my mom reminding me to phone my gran for her birthday. No big deal,' she lied.

She knew Julia would support her whether she got the role or not, but she was just so sick of being 'Poor Peggy'. She couldn't bear to have Julia and the others crossing their fingers for her to get the part; telling her they were sure she would be successful *this time*. Or, worse than that, having to face them all afterwards if she didn't get the role.

Julia's arrival at the Studio Club had given Peggy something she'd always wished for – a group of friends to call her own. As wonderful as it was, friendship had brought about some surprising emotions that she could never have predicted. Peggy loved her friends and wanted the best for them. She was truly happy for their success. But she'd be lying to herself if she didn't admit that sometimes jealousy reared its ugly head. It wasn't easy to keep smiling when it never, ever seemed to be her turn.

Sometimes it was hard to keep believing in herself. Her mom, who swore that Hollywood was the creation of the devil, saw Peggy's lack of success as proof God was protecting her. Just last week she'd written, imploring Peggy to come home before it was too late.

You're still young and there are plenty of decent, eligible men who'd be happy to have you as their wife. Come back before your reputation is damaged irreparably. Your father and I love you and want the best for you. I fear you will never know the joys of holy matrimony and the blessing of children if you stay in that place much longer. No God-fearing man wants a wife whose virtue is uncertain. Remember that.

Peggy understood her mother's fears. Hollywood was filled with opportunities to sin, but her parents underestimated her strength. She was doing her best to live her life in a way that would make God happy. She went to church every Sunday, prayed every night, and had never once let herself be compromised. She made sure every man she dated knew that if they wanted to do more than kiss her, they'd need to put a ring on her finger.

She'd done everything right. She'd worked hard to improve upon her God-given talents. She'd taken classes and spent hours rehearsing all on her own. She'd gone to audition after audition and tried so hard to take the rejections in her stride, choosing to believe they were all part of God's plan. But it was hard when her friends – whose behaviour wasn't always as virtuous her own – were the ones reaping rewards.

Performing at Ciro's gave her a small taste of what it felt like to be in the spotlight. Sometimes, after the show, people came up and complimented her on her performance. Once, Montgomery Clift had come over to pay his respects. *Montgomery Clift!* As wonderful as that attention was, it wasn't the same as the adoration reserved for bona fide movie stars.

She was tired of being the recipient of sympathy. Of being the one always having to pick herself up and dust herself off. If she told the others about the callback and then didn't get the role, the pity would return to their eyes. This way was better. She'd go to the audition and do her best. She'd read *Agnes Grey* this week and now realised why her dejected demeanour had helped her audition. With a fresh understanding of the character, she was ready to give it her all. If she got the part, her friends would be delighted and surprised.

And if she didn't, they would be none the wiser.

Peggy gave her name to the security guard at the gates of Paramount Studios. 'They're expecting you on sound stage four, Miss Carmichael. Do you know where to go?'

Peggy nodded. 'Yes, thank you.'

'Best of luck to you.'

Peggy was early. From her visit the week before she remembered there was a bathroom near the commissary, so she made her way there to check her appearance. She'd be in costume today – it was a full screen test, which meant wardrobe and make-up – but she wanted to be sure she went in looking the part anyway. She'd chosen a woollen suit in olive green, which she thought suited the character, and had fashioned her hair into a conservative bun. She'd kept her make-up light, but now that she was here she decided even her soft pink lipstick was too much. She used a tissue to blot the excess sheen from her lips, then stepped back and took a last look in the mirror.

Agnes Grey stared back at her.

Once she reached the sound stage and had her name marked off, she was taken to wardrobe. The wardrobe assistant sized her up and handed her a drab grey ankle-length dress. 'Put this on and then report to make-up over there.' She pointed to a curtained-off area.

In the make-up space there were three high swivel chairs, two already filled. The girl in the end chair didn't look up from the script she was reading, and the make-up artist was busy with the actress in the centre seat. Peggy took the empty chair and closed her eyes to focus on memorising her lines while she waited. She wanted to impress the director by being word perfect without needing to consult the script.

'Peggy! What are you doing here?'

She opened her eyes and was startled to see Vivienne – was that really her? – seated in the chair beside her. Viv's bouncy blonde waves had been dyed dark brown and were pulled back into a severe bun. Her make-up was muted. There was no sign of her signature cherry-red lips. If Peggy hadn't recognised her friend's voice, she would never have known it was her.

'Oh my goodness, Viv, your hair!'

Vivienne's hand went to the top of her head and she laughed self-consciously. 'Do you like it? I did it last night. I thought perhaps people would take me more seriously as a brunette.'

'You certainly look different. I didn't realise it was you at first. But yes, I *do* like it. It suits you.'

'I didn't know you'd auditioned for this. Why didn't you say something?' Vivienne asked.

Peggy's heart sank as she realised she'd have to compete with her friend for the role. 'When did *you* audition for this? I didn't see you here last week.'

'I wasn't, but you remember Jack Porter, that reporter I dated for a while? I brought him to the club to watch you perform a couple of times. Well, he suggested I try out for the part and here I am.'

'But these are screen tests for the callbacks. How . . .'

'Jack put in a word for me – he knows the director personally. How lucky is that?'

'*Very* lucky.' Peggy tried to keep her voice light.

'I honestly don't think I have much of a shot, though.' Vivienne's words tumbled out quickly. 'And especially now I see you're here. In fact, if I'd known you were trying out for it I wouldn't have taken the audition. It's a bit awkward, us vying for the same part, isn't it? I would hate a silly audition to come between us.'

Peggy sighed inwardly. This was what came of keeping secrets from her friends. 'Don't worry about it. It was bound to happen sooner or later.'

'Close your lids please, Miss Lockhart, so I can do your eyeshadow,' the make-up artist said.

'I mean, I'm not sure anyone is going to buy me as Agnes Grey, even with my hair this colour,' Vivienne continued, as her lids were painted with a soft brown powder. 'I'm sure you're much more suited to the role.'

Peggy relaxed a little then. Vivienne was right. Agnes Grey was not the role for a sexpot. It was a serious part, and Vivienne was anything but serious. Peggy might not get the role, but there was no way she'd lose out to Vivienne.

'Well, if I don't get the part, I hope it goes to you,' Peggy said. It never hurt to be magnanimous in these situations.

'Oh, thank you, honey. I feel exactly the same way. But you didn't answer my question. Why didn't you tell us you were auditioning? I could have run lines with you.'

'I thought it would be nice to surprise you all if I did happen to get the part.'

'Maybe just keep us informed next time. It's a shame for us to be competing against each other.' Vivienne closed her eyes again while the make-up girl dusted her face with powder, then opened her mouth while a slight sheen of pink lip colour was applied.

'There,' said the make-up artist. 'You're all done, Miss Lockhart. You can head on in to the audition space. Just wait in the holding area until your name is called.'

'Break a leg, Vivienne,' Peggy called after her.

Chapter 15

Julia

Julia's first reaction when Sadie relayed Harry's directive to cool the friendship with Charlie Hudson was to tell Harry to go jump! Who was he to tell her who she could be friends with? But after Sadie quietly reminded her about the clause in her contract that required her personal relationships to be endorsed by the studio, she had second thoughts.

She and Charlie would need to be more careful.

Not that anything had actually transpired between them, but each time they met her desire for him grew stronger. It seemed inevitable that the friendship would become something more physical if they continued to see each other.

In the meantime, if she had to play out this charade with Cal, why not do it where she could at least see Charlie? Harry couldn't possibly object. Well, he could, but he wasn't getting *everything* his own way. He'd forced her to have lunch with Cal and be accidently caught out by Jack last week. A follow-up dinner would only cement the rumours that she and Cal were still a couple, even if it was at Ciro's.

She'd sent a note to Charlie via Peggy, explaining the situation and asking him not to sit at their table tonight, just until things cooled down a little, and late this afternoon a bouquet of roses from a 'secret admirer' had turned up at the Studio Club for her. She was certain that Charlie understood.

Cal was happy enough with the arrangement. It meant that his fledgling relationship with an up-and-coming screenwriter was flying well under the radar. His fellow was in the middle of writing a new script and not up for partying right now, which left Cal free to carry on his 'affair' with her.

Now her problem was what to wear. None of the five gowns she'd tried on and discarded seemed quite right. She wanted to look glamorous and sexy but in a way that wasn't too obvious or revealing. She rifled through her wardrobe again and pulled out a pale pink satin dress. The floor-length gown was strapless, with a fitted bodice and gentle ruching at the waist. Yes! This one was perfect. It showed enough skin to be sexy and yet was still elegant. She stepped into it and pulled up the zip as far as she could. With pearls and a pair of kitten heels this would do the job nicely. The photographers would get pics worth printing tomorrow. Hopefully she and Cal would get good mileage out of this outing.

And hopefully Charlie would know that the outfit was all for him.

Julia and Cal were the first of their party to arrive. She'd booked for six people – Sadie was unexpectedly bringing a date! Vivienne had invited Jack Porter, who she'd dated for a while last year. Those two seemed an unlikely match and Vivienne had insisted they were just friends, but that could mean anything. Vivienne's definition of friendship seemed quite fluid when it came to the opposite sex.

Sadie hadn't mentioned who she was bringing. 'Someone from work' was all Julia managed to get out of her. Not that it mattered. It was great to see her dating anyone. Lately Sadie had been so obsessed with finishing her screenplay that it was hard to get her to come out with the rest of them, but she'd agreed to come to Ciro's a few times. Julia had assumed it was to support Peggy, but in light of recent developments she now wondered if Harry had sent Sadie to babysit her.

Cal had only just finished pulling out Julia's chair for her when he let out a low whistle. 'Wow. Vivienne's dressed to kill tonight.'

It took Julia a moment to spot Vivienne – she was briefly thrown by her friend's new hair colour, which was taking some getting used to. Eventually, she spied Jack Porter heading towards her with Viv by his side. Cal wasn't wrong: Vivienne wore a shimmering gold dress with a plunging neckline. She and Jack were laughing, clearly sharing some private joke, as they approached the table.

'What's so funny?' Julia asked as Vivienne leant in to kiss her cheek.

'What? Oh . . . nothing, really. Jack and I were just talking about a mutual friend.'

'Speaking of mutual friends,' Cal interrupted, 'are my eyes deceiving me or is that Sadie?'

Julia looked up to see Sadie sailing across the room on her date's arm. She was dressed in a fitted red satin gown that had once belonged to Julia. Her long dark curls hung loose, with just one section pulled back off her face and contained by a bejewelled comb. Her lips were painted fire-engine red. The result was simply breathtaking.

When they got to the table, Sadie introduced her date. Tony Astor worked in some capacity at Goldstar, but Sadie didn't elaborate further than that. He didn't look familiar to Julia, so she presumed he wasn't an actor.

Julia kissed her friend's cheek. 'You look gorgeous tonight, Sadie.'

'Thanks, Jules.' Sadie reached over and took Tony by the hand. 'I figured I should make a special effort for my date here.' As Tony looked at Sadie, his cheeks flushed pink. He was really quite adorable.

'I don't know about the rest of you, but I could use a drink,' Jack said. He caught the eye of a nearby waiter and nodded to him. 'What would you like, ladies? Pimm's and lemonade perhaps, or are we in the mood for champagne?'

'Pimm's for me,' Sadie said.

'Make that two,' Vivienne chimed in.

'I'm sticking to the non-alcoholic stuff,' Julia said. 'I've got a meeting at the studio with Harry Gold at the crack of dawn.'

Ever the newshound, Jack homed in on this information. 'What's so important that Harry needs you to get up early?'

'Who knows? I'm probably being told off for something. Perhaps Harry wants to get my scolding out of the way before his golf game.'

'I'm sure that's not the case,' Sadie said. 'He probably just wants to chat about your next movie. You know what he's like. He works seven days a week and is shocked that others expect their weekends off.'

'What have you done to deserve a scolding, Julia?' Jack asked.

'Be careful what you tell him, Jules,' Sadie cut in before she could answer. 'Don't forget he's a reporter.'

'I'm an open book. Besides, Jack is our friend,' Julia said, looking at him pointedly. 'We know he would never write anything that would harm us.'

'Thank you, Julia,' Jack replied. 'I'm pleased to see *someone* appreciates me.'

Vivienne threw an arm around his shoulders. 'Oh, Jack, we all adore you. You must know that?'

Jack's answer was interrupted by the waiter. Cal took the opportunity to change the subject by asking Tony what he did for a living. The poor man looked uncomfortable, and no wonder; his answer was decidedly dull – something to do with accounts – but Sadie seemed completely enamoured of her date. Her gaze never once left his face. Julia had never seen her friend so smitten. Good for her!

As their drinks arrived, Peggy came out from backstage to greet them. 'I'm so happy to see you all here tonight.' She placed her hand on Julia's shoulder. 'Especially you, roomie. I feel as if we hardly see each these days.'

Cal's head swung around. 'Wait, what? You two share a room?'

Julia nodded. 'We do.'

'Wow. I had no idea. It's bad enough that Harry makes you live at the Studio Club, but you're a huge star now. Why do you have to share a room?' He glanced at Peggy. 'No offence, Peggy.'

125

'None taken.'

'We don't *have* to share a room,' Julia said. 'We want to. When I first moved to the club, all the single rooms were taken. I agreed to share with Peggy until one became free. By the time that happened we'd become used to sharing. It's just so nice to have someone to talk to about all the things that happen in the day, someone who understands.'

'It really is,' Peggy said. 'And we help each other out with everything from learning lines to doing hair and make-up. It's a lot of fun.'

'I think I'd be lonely without Peg,' Julia said. 'In fact, I know I would. We barely see each other since she started working here. I'm asleep before she gets home from work, and most days I leave for the studio before she wakes up. I miss our nightly bedtime chats and having breakfast together.'

'You still have us,' Sadie said.

'Yes. I'm thankful for all of you. I don't think I would have stayed in Hollywood this long if I hadn't made such wonderful friends. Being surrounded by people you can trust really makes a difference in this business.'

'Well, let's make the most of our time together now.' Peggy patted Julia's shoulder. 'There's still another hour before showtime. Would you gents mind if I stole the ladies away for a few minutes? The Ciro's dancers would love to meet you, Julia, and I'd love to catch up with you girls in my dressing-room before the show.' She looked at Jack, and then to Cal and Tony. 'If that's okay with you fellas? I promise I won't keep them from you for too long.'

'Fine by me,' Cal said. 'I see Glenn Fordham is here. I might avail myself of the opportunity to say hello.'

'You ladies go ahead.' Jack looked at Tony. 'We'll be fine. Won't we, Tony?'

Tony's face was beet-red and he was staring at Peggy. 'Yes, yes, of course.'

Julia stole a glance at Vivienne, who raised her eyebrows. So she wasn't imagining it – Tony couldn't take his eyes off Peggy. Hopefully Sadie hadn't noticed.

Vivienne jumped up and took Sadie by the hand. 'Come on, girls. Grab your drinks and let's go.'

Peggy led them backstage to the girls' dressing-room – a long, narrow room with a bench running the length of it. A dozen lighted mirrors sat atop the counter, which was littered with wig stands and cosmetics. Around ten girls were seated there in various states of undress. Julia's arrival caused quite a sensation. All the girls wanted to talk to her and ask about her clothes, her make-up and her gorgeous co-stars. Four extra bodies in the cramped quarters made for a claustrophobic atmosphere, so after a minute or two Peggy took Vivienne and Sadie to her dressing-room, leaving Julia to fend for herself. It was a good ten minutes before she managed to extract herself from the adoring dancers.

When she finally got to Peggy's dressing-room, she found Sadie perched carefully on the edge of a green velvet sofa – from memory, that close-fitting dress was not the most comfortable garment to sit in. Vivienne sat regally in an oversized armchair, like a queen on her throne. Peggy was at her make-up table with her chair swivelled to face the others. Julia plonked herself down next to Sadie. 'Good grief, I thought I'd never get away.'

'Now that you're here, let's not waste another second,' Peggy said. 'I feel as if I'm losing touch with what's happening in everyone's lives, we all see so little of each other these days. Sadie, let's start with you. You're a dark horse. What's the deal with you and Tony?'

'Isn't he lovely?' Sadie said, brightly. She took a swig of her Pimm's.

'He's certainly handsome,' Julia replied. 'How do you know him?'

'He works at the studio in the finance department and is in and out of my office quite a bit.' Sadie sipped her drink again, ignoring the inquiring looks on the others' faces. 'But enough about me. Vivienne, tell us how your screen test went today.'

'Oh, I don't know. I'm not sure that I'm right for the part. Especially not when . . .' She glanced up at Peggy and cocked an eyebrow.

'Okay, okay,' Peggy said. 'I have a confession to make. I auditioned for *Agnes Grey* last week and I got a callback. I had a screen test today too.'

'What—' Sadie started.

'Why—' Julia said at the same time. Sadie motioned for her to go ahead. 'Why didn't you tell us?'

'I didn't think I'd get anywhere, and I didn't want to burden you all with yet another failure.'

Sadie looked aghast. 'Oh, Peggy—'

'No, Sade, don't. It's fine. I don't need your sympathy. In fact, that's why I didn't say anything. I just couldn't bear to see the pity in your eyes if I got another knockback. But as it turns out I did okay; I think the screen test went well.'

'That's fabulous, Peggy. I hope you get it. Oh . . .' Julia looked up at Vivienne. 'You too, Vivienne. This is a bit tricky, isn't it?'

'Not at all. I'm sure Peggy's right for the part. If I'd known she was auditioning, I wouldn't have bothered. But I didn't know until after I arrived at the studio and it would have been rude to pull out then, especially as they were really only seeing me as a favour to Jack.'

'Speaking of Jack, shouldn't we be getting back to our dates?' Sadie's voice had an edge to it. She sounded anxious, or perhaps irritated.

'Ah, they can wait a little longer. What's that saying? "Treat 'em mean, keep 'em keen"?'

'I hardly think that's the way you should be treating Jack, especially after the huge favour he's just done you.' Sadie was definitely annoyed.

'Jack won't be missing *me* one little bit.'

There was a knock on the dressing-room door. 'Thirty minutes, Miss Carmichael,' a male voice called.

'Thanks, Ernie,' Peggy replied. She screwed up her nose. 'I probably should finish getting ready. I'll come sit with you all when my set is done. Charlie and I do a closing duet and tonight I have another number with him halfway through his set, but I can sit with you while he's doing the rest of his show.'

'Knock 'em dead, Peggy,' Vivienne said as she stood up.

Sadie kissed Peggy's cheek. 'I'm so proud of you, Peg. Your star is definitely on the rise.'

Julia kissed Peggy and followed the others out of the dressing-room. 'You two go ahead,' she said. 'I'm just going to powder my nose before I head back in.'

'Do you want us to come with you?' Sadie asked.

'No, no. You've both kept your dates waiting long enough as it is. Cal won't be missing me. Besides, I promised I'd pop my head into the dancers' dressing-room before I left. One of the girls was running late and the others said she'd be sad not to have met me. I'll just quickly do that and then go to the bathroom. I won't be too long, I promise.'

Vivienne gave her an odd look but said nothing. Instead, she linked arms with Sadie and strode towards the club's main room.

There was no time to waste. Julia continued down the corridor hoping to find the room she was looking for. It didn't take long before she was standing in front of a door adorned with a gold star. This had to be it. Her pulse thudded in her ears. If she knocked, there would be no going back. Was she about to make the biggest mistake of her life?

To hell with it. She was so sick of doing what everyone expected of her. For once in her life she was going to do what *she* wanted. She knocked on the door.

Chapter 16

Sadie

From the moment Peggy came on stage she had Tony's undivided attention. Sadie worked hard to bring his gaze back to her – flicking her hair, leaning closer to him, touching his forearm when she spoke. She went as far as beckoning the cigarette girl over and purchasing a packet, simply so she could ask Tony to light one for her. This backfired spectacularly when she inhaled deeply and began to cough. Hardly surprising, considering she wasn't a frequent smoker.

All her efforts were in vain. Tony was a gentleman and unfailingly polite, but he was not interested. Who was she trying to kid? He wasn't even her type. So why was she so desperate for him to want her?

Jack. That was why. How many times had Jack asked her out on a date? It had to be dozens. She'd pegged him as a smooth operator; a man who would do whatever it took to get the latest scoop. And if he managed to get into her panties along the way, all the better. But these past couple of weeks she'd seen a different side of him. He'd taken the time to get to know Vivienne and gone out of his way to help her when he didn't need to. Not only that, it turned out the man was educated and intelligent.

And totally besotted with Vivienne, by the looks of things.

Why had it taken her so damned long to see Jack's good points? If only she'd taken more notice of him instead of shooing him away every chance she'd had. Too late to worry about that now. He'd obviously moved on. Her date with Tony hadn't caused even a flicker of interest from Jack. She had to concede defeat. That ship had sailed. Besides, Vivienne seemed to like Jack too. Maybe they were meant for each other, and who was she to stand in their way?

Vivienne deserved a bit of happiness in her life. Especially if she didn't end up getting the part of Agnes Grey. From all accounts Peggy was a certainty to snag the role. Sadie sighed inwardly. If the part went to Peggy, Vivienne would laugh it off and tell everyone she was fine, but there'd be a wound beneath that tough outer layer.

Whatever way Sadie looked at it, there was no good solution to this problem. She'd hoped to catch a moment alone with Julia, to see what she thought about the whole dilemma, but when she'd tried to accompany Jules to the bathroom earlier, Vivienne had whisked Sadie away, chattering so incessantly that there hadn't been an opportunity to protest. Julia had taken forever to make her way back to the table. She'd rushed in just before Peggy came on stage, looking flustered. 'Sorry,' she'd said to no one in particular. 'I got caught up chatting to the dancers and I lost track of time. Goodness me, those girls were hard to get away from. Every one of them wanted to tell me their life story. I was worried I wouldn't make it back in time for Peggy's first number.'

Sadie glanced over at her now, hoping to catch her eye. Perhaps they could steal a few minutes together before the night's end. But Julia's gaze was fixed on the stage. Peggy was doing the final number of her set – the duet with Charlie – and Julia seemed enthralled by it.

Cal touched her arm. 'You're the belle of the ball tonight, Miss Sadie,' he whispered.

'Thanks, Cal.'

'Someone needs to say it. Looks like your date – and mine, for that matter – have their sights set on others this evening. I can't say

131

that I blame Julia, but young Tony's a fool. If I . . . well, if I was looking for a lady, you'd be my choice tonight.'

She patted his hand, not trusting herself to speak. It was bad enough to watch Vivienne and Jack falling for each other across the table, but now she realised everyone had noticed Tony's complete disinterest in her. Not only had she failed to make Jack jealous, but he'd witnessed her humiliation. *Great. Just great.*

Sadie reached for her drink. She'd ordered a second Pimm's, which she'd probably regret in the morning, but right now the warm buzz she felt was the only pleasure she was taking from this evening. It took a few moments but as the alcohol began to work its magic, the meaning of Cal's words became clear. It wasn't just Tony who was looking towards the stage with adoration in his eyes. It seemed Julia could not take her eyes off Charlie Hudson.

Suddenly it all made sense. Julia's late return to the table, her flustered appearance and her careful and overly detailed explanation of where she'd been.

This really couldn't be happening. Harry Gold would have a stroke if there was even a hint of a relationship brewing between them, and the press would have a field day. Mr Gold didn't want Julia dating anyone at all unless the studio sanctioned it. Of course, that was unfair and ridiculous, but Julia had always gone along with it. 'It's just for show,' she'd said when Sadie had asked her whether she minded. 'And it helps my career. The fans love to see a relationship between the two leading actors.'

'But what if you fall in love with someone else?'

'I'm not sure I even know what love is. Besides, I'm not ready for all that just yet. Right now, I'm focusing on making the most of my career.'

Sadie couldn't argue with that.

So what was Julia thinking? A flirtation was bad enough, but a full-blown relationship with Charlie Hudson would be career-ending. Was she really willing to risk everything for him? Because, like it or not, it wasn't just the studio she'd have to answer to if this got out.

The movie-going public was not likely to stand for their golden-haired girl cavorting with a Black man. It might not be fair or right, and things might be changing, but for now a white woman and Black man going out together was bound to cause controversy. And if that white woman and Black man happened to be huge stars? That was simply trouble waiting to happen.

29 December 1999

Vivienne is still sleeping when Peggy calls. Even so, I take the cordless phone out onto the terrace so she won't hear us talking. Weenie follows, tugging at my robe. She hasn't been walked yet and is no doubt displeased at this disruption to her normal routine.

'How did you end up last night?' Peggy asks. 'Did you manage to get Vivienne to leave?'

'Yes and no.' I shift the wicker outdoor chair slightly to avoid squinting into the morning sun.

'Don't be cryptic, Sadie. Say what you mean.'

I glance through the sliding glass doors into the light-filled living area to make sure Vivienne hasn't suddenly appeared. She's nowhere to be seen but I keep my voice low, just in case. 'She left the Studio Club but she's here with me.'

'You're kidding?'

'I most certainly am not.'

'I can't believe you brought her home with you. Good grief, Sadie, what were you thinking?'

'I didn't have a choice. She's not well and she had nowhere else to go. I couldn't just leave her there.' Weenie barks and I lift her onto my lap, which calms her.

'You should have called the police. I mean, I'm sorry that she didn't have anywhere to go, truly I am, but you're not responsible for her. There must be someone else.'

'There's not. We're all she has left. Peggy, we loved her once and now she needs us. She has dementia.'

'Dementia . . .' Peggy pauses for a moment and then says quietly, 'How do you know?'

'Her assistant left a letter. I'll read it to you if you like. Just hang on a moment while I find it.' I take the phone back to my bedroom and grab the letter from the nightstand. Weenie, possibly realising that her walk is not forthcoming, jumps up onto my bed and digs into my bedcovers as punishment. 'Shoo!' I say. 'Get out of there, right now.'

'Sadie?'

'Sorry, Peg, just talking to the dog. Here's the letter.' I slide my glasses on and begin to read.

Dear Ladies of the Hollywood Studio Club,
My name is April, and I am writing to you because I simply don't know what else to do. By now you will have realised that I am gone, and my darling Vivienne has been left in your care.

For the past twelve months, I have been Vivienne's assistant. I was employed by her beautiful partner, Georgina Fellows, to help Vivienne compile her memoir.

'A woman!' Peggy interrupts. 'Vivienne's partner was a woman!'

I sigh impatiently. 'Does that really matter?'

'No, of course not,' she says in a petulant tone. 'I'm just surprised, that's all. I mean, she was a bit of a floozy—'

'Peg!'

'Oh, Sadie, don't be so sensitive. Go on.'

George had noticed that Vivienne was talking more and more about her movie career and her time at the Hollywood Studio Club. She wanted Vivienne to have the chance to write her story before it was too late, and she gave me the job of turning Vivienne's memories into something readable.

As you might have noticed, Vivienne is unwell. She has a progressive form of dementia—

'Oh, dear god.'

—and is not able to care for herself.

George was her partner and her main carer until she died suddenly last summer. I moved in on a short-term basis, thinking that there would be family, friends or someone to help, but I haven't had luck finding any.

That brings me to you. She speaks so fondly of her time at the Hollywood Studio Club and of the friends she made there. She refers to her 'sisters' Sadie, Peggy and Julia often, and says how much she misses them. So I am turning her care over to you.

There's a house in Three Rivers – I've printed the address on the back of this letter – but you should know there's no money. George and Vivienne ran a shelter for injured wildlife, and unwanted pets and livestock. When George died we had to close the shelter and pay off all the remaining debt. (In case you are wondering, I haven't drawn a wage since George died, and the small amount of money that was left in Vivienne's accounts has gone entirely towards her care.)

You'll find an overnight case containing clothes, personal care items and all the basic information you will need – bank account details, financial records and so on – behind the reception desk at the Studio Club.

My notes on Vivienne's memoir and all the documents you will need to help her finish her story, should one of you choose to do so, *can be found in the office at Vivienne's home. Vivienne is always talking about her talented writer friend Sadie, so perhaps Ms Shore would be interested in taking on the job.*

Please don't think badly of me for abandoning her. I have done my best, but I am out of money and out of ideas. I'm heading to New York, where I've been offered a job, but I couldn't just leave Vivienne in the hands of the authorities. She's the kindest, sweetest woman I've ever known and she deserves better. I'm sorry for the deceitfulness of my actions but I couldn't think of another way to force your hands. I knew if I asked you there was a chance you'd say no, but I am quite sure you ladies won't leave your friend to fend for herself when she's so vulnerable.

Please look after her. You're all she has. Tell her that I love her and I'm sorry.

April

When I'm done I take a breath and wait for Peggy's response, but there's silence on the other end of the phone.

'Peg? Are you still there?'

Peggy sighs. 'I am. That's terrible news. I know she's made some mistakes in her life, but I wouldn't wish that fate on anyone. My grandmother had dementia. It's a terrible disease. And Vivienne's so young.'

'Now do you understand why I brought her home?'

'I understand why you would want to help, but what now? I mean, you can't let her just move in with you.'

Peggy's right, I suppose. I can't look after Vivienne forever, can I? I have no idea what I'm going to do and have been pondering my next move ever since the taxi dropped us off last night. But Peggy's insistence that Vivienne is not my problem riles me. 'Why not?'

'Your work, for one thing. Sure, you might work from home some of the time, but what about when you have to do site visits? Are you going to take Vivienne with you and give her a shovel? And what about when you have important client meetings?'

Of course, she is right. 'Look, I know it's not a long-term solution,' I concede, 'but it won't kill me to have her here for a few days while we work out what to do.'

'Sadie, you do realise Julia will have a fit when she finds out? I'm sorry this has happened, but I don't think it's up to us to care for Vivienne.'

'Maybe you're right. It's just when April said she called us her "sisters" it got to me, you know?'

Peggy huffs. 'You're not actually thinking about writing that memoir, are you? I mean, heaven forbid!'

'Of course not. I haven't written anything for years and I'm not about to start again now. But I can't just throw her out on the street. We did once promise to be there for each other no matter what.'

'Vivienne's the one who broke that covenant. I'm sorry this has happened to her, but I'm not going to risk Julia's friendship by getting involved. Although . . .'

'Yes?' I ask hopefully.

'Look, if it's simply a matter of throwing some money at the problem, I'd be happy to help. Of course, I don't want Vivienne to end up on the street, but we have to be realistic about what we can do. Perhaps we could pay for private care. That's something you could look into if you like and, as I said, I'm happy to pay. In the meantime, please, Sade, for all our sakes, just hand Vivienne over to the authorities. Take her to the nearest hospital. And if I were you, I'd do it quickly, before Julia gets wind of the fact she's there.'

'But—'

'Sorry, my love, I must go! I'm meeting up with the water aerobics girls for coffee – I'm already late. I'll call you back this afternoon.' She rings off, leaving me holding the phone.

It's almost eight-thirty and not a peep from Vivienne yet. Usually, I'd be heading out to walk Weenie but I don't want to risk leaving Vivienne alone. What if she wakes up and doesn't know where she is? Instead, I shower quickly and dress casually in jeans, a T-shirt and a lightweight zippered jacket to guard against the morning chill. I have no clients today; I'm on a break until after New Year, so there's no need for anything more businesslike. I pull my hair up into a loose bun and head to the kitchen to make a fresh pot of coffee, so it will be ready for Vivienne when she finally wakes. But I'm too late. I emerge to find Vivienne standing at the sink drinking a glass of water. She has the dog tucked under one arm, which is quite astonishing really, as Weenie usually takes ages to warm up to strangers.

Her back is half-turned and she doesn't see me at first, but Weenie gives an excited little bark, and Vivienne swivels round. 'Who are you?' she demands.

I stop where I am so as not to alarm her further. 'Good morning, Vivienne. I hope you slept well. I'm Sadie. I brought you home with me last night.'

She looks me up and down. 'Are you the housekeeper?'

I can see how she might think that. Even in her pyjamas and robe, Vivienne is somehow more glamorous than me. 'I'm your friend Sadie. Sadie Shore. We were at the Studio Club together when were girls.'

Vivienne's face falls. She peers at me for a moment, looking truly bewildered. Weenie has started to wriggle and whimper, so I cross the floor and gently extract her from Vivienne's grip.

'She hasn't had her walk yet, so she's probably a little wound up.'

'Oh, dogs do need their exercise.' A smile lights her face as she watches Weenie chasing her tail at my feet. 'What's her name?'

'Edwina. Weenie, for short.'

Vivienne crouches down – she's still remarkably flexible – and croons, 'Do you want a walk, little Weenie?'

Weenie runs and jumps into her arms again, her little tail wagging furiously.

'We'll take her soon. Would you like some coffee and breakfast first?'

She looks confused again. 'No, thank you. I must be getting home. Perhaps you could call me a taxi.'

Chapter 17

Julia

When he'd opened his dressing-room door half an hour ago, Charlie hadn't seemed the least bit surprised to see her. He'd simply taken her by the hand and drawn her into the room. 'I hoped you come.'

'I was back here with Peggy and I just thought I'd come by and wish you luck for the show.'

A languid smile settled on Charlie's face. 'I don't need luck, honey, and you don't need an excuse to see me.'

'Oh . . . no, I know. I just . . .'

'You wanted to see me,' he said. 'Admit it. There's no shame in talking about what you want.' He let her hand drop and leant over to snib the door behind her. He was so close she could feel the heat of his breath on her neck. 'Let me make it easier for you. I'll go first.' He put his hand on the small of her waist and drew her to him. 'I want you, Julia,' he whispered in her ear. 'So bad it hurts. I haven't stopped thinking about being alone with you since the first moment we met. I'm not going to push or ask you for anything you're not ready to give. I can be patient. But I need to know: do you want me too?'

'Yes,' she breathed. He was so close but not close enough. Her whole body was humming with anticipation, aching to be touched, but he didn't move a muscle.

'Tell me,' he said. 'Tell me what you want.'

Julia had been with men before. Not many, but enough to be surprised by his question. This wasn't how it usually went. First, they would kiss her. Then came the breast fondling, which she quite liked but it was usually over in the blink of an eye. The awkward bra fumbling part came next and eventually they both ended up naked on the bed. The part that followed was largely to be endured. Not entirely unpleasant, but not mind-blowing either. No man had ever asked her what she wanted. She had no idea what to say. 'I . . . I don't know what you mean.'

'It's simple. Just tell me what you want. You can say anything, even tell me to make you a cup of coffee. Whatever you want, baby. Just say the word.'

'I want you to kiss me,' she said.

'Where?' He kissed her earlobe. 'Here?' He moved his mouth to her neck. 'Here?'

'Yes,' she heard herself say.

'How about here?' He pressed his lips to hers and kissed her softly.

She responded by putting her hand on the back of his head. Her desire to be closer to him was insatiable. Even this – their mouths meshed together – was not enough.

He drew back and cupped her face in his hands before gently kissing her again. His hand moved to her neck and then caressed the bare skin of her shoulders. 'Do you like this?'

'Yes,' she murmured. His mouth followed his hand and her skin quivered beneath his lips. She wanted to be free of her dress, to stand naked before him so he was able to move his hands – and those lips – wherever he wanted. 'Touch me,' she heard herself say. Dear god, where had this need, this voice, come from?

'Where?'

She moaned in response, as his hand slid over the satin bodice to cup her breast. It wasn't enough. 'Take it off,' she whispered.

141

'Are you sure?'

'Now!' she demanded. 'I need to feel your skin on mine.'

'Whatever you want, baby.' His hand went to her zipper and pulled. As the dress slid to the floor he looked at her in her strapless lace bra and matching panties. 'You truly are the most beautiful woman I've ever seen.'

She stepped forward, still in her heels, and pressed herself against his chest while he unfastened her bra. And then his hands and his mouth were everywhere, *everywhere*, and Julia could barely breathe. She willed herself to be quiet. If they were caught . . . No, she wouldn't let her mind go there. She couldn't bear to think about the consequences.

By the time he lowered her onto the couch she was so lost in her own desire that she no longer cared about anything beyond the man above her, and when he entered her she cried out in ecstasy.

Charlie stopped dead still. 'Am I hurting you?'

'No,' she panted, 'don't stop.' She rocked her hips against his. 'I want you. All of you.'

Now, sitting at the table next to Cal, the memory of her abandonment drew heat to her cheeks, yet she was not ashamed. This was what love felt like.

She wasn't a fool. There was every chance that Charlie did not feel the same way; that he had been driven purely by lust. Her desire was every bit as strong as his, but she knew that there was more to it than physical attraction. She'd fallen for him long before he'd touched her. It was his attention, his ability to see her for herself – that was the drug.

Dear god, she was in trouble. She was ridiculously, *stupidly*, head over heels in love with Charlie Hudson.

Chapter 18

Peggy

In the break between her set and Charlie's, Peggy joined her friends at their table. Sadie asked the waiter to bring an extra chair and she had her date move over so Peggy could sit between him and Vivienne. 'There you go, Tony. Enjoy,' Sadie said, cryptically.

Peggy raised an eyebrow at her, hoping for at least a hint of an explanation, but Sadie just shrugged and turned her attention to Cal on her other side. Vivienne was deep in conversation with Jack, which left her to entertain Sadie's awkward date.

'Can I just say, Miss Carmichael, that was a wonderful performance. Simply breathtaking.'

The compliment warmed her. 'Please, Tony, call me Peggy.' He was certainly handsome enough. She hadn't taken much notice of him when they were introduced earlier, but now she could see why Sadie had chosen him. Obviously, he wasn't someone she would consider dating herself – low-level management types weren't nearly useful enough. Successful actors, directors and studio executives were more suitable. Still, this fellow seemed nice enough and he was easy on the eye. Sadie could do worse, she supposed.

'Peggy it is. I have to say, I've been to lots of shows here and I can't remember ever enjoying one as much as yours. You have a beautiful voice.'

'You flatter me, Tony.'

'I'm quite serious. Where did you learn to sing?'

'I didn't. Not really. I've always been able to hold a tune, ever since I was a little girl. A gift from God, I guess. But I did sing in the church choir back home for quite a few years, so I guess I have had some instruction.'

Tony went on to ask where home was and followed up with another question and another. It seemed he had forgotten about Sadie altogether. Not that Sadie seemed bothered. She'd barely even glanced in Tony's direction since Peggy had taken a seat.

As lovely as Tony's attention was, she really wanted to talk to Sadie and Julia about her audition. She wanted to go over everything that had happened and get their opinions on how to handle Vivienne. The whole situation was unfortunate. Vivienne auditioning had taken the shine off the possibility of getting the part. Not that she was counting her chickens, of course; it could go either way. But if she *did* get the part, how on earth could she celebrate when she knew it came at her friend's expense? Vivienne had assured her that she would be fine if she didn't get the role, but hadn't she told Vivienne the very same thing? And the truth was, she wouldn't be fine at all. She'd be devastated.

Catching a moment alone with Sadie and Julia seemed impossible tonight, though. She couldn't talk freely here at the table, not with Vivienne right there, and if she asked Julia and Sadie to come to the ladies' room Vivienne would no doubt tag along too.

She suddenly realised Tony was looking at her expectantly. 'Sorry, Tony, I was miles away. I missed your question.'

'I was just asking if you needed a ride home later?'

'Oh, you're sweet to ask, but I wouldn't want to cramp your style with Sadie.'

'I'm pretty sure Sadie won't mind.'

'Maybe not, but you'll need to get her home before curfew, and I won't be ready to leave in time for that. The show finishes around eleven-thirty. After that I need to go backstage to change and then we have a quick meeting and a drink with the club manager. I can catch a ride with one of the band members, or Charlie's driver will take me home. I usually don't get home until an hour after curfew.'

'How do you get away with that?'

'I have an exemption . . . and a key. I'm very trustworthy, you see.'

'Well, perhaps another time, then.'

Thankfully, the band started up and Charlie burst onto the stage, saving her from having to answer.

⟲

After the show and post-show debrief, Peggy and Charlie gave in to the club manager's pleas to have one for the road with him.

Charlie swirled the whiskey in his tumbler and then downed it in one gulp. As he placed the glass back on the bar with a thud, he glanced at his watch. 'Hell, Peggy, it's late. I'll have my driver drop you home.'

Billy unscrewed the lid from the whiskey bottle – the good stuff he kept hidden behind the bar – and nodded at Charlie. 'Another?'

Charlie shook his head. 'I probably should get going.'

'What about you, Peggy? Come on, just one more. It won't be long before Charlie's no longer with us. We have to make the most of these last days together.'

Charlie laughed. 'I'm going to work on a TV special, Billy, not dying. I'm not even leaving LA. I'll be visiting the club as a patron all the time.'

'Still, it won't be the same, will it?' Billy poured whiskey into a glass and downed it himself.

Peggy slid off the bar stool and smoothed out her skirt with her palms. 'We still have a few more shows to do together and I want to be at my best for tomorrow's, so I'm going to need my sleep.'

Billy looked so crestfallen that Charlie relented. 'Okay, I'll stay for one last one. Peggy, you take the car. Leon can come back for me after he's dropped you home.'

'Thanks, Charlie, you're an angel. I'll see you both tomorrow night.'

It was almost one-thirty by the time the car turned into Lodi Place. The driver stopped in front of the Studio Club and got out to open Peggy's door. As she stepped from the car she was surprised to see another girl exiting a similar vehicle on the opposite side of the street. Was that Vivienne? *What on earth?* She and Jack had left before the end of Charlie's set. Vivienne said she had things she needed to do, and Peggy assumed Jack was taking her directly home. Evidently she'd made the wrong assumption.

The car's driver, who seemed somehow familiar, took Vivienne by the hand and then kissed her on the cheek before closing the passenger door. He got back into the driver's seat and drove away.

As Vivienne crossed to her side of the street, Charlie's driver looked at Peggy. 'Let me walk you to the door, Miss Carmichael.'

'There's no need, Leon. My friend, Miss Lockhart, is right there and I have my key. We'll be perfectly safe.'

'As you wish, miss, but I'll stay here until you're inside. Just in case.'

'Thank you. That's very kind.'

'Peggy!' Vivienne called. 'I thought you'd never get here.'

'Shh,' Peggy said, alarmed. 'You'll wake up the whole club.' She ushered Vivienne up the steps to the entrance. 'What are you doing out past curfew?'

'I didn't mean to be, scout's honour,' slurred Vivienne. 'It's jus', well . . . I lost track of time. You know what they say, right? Time flies when you're having fun! I didn't think to look at the clock and when I did it was almost midnight. I figured I would be locked out for the night. Then I remembered you had a key. I tried ringing Ciro's to leave you a message but the phone rang out. So I decided to just come here and wait. But you were later than usual. I was worried I'd missed you.'

'Keep your voice down. We could both lose our places at the club if we get caught. Don't ever do this to me again, Vivienne, you hear?

146

I'll cover for you this time, but never again.' Heaven help them both if Miss McGovern woke up.

They crept inside, Peggy shushing Vivienne as she signed her name in the register. 'What about this?' she whispered to Vivienne, pointing to the record of comings and goings. 'You know Miss McGovern checks this personally before bed, right?'

Vivienne giggled. 'Sadie fixed it for me. I called her and had her sign in for me. So old Florrie will never know unless you spill the beans.'

'Or unless you wake her up. Go upstairs and don't say another word, all right? I'm right behind you.'

Miraculously they both made it to their rooms without incident. Normally Peggy would be furious about being put in such a perilous situation, but Vivienne was clearly drunk. Perhaps she was feeling a bit low. She'd admitted that her audition for *Agnes Grey* hadn't gone well, so maybe she'd been out drowning her sorrows. In which case, Peggy had no option but to forgive her this time. Tomorrow, when Vivienne was sober, she'd reiterate that this was a one-time-only pass. They might have got away with it tonight, but Miss McGovern was no fool and Peggy couldn't afford to lose her place at the Studio Club.

When she made it safely to her room, she saw there was an envelope taped to the outside of the door. She tore it open right there in the hallway.

Please call Sam Hayden tomorrow at 9 am.

Sam Hayden! Not someone from the casting department, but the director himself. She scanned the note again and saw he'd left a number. Sam Hayden wanted her to call on a Saturday morning. This could only mean one thing. She most definitely had the part!

29 December 1999

Three hours after Vivienne's first plea to take her home, our suitcases and a small box of groceries are packed in the car's trunk and Weenie's in her basket on the backseat. Vivienne's riding shotgun and we're heading north.

Peggy and Julia will no doubt think I've lost my marbles, but I'm taking Vivienne home to Three Rivers. Maybe I *have* lost the plot, but after several hours of Vivienne's increasingly desperate appeals to go home – which even a walk in the park with Weenie could not distract her from – I figured, why not?

I'm on vacation until next week so I have the time, and I'm curious to see where Vivienne's been living all these years. Maybe seeing her in her home environment will help me make up my mind how to best deal with the current situation.

Not that I would admit this to the others, but April's talk about the memoir has piqued my interest. It's ridiculous to think that I could finish writing it for her, but I would like to see the notes that April's compiled and the documents she talked about. Maybe reading those will give me some insight into Vivienne's life after she left Hollywood and, more importantly, if she regrets what she did all those years ago.

I couldn't leave town without letting the girls know my plans, but I had no desire to be talked out of them either, so I was relieved that Peggy didn't pick up when I called to say we were heading off. I took the coward's way out and left a message on the machine – ignoring the recorded message instructing me to try her cell.

I take Hollywood Boulevard to North Highland, which will take us to the highway to Bakersfield. As we cruise past our familiar old haunts – The Chinese Theatre, El Capitan and The Hollywood Roosevelt – Vivienne's face lights up.

'Oh,' she says. 'Are we going to the movies?' She looks down at her navy cargo pants and white T-shirt. 'I'm not dressed for a premiere.'

'Not today. I'm taking you home, remember?'

Her face clouds with confusion momentarily and then she smiles. 'George will be pleased.'

I don't know what to say to that, so I click on the radio. The announcer is talking about the end of the millennium and the uncertainty around Y2K. Just thinking about this makes my head hurt. I have to admit to being a bit of a Luddite as far as all this new technology is concerned. I'd rather speak on the phone or meet a client in person than send an email, and don't even get me started on being contactable twenty-four hours a day via a cell phone. Suffice to say, I can't see the advantage of that. I've employed a young accountant to do my books and have recently put on an admin assistant. They both assure me that the business is Y2K compliant – whatever the hell that means – but every time the story pops up on the news it worries me.

I switch stations until pop music blares from the speakers. It's a song I know from too much time spent on building sites with young trades-people, so I enthusiastically sing along.

Vivienne chortles and then wrinkles her nose.

'What? Am I flat?' I was never a great singer – not compared to Peggy, Vivienne or even Julia – but I pride myself on being able to hold a tune.

'It's not that. Your singing is . . . perfectly adequate.'

I laugh. 'Don't go mad with the compliments there. I might get a big head.'

149

She joins in my laughter. 'It's not you. It's the song.'

'Not a Britney fan, huh? I quite like her. But each to their own. Hang on a minute, I might have something more to your taste in my CD collection.' In fact, I know I have just the thing. Last year, in a fit of nostalgia, Julia gave me a CD filled with famous show tunes. There's even one of her songs from *Love Like the French* in the mix. At the next traffic light, I open the console and flick through the cases. I quickly find what I'm looking for and slide the disc into the player.

Vivienne claps her hands together as the first song, 'Diamonds Are a Girl's Best Friend', blasts through the speakers. I turn the volume up even louder and the two of us begin to sing. In a strange way, this is just like old times – the two of us laughing and singing.

We've been driving for almost two hours when the sign for Bakersfield comes into sight. Singing the show tunes on repeat has kept Vivienne happy and the time has flown by. It's past lunchtime, and my stomach is growling, so I pull off the interstate to fill up on gas and get us something to eat. Weenie could probably use a toilet break, too. It doesn't take long to find a burger joint with outdoor picnic tables. It's so much colder here than it was back home. I open my suitcase and grab the sweater and woolly hat I threw in, and get a sweater for Vivienne from her bag too. 'Are you okay to sit out here? We can eat inside if you like. I can tie the dog up outside in a spot where we can see her.'

'And leave her by herself? Oh no, I wouldn't do that. I have my sweater. I'll be fine.'

Vivienne sits with the dog while I go in and order. I get burgers, fries and extra-large shakes. Julia would be horrified.

Before we've finished eating Vivienne has taught Weenie to sit up and beg for fries. It's both adorable and astounding. Weenie is not a dog who performs tricks – in fact, in our relationship it seems to be me who is under her command.

'You're so good with her,' I say.

Vivienne strokes Weenie's head and then looks up at me. 'Animals can always sense a kindred spirit. George taught me that.' She looks down at Weenie. 'George is just going to love you.'

Every time Vivienne mentions George, I'm uncomfortable. I don't know how to handle the situation. Is it better for Vivienne to live happily in the past or should I tell her the truth about George? I'm worried that when we arrive in Three Rivers and George isn't there, Vivienne will be distraught. Maybe it's better to say something now. But why burst her bubble when in twenty minutes' time she might not even remember this conversation?

My teeth chatter – I should have ordered coffee instead of the shake. 'Are you done?' I say. 'I think it's time to get back on the road.'

Vivienne nods and picks up Weenie while I collect our empty cups and wrappers and put them in the trash.

Twenty minutes out of Bakersfield, with her belly full of food and the winter sun streaming into the car, Vivienne falls asleep. I turn off the car's stereo and enjoy the peace and quiet for a while. I'm really not sure what I'm getting myself into here, but I know in my gut that sticking by Vivienne is the right thing to do.

Chapter 19

Peggy

'This is Peggy Carmichael calling for Mr Hayden.'

'Ah, Peggy, it's me, Sam Hayden. Thanks for calling back. I wouldn't normally do this sort of thing on a Saturday, but I wasn't able to contact you last night and, er . . . well, I wanted to talk to you before the news got out. That is, I wanted to tell you personally.'

Peggy held her breath. This was it. He was going to give her the news that would change her life.

'I'm sorry to have to tell you that we decided against you for the part of Agnes Grey.'

What? This couldn't be happening. Why on earth was the director ringing her personally to give her *bad* news? Perhaps she'd misheard. 'I'm sorry, did you say I *didn't* get the part?'

'That's correct.'

'But I thought the audition went well. Did I do something wrong?'

'Your audition was great, almost flawless, in fact, but we decided to go with another actress this time. I would be happy to offer you one of the supporting roles, though. I thought perhaps Mary Grey.'

Mary Grey! It was a tiny part – a speaking part, yes, but hardly compensation for missing out on Agnes. She couldn't bear to be on the set playing second fiddle. She sucked in a steadying breath before responding. 'That's very kind of you, Mr Hayden, but I do have other irons in the fire and now that I know I won't be playing Agnes, I'd like to be free to explore those options.'

'Yes, of course. I'd certainly be open to working with you on future projects, so please keep that in mind.'

'Thank you. I appreciate that. Could I just ask why you decided not to go with me this time? Is there something I could do to improve my performance at my next audition?'

'No, really, Peggy, you were great. It's just that the actress we decided to go with brought something extra to the role, something I didn't even know I was looking for until I saw her.'

He was talking about Vivienne. She was sure of it. Peggy's gut roiled. 'Can I ask who *did* get the part?'

Sam Hayden hesitated.

'Is it Vivienne Lockhart?'

He sighed audibly. 'Yes. I'm sorry. I know you two are friends, which is why I wanted to call you personally. I've told Vivienne the news already and I wanted to make sure that you knew as soon as possible. I'd hate for this to cause any friction between you.'

What he meant was he didn't want her to make a fuss and cause an upset for his precious star. 'I can assure you there will be no friction, Mr Hayden,' she said primly. 'Vivienne and I are friends, as you say, and I am a professional. If I can't have the part, I'm thrilled to see it go to her.'

'Oh, that is very good to hear.' The relief in his voice was obvious. 'Vivienne said you were a sweetheart and that you'd be a good sport. She talked about you and your friends quite a lot last night. You're obviously very important to her.'

Last night? Suddenly the pieces all fit together. It was Sam Hayden who'd dropped Vivienne off in the early hours of the morning. The one who'd kissed her! Well, now she knew what the 'something extra'

153

was that Vivienne had brought to the part. It seemed that opening your legs was the only way to get a decent role in this town.

'As I said, Peggy, I'd be open to working with you on another project. Let's keep in touch, okay?'

She hung up the phone without bothering to answer.

Chapter 20

Julia

On Monday, when Julia's driver dropped her off at the Studio Club after a long day of filming, all she could think about was having a nice hot bath and climbing into bed. She hadn't had a full night's sleep in days.

Her appearance at Charlie's final shows at Ciro's over the weekend probably had tongues wagging, but she couldn't stay away. Luckily, Tony Astor had been there every night too, and she'd made sure they sat together. Better for the gossips to think she was stepping out on Cal with a mystery man than know what was really going on.

She and Charlie were careful not to be seen together – keeping their contact to quick trysts in his dressing-room. If Tony was paying her any attention, he might have figured out something was up, but he was too busy pining after Peggy to notice.

They were playing a dangerous game, but what other choice did they have? If she could walk away, she would, because having to conceal her feelings was almost unbearable. The thrill of meeting secretly was wearing thin already. But the thrill of being with him? That only grew more each time. He could make her quiver with just a look.

155

The anticipation of what he could do with his hands, with his lips, with his tongue, left her breathless. Even the mere thought of him caused desire to bloom within her. She had to work hard to push him from her thoughts while she was on set. More than once today her mind had wandered, and she'd caught herself blushing. Although, conjuring Charlie had helped her to be more convincing in her love scenes with her current co-star – a tedious man who left her cold.

What she had with Charlie wasn't just physical, though. It went way deeper than that. In fact, it was because of how he treated her when they *weren't* between the sheets that she found him so desirable. Before their relationship had become physical, a real friendship had blossomed between them. When she talked, he listened – really listened. He saw the best in her, knew she was more than just a face or a body.

She couldn't give him up, not for anything. But she wasn't sure how she was going to keep seeing him now that his time at Ciro's was over. Charlie had promised they'd work something out and that he'd be in touch in a day or two. It wouldn't be as easy now. They'd have to be extra careful not to be caught. Harry had made it quite clear than any liaison between her and Charlie would be considered a breach of contract.

She signed in at reception and then dragged herself up the stairs, thinking of the long soak she was about to take. As she walked down the corridor, she heard laughter coming from her room. Peggy was obviously entertaining friends in there. Hopefully they'd be gone by the time she'd had her bath. She hated to be such a grump, but she really wasn't in the mood for company.

'Why, hello you,' Vivienne said as Julia opened the door. She was sprawled out on Julia's bed. Peggy and Sadie – who was home remarkably early for once – sat cross-legged like school children on Peggy's bed.

She tried her best to smile. 'Hello, yourself.' She looked at Sadie. 'What are you doing here at this time of day?'

Sadie chuckled. 'Playing hooky! No, not really. I have a business dinner with Mr Gold later tonight. He let me off early so I could come home to change.'

'Sounds important,' Julia said. 'Which big fish is Harry trying to hook?'

Sadie touched the side of her nose. 'Sorry, sworn to secrecy on this one. But I'm glad to see you. You've been so busy lately. Peggy says she sees more of you at the club than she does here.'

Vivienne sat up and patted the bed. 'Don't be a stranger, Jules. Come sit with us for a minute.'

'Sorry, I'm exhausted. I'm going to have a bath and hit the hay.'

'Without dinner?' Peggy asked.

'It won't kill me to go without one meal. This director is firm about my character being petite, and you know how easily I put on weight.'

Sadie frowned. 'Julia, there's nothing of you. You have to eat.'

'Okay.' Julia's shoulders slumped in resignation. 'I'll have the girls in the kitchen fix me a tray I can bring up here.' Anything to get them off her back. 'I really am tired, though, so if you'll excuse me, I might just go and have that bath.'

'No,' said Vivienne firmly.

'Excuse me?'

'No, you're not excused. You need to sit down. We want to talk to you about something.'

'Please, Jules,' Peggy said softly. 'It's important.'

Reluctantly, Julia sat down next to Vivienne. 'All right, just for a minute. What seems to be the problem?'

'It's not necessarily a problem,' Sadie said carefully.

'People are talking,' Peggy said.

Julia got a sick feeling in the pit of her stomach. 'About what?'

'About you and Charlie, Julia,' Vivienne said. 'Rumour has it that the two of you are an item.'

'Who's saying that?' Not that it mattered, but maybe the answer would buy her some time. Her instinct was to protect what she and Charlie had, but on the other hand these were her friends and she hated lying to them.

Sadie glanced at Peggy before looking Julia in the eye. 'I've been asked quietly by members of the press.'

157

'You mean Jack?' Julia relaxed a little. Jack was a good guy. Maybe if Sadie told him there was nothing going on, he'd leave it alone.

'It's not just Jack,' Peggy said. 'Some of the dancers at the club have been talking too. One asked me if it is true that you are dating Charlie.'

'What did you say?'

'I denied it, of course, but then one of the other girls said she'd seen you coming out of Charlie's dressing-room while I was on stage – more than once. I didn't know what to say to that, because there's been several times when you haven't been in your seat at the beginning of the show.'

Julia's pulse thudded in her head.

'Well?' Peggy insisted. 'What should I tell her, Julia?'

'You should tell her to mind her own goddamned business!'

'Julia!' Peggy's face flushed. 'There's no need for that sort of language.'

'What there isn't any need for is this interrogation.' Julia's voice rose, along with her fear. 'I thought you were supposed to be my friends.'

Sadie looked alarmed. 'We *are* your friends. We're worried about you.'

'Well, you needn't be.' She moved to stand but Vivienne caught her arm.

'Julia, relax. No one here is accusing you of anything, I promise. We're not trying to catch you out. You can trust us, you know that. It's just that talk about this type of thing can be damaging – for both of you. We can't help you if we don't know what's going on.'

Julia eased herself back down onto the bed and looked at her friends' concerned faces. 'It's not a "type of thing",' she said, her voice breaking. 'It's . . . well, I think . . . I'm in love with him.'

Peggy gasped. 'It's true?'

Julia placed her head in her hands and nodded.

Sadie looked aghast. 'Oh, Jules, if Mr Gold finds out about this . . .'

Julia looked up, tears stinging her eyes. 'Don't you think I know that?'

'You need to put an end to this madness right now,' Peggy said. 'Before it's too late.'

'It's already too late. I can't stop seeing him. I don't want to.'

'Julia, can't you see this is foolhardy? It's worse than that'—her voice took on a sanctimonious tone—'it's wrong.'

'*Wrong?* Peggy, how can you say that? You of all people? You know what a good and kind man Charlie is. He's been so generous to you.' She looked at each of her friends individually. 'You all know what men in this town can be like. How is it wrong to want to be with a man who treats me with respect?'

'Charlie's character is not in dispute. He's a wonderful man and a good friend.' Peggy lowered her gaze. 'It's not about that.'

'What is it then?'

'You know what it is.'

'Say it, Peggy. I want you to explain to me why dating Charlie Hudson is so very wrong.'

Sadie looked dismayed. 'Julia . . .'

Peggy's cheeks turned crimson. 'You want it spelled out? All right then. It's because he's Black.'

Julia said nothing. Peggy's words hung in the air between them for what seemed like an eternity. When she finally opened her mouth to speak, Julia fixed her gaze on Peggy. 'I've always known you had conservative views on things, Peggy, but I never picked you for a racist.'

'How dare—'

'Peggy, Jules, stop,' Sadie pleaded. 'There's no need to turn on each other.'

'No, Sadie, we need to talk about this,' Peggy insisted. She took a deep breath and continued in a calmer voice. 'I'm not a racist. I believe God created us and loves us and we are all equal in his eyes, but *different*. A lot of folks think that, as far as marriage and babies are concerned, people should stick to their own kind.'

'A lot of folks also think the Earth is flat.' Vivienne reached over and squeezed Julia's hand.

'And some people have no morals.' Peggy looked pointedly at Vivienne.

159

Julia's body pulsed with rage. How could Peggy, who was supposed to be her best friend, say such a thing? 'No morals? You think me falling in love with Charlie makes me somehow amoral? I can't believe you'd be so small-minded, Peggy.'

Peggy looked crestfallen. 'Julia, no, I didn't . . . that's not—'

'I think you'll find that comment was directed at me,' Vivienne said. 'If the shoe fits . . .'

'Wait, what's happening here?' Sadie looked from Peggy to Vivienne and back again. 'What's going on between you two?'

'I presume this is about me getting the role of Agnes Grey,' Vivienne said. 'I never took you for the jealous type, Peggy.'

'I'm not jealous. I'm just wondering what special quality you have that I don't? I saw you kissing Sam Hayden when you were loaded the other night, Vivienne.'

Julia had been so caught up in her own life these past few days she'd missed what was going on between her friends. But Vivienne wouldn't have slept with Sam to get the part. Or would she?

'Don't be such a child, Peggy. Sam kissed *me*. On the cheek. He's a gentleman. He took me out to celebrate getting the role and I got a little tipsy, so he made sure I got home safe. That's what you saw. Nothing more.'

'But . . .'

'You can apologise anytime you like.'

'If I misinterpreted what I saw, I'm sorry,' Peggy said flatly.

'Apology accepted.' Vivienne smiled brightly, clearly choosing to ignore Peggy's implication. 'Now, back to solving Julia's problem.'

'I don't think there is a solution. At least not one where I can keep my job.' Julia momentarily covered her face with her hands.

'Does anyone else know about the relationship?' Sadie asked. 'What about your agent?'

'Lester? Good god, no. He'd have a stroke! I can just imagine the lecture I'd get. I'm sure he'd say I was committing career suicide.'

'There's more at stake than just your career, Julia,' Peggy said. 'It could be dangerous if people found out. For you *and* for Charlie.

A lot of people won't tolerate mixed relationships. I mean, interracial marriage isn't even legal in some states. You know that, don't you?'

'It's legal here,' she said, defiantly.

'Jules,' Sadie said softly, 'we all love you, and as far as I'm concerned whatever makes you happy is all right by me. But if you date Charlie in public, it will cause a huge scandal. There could be serious consequences for both of you. Are you willing to risk that?'

Hot tears slid down Julia's cheeks and she covered her face with her hands once more. 'I don't know, I don't know. All I know is that I can't give him up.'

Vivienne placed an arm around her shoulders. 'Well, best you don't get caught, then.'

Julia lifted her head, tears still streaming down her face. 'I don't see how we can avoid it. As you've all pointed out, people are already talking. And Charlie's run at the club is over, so our safe haven – such as it was – is gone. It's not like he can meet me here, or even call me on the phone.'

'Honey, there are plenty of places in this town to carry out discreet liaisons. Believe me, I know.'

Peggy looked at Vivienne as if she'd caught her out somehow. 'Pray tell, Vivienne, who have you been dating that you need to keep under wraps?'

'Give it a rest, Peggy. Nobody you need to worry about, that's for sure. But I do know a thing or two about how to keep an affair out of the headlines. Jules, if you're serious about sticking with Charlie, I can help you. Hopefully you can keep things quiet for long enough for the two of you to decide whether you have a real future together.'

The tension in Julia's shoulders eased a little. 'Really? You think you know a way we can keep seeing each other secretly?'

'Sure I do. But that's not the immediate issue. First, we need to shut down those rumours. If I were you, I would lie low this week. Don't worry – I'll make sure you and Charlie get some alone time on the weekend. In the meantime, you should go on a very public date

161

on Friday night, with Cal perhaps? Or anyone, it doesn't really matter who. A big name would be ideal, if you can manage it.'

Julia nodded. 'Okay.'

Vivienne looked at Sadie. 'Can you call Jack off?'

'I can ask him to back off, although whether he will or not is another story. We already got him to plant that story about you and Cal. He might not go for it again. Maybe he'd pay more attention to you, Vivienne?'

'Me?' Vivienne looked confused. 'I don't think I'd have more influence than you. Sure, we dated a few times but nothing came of it. I've got a feeling if *you* ask him nicely he'll do anything.' Vivienne winked at Sadie, who blushed.

'For heaven's sake, Vivienne.' Peggy huffed. 'Not everyone is prepared to use their body to get their own way.'

Vivienne's eyes narrowed as she stared at Peggy. 'I'm not suggesting she sleep with him.' She turned her attention back to Sadie. 'But maybe bat your eyelashes a little, honey. Flatter him a bit. Fellas respond well to that.'

'Jack and I are friends. I'm not sure any eyelash batting on my behalf will get us across the line, but I promise to give it my best shot.' She gave her lashes a dramatic flutter and Vivienne tossed Julia's pillow at her head, which broke the tension in the room and made everyone giggle.

As the relief of sharing her secret set in, Julia's laughter turned to tears. 'I'm so sorry I didn't tell you all right away. I was worried you wouldn't approve, that you'd try to make me stop seeing him, and maybe even make me choose between Charlie and our friendship. And that would be an impossible choice.'

Vivienne pulled her in for a hug. 'We're your friends. Of course you have our support. No matter what.'

'We love you, Jules,' Sadie added. 'We would never make you choose.'

Peggy's lips were set in a hard line.

'What about you, Peg?' Julia asked.

'Honestly? I think this is a bad idea. I can't say I support it because that would be lying. But I do support *you*, Julia, and I want you to be happy.' Peggy looked at Vivienne. 'Whatever crazy scheme you're cooking up, you'd be better be sure about it because you're holding Julia's – and Charlie's – future in your hands.'

'Don't worry, I know what I'm doing.' Vivienne chortled. 'You might even say I'm an expert in the field.'

'That's nothing to be proud of, in my opinion. In any case, leave me out of your plans, whatever they are. I don't want to know the details. That way I won't have to lie.' Peggy looked Julia in the eye. 'You're the best friend I've ever had. I would never betray you and I won't stand in your way, but please don't ask me to help.'

Julia nodded. 'I understand, Peg. I promise you I'll be careful. For all our sakes.'

Chapter 21

Julia

'Peg.' Julia sat on the end of the bed, hoping that the movement would be enough to rouse her sleeping friend. When there was no response, she gently shook Peggy's foot through the bedcovers. 'It's nine o'clock already. We're supposed to be at breakfast in half an hour. Are you coming?'

Peggy groaned, rolled over and rubbed her eyes before sitting up. 'I'm so tired. Our show went over time last night. I didn't leave Ciro's until after one. Maybe you should just go without me.'

Saturday morning breakfasts at Sal's Diner had become their new routine over the past few weeks. Sadie had come up with the idea after the night Julia had told them about Charlie. Vivienne and Peggy arguing the way they'd done had upset Sadie. 'We need to spend more time together,' she'd said. 'That way, misunderstandings like this can't take hold. Let's make a commitment to have a meal together once a week. Away from the club, just us.'

Saturday morning was the one time of the week everyone was likely to be free.

'Peggy, come on. We promised each other we'd do this every week.

164

No excuses, remember? In fact, weren't you the one who made that rule?'

'All right, all right. You've made your point. I'll have a quick shower. You should go on ahead and I'll meet you there.'

'Don't be too long.' Julia picked up the oversized tote at her feet and walked to the door so she wouldn't have to look Peggy directly in the eye as she delivered the next bit of news. 'Vivienne and I have an appointment at the beauty parlour at eleven, so we'll need to leave before then.'

'Really? What are you getting done? Maybe I should come too. I haven't had a proper manicure in forever.'

Julia bit her lip and turned to face her friend. She'd hoped not to have to spell this out to Peg. She'd only managed a couple of clandestine meetings with Charlie since he'd left Ciro's, both of which had been far from satisfactory. Vivienne had come up with a more workable solution, and today was the first opportunity they'd had to try it out.

'Peg, I don't think you'd want to come to this particular appointment with Vivienne and me.'

Peggy looked confused for a moment. 'Why not?'

Julia was silent as she waited for Peggy to catch up.

'Oh . . .' Peggy's expression changed as the truth dawned on her. 'Right. Say no more.' Her words came out tight and unforgiving, creating a tension that hadn't existed only moments before.

Julia ignored Peggy's thinly veiled disapproval. Peggy was doing her best, that was enough. At least for now. 'See you at Sal's.'

Forty minutes later, the four of them were seated in their favourite booth in a secluded corner of the diner, with coffees in front of them.

'I ordered the special for you, Peg,' Sadie said. 'I hope you don't mind, but it's waffles and I know how you love them. I didn't want you to miss out.'

'Thanks, Sade.'

Thank goodness for Sadie. She was keeping the conversation alive by recounting studio anecdotes. Apparently, the typing pool was putting together a list of 'handsy' directors, producers and other executives for the benefit of aspiring young actresses. Not that it would make much difference. Those men had a way of taking what they wanted, one way or another.

Julia noticed Peggy's dark expression. Maybe it was because of Julia's plans to see Charlie, or perhaps Sadie's anecdote had rekindled Peggy's suspicion regarding how Vivienne got the lead in *Agnes Grey*. Lately, every time the subject of the casting couch came up, Peggy gave Vivienne a pointed look. Fortunately, Sadie had now moved on to an anecdote about Harry Gold's wife.

The change in topic allowed Julia to relax a little. She eased back in her chair and let her mind wander to Vivienne's plan for the day, which she was both nervous and excited about. She hadn't seen or spoken to Charlie since last weekend, but Vivienne assured her everything was on track for their rendezvous this afternoon. At Vivienne's suggestion, Charlie had moved out of his hotel room at Chateau Marmont and rented one of the Chateau's private bungalows. He would be waiting there for her today.

In all the time she'd lived in Los Angeles, Julia had never set foot inside the Chateau, which sat near The Garden of Allah on Sunset Boulevard. Unlike its infamously wild neighbour, the Chateau had a reputation for discretion, but rumours of quiet debauchery abounded nonetheless. Everyone was welcomed at this European-style hotel. Julia had been shocked to discover that, like many other Black performers, Charlie found it difficult to secure accommodation in most of the first-class hotels in Hollywood. But not at Chateau Marmont. He'd been staying there for some months now.

Sadie's voice cut into her thoughts. 'Julia, you were having the omelette, weren't you?'

She looked up to see a server standing in front of her, holding a plate. 'Yes. Sorry. I was miles away.'

ome

'You'll be fine once we're inside the hotel,' Vivienne said, as they drove away from the diner in Vivienne's pride and joy, her cherry-red Buick. How she came by the car – which was well beyond the means of a struggling actress – had been a topic of great discussion among the other girls at the Studio Club. Vivienne lovingly referred to the car as 'my baby' but was coy about its origins, saying only that it was a gift from an admirer and not a word more. Peggy had noted on several occasions that the car had arrived on the scene around the same time as Vivienne landed the role in *Agnes Grey*, but Vivienne refused to be drawn on the subject.

Right now, Julia didn't care where the car came from. She was just grateful for its existence. Without Vivienne and her car, she'd have no way of getting to Charlie. She could drive, of course – she'd learnt on the farm – but that was an entirely different prospect to driving in Los Angeles. Here, the traffic terrified her. Besides, there was no point owning a car when the studio provided her with a driver.

Julia leant forward and placed her arms on top of the front seat. She was sitting in the back to make it easier to conceal her presence as they approached the hotel. Vivienne had placed a picnic rug in the back and advised her that she should scoot down onto the floor and cover herself once they got closer.

'Are you sure this is safe? What if someone sees me?'

'They won't. The bungalows are completely private. And set away from the hotel itself. In any case, Marmont is a sanctuary of sorts. Nearly everyone there has a secret of their own, so no one will ask questions. We just need to be careful getting you in and out.'

'And you'll pick me up at five?'

Vivienne glanced at her in the rear-vision mirror. 'I'll be there the whole time. I have my own reasons for visiting the Chateau.'

'You're seeing someone?' How had she not noticed this? 'Is it serious?'

'Maybe . . .'

'What? Viv, tell me more! Why haven't we met him yet? Why are you hiding him away?'

'It's just . . . well, Jules, I can trust you not to tell anyone, right? Especially not Peggy?'

'Of course!'

'It's Sam Hayden.'

'Oh . . .' Dear god, Peggy was right!

'It's not what you think, Jules. We like each other. He makes me laugh. He asks me what I've been reading. Anyway, I didn't sleep with him to get the part. Even if I had, it wouldn't have helped. This movie's a big deal to Sam. He wouldn't have cast me – or anyone for that matter – unless he thought I was perfect for Agnes.'

'I don't doubt you are the best person for the part, but you must know—'

'I know how it looks,' Vivienne interjected, 'and so does he. That's why we're keeping it so quiet. To be honest, I'm used to people judging me for things other than my acting, so I wouldn't even care if it wasn't for Peggy. I don't want her to feel any more aggrieved than she already does. I hate that this role has put a wedge between us, but it's such a big opportunity for me. If I'd passed it up I might never get another one like it. Sam's the first person to see beyond my looks and notice my potential as an actress. And I really like him.'

Julia heard the sincerity in Viv's voice and couldn't help but be moved. Maybe Vivienne slept with Sam to get the role, maybe she didn't. Either way, Julia couldn't begrudge her taking her shot at success. Vivienne didn't talk much about her past, but from the snippets she had divulged, Julia suspected that her life hadn't been a bed of roses. Still, if Peggy discovered Sam and Vivienne were an item, she was unlikely to be as sympathetic.

'You're perfect for the role, Viv, but you're right – people might get the wrong idea if they see you together. Peggy especially.'

Vivienne nodded slowly. 'Look, I'll tell her the truth eventually. We just want to get the shoot over and done with before we go public. In the meantime, we're being discreet, which means it suits me to chauffeur you to and from Chateau Marmont whenever you need me to.'

168

'Thank you, Vivienne. Your support means the world to me. There's no way I could do this without you.'

'Of course. Don't mention it. Now, I think it's time for you to get under the blanket. We're almost there.'

Julia had dressed in capri pants, a T-shirt and a pale pink sweater. She figured it wasn't practical to be wearing a dress and heels when she'd have to spend time on the car's floor. She hoped Charlie would forgive her lack of glamour.

'Not long now. We're pulling in to the hotel driveway,' Vivienne called from the front. 'Just stay put until I give you the all clear.'

Her stomach churned with a mix of excitement and nerves. She and Charlie would have five whole hours together, and she had to admit a hotel room was far preferable to their early encounters at Ciro's. At first, the thrill of making love to Charlie had been so overwhelming that the confines of his dressing-room hadn't mattered. In fact, if she was honest, she'd even been a little turned on by the setting. Especially that time when he'd sat her up on the dresser, pushed her dress above her hips and then kissed her from her ankles all the way up until he reached her panties. God, she felt hot just thinking about it. But as arousing as their illicit lovemaking had been, Julia wasn't content with that. She longed for the luxury of time and a location where they didn't have to worry about getting caught.

The car stopped. She heard Vivienne open and close the car door and then the crunch of gravel under her feet as she walked away. Moments later she was back, opening the rear passenger door.

'Out you come.' Vivienne pulled the rug aside and offered Julia her hand. When she was out of the car, Vivienne gave her the once-over.

'How do I look?'

'Just fine, honey. It was a smart move to wear your hair in a ponytail today. Now follow me. Your man is waiting.'

Vivienne took her by the hand and led her into the bungalow. Charlie was just inside the door, and he grabbed her and picked her up off her feet as soon as he saw her. 'Oh, baby, I'm so happy to see you.'

He kissed her, and then pulled back for a moment to look at Vivienne. 'How can we thank you?'

'Julia's happiness is thanks enough. Now, I'm going to find some happiness of my own. If you two lovebirds need me – and I'm pretty sure you won't – I'll be up in room thirty-six.' Viv nodded her head towards a sliding glass door at the rear of the bungalow. 'I'm going to head out this way. I'll be back around five. Be ready, Cinderella. My coach turns into a pumpkin after that.'

29 December 1999

As Vivienne sleeps beside me in the passenger seat, my thoughts turn to the end of her time in Hollywood. She was well on her way to being one of the era's biggest stars, and with her innate talent I have no doubt she would have eclipsed all the others – even Julia – if she'd stayed.

When we parted, I had no idea it would be decades before I'd see her again. Even when I realised she'd left LA, I always thought she'd return. I thought she'd lick her wounds for a while, but that eventually the lure of the marquee lights would pull her back. I was wrong, and now I'm curious to see the place she chose to call home for all these years.

She's still sleeping when we drive through the open gate at the address April provided. I stop on the gravel drive for a moment to take in the house and its surrounds. The scenery here is breathtaking – mountains in the distance and dense forest all around. Vivienne's home is a two-storey log cabin built into the side of the hill. The house itself is cute, but the garden surrounding it is overgrown and full of weeds. In my mind's eye I can see what it could be like with some care, but sadly I won't be here long enough to work on it. I stop fantasising about what I would plant if I lived here and turn my attention to where to park.

The upper level of the house has a wraparound balcony, which doubles as a carport on one side of the house. There's a dusty old van parked there already. I move my car forward and park behind the van before gently nudging Vivienne.

'Hey,' I whisper. 'We're here.'

Her eyes flicker open and she jolts backwards, leaning as far away from me as possible. 'Who are you?'

'I'm your friend Sadie.'

She looks at me suspiciously and doesn't move an inch.

'Look where we are,' I say.

She turns her head. 'Oh! Oh! Home. We're home.' She opens the car door and steps out as Weenie barks excitedly. Vivienne runs through the carport to the rear of the house and starts climbing the stairs.

I get out of the car and inhale the fresh mountain air. It's cold here and I'm grateful for the sweater I'm wearing. I didn't think to pack a coat, though. That was probably a mistake. I round the car so I can let Weenie out, and as soon as she's free she dashes after Vivienne but is confounded by the open-riser stairs. She barks at me to hurry up. I grab my purse and follow Vivienne, scooping up Weenie at the foot of the stairs. Vivienne is trying the doorhandle with no luck.

'I don't understand,' she says. 'Why is it locked?'

'It's okay. Just hold on a moment.' I fish in my purse for the set of keys April left. I try one and then another without luck. Third time's the charm. I turn the handle and the door springs open and Vivienne rushes inside.

This back entrance brings us into the kitchen, which opens onto a large living and dining area. All the curtains are drawn and it's colder in the house than outside. Vivienne has disappeared – perhaps headed for the bathroom, which I could also use. For now, I busy myself with pulling back the curtains to let in some light. Now the place is illuminated I can see that every cupboard, every drawer and every container on the countertop is labelled with a name and a picture. It looks like a kindergarten classroom. My heart sinks. Clearly Vivienne's memory is even worse than I thought.

As I move from the kitchen to the living area, the sound of my boot heels striking the worn timber floors echoes slightly. Weenie scampers behind me, her paws also clattering on the boards, as I head for the large window that looks out onto the front balcony. I pull back the curtains and gasp as I take in the view – a postcard-perfect lake shimmering with the light of the late afternoon sun, framed by mountains.

'Pretty, isn't it?' Vivienne's voice comes from behind me.

I turn to look at her. 'Breathtaking.'

'I can't find George,' she says. 'I've looked everywhere.' There's a note of concern in her voice.

I had hoped that coming here might help Vivienne remember that George is gone, but I suppose that was wishful thinking. 'I'm looking after you while George isn't here,' I say, hoping this will mollify her.

A deep and throaty laugh escapes her lips. 'I look after George, not the other way around, silly!'

'Oh. Well, perhaps you can look after me while George is away.'

She considers this. 'Hmm. Okay. Maybe she's out on a call and will be back soon.'

'You're probably right. In the meantime, it's cold in here. Do you know where the thermostat is?'

'Um . . .'

I point to the open fireplace in the living room. 'Or we could light the fire if you have firewood.'

'Maybe.'

I smile to reassure her. 'I know. Why don't we have a look together? You can show me around your house at the same time.'

'That's a great idea . . . Sorry, I don't believe you told me your name.'

'Sadie,' I say and think I see a flicker of recognition in her eyes.

'I'll remember that,' she says, with a smile. 'I used to have friend called Sadie.'

I know I shouldn't ask this, but I can't help myself. 'Was she nice?'

Her smile fades a little. 'Oh, yes. She was the best friend I ever had. Other than George, of course.'

173

'Of course. Shall we?'

She places one hand on her hip and makes a sweeping motion with her other. 'This,' she says, adopting the tone of a spokesmodel or a real estate agent, 'is the living and dining area.'

I chortle. 'You could be in TV commercials.'

'Well, I *am* an actress, after all.'

'I see. And how do you like that?'

She chews her lip. 'I don't really. I didn't, I mean. I stopped. I don't do it anymore. It's not . . . I don't know . . . I thought when I was up there on the big screen everyone, *everyone*, would love me. But it's not like that.' She shakes her head. 'It's not like that at all. They like my face and my body, but they don't really like *me*. Nobody takes me seriously, which is why . . .' As she trails off, looking forlorn, I feel ashamed for having asked the question.

I walk over to one of the floor-to-ceiling bookcases that flank the stone fireplace and run my eyes over the varied titles. I've always been a sucker for other people's bookshelves and this eclectic collection doesn't disappoint. There's everything from recent bestsellers – *Bridget Jones's Diary* and *Outlander* – to the classics I remember Vivienne loving when we roomed together. There's also a whole shelf dedicated to reference books about plants and animals. 'I see you still like to read.'

'Oh, yes, we both do.' She picks up a photograph of a smiling woman dressed in overalls and a wide-brimmed straw hat. The woman has a kind, weather-beaten face and she's holding a chicken in her hands. George, I presume, but I don't want to ask.

'Well, it's a lovely living room. A view, a brimming bookcase and a fireplace. Who could ask for more? What's next on the tour?'

Vivienne guides me through the timber kitchen. It's light on appliances – there's a decent enough oven and cooktop as well as a small microwave, but no dishwasher that I can see. There is, however, a well-stocked pantry. As well as the usual staples there are jars of homemade jams and preserved fruits, pickled vegetables and relishes. By contrast, the fridge is almost bare – just a couple of bottles of wine and some basic condiments. We can get by for tonight on what I brought with me, but tomorrow I'll take Vivienne into town for some more groceries.

We walk past the farmhouse-style dining table with six mismatched, yet somehow perfect, chairs, to the hallway that leads to the main bedroom, an office and a bathroom. The bedroom takes me back to our days together at the Studio Club. There's a dresser, strewn with make-up, jewellery and an assortment of photos and knick-knacks. The dresser drawers are labelled, not that it seems to make much difference. Vivienne never was great at putting things away.

Next stop on the tour is the office, and there, as promised by April, I find an archive box labelled *Memoir* sitting on the desk. I'm itching to take a look at what's inside that box, not only to read Vivienne's version of the events leading to her exit from Hollywood but also to discover what her life has been like since then. Has she been happy here? Fulfilled? It's hard for me to imagine the luminous star I once knew being content in this tiny village, but she's lived in the foothills of the Sierra Nevada longer than she stayed in Hollywood. And it appears that she found love in this unlikely location.

As eager as I am to read April's notes, I'm not sure that Vivienne should be present to witness my reaction. Perhaps if she has an early night I'll get a chance to read and digest the information alone.

The lower floor features a neat-as-a-pin guest bedroom, which will do nicely for me and Weenie. There's another small bathroom, a tiny sitting room and a laundry room, which is where I find the thermostat. I spend a few moments figuring out how it works and then turn it on. Hopefully it won't take too long for the heat to filter through the house, because it's getting colder in here by the minute.

I step outside and poke around a bit to see if I can find any firewood but have no luck. Vivienne, who has followed me, is picking wildflowers – most likely weeds.

'Come on,' I say. 'Let's go inside and find a vase for those.'

Upstairs I head into the kitchen to start making dinner. Vivienne puts her flowers on the counter and looks for a vase, but there's no label depicting vases anywhere. After opening every cupboard in the kitchen, I discover a jar that will do the trick. Delighted, Vivienne fills it with water and arranges her blooms.

'These will look lovely on the coffee table, don't you think?'

I agree and she heads off to set down her arrangement with Weenie at her heels.

My quest for dinner ingredients reminds me that I have a bag of pasta and a bottle of pre-made sauce in the car. I'm yet to bring in the suitcases and groceries I packed. Vivienne is now happily cuddled up with Weenie on the sofa and I don't want to disturb her, so I slip out without saying anything. As I step through the kitchen door I notice two steel boxes sitting up against the outside wall. I open the first and find it filled with chopped wood. The second box has small sticks suitable for kindling. We will have our fire after all!

The first two trips to the car are without incident, but when I go to retrieve my suitcase a gust of wind catches the door and slams it shut. The sound startles Vivienne and she jumps up. Spying me through the kitchen window, she shouts, 'Get out! Get off my property now!'

My heart sinks as I watch her latch the door.

I panic momentarily. I can't leave her in the house all alone. I knock on the window. 'Vivienne, please, let me in. It's me, Sadie. I'm your friend.'

She comes to the window and looks at me with terror in her eyes. 'I don't know you. Go away!' She closes the curtains so I can no longer see her.

Damn. Peggy was right. I'm not equipped to deal with this and I'm not sure I'm making things better.

At least I have my car keys in my hand. I guess I could drive into town and seek help. But from who? The medical centre? Maybe she's a patient there. It's almost six now, I doubt they'll be open. Perhaps the police or fire brigade? What will they do, though – break in? I can do that myself easily enough. And I'm not sure I want to get the authorities involved just yet. I haven't driven all this way to give up at the first hurdle. I just need a minute to think this through.

I take the now damp and slippery stairs back down to the carport so I can sit in the car, out of the cold. It occurs to me that I'd left my suitcase until last because I'd planned on setting it down at the laundry room door on the lower level, which I'd opened earlier when I was looking for firewood. There's a chance the laundry room door might be unlocked! I leave the car and run to see.

I try the handle and it gives immediately. *Yes!* Crisis averted.

After retrieving my suitcase from the car, I slip back inside the house as quietly as I can, not wanting to alarm Vivienne even further. I stand at the foot of the stairs and hear her talking to Weenie.

'You're such a good dog. Yes you are, yes you are!'

She seems calm enough right now. Perhaps if I give her a moment, she will have forgotten about the earlier incident. I take my case to the guest room and start unpacking as quietly as possibly. For a few minutes all is quiet upstairs, but then I hear movement. The sound of Vivienne padding across the floor from the living area to the kitchen is unmistakable. The refrigerator door opens.

Something clatters on the floor and is followed by Vivienne cursing. 'Goddammit!'

Time to make my presence known. I walk up the stairs quietly and then call to Weenie, who jumps from her cosy position on the couch and bounds over to me. I pick her up, reasoning that if Vivienne is still feeling hostile towards me, Weenie's ease in my company might help to convince her I'm not dangerous.

I find Vivienne crouched in the kitchen, retrieving a corkscrew from the floor. She has a bottle of wine in her hand.

'Can I help?'

She stands up and smiles at me, her earlier fear completely evaporated. 'I want a drink but I can't seem to make this damn thing work.' She waves the corkscrew in the air.

A vision of April trying to prevent Vivienne from drinking at the reunion comes to me. Maybe I should try to dissuade her, but quite frankly I could use a glass of wine myself. I figure one can't hurt. We're at home, where she'll be safe. It might help her relax. 'Here, give it to me. Perhaps I can work it out.'

'Oh, that would be great. Thank you. What did you say your name was again?'

'Sadie,' I say. 'My name is Sadie and I'm your friend.'

Chapter 22

Peggy

Peggy returned to the Studio Club feeling flat after her dinner meeting with Billy. It was a sultry June night and after almost a year being the support act at Ciro's, she'd just accepted an offer to be the headline for the next month, so she had no reason to be glum. She inwardly chided herself, knowing she should feel excited or, at the very least, grateful, but she couldn't honestly say she was even pleased about this latest development.

After kicking off her heels and removing her stockings, she flopped down on the bed and sighed. She was too wound up to sleep or even read. What she wanted was someone to talk to about all of this. Where was Julia when she needed her? The French Riviera, filming her next smash-hit movie, that's where.

And that was the problem.

Not Julia being away, but that *she* wanted to be the one off filming in an exotic location. She didn't want to be a nightclub singer. She wanted to be a star like Julia. She'd paid her dues, hadn't she? But where had that got her?

179

Maybe Sadie was around. She would understand. Sadie knew what it was like to have dreams that hadn't started to come true yet.

Peggy washed her face, slipped on her pyjamas and robe and headed off down the corridor. She heard the sound of Elvis Presley singing 'Heartbreak Hotel' as she neared Sadie and Vivienne's room.

She tapped on the door. 'Sadie, you in there? I've got news.'

'Come on in,' Sadie called.

Peggy pushed the door open and her nostrils were immediately assaulted by the smell of cigarette smoke. Sadie and Vivienne were sitting on their respective beds facing each other. Sadie had a glass in one hand and bottle of gin in the other.

'Vivienne,' Peggy said. 'I didn't expect you to be here. Didn't you have a date tonight?'

'We broke up.'

'Ah.' That explained the music. 'I'm sorry to hear that.'

'Oh, don't be, honey. He's not worth mourning. Sadie and I are celebrating the end.' Vivienne's voice was bright, but her eyes were red-rimmed and her cheeks were tear-stained. 'In better news, Sadie has finally finished her screenplay!'

'Really? Wow! That's quite an accomplishment. Congratulations!'

'Thanks. But it's not really finished. It's only a draft. I need to rework it before I can show it to anyone.' Sadie's words were slightly slurred. Obviously, they'd been drinking for a while.

Vivienne beckoned for her to come in. 'Shut the door behind you, before McGovern hears the music and comes to investigate.' She got up from the bed and went to the record player to turn the music down a notch. 'So, what's your news?'

Peggy pulled the door closed. 'Oh, nothing important. Just, well . . . Billy has asked me to be the headline act at Ciro's after Margaret Whiting's show closes.'

Vivienne flopped back onto her bed and grabbed a teacup from her nightstand. 'Wow! I think that news deserves a toast.' She looked down at her cup. 'I'm empty, though.'

'No. It's not a big deal. I mean, I wasn't even sure if I wanted it when he asked, but then I figured, why not? It's not like I've got any other offers on the table. At least the money is okay.'

Sadie poured a slosh of the illicit gin into a cup and held it out for Peggy to take. 'This is good news, isn't it? You're the headline act, Peg. That means you're a star in your own right now.'

Peggy sighed as she took the teacup from Sadie's hands. Once upon a time she would have frowned upon this flagrant disregard of the Studio Club's rules, but right now she couldn't care less about doing the right thing. 'I guess.'

'You don't seem very excited, hon.' Vivienne shuffled her bottom along the bed to make room for Peggy to sit. She patted the space beside her and held out her empty cup for Sadie to fill. 'I thought you'd be happy.'

Peggy sat on the bed, spilling a little gin onto Vivienne's bedcover as she did. 'Oops. Sorry.'

'If I didn't know better, I'd think you were drunk.' Vivienne giggled.

'That would be the pot calling the kettle black.'

Sadie refilled her own glass and sat cross-legged on the bed. 'What's up, Peg? You've just come in with this great news but you're acting as if someone died.'

Peggy knew she should be grateful to Billy, and she was – grateful for the work and for the opportunity. But headlining at Ciro's wasn't the big deal it used to be. Like a lot of the clubs on the strip, Ciro's was struggling. All the big acts were playing Vegas now and getting paid ridiculously good money to do so. Old-style Hollywood clubs like Ciro's just couldn't compete. Billy wasn't paying her because she was some kind of star in the making. He'd promoted her to headline because she was all he could afford. It wasn't as if one of the big Las Vegas clubs like the Sands was pursuing her. And the way things were going, who knew if Ciro's would even be open in a month or two? Audience numbers had been slowly decreasing over the past few months. The last time they'd had really big audiences was when Charlie was performing. Peggy had opened for a number of acts since then – some of them top performers – but each week the crowd got smaller and the takings lower.

'This just isn't where I expected to be when I came to Hollywood. I know I shouldn't complain; I have steady work doing something I love. Some people would give their eye-teeth to be so lucky. But it's not what I dreamt of. I've worked really hard, you know? I thought by now I'd be on my way to being a star. I guess I'm not as special as I thought I was.'

'That's not true at all!' Sadie said. 'You *are* special.'

Good old Sadie. Her loyalty was never in question. 'Thank you. That's sweet of you, but I'm trying to be honest here, with myself as well as you. I think maybe it's time for me to face up to the fact that I'm never going to make it here, not in the way I thought I would.'

'I don't get it,' Viv said. 'You have your own show at a major Hollywood club. That in itself is a success. I know you want to be on the screen, but you just need to hang in there a bit longer. It's only a matter of time until you get your big break.'

'Peg, you've worked so hard to get where you are.' Sadie said. 'Are you just going to give all that up and go on home to Wisconsin?'

'I don't know . . . I'm not getting any younger and I don't want to be a nightclub singer for the rest of my life. I know I have things going for me. I'm pretty in a girl-next-door kind of way, but I'm not breath-takingly beautiful like Julia, or a sexpot like this one.' She inclined her head towards Vivienne.

'That's not true at all,' Sadie protested.

'Please, let me finish. I have got a good voice, I'll grant you that. But it's not unique. I can copy the greats but I'm not truly great myself. I guess I've always known this, which is why I wanted to be an actress. I thought I was a sure thing – a pretty girl who can sing and dance. Back where I come from I was a standout. But the truth is, out here I'm just like everyone else. I don't have that extra special something, and that's the thing that makes the difference. My parents were right. My vanity is a sin and it hasn't got me anywhere at all. Maybe I should go home and find myself a husband before it's too late.'

Vivienne blew a smoke ring into the air. 'Pah. Cry me a river. None of that is an excuse to give up.'

'I'm sorry?' Peggy was taken aback.

'You're a pretty and talented singer in a club where lots of Hollywood directors and executives hang out. Use that to your advantage. What's the worst that could happen? If you don't get a role, then you might at least find yourself a rich husband.'

'Vivienne!' Sadie admonished. 'Peggy's got what it takes to be a star. She doesn't need to a rely on a man.'

Vivienne laughed. 'Oh, Sadie, don't be so naive. In this town, and in every other town I've known, everything depends on the whims of men. Smart women know this and use it.'

'I don't believe that. Look at Julia,' Sadie said. 'She made it on her own. She's making good money now, and once her contract with Goldstar is up she'll be able to do whatever she wants.'

'But in the meantime, she's forced to live here and see the love of her life in secret, all because of rules made by men. And you, Sadie, too. You've written a brilliant screenplay – one that deserves to become a hit movie – but that will only happen with the backing of a man. How many women producers and directors do you know?'

Sadie's cheeks flushed pink. 'What about Ida Lupino?'

'Okay, there's one. One female director you can think of. Look, I'm not saying things aren't changing; they are. But not quickly. Right now, if Peg doesn't want to end up a housewife in Wisconsin with a houseful of hungry brats and an ungrateful husband, she needs to be smart and hedge her bets.' She turned to look at Peggy. 'All I'm saying is stay here, Peg. If you don't end up being a star, there's nothing wrong with being married to one. If you're going to end up a housewife, you may as well be a rich one.'

Peggy laughed and raised her teacup in the air. 'I'll drink to that.'

Sadie refused to toast, but Vivienne raised her cup. 'To rich husbands,' she said, as she fished for something under her pillow. After a moment, she pulled out her dog-eared journal and opened it at a page near the front, lifting it up so Sadie and Peggy could see. In the middle of the page was a photograph of the four of them in this very room. Only Julia was looking at the camera and they were all laughing. The window behind them was decorated with tinsel.

'Remember this? It was our very first Christmas here.'

Sadie smiled. 'Who took this?'

'It was Janet, from across the hall, wasn't it?' Peggy said. 'She snapped it just before she left for Sacramento.'

Sadie nodded. 'I'd forgotten about that. It was the first Christmas I'd ever had away from home. I was sad about it, but those few days here with you girls made for one of the best holidays I'd ever had.'

'It was the first Christmas I'd had with family since my mom died,' Vivienne said. 'And it was wonderful. This is what I wrote.' She smoothed down the paper.

'*Sadie had brought home a little Christmas tree and some tinsel from her office to decorate our room. We made paper chains and sang Christmas carols while we worked. When the others talked about how different this was to their usual Christmas Eve celebrations, I nodded along. What I didn't tell them was that I usually spend the evening alone. Let's face it, I'm not the kind of girl a fella takes home for Christmas. And with no family of my own, that usually leaves me at a loose end. But not this year! I finally feel as if I have people in my life who really care about me.*'

Peggy's eyes misted over. She and Viv hadn't always seen eye to eye, but they were as good as family. Better, really, because they'd chosen each other.

Vivienne looked up from the page with glassy eyes. 'This is the real reason I don't want you to ever go back to Wisconsin, Peg. We love you and we need you here.'

Sadie raised her teacup in the air. 'Now that's something *I* can drink to. Cheers!'

Chapter 23

Julia

'I still can't believe you're here.' Julia drew up the bedsheet and tucked it under her arms to cover her nakedness as she sat up. She positioned herself against the hotel's oversized pillows so she could look out at the lit-up shoreline. She was the luckiest woman on Earth. She was in beautiful Nice, staying at the luxurious Negresco Hotel, and to top it all off Charlie had arrived earlier that evening. 'It feels like a dream.'

Charlie rolled onto his side, propped himself up on one elbow and stared at her. 'Do I frequent your dreams often?'

'Now, that would be telling.' She laughed. 'But seriously, Charlie, this is magical. I can't believe our luck. I mean, I'm not surprised that the prince would choose you to entertain his wife, but how lucky that the party coincides with our shoot. What are the odds?'

'Pretty good, actually.'

'What do you mean? It's an amazing coincidence, don't you think?'

'Oh, my darling, how sweet you are. It's not a coincidence. Grace and I are friends. I asked her to get Rainier to invite me to perform while you were here on the Riviera.'

'You asked Princess Grace? Charlie!'

'What? Just because she's a princess now doesn't mean we can't be friends. She's still the same person she was before she married him. I thought you knew her too?'

'Not really. I was in a movie with her once when I was just starting out. She seemed lovely, but we only had a few scenes together and our paths haven't crossed much since.'

'Well, she's a doll. You two are going to love each other, take my word for it.'

'I don't expect we'll get a huge amount of time to chat; she'll be busy entertaining all her guests. It is kind of the royal couple to invite the cast to the party, though.'

Charlie chuckled. 'The cast *is* the party. Grace is always happy to see her Hollywood friends. When she found out you were filming here, she jumped at the chance to have some showbiz people to the palace. It's an intimate affair, and mutually beneficial. Grace gets to hang out with some pals and I have an excuse to be here with you.'

'Are you telling me you concocted this whole thing so we could be together for a few nights?'

He rolled onto his back and clasped his hands behind his head. 'What can I say? I couldn't bear the thought of being away from you for three whole weeks.'

'Oh, Charlie, I love you.' The words slipped out before she had the chance to think about them, to stop them. Never had she uttered these words to another human being, at least not in real life.

Plenty of men had expressed their love for her – usually as a ploy to get her into bed – but she'd never considered saying it back. Then again, she'd never felt like this before.

Her whole life she'd been waiting for someone to notice her, the *real* her, and love her for who she was. Her father's love was conditional on her being the daughter he wanted – dutiful and reserved. Men, even the ones who had professed their love, really only wanted her for her body.

But Charlie was different. At least it felt that way.

And now he'd orchestrated an elaborate plan, one involving

European royalty no less, and flown across the Atlantic to be with her. Surely that meant something.

So why wasn't he saying anything?

Her face burned despite the gentle sea breeze cooling the room. 'I'm sorry. I shouldn't have—'

Charlie sat bolt upright and grabbed both her hands. 'Julia,' he said, looking her in the eye. 'Don't apologise. Dear god, I can't believe you said it out loud. I feel the same way. I haven't said anything because I thought it was crazy. I thought I'd scare you off. Heck, *I'm* scared of how I feel. But I *do* feel it. It might be crazy and scary, but I love you too.'

They stared at each other without speaking for what seemed like an eternity – the gravity of what they'd each said permeating the space between them. Julia had imagined this scenario countless times. Although, in her fantasy, Charlie was the one who uttered the words first. She'd imagined the moment to be euphoric, but the reality was sobering.

How could they ever have a proper relationship? One that took place outside of the confines of luxurious hotel rooms?

The studio would never tolerate it. And neither would the public. It might be 1957, and things might be slowly changing, but segregation was still very much alive in America. If they went public it would be the end of her career.

Would that really be so bad? It wasn't as if she was a great actress – in fact, according to her many critics, she was actually terrible at her chosen career. Her stardom had come on the back of her looks. The camera loved her face and she had a perfect figure – provided she didn't eat too much. But looks fade, and the public was always on the lookout for the next big thing. What then?

Having him love her, saying the words out loud was what she'd wanted – but now that he had, what they were up against suddenly became very real. What they had seemed perfect, but how long could it last? Right now, the secrecy of their relationship, sharing something between just the two of them, felt intimate and delicious.

But eventually she'd want the freedom to see Charlie publicly. To have dinner together, dance cheek to cheek, hold hands as they walked along the street. Even if she left her career behind, these things would be frowned upon back home. A ring on her finger wasn't important to Julia; being with Charlie would be enough. But what if he wanted more? Marriage and babies, for instance. Mixed marriages weren't legal in some states. Her father would never approve. Maybe Charlie's family wouldn't either.

He reached out and brushed away the tear that had slipped down her cheek. 'I know, baby. I know. It seems impossible right now, but we have to have faith. I truly believe things will work out for us in the end.'

'I just want to be with you like this forever, but next week I'll be back in Paris and you'll be back home. What then? How can we ever make this work?'

'We'll find a way.'

'How, Charlie? No studio would allow me to date you. Goldstar would tear up my contract. I mean, I'm barely allowed to date anyone let alone . . .' She stopped, unsure of how to finish the sentence.

'A Black man?'

'Yes.' She averted her gaze, deeply ashamed of the prejudice Charlie had to endure at the hands of white people.

'Do you want to make this work? Is being with me long term – being married to me one day – something you would consider, even if it meant sacrificing your acting career?'

'Of course, but I can't see how that can happen. My own father will disown me. We'll be shunned.'

'Things are changing. Look at what's happening in Alabama because of Ms Rosa Parks. One day soon, things will be different. We just need to be patient.'

Julia wanted to believe him, but in her heart she didn't know if she was up to the task. All she wanted was to be loved and appreciated. With Charlie she had that, but would it be enough if the whole world was against them?

'I love you but I'm not a rebel, Charlie.'

'Oh, baby, I beg to differ. Aren't you the girl who defied her dad and crossed the country to work in an industry he disapproves of?'

'Well, yes, but—'

'And aren't you here, right now, in bed with a proud Black man despite knowing that if we are caught it will cause a huge scandal and possibly cost you your studio contract?'

'Yes, but we're being careful not to be caught, aren't we? And that's the point. I don't want to stop seeing you, but it's only a matter of time before we get found out. What happens then?'

'Julia,' he said, drawing her into his arms, 'I'm not suggesting we go public, not yet. I'm suggesting we make a commitment to each other. I don't want to think about you seeing other men. And I'm certainly not interested in seeing other women. I want us to be exclusive, a proper couple. We'll work out a way to have a future together. If America won't accept us, we'll find someplace that will. Here, for instance. They seem to be more tolerant, more forward thinking, don't you think?'

She nodded, because more than anything she wanted to believe him.

He kissed her cheek. 'Be happy, mon amour. We don't have to rush into anything, but I believe in us. It won't be easy, but please tell me you are willing to try.'

'Oh, my darling, of course I am.'

She loved him. What other choice was there?

30 December 1999

I wake just before seven in the morning. After yesterday's events I'd anticipated a restless night, but somehow I seem to have slept soundly. Perhaps
it's all the fresh mountain air . . . or the wine.

The house is toasty warm now that the heat has kicked in. I rise
quickly and dress in jeans and a light sweater. Hopefully I'll have time
to have a browse through April's notes before Vivienne gets out of bed.
I pad up the stairs in my socks, trying to make as little noise as possible.
There's no fooling Weenie, though. The little traitor slept in Viv's room
last night, but now she wants out. She starts whining and scratching at
the door as soon as she hears movement. 'Shh,' I say as I open Vivienne's
bedroom door, as if it will make a difference. I needn't worry. Vivienne is
snoring; her slumber in no danger of being disturbed despite the loud
scrabbling sound Weenie's paws make on the floorboards in her mad
rush to get out. I scoop her up and take her downstairs to the laundry
room, where I find an old coat and a pair of waterproof boots just big
enough to squeeze my feet into.

'Come on, girl. Let's go outside.'

While Weenie relieves herself, I take the opportunity to poke around a little. There are several small fenced-off yards and an old chicken coop. I wonder what has happened to all the animals. It hurts my heart to think of Vivienne losing the love of her life at the same time as all the creatures that were obviously so dear to her too.

Weenie has found me and is trotting along at my heels as I explore. The barn is a huge structure. As well as the massive barn doors, there's a smaller entrance to the side. I try the handle and find it's unlocked. Inside, there's some machinery, a small tractor and dozens of labelled bins. At the rear there's an office with a desk and a phone. This room leads to another large room, which is set up as a veterinary surgery. On the desk in the office there's a framed photo of Vivienne holding a black-and-white cat and another of Vivienne and George, both in ankle-length floral dresses. I pick up the second photo and stare at it. A floral crown adorns Vivienne's head and George has a daisy chain around her neck. Their feet are bare and they're holding each other with both hands and staring into each other's eyes. The photo makes me well up.

Behind me, Weenie whimpers a little. I carefully place the photo back where I found it. 'Come on,' I say. 'Let's go get breakfast.'

Once Weenie's fed and I'm properly caffeinated, I make a start on the day's tasks, with the memoir box as my first priority.

April's notes are a bit of a mess. Some are handwritten, but others are printed out. Thankfully each page is dated, and I quickly scan each one to get a feel for its content as I put them in order. Most of the notes I've found refer to Vivienne's early life, or after she arrived here in Three Rivers. There's nothing about her time in Hollywood yet. Not printed, at least. But underneath the manila folders that hold April's notes is a plastic box, which contains half-a-dozen cassette tapes, each one carefully labelled. One jumps out at me: *Vivienne – H.S.C.*

Hollywood Studio Club. Bingo!

I look around the office for something to play the tapes on, but after searching the desk drawers, the bookcase and even the filing cabinet, I find myself out of luck. I could take the tapes out to the living room and play them through the stereo, which I'm pretty sure has a cassette player, but I don't want to risk Vivienne overhearing. Instead, I head down to my car and retrieve my Walkman from the glovebox. Once I'm back in the office, I slide the cassette into the player, adjust the volume and press play.

'Interview with Vivienne Lockhart. 22 May 1999.' It's April's voice coming through the speakers.

April: *Vivienne, I want to talk to you today about how you ended up living here.*

Vivienne: *[Giggling] Why, you know that already, silly.*

April: *Yes, I do, but this is for your book. Remember? I have the tape recorder on and it will record our conversation. I just need you to answer the questions I ask, even if you think I already know the answers. Is that okay?*

Vivienne: *Yes, of course. Sorry . . . So, you want to know how I came to live with George?*

April: *Go back before that. Why did you come to Three Rivers?*

Vivienne: *To be left alone.*

April: *Where were you coming from?*

Vivienne: *I'd been living at the beach, up near Monterey.*

April: *What year was this, Vivienne. Can you remember?*

Vivienne: *Oh gosh, I'm not really sure. It was just after I filmed my last movie for Goldstar, probably around 1958. A lot of things had happened in my personal life and I just wanted to get as far away from Hollywood as I could. I thought Monterey would be perfect, but I was wrong. I couldn't get away from people. They were always there, always wanting to take my photo. Always calling out, 'Vivienne, Vivienne!' I hated it.*

April: *Why was that?*

Vivienne: *Why did I hate it?*

April: *Why did they call out your name?*

Vivienne: *Well, I was sort of famous you see, back then. [Laughter] I was kind of a big deal. In fact, I was on track to be one of the biggest stars in Hollywood. You know Julia Newman, right?*

192

She and I were the best of friends once. Back in 1958 she was the hottest actress in America, maybe even the world, and I had the potential to follow in her footsteps. Back then, all the directors in town wanted us in their movies – and in their beds. [Laughter] Julia, she was a princess. Harry Gold's princess. So, she was off-limits in that department.

April: *What do you mean? Was Miss Newman having an affair with Mr Gold?*

Vivienne: *[Giggling] No, silly! Harry didn't want anyone going near his golden girl. Didn't want her getting herself knocked up, or worse, married! Because the studio can get rid of unwanted babies, you know . . . but a marriage to the wrong person? Well, that could do some damage. Harry had invested a lot of money into Julia, and he didn't want to risk her reputation – and his investment – by letting her date just anyone. He had all kinds of rules for her. She even had to live at the Studio Club while she was working for Goldstar.*

April: *Why was that?*

Vivienne: *I expect it was easier to control her that way. There was a curfew and someone could keep an eye on her. I guess ol' Harry figured it would be almost impossible for her to get into trouble while she was in that supervised setting. Kind of ironic when you think about it.*

April: *What do you mean by that? Ironic how?*

Vivienne: *I don't want to talk about that right now. I'm not sure if I should. I promised Julia I wouldn't.*

I stop the tape and rewind it a little to listen to this part again. To me it's an odd remark to make – Vivienne claiming to be loyal to Julia after what happened between them – but perhaps Viv's dementia has warped her memory of their falling out.

April: *Okay. So, you said Harry Gold kept a close eye on her. What about you?*

193

Vivienne: *I was contracted to a different studio.*

April: *Did your studio have strict rules for you? Was that why you went on living at the club after you started to star in movies?*

Vivienne: *. . . No . . . there were no rules for girls like me. I was a different kind of actress to Julia. I was . . . [self-conscious laughter] . . . kind of a sex symbol. You see, I was a girl who'd grown up knowing how the world works. I had no money, no family and no connections. I only had myself to rely on. Thanks to my foster daddy, I was well and truly damaged goods by the time I arrived in Hollywood. Men can tell that sort of thing. Girls like me, well . . . we know the score. If you're going be used and abused anyway, might as well get something out of it. I did do one serious movie, Agnes Grey, and I was good in it. But even that didn't change people's minds about me. Everyone assumed I'd slept with the director to get the part. I was famous for a moment when that film came out, which was what I'd always wanted. But fame wasn't what I thought it would be. I didn't feel loved, I felt consumed. I only made one more movie after that . . .*

I press stop and take a deep breath. Of course, I already knew most of this and what I didn't know, I suspected. But the melancholy in her voice combined with her acceptance of her situation punctures my heart.

Back then we were all so quick to judge, when none of us really understood what it was like to be her. Me least of all. I ran away from a loving home, where I'd grown up with everything a young girl could ever want. Yes, my father was controlling, but he loved me and wanted the best for me. And no matter how vehemently we disagreed, he never once made me feel afraid.

God, when I think of how damn proud I was of making it on my own, all the while ignoring the advantages I'd been given – my education, the freedom to have a childhood, and above all the safety net my family afforded me. I was never truly on my own.

The floorboards creak in Vivienne's room. I look at my watch to discover that over two hours has passed since I woke. No wonder my

194

stomach is growling. The bedroom door opens and Vivienne appears in the hallway. I smile, hoping to reassure her, but there's no need to worry. This morning she is unperturbed by my presence.

'I see you've started work already,' she says. 'Did I miss breakfast?'

She seems to have accepted me as April's replacement. Or maybe she thinks I *am* April. I don't know, but I'm grateful for her serene demeanour.

'Not at all. I haven't eaten yet. I'll come and make us some breakfast.'

'Eggs?'

I laugh. 'Sure, I can do that. How do you like them?'

'Scrambled, please,' she calls as she disappears into the bathroom.

I carefully place my Walkman in the desk drawer before making my way to the kitchen.

Vivienne reappears twenty minutes later, wearing jeans and an over-sized black sweater. Her hair is pulled back into a small ponytail and her eyes are clear and bright. She seems more alert than yesterday.

'Breakfast is almost done.' As I speak, the toaster pops up two slices of golden brown toast. I plate these and scoop the freshly scrambled eggs on top, then we move to the table. 'Juice?' I ask, and she nods, so I pour us both a glass.

She smiles at me. 'Thank you . . . I'm sorry, I've forgotten who you are. You're the woman taking care of me, I know, but I can't remember your name. You must forgive me. My brain doesn't quite work the way it used to.'

This is the most grounded in reality I've seen her. Perhaps she'll be able to answer basic questions about her care today. I don't want to push her too hard though, so I begin gently. 'I'm Sadie. And, yes, I'm here to look after you. What would you like to do today? What would you normally do with April?'

She frowns. 'April?'

'April is the girl who usually looks after you, but she's got a new job now.'

'Oh. The girl. Yes. George . . .' Her face crumples. 'George is gone. She died.'

195

'Yes,' I say softly. 'She did. I'm so sorry for your loss. But I want you to know, Vivienne, that you don't need to worry. I'm here for you now.'

'You're very kind . . .' She prods the eggs with her fork and then looks up at me quizzically. 'What's your name again?'

1958

Chapter 24

Peggy

The loud rap on her dressing-room door startled Peggy. Thankfully she had just finished applying her lipstick, otherwise she might have ended up with a cherry-red stain on her face. It was hard enough getting ready in this cramped little dressing-room, with its cracked mirror and poor lighting; the last thing she needed was having to start all over again. Not for the first time she thought longingly about her old dressing-room at Ciro's. She hadn't known how good she'd had it until the club closed down and Ernie convinced her to come over to Mickey's Supper Club with him.

'Yes?'

Ernie opened the door just a crack. 'You have a visitor, Peggy. Mike Schofield?'

Peggy turned from the mirror. 'Never heard of him.'

'Says he's a TV producer.' Ernie stepped into the dressing-room – something he never did – and pulled the door closed behind him. 'Look, Peg, I'm pretty sure this guy's the real deal. He was at the show last night with some bigwig from Columbia.'

'Hmm. What does he want with me?'

'Honestly, I don't know. Maybe he thinks you're cute and wants a date. Or maybe . . .'

'What?'

'Look, Peggy, I shouldn't be saying this, but I'm probably not telling you anything you don't already know: this club is going the same way as Ciro's. All the clubs on the strip are looking for ways to reinvent themselves or they'll have to close. I'm not sure how much of a career there is in nightclub singing anymore. Not unless you want to move to Vegas.'

Ernie was right. This wasn't news to her. The writing was on the wall when Ciro's shut up shop. She'd only taken this gig because she wasn't getting acting work. It was this or go back to being an extra.

'Your point being?'

'Maybe you see the guy. Worst case scenario, he wants to date you and who knows where that might lead? Or maybe he has you in mind for something. You never know.'

Peggy stood up and walked over to her stage manager and cupped his unshaven cheek. 'You're good to me, Ernie.'

'Ah, get out with you, Peg. I'm only doing what's right.'

'All right. Send him in.'

'Don't you worry. I'll be right outside the door. If he gets too fresh, you call out, okay? If he sets a foot wrong, he'll be dealing with me.'

Peggy chuckled. 'You big softie.'

Five minutes later there was another rap at the door. When Peggy answered it she found herself staring at a man every bit as handsome as Cary Grant. He was wearing a well-cut suit and highly polished leather shoes, and he carried a sheath of long-stemmed red roses. When Ernie had said TV producer, she'd pictured a short, rotund, balding man. Mike Schofield was the opposite of that.

'Hello.' She looked at the flowers. 'Are those for me?'

'Hello, Miss Carmichael. I'm Mike Schofield and yes, these are for you.'

'Why, thank you, Mike, they're gorgeous. Please come in, and do call me Peggy.' She placed the roses on her dresser and then led Mike to the lumpy sofa and invited him to take a seat.

'It's good of you to see me without notice. I appreciate it.'

'Not at all. Although, I must warn you, I go on stage in twenty minutes so we don't have long.'

'That's fine. I'll get right to the point. Peggy, I'm here to offer you a job.'

'A job? Doing what?'

'Over at Columbia, we're about to produce a new TV series called *My Mermaid Wife*. The lead role is Sirena, a mermaid who takes on human form to lure men with her siren's song. She ends up caught between worlds when she falls in love with a human man. I think you'd make a perfect Sirena.'

Peggy's stomach flipped. Was this really happening?

'Obviously I don't expect you to give me an answer right now. I'll have my office send over a script to you tomorrow morning, if you'd like to read it.'

'When are you holding auditions?'

'There's no need for that. If you want it, the role is yours.'

Peggy stared at him wordlessly for a moment. This really was too good to be true. What was going on here?

'Why me? Who put you up to this? Was it Julia Newman? Vivienne Lockhart, perhaps? I know they mean well but I'm not a charity case, Mr Schofield. I don't want you to take me on as a favour to someone at your studio or to a friend, only to have you drop me after the pilot because it "just didn't work out".'

'Wow. Someone really has done a number on you.'

She continued to stare at him. 'You haven't answered my question.'

'I want you because you are perfect for the role. I was in the room the day you auditioned for *Agnes Grey*, so I know you can act. Not only that, you can sing. Sirena is a mix of girl-next-door beautiful by day and sexy singer at night. I think you meet that description exactly. And the fact that you'll be able to sing your own numbers is a real plus. I want you, Peggy, and I'm here to tell you I'm prepared to pay. We think we could have a big hit on our hands and I want someone who can commit to the job. I know a lot of girls see TV as second to the movies but I'm telling you, TV is the way of the future. If you take this role, this time next year you'll be a household name.'

'I don't know what to say.'

'Say you'll read the script. Have a look and then, if you're interested, have your agent give me a call.'

'Okay, I'll read it. Now, forgive for being rude, but I really need to get ready for my act. It was a pleasure to meet you, Mike.'

His eyes met hers. 'Believe me, the pleasure's all mine.'

What a difference a month made. Only a few short weeks ago, Peggy had been wondering what her future held. This week she'd started shooting the pilot episode of *My Mermaid Wife*, and right now was on her fifth date with Mike Schofield.

He'd just taken her for a delightful (and expensive) dinner at Chasen's. It was a warm night for March, so Mike had lowered the top of his convertible. As they wound their way through the Hollywood Hills, the wind blew her hair back and the radio blared. When her favourite song, 'You Send Me', came on, she took it as an omen. Mike was *the one*.

She mentally checked off all the ways he was perfect for her.

He was wealthy *and* his career was on the rise.

He wasn't an actor. She wouldn't have to watch him kissing other women on screen, and there was no chance of him falling in love with his co-star.

He could help her career. He'd already got her the best role she'd ever had. If things went well – and Mike was confident they would – she would soon be famous. And the great thing about TV was that it was more stable than movies. If the series was a long-running one, she'd be guaranteed work (and fame!) for years.

He was handsome and made her belly fill with butterflies when he kissed her.

He was at a point in his life where a wife would be advantageous. Peggy was still young enough that she could hold off on having a family for a little while – long enough to get a couple of seasons of the show under her belt – but she didn't want to end up an old maid. Mike, a man who understood the industry, would be the perfect match in this regard. As the show's producer, he would want her to keep working. Then, when the time was right, she would have her family. With Mike she could have her cake and eat it too!

This was the life she'd dreamt of. Everything she'd hoped for was coming true.

After a while Mike found a place to pull over. From this vantage point high in the hills they could see LA lit up in all its glory. With her favourite song still playing, Peggy sang along, directing her melodic declarations of affection to the city below.

'God, I love it when you sing.'

'You'll be sick of it soon with all the singing I do on set.'

He nuzzled her neck. 'Never. I will never be sick of your voice, or anything else about you.' He pressed his lips to hers.

Her heart leapt. *Never.* That was a good sign.

After a minute, Mike's lips moved to her earlobe and his hand drifted to her breast. She let the hand linger just long enough for him to appreciate her pert perfection before pulling away. 'Mike, I'm sorry, no.'

'Oh, Peggy, we've been dating for weeks. Come on, you must know what you're doing to me.'

She drew back in her seat. 'I'm sorry, Mike, I'm not the sort of girl who fools around just for the sake of it. I have my beliefs, and those beliefs don't allow for relations between unmarried couples. Besides, I can't risk it at the moment. Imagine if I were to get pregnant. Where would that leave the show?'

'Honey, a little bit of fondling isn't going to get you pregnant.'

'I know that,' she said coolly. 'But a little bit of fondling leads to more. I'd rather say no now than let you get all hot and bothered, and then not follow through.'

He was silent for a moment and then leant across and pecked her on the cheek. 'You know what? I respect that.' He took her hand and squeezed it. A huge grin spread across his face. 'But, baby, you've got to know, just looking at you makes me hot and bothered.'

She chuckled. 'I'm sorry, but there's not a lot I can do about that.'

Chapter 25

Sadie

'You need to push Harry harder, Sadie. He's had your script for a month and not said a word. March on into his office tomorrow and ask him what his thoughts are.' Vivienne's voice was matter of fact, as if demanding something from Harry Gold was a commonplace thing, not an impertinence that could cost Sadie her job.

Sadie stared out at the breaking waves in front of her. She and Vivienne had taken a drive out to Malibu after depositing Julia at Charlie's bungalow. Since Vivienne's break up with Sam Hayden she had no reason to while away the afternoon at Chateau Marmont, but she was committed to dropping Julia off nevertheless. Sometimes, Sadie would tag along for the ride. It was too breezy to sit on the beach, but they'd been for a walk on the sand and now were sitting in Vivienne's car, enjoying the view as they passed the time. They weren't due back at the Marmont for at least another hour.

'I'm serious, Sadie. You didn't come out here to be someone's secretary.'

Funnily enough, Jack had said almost the very same thing to her just days earlier. It was one of the rare days when she'd had time to grab a bite at the commissary. She was halfway through her sandwich when Jack appeared at her table, tray in hand.

'Why, Sadie Shore, it must be my lucky day. Mind if I join you?'

'It's a free country.'

'As usual, I'm overwhelmed by your delight in my company.'

She chuckled. 'Sorry, Jack. I guess I wasn't expecting to see you here. What brings you to Goldstar today?'

'Just finished an interview with one of the studio's up-and-coming starlets.' He screwed up his face. 'Poor thing. The movie she's doing sounds like a real stinker. I've read the script and it's terrible.'

'How did you come to read it?'

'A friend was auditioning for a part and asked me to take a look.'

A *female* friend, no doubt.

'Anyway, it got me thinking about you and your screenplay. I know yours will better than the garbage I just read, Sadie. You should hurry up and finish it, because I'm sure it'll get snapped up.'

When she explained that it *was* finished and was sitting on Harry Gold's desk, waiting to be read, Jack had looked like a proud parent. 'Well, that's just great news. I have no doubt we'll have an excuse to hit the town and celebrate soon. Of course, I'll miss seeing you on my regular visits to harass Harry, but I've always known you wouldn't be there forever. You're too talented to be someone's secretary for the rest of your life.'

At the time, Jack's words had caused a lump to form in her throat. His absolute confidence in her success warmed her heart.

'Sadie! Are you listening to me?' Viv's voice cut into her thoughts. 'This is important. We're talking about your future.'

'Sorry. What were you saying?'

'The screenplay is good. No, it's brilliant, and I've read enough of them to know. If Harry Gold doesn't want it, one of the other studios will. Huh . . .' She stopped mid-sentence and threw her hands in the air. 'I'll bet that's it. Old Harry has probably read it already and knows it's a masterpiece, but if he buys it, then he'll lose you as his personal secretary and he doesn't want that now, does he?'

'I'm sure Mr Gold wouldn't stand in my way like that. He knows writing is my dream.'

'Sadie, for someone who is so smart, sometimes you can be quite dense. Harry Gold doesn't give two hoots about you. Just like practically every other man in this industry, he only cares about himself. He's holding on to that script so no one else can produce it, but he's stringing you along so he doesn't have to replace you in the office.'

'You're reading too much into it. He's a very busy man.'

'You have to be pushy about it, make him think that you're going to send it elsewhere. That'll hurry him up.'

Sadie opened the window and sucked in salt-laced air. God, she loved it out here. The climate, the beach, the freedom to be anything she wanted. She didn't want to give any of that up, but Vivienne was right; she didn't move all the way across the country to be someone's secretary.

'Yeah, I know, I probably should be more assertive. It's just . . . well, I'm scared. What if he tells me it's no good? So long as it sits on his desk unread there's still hope, you know?'

'If Harry doesn't want it, he's a fool. And you're better off knowing, right? Because then you can take it to someone else.'

'What if no one wants it?'

'Then you write another one. And another after that. I know it's not exactly the same thing, but look at me – how many knockbacks and dud roles did I have to cop before I landed *Agnes Grey*?'

Vivienne had certainly landed on her feet with that movie. The film hadn't been released yet, but there was plenty of buzz about it.

'Not long before you're a household name.'

'Let's hope so. But that wasn't my point. My point was that even when the best job I could get was as a bikini model, I didn't give up. You shouldn't either. If you need another example, how about Peggy? She's had her moments of doubt, I know, but she hung in there. Now she's on her way to being a TV star.'

'Do you really think the show will be a hit?'

207

'I'm sure of it. And you know what? The way things are going, TV is a much safer bet than the movies, don't you think? This could be the best thing that's ever happened to her. She might end up being the most successful of us all.'

'Oh, how she'd love that.' Sadie chuckled.

'I think you're brilliant, Sade, I truly do, but if this script doesn't make it, you just have to keep going until you get one across the line. Hollywood isn't for the faint-hearted.'

'You know what? You're right. I'm going to ask Harry about it tomorrow.'

Chapter 26

Julia

Julia sipped her water and looked at her three best friends in the world. It seemed like ages since all four of them had been in the dining hall together and she wanted to savour the moment. These halcyon days wouldn't last forever. Eventually, the four of them would go their separate ways.

Sadie hadn't sold her screenplay yet, so she would most likely be here for a while to come, unless a better option presented itself. Peggy's star was on the rise, though, and Julia was sure that soon she'd be making plans to move out. It was inevitable, really. The Studio Club had been a haven when they were Hollywood fresh meat, but they'd outgrown the boundaries designed to keep them safe.

Of all of them, Vivienne was the one who'd found the confines of the club the most repressive, and she flouted the rules every chance she got. *Agnes Grey* was about to be released and the word about town was that it would be a huge hit, which made Vivienne just about the hottest property in Hollywood right now. Warner Brothers had signed her for her next movie; soon she'd have the money to buy her own place, if that's what she wanted. She'd often talked of them all getting a place together. If Vivienne bought a house maybe Sadie would move in with her. Those two were as close as sisters.

But for Julia, leaving the Studio Club was a pipe dream. While she was under contract to Goldstar, she was going to be stuck living here. At least until she and Charlie were ready to go public. And who knew when that would be?

The press were often incredulous that she lived here. In every second interview she was asked, 'What keeps a big star like you living in a house designed for young hopefuls?' She wasn't at liberty to talk about her contract, so she explained it by saying she chose to live at the Studio Club because she liked it, and her friends lived there. That wasn't a lie. She'd loved being part of this household full of talented young women, and without the Studio Club she would never have met Peggy, Sadie and Vivienne.

Still, she had to admit that she was now yearning for a place of her own, a place she and Charlie could call home. She wanted nothing more out of life than to be Mrs Charlie Hudson. If it were up to her, she'd happily give away her career this very minute to make that dream a reality, but Charlie had convinced her not to do anything just yet.

They'd argued about this very thing earlier that day. 'I'm not sure how much longer I can keep doing this, Charlie,' she'd said.

Charlie, whose nakedness was barely covered by the bedsheet, looked at her with alarm in his eyes. 'What are you saying? Are you breaking up with me?'

She placed a hand on his freshly shaven cheek. 'Oh, baby, of course not! I just meant that I hate sneaking around like this. I love spending time with you here, but I want to do things that normal couples do as well – go out to dinner or to a show.'

He drew her close, and she rested her head on his bare chest. 'I want that too. More than anything. But we just need to be patient, my love. We need to be sure we have the resources behind us to deal with the fallout from going public.'

'I don't care what people say, Charlie. The only resource I need is you.'

'Oh, my darling, if only it was as simple as that. It's not just about people calling us names. You'll lose your career. Maybe I will too. Best case scenario is that I hang on to some of my shows. But it could be much, much worse than that.'

'I've got plenty of money and so do you. What does it matter?'

He puffed out a long breath of frustration. 'A man needs to work, Julia. *I* need to work. Entertaining people is my life. I could never give that up, and you shouldn't have to either. But more than that . . . I'm afraid of something happening to you. There are bad people in this world. People who think they have the right to a say in how others live their lives.'

Her eyes filled with tears of hopelessness. 'Is this it, then? Illicit meetings for the rest of our lives?' She sat up and looked at him. 'I mean, you keep saying "not yet" but when, Charlie, when? What the hell are we waiting for?'

'Things are changing, Julia. Every day is one day closer to couples like us being accepted.'

'God, Charlie, the sort of change you're talking about could take years. Decades even. Do you really expect me to just wait for a day that might never come? We need to be brave. It's people like us, people with money and fame, who can help bring about the change you're talking about.'

He pulled away from her then and swung his legs over the edge of the bed, facing away from her. Resting his elbows on his knees, he dropped his head into his hands. After a few minutes he turned to face her again. His eyes shone with tears. 'Maybe you're right. Maybe I am a coward. I *do* want to stand up for us, to announce our love to the world, but the thought of some bigot harming you fills me with terror. I only want to keep you safe.'

She scooted across the bed and draped her arms around him, pressing her chest to his back. 'I don't think you're a coward, Charlie. I just want us to have a normal life.'

He laughed then. 'No matter what happens, I don't think we're ever going to have a normal life.' He drew her onto his lap. 'I promise you this won't be forever. We just need to plan. I've been offered a limited run on TV – six musical specials. The money is phenomenal. Let me record those. By the time I'm done you should be almost finished shooting the current movie. Let's look at our joint finances after that. Maybe we can look at moving to Europe – at least for a while. We just need to ride this out for a little bit longer.'

That was all very well, Julia thought, as she took a bread roll from the basket Peggy offered, but finding ways to see Charlie without arousing suspicion was getting harder. They used Chateau Marmont as often as they could – Charlie still had a bungalow there – and occasionally she was able to see him as part of a larger group at a club or a dinner, but it was far from ideal.

'Jules!' Peggy snapped her fingers. 'Are you even listening?'

'Sorry. I was miles away.'

'Peggy was telling us all about her new *lover*,' Vivienne said. She proceeded to make kissing noises and Sadie chortled.

Peggy frowned. 'Stop it. He is *not* my lover. That's precisely the point.'

'Who isn't?'

'Her producer.'

'Mike Schofield?' It was Julia's turn to frown. 'Hang on, I'm confused. I thought you *were* dating him.'

'I am.' Peggy sounded exasperated.

'But you just said—'

'I said he wasn't my lover and he isn't. But I do think he's *the one*.'

'The one . . . oh! Peggy, are you telling us you're in love?' Julia said.

A satisfied smile settled on Peggy's face. 'Yes . . . yes, I think I am.'

'Tony will be devastated.' It was only when Sadie kicked her under the table that Julia realised she'd said the words out loud.

Peggy seemed indifferent to Tony's pain. 'He'll get over it.'

Julia wasn't sure he would. For the past year he'd been Peggy's 'plan B' – the guy who accompanied her to events when she needed an escort but couldn't be bothered with all the romantic expectations that

212

came with a real date. Somewhere among the many group outings, Julia and Tony had struck up a friendship.

Julia couldn't understand why Peggy hadn't snapped Tony up. He was a lovely fellow, quiet and unassuming. And wealthy to boot! When Julia had discovered Tony was an Astor – and heir to the Astor Candy Company fortune – she'd expressed her surprise at his insistence on working in the movie industry. Or at all.

Tony had told her his father had encouraged him to take a job, saying he would never appreciate his wealth properly until he understood what it took to earn it. This had impressed Julia greatly and she'd tried to steer Peggy towards him, but Peggy simply wasn't interested.

She'd tried to gently warn Tony that Peggy would never fall for him. He'd smiled and said he wasn't a quitter. 'While she's not married, there's still hope.'

The way Peggy was talking, it looked as if Tony was about to be out of luck.

Chapter 27

Julia

Julia's shoulders ached and perspiration dampened her hairline and trickled between her breasts. She'd been standing on a block with her arms out like a scarecrow for what seemed like an eternity. The joys of being fitted for a period gown on a warm April day.

Harry kept telling her *Ma Cherie* – a film about Marie Antoinette – would cement her as a serious actress. Julia loved his confidence but had no expectations of critical acclaim. She was a beautiful clothes-horse in this film, but not much more. She learnt her lines diligently and did her best, but she was no Vivienne.

Agnes Grey had premiered the previous month and immediately became one of those universally loved films. The critics raved while the public queued at the box office. Vivienne's face was suddenly in all the magazines. Even better than that, her name started appearing on the casting wish lists of several well-known directors. If there'd ever been any doubt about her suitability for the role, it was washed away the moment her face appeared on the screen. She ceased to be Vivienne and *was* Agnes. It was a breathtaking performance, and even Peggy agreed that Vivienne was perfect in it.

Thank god Peggy had been offered the TV series, otherwise the film's premiere might have reopened old wounds. With the hype about *My Mermaid Wife* still fresh, Peggy's confidence was at an all-time high, which clearly made it easier for her to be magnanimous. The fact that Sam Hayden had sought her out on the opening night of *Agnes Grey* to tell her he was still keen to work with her in the future had helped somewhat. Peggy had not hidden her pleasure when telling him she was fully booked at the moment but to give her agent a call if he had something specific he wanted to discuss.

Vivienne shone on the night, looking every bit the star she now was in her form-fitting strapless silver gown. She smiled and posed for the bevy of photographers outside the cinema. Laughed and signed autographs for the adoring fans who lined the red carpet. But afterwards she was pensive. She'd sat on Peggy's bed in the early hours of the morning after the premiere looking at Julia with puzzled eyes.

'I don't know what I was expecting,' she'd said, 'but it wasn't that.'

'What do you mean?' Julia had asked her.

'It's all so . . . fake. I mean, it's what I've wanted for so, so long. I always thought that if I could be famous, really famous, I would know what it was like to be truly loved. Tonight couldn't have gone better. People loved my performance, and they were happy to tell me so. Everyone wanted my photo or an interview with me. It was what I'd always dreamt of. It's just . . .' She left the thought unfinished, as if she couldn't quite articulate the problem.

'That's good, though. It means you're getting the recognition you deserve.'

'Am I though? It doesn't feel that way. All anyone cares about is the image, the star. *Who designed your dress, Vivienne? Are you going to go back to being blonde now the movie's out? Do you have any make-up tips for the girls out there?* Agnes is a serious role, and all anyone cared about was what I was wearing. Nobody cares what I think or what I have to say. So long as I look pretty and smile for the camera, they've got what they came for. All that attention didn't feel like love. It felt like consumption. Like I was a piece of meat. A nice juicy steak to be enjoyed.'

Julia knew exactly what she meant. Fame wasn't all it was cracked up to be, but nobody knows that beforehand. On the night of her movie's premiere, Vivienne was one of the most looked-at women in the country and yet she didn't feel seen. Julia, on the other hand, felt as if every single one of her inadequacies was on show for all to observe. The camera saw past her looks and exposed who she really was. *Nobody*. A girl who was completely unremarkable. Not smart, not funny, not good enough.

The only time she didn't feel this way was when she was with Charlie. The way he listened to her, sought her counsel and so often took her advice made her believe that she just might be worthwhile after all. When they were together she felt complete.

Her heart broke a little for Vivienne. There was no Charlie in Vivienne's life to keep her grounded, to let her know that she was seen and loved for who she was. No one apart from her friends. Julia was determined to make sure Vivienne knew that she had someone who truly cared.

As soon as wardrobe were done with her today she planned on surprising Vivienne on the set of her new movie. She had a gift for her – a notebook that Julia had found in an adorable little shop in Malibu. She and Charlie had spent the whole weekend in a holiday house there, courtesy of one of his friends.

'All done, Miss Newman. You can step down now and I'll get you out of this thing.'

It was another hour before Julia made it across town to the Warner Brothers studios. At the gate she told the security guard that no, she didn't have an appointment. 'The thing is'—her eyes flitted to the guard's name tag—'the thing is, Stanley, I want to surprise my very good friend Vivienne Lockhart.' She held up the wrapped notebook for him to see. 'I have a gift for her. I don't want her to know I'm coming. But please do feel free to call ahead to the sound stage and get permission. I'd hate to get you in any trouble.'

'Oh, no need for that, Miss Newman. You're more than welcome here at Warner Brothers anytime.'

She smiled. Fame did have some perks.

'I will just call ahead and let them know you're coming, though. I'll have them send someone to greet you outside sound stage seven.' He leant out of the window and beckoned to a nearby studio page. 'Steve here will escort you. And don't worry, I'll make sure no one lets Miss Lockhart know you're coming.'

'You're too kind, Stanley. Thank you so much.'

True to his word, Stanley called ahead and Andy, a young production assistant, waited to greet her. 'They're shooting a scene that doesn't require Miss Lockhart,' he said.

'Oh!' Julia hadn't counted on Vivienne not being there. 'Has she gone for the day?'

'No. I believe she's in her dressing-room. Mr Gleeson asked her to stay put for a little while because she's required for the next one. I can show you to Miss Lockhart's dressing-room if you like,' Andy said.

'That would be lovely. Thank you.'

Andy led her from the sound stage to a nearby building and escorted her to reception. 'Miss Newman for Miss Lockhart,' he said, with great authority. 'She's been cleared to go straight through.'

'Welcome, Miss Newman. We're thrilled to have you here at Warner's,' the receptionist gushed.

'Thank you. Can I go on in now?' She lowered her voice as she held up the gift. 'I want to surprise Vivienne.'

'Of course, Miss Newman. Down the corridor to the right. You'll see Miss Lockhart's name on the door.'

This was so much fun! She'd never visited Vivienne on set before – her schedule didn't usually allow for it – but it was a great idea. If Vivienne didn't mind, she might hang around for the afternoon shoot. She'd love to see her friend at work in front of the camera – maybe she could even learn a thing or two.

She stopped outside the door bearing Vivienne's name. She turned the doorknob – it wasn't locked – and then pushed the door open.

'Surprise!' she called and then stopped dead, momentarily unable to speak or move.

Vivienne was seated on top of her dresser. The buttons of her dress were undone to her waist, her skirt bunched up around her hips. Her legs were spread wide apart and between them was a man.

'Oh god, I'm so sorry,' she started as the man's face turned towards her.

Julia gasped. It was Mike. Mike Schofield. *Peggy's* Mike.

Vivienne cried, 'No!', which was enough for Julia to regain her senses. She dropped the notebook on the floor and fled.

Chapter 28

Julia

The following week, Julia was back in wardrobe when Sadie appeared and asked her if she had time for lunch. One of the great things about being on set at Goldstar was that she and Sadie occasionally got to grab a coffee or share a meal together.

'That would be great, Sade. I'll be done here in about half an hour. Shall we meet at the commissary?'

'Harry's feeling magnanimous. He told me to take a whole hour, so maybe we could go to Sal's Diner instead?'

Huh. This wasn't just a casual catch-up, then. Sadie wanted to talk in private, away from the studio gossips. Maybe it was something to do with the film?

'Sure, that suits me.'

'I'll call ahead and see if they can reserve our usual table. Come by my office when you're ready.'

An hour later, they were safely tucked up in their regular booth at the back of Sal's. They'd ordered – a burger and fries for Sadie and chicken salad for Julia – and now it was time to find out why Sadie had invited her for lunch. 'Spill the beans, Sade. What are we doing here?'

'Am I being that obvious? Sorry, but yes, there is something.'

'Okay, what's old Harry got you softening me up for now? What do they want me to do?'

'What? Oh no, Jules, it's nothing like that. And you must know I'm *always* on your side when it comes to Harry.'

'I know. I was only teasing. But if you're not on a mission from Harry, what is it? What do you want to talk about?'

'I want to know what's going on with you and Vivienne.'

The blood drained from Julia's head and pooled in her feet, and a wave of nausea washed through her as the image of Vivienne and that bastard Mike going at it flashed into her mind.

'Jules, are you okay? You've gone pale.'

'I don't know what to tell you.'

Sadie put her water glass down on the table. 'Please tell me *something*. I don't know what's going on, but I know Vivienne's in a bad way. She has barely left her room all week, other than to go to work. And twice now I've heard her crying at night when she thinks I'm already asleep. I haven't seen her like this ever – not even when Sam Hayden dumped her.'

Julia sighed. There was nothing she wanted more than to share the burden of this secret with someone. The weight of it was crushing her. For days she'd been tossing up what to do.

Vivienne had come after Julia as she ran through the studio's backlots, desperate to put distance between herself and the awful scene she'd witnessed. She'd had a head start while Vivienne buttoned herself up, and probably would have got away if she hadn't been wearing heels. Vivienne hadn't bothered to put on shoes and was faster in bare feet. It hadn't helped that Julia had also been forced to stop when nausea came over her. She'd purged the contents of her stomach into the nearest garden bed before running on. It hadn't taken long for Vivienne to catch up.

'Julia, stop. It's not what you think.'

Julia turned to face her. 'Were you not just having sex with Peggy's boyfriend?'

220

'Yes, but I didn't . . . It wasn't what it seemed. I mean, I didn't want . . .' Rivers of mascara streamed down her cheeks.

Julia frowned, trying to make sense of what Vivienne was saying. 'Do you mean he was *raping* you?' She tried to marry that accusation with what she had seen. She supposed it was possible. Vivienne was pushed up against the mirror and partially clothed. Dear god, had Mike just assaulted Vivienne? 'Vivienne, you must tell me. We should get the police.'

Vivienne opened and closed her mouth, seemingly unable to make up her mind what to say. 'Not exactly . . . he . . . I . . .'

'Not exactly? He either assaulted you or he didn't. If a crime has been committed, we need to go to the police right now. Otherwise—'

'No! No police! That wasn't what I meant. I only meant I . . . I . . . I hadn't planned on it. It just kind of . . . happened.'

'How could you do this to Peggy?'

'I'm sorry.' Vivienne sobbed. 'Please, Julia, promise me you won't tell her. It'll break her heart.'

'You should have thought about that before you fucked her boyfriend.' Julia had been shocked by the vehemence of her own language. She wasn't fond of vulgarity. But what Vivienne and Mike had done *was* vulgar. And it was unforgivable.

A week had passed and she hadn't spoken another word to Vivienne. And she still hadn't decided what to do about Peggy.

If she told her about Vivienne and Mike, all of their lives would change forever. Peggy would never forgive Vivienne, and Julia couldn't blame her for that. It would be the end of the lovely friendship the four of them shared. But things had changed anyway, hadn't they? Because no matter how hard she tried to justify what Vivienne had done – it was a mistake, she was vulnerable and looking for comfort, her lack of self-worth led her to make poor decisions – in the end, there was no excuse. Vivienne could have any man on the planet. Seducing, or being seduced by, Peggy's boyfriend was inexcusable.

The friendship was already broken. She couldn't look Vivienne in the eye, let alone have a conversation with her. Was burdening Sadie with all that worth it? She simply didn't know. On the one hand, she didn't want Sadie to feel the way she did right now. On the other hand, maybe Sadie would know what to do.

'You should ask Vivienne.' She focused on smoothing the napkin on her lap, avoiding Sadie's gaze.

'Don't you think I've tried that? It's clear that whatever is going on has something to do with you. Every time she enters the room, you leave. When her name comes up in conversation, you change the topic. Obviously you two have had some sort of falling out. Is there nothing I can do to help? I hate this. We're friends, practically family. We should be able to talk about our differences and solve them. Vivienne's really hurting, Julia, and I'm sure you are too.'

'It's more about who Vivienne has hurt, than whether she's hurting, frankly,' Julia blurted out.

Sadie's forehead creased in concern. 'I really think it would do you good to talk about it. You two have been so close. Vivienne has gone out of her way to be a good friend to you. That must count for something. I don't know what she's done, but none of us are perfect. We all make mistakes at times. Whatever it is, can't you find it in your heart to forgive her?'

Vivienne's past generosity was part of what made this current situation so unbelievable, so unbearable. 'It's not up to me to forgive her.'

'For god's sake, Julia. You're talking in riddles. Whatever it is, you can tell me. You know you can trust me.'

Julia blew out a long, exasperated breath. 'It's not about trust, Sadie. I'm trying to protect you. I'm not sure this is something you want to know. I sure as hell wish I didn't.'

'Okay, okay.' Sadie raised her palms in a gesture of surrender. 'I can't make you tell me. But just know, I'm here if you need to talk. I love both of you and I hate to see you like this.'

'Thanks, Sadie. I'll let you know if I change my mind.'

∾

Worn out by the week's drama, Julia decided an early night was in order. She wasn't seeing Charlie this weekend – he was in Vegas for a show – so she figured a hot bath followed by a good sleep might help her to decide whether to come clean to Peggy. Even though she hadn't set foot inside a church since she'd left Nebraska, she found herself praying as she drifted off to sleep. 'Please God, I don't know what to do. Send me a sign.'

The next thing she knew she was being woken by Peggy. 'Jules, Jules, wake up.'

Her eyelids flipped open. 'What? Is it morning?' She sat bolt upright, still confused. The room was dark.

'No, silly.' Peggy giggled. 'It's the middle of the night.' She turned on Julia's bedside lamp.

'Why are you waking me, then?'

'Get up and come with me,' Peggy whispered. 'I've got big news that I can't wait to tell you.'

'So tell me here.'

'Uh-uh. All four of us need to be in the room together when I share this.'

Julia's pulse quickened. Being in the same room as Vivienne was not ideal at this point. 'Peg, whatever this is, can't it wait until morning? I'm really tired.'

Peggy pulled back her bedcovers. 'No! I promise it will be worth it.' She grabbed Julia's robe from the end of the bed. 'Come on, put this on and let's go.'

Julia got up, took the robe and jammed her feet into her slippers. As she silently followed Peggy down the hall to Sadie and Vivienne's room her gut clenched in nervous anticipation. What on earth had got into Peggy? Was she drunk?

When they arrived at Sadie and Vivienne's room, Julia could hear talking.

'They're still awake,' said Peggy, gleefully clapping her hands. She rapped on the door and waited to be let in.

Sadie opened the door a crack and then, when she realised who was standing there, beckoned them in. Vivienne was sitting cross-legged

223

on her bed with her journal resting in her lap and a pen in her hand. Her eyes widened at the sight of Julia. Julia averted her gaze. Peggy planted her bottom on the end of Vivienne's bed and looked at Sadie and Julia. 'Sit down, you two. I've got something to say.'

Sadie and Julia silently obeyed, both perching themselves on the edge of Sadie's bed.

It seemed Peggy could contain herself no more. 'Girls,' she said, grinning from ear to ear. 'I have the best news. Tonight is unequivocally the most wonderful night of my life.' She waved her left hand in the air. 'I'm engaged! Mike and I are getting married! And I want all of you to be my bridesmaids.'

As Sadie stood up to congratulate her, Julia and Vivienne briefly locked eyes before Vivienne dropped her gaze.

Well, she'd asked for a sign and God had delivered. There was no way Julia was going to let Peggy walk down the aisle with that lecherous toad without her knowing what he'd done.

But not tonight. She'd let Peggy have this one night of happiness, because tomorrow her world would be shattered.

Chapter 29

Peggy

'Baby, please, you have to listen to me. Vivienne Lockhart means nothing to me. Nothing! She's a tramp, Peggy. I never did understand how the two of you could be friends.' It was less than twenty-four hours since he'd asked for her hand in marriage, and now Mike was on his knees again. He stared up at her with pleading eyes from his position on the thick mint-green rug that covered his living room floor.

This was the first time Peggy had been inside his house. She'd resisted all attempts to get her to come in for a 'nightcap', knowing that once inside he'd be expecting much, much more. Even in the midst of her fury, Peggy noted the modern and expensive furnishings, and the floor-to-ceiling windows, which revealed a spectacular view of the valley below. At the rear of the living area, a set of glass doors led to a large in-ground swimming pool surrounded by timber sunlounges and Adirondack chairs. This is where she could have been living in a few short months if not for Vivienne.

And Mike. He had plenty to answer for too.

Earlier that morning, Julia had taken her hand and gently told her what she'd seen.

At first she'd refused to believe it, arguing with Julia that she must have misunderstood, because neither Mike nor Vivienne would do that to her. But Julia had been insistent. 'My darling girl, why would I make this up? I hate that it is the truth and I wish that it wasn't, but I know what I saw.'

Determined to get to the bottom of the matter, Peggy marched up to Vivienne's room and pounded on the door. When Sadie opened it, Peggy pushed her aside and yelled across the room at Vivienne, who was still in bed, '*How could you?*'

Sadie looked confused. 'What's going on?'

'Did you?' Peggy shouted. There was a touch of hysteria in her voice, but she didn't care. If ever there was an appropriate time for hysteria it was now. 'Did you have sex with Mike? Don't lie to me, Vivienne.'

Vivienne dropped her head into her hands and began to cry.

'Well? Have you nothing to say for yourself?' Peggy scowled in disgust.

'I promise you, it's not what you think. I didn't want . . . I didn't mean . . . it was a mistake. I can explain.'

'You've told me everything I need to know already.' Revulsion overtook her in the form of nausea. She needed air, but she couldn't resist firing a parting shot in her former friend's direction as she left the room. 'You're dead to me, Vivienne. Don't ever speak to me again.'

Now to deal with the other offending party. She wanted to slap his pathetic face. 'Get up,' she said, 'and act like a man.'

He stood and moved to the couch. 'Come and sit with me. Let's talk about this.'

Her feet were killing her. She'd dressed in her highest heels, a skin-tight skirt and the lowest cut blouse she owned, which wasn't particularly revealing but did give a hint of her impressive cleavage. She'd taken the time to style her hair and carefully apply her make-up. If she was breaking up with Mike she wanted him to see just what he was missing out on. She wasn't about to give him the satisfaction of a cosy chat on the couch, no matter how much her feet were hurting.

'I'm so, so sorry, baby.'

Peggy scoffed. 'Sorry you got caught, you mean.'

'Peggy, what do you want from me? I love you, I want you to be my wife. That's what matters, isn't it? That whore means nothing to me, you must know that. Please sit down and let's discuss this like adults.'

Peggy didn't move. 'What I want from you is for you to give me the courtesy of telling the truth. I want to know why.'

'Honey, you know how much I respect your decision to save yourself for marriage. It's part of the reason I love you so much. But you must understand that it's different for men. I have needs; needs you can't meet until after we're married. I thought you'd understood that I'd be seeking satisfaction elsewhere.'

Peggy's cheeks burned with humiliation. He was right. Sort of. On some level she'd known that a red-blooded male like Mike couldn't be expected to totally abstain from sex for months on end. She'd chosen not to think about it. But if she *had* thought about Mike having his needs attended to, she would have imagined it being with some nameless, faceless woman. Not with one of her best friends.

'Why her?' she said, struggling to keep the waver out of her voice. 'Of all the women you could have chosen, why did you have to go and pick Vivienne?'

He covered his face with his hands for a moment and then lifted his head. 'That was a terrible, terrible mistake, and I don't blame you at all for being angry.'

'A mistake? A mistake is forgetting to pick up the dry-cleaning or spilling a drink. You don't just trip over and end up screwing one of my best friends.' She closed her eyes for a second and remembered the scene Julia had described. Poor Jules had turned crimson when Peggy had insisted on hearing the details. She'd needed the specifics to be convinced that Julia hadn't misinterpreted what she was seeing. Foolishly, she'd even suggested that Mike might have been helping Vivienne rehearse a scene. But when Julia described exactly what she'd seen Peggy knew that there was no explaining this away.

'She came on to me and, I admit it, I was weak.'

227

'What were you even doing there? What possible reason could you have for being in Vivienne's dressing-room?' A fresh wave of nausea took hold as a new possibility dawned on her. Vivienne was always out on dates, and they rarely picked her up at the Studio Club. 'Please don't tell me you've been seeing her all along? How long has this been going on?'

'What? No, I'm not having an affair with that tramp. It was just one time. I swear on my mother's grave. And *she* was the one who orchestrated it. She threw herself at me. Wore me down. Peggy, baby, you gotta believe me.'

Her pinched toes were screaming at her to take the weight off her feet. She sighed and walked to the sofa, taking a seat at the opposite end to Mike. 'Maybe if you explain what you were doing there I'd have a better chance of understanding.'

He leant back into the sofa and turned his head to face her. 'It was my idea to go there, to ask her opinion on the ring I'd bought for you. I wanted the ring to be a surprise, but I also wanted to get it right; for you to love it. I thought I'd show each of your girlfriends and get their thoughts. Vivienne's studio is closest to the TV station, so I figured I could dash out at lunchtime and get her to take a look. I called ahead and organised to meet Vivienne in her dressing-room. That was her suggestion. I would have been just as happy to meet her for lunch or anywhere where I could show her the ring without anyone else seeing it.'

'So you went to her dressing-room and she came on to you? Is that what you're saying?'

'That's exactly what I'm saying and it's the truth. I'm sorry, I know I should have resisted, but she started talking about how hard it must be for me not to be able to sleep with you until we were married, how she understood and how it would be her pleasure to help. Then she unbuttoned her dress. I'm so sorry, Peggy. I know I've been a fool, but if you can forgive me, I swear I will never so much as look at another woman again.'

Peggy was silent. If she walked away right now, who would be the biggest loser? Mike would lose out on her, and that would be a shame for him, because Peggy would make an excellent wife. But if they broke up, he would find himself someone else quick smart. She, on the other hand, was almost twenty-one years old. She wouldn't have trouble finding men to date her, but marry her? That was another thing altogether. If she threw away the opportunity to marry Mike, what if another chance didn't come her way? What she wanted more than anything was to have a family of her own. If she left it too long that might not be possible. What if it took her years to find the right man and then she was too old to have children?

Apart from this one tiny indiscretion, Mike was the perfect catch. He worked in the industry. He understood what she did and respected the work. And he was rich. She could work if she chose to but she wouldn't need to. She'd never have to worry about money.

Damn Vivienne for ruining what should have been a triumphant moment in her life. She should never have let down her guard with that one. Once upon a time, she'd had a low opinion of Vivienne, but then Sadie and Julia had come along and convinced her that Vivienne was sweet and misunderstood. And she'd allowed herself to be swayed. She should have trusted her gut.

Vivienne might have covered it well, but she'd never liked Peggy. There were always the little barbs about Peggy being too uptight and prudish. And she'd stolen *Agnes Grey* without a peep of remorse. It was blatantly clear that she had slept with Sam Hayden to secure the role. Yes, she was good in it, but that was hardly the point. She'd known how desperately Peggy wanted the part. A true friend would have stepped aside and most certainly wouldn't have slept with the director to ensure she was cast.

It was clear to her now. Vivienne was jealous. She'd deliberately set out to ruin Peggy's relationship with Mike. If she broke off this engagement, Vivienne would win.

Well, if Vivienne Lockhart thought she was that easy to break, she was mistaken.

She kicked off her shoes and settled back onto the sofa. 'If I were to forgive you – and it's a big if – I would need your word that you will never have anything to do with Vivienne again. Not in a personal or a professional capacity.'

He looked at her hopefully. 'Oh, Peg, are you saying—'

'Hold your horses. I'm not saying anything yet. But could you promise me that if I asked? No exceptions.'

'Hand on heart, I swear.'

Peggy nodded slowly. She'd already made up her mind to forgive him, or at least not to break the engagement – after all, she did love her sapphire-cut diamond engagement ring – but she wasn't going to let him off the hook just yet. Besides, he'd hurt her and ruined her special moment. There was a price to pay for that. 'Seeing as you find it so hard to control yourself, if we were to be married, I'd want to do it right away. As soon as the wedding could be organised.'

His head bobbed up and down vigorously. 'Of course. We could fly to Vegas tonight and get married immediately.'

'No, not like that. It has to be big. In a proper church and with a reception somewhere fancy like the Beverly Hills Hotel.' She'd initially planned on a year-long engagement but this would work just as well. A big wedding coinciding with the pilot of the show airing would be great publicity and ensure that the show was a success. 'My whole life I've dreamt of being a bride. I'm not giving that up because of a "mistake" you made. It will take a few weeks to arrange but that's what I want. And I want our engagement to be big news – a feature in *TV Guide*, at a minimum.'

'Of course, my darling. That was always going to be the case. Anything else?'

'My feelings have been very hurt by this, Mike. I think you'll need to find a way to ease that pain. I'm not going to give you instructions on how to do that. Use your imagination. I'm sure you'll figure something out.'

30 December 1999

It's quiet when Vivienne and I head into town for supplies. Most likely people are still holed up for the holidays, and many of the town's businesses are closed.

We park outside the supermarket and Vivienne shivers as we collect a cart from the rack outside. She smiles and links her arm in mine. This small display of trust warms me every bit as much as the rush of heated air that hits us as we enter the store.

A few people say hello to Vivienne as we amble around the aisles, and she replies politely without really engaging. I'm not sure that she recognises any of them. They look at her briefly with pitying eyes before hurrying away.

We finish our shopping quickly and head back to the comfort of home. Vivienne's quite settled today and she's keen to help me make lunch. We've bought the ingredients to make vegetable soup, and before long we're chopping vegetables side by side while singing along to the boppy tunes we've got pumping from the stereo. We sing a duet to 'Baby, It's Cold Outside' and end up laughing ourselves silly. Vivienne hasn't lost her singing voice or her sense of humour.

Later, over lunch, she smiles at me. 'This is nice.'

I nod my agreement. 'Yes, the chilli flakes give it a lovely little kick, don't you think?'

'I don't mean the soup, silly! I mean us, here together, Sadie. I like having you here.'

There it is again. A sliver of hope that she knows who I am. 'Do you remember me, Vivienne? From the Studio Club?'

'Of course I do!' she says. 'I used to live there, you know.'

'Yes, I know.'

She smiles. 'The good old Studio Club. I had the time of my life there. I wish . . . I wish things had been different.' The smile disappears from her face, and she pats her stomach and then yawns dramatically. 'I might have a catnap.'

She clearly doesn't want to say more and, reluctantly, I decide not to push her. 'Excellent idea.'

Once Vivienne retires to her room I clean up and head back to the office.

Even though I'm keen to listen to more of the tapes, I need to start sorting out what can be placed into storage and what we should take back to LA with us. I'm not sure what will become of Vivienne – whether I can viably care for her at my home on a long-term basis or not. Perhaps I will have to do what April couldn't and find her an appropriate care facility. Whatever happens down the track, though, it has become clear that she can't stay here alone.

I remember seeing a stack of folded cardboard cartons in George's surgery. I go downstairs and grab Vivienne's coat from the peg in the laundry room, then retrieve the boxes and a roll of tape and start the job of packing. I carefully place Vivienne's books into cartons to go into storage. I'm not sure how much she's reading these days, but I have many of the same titles on the shelves at my place, so it seems silly to double up.

Inside the cupboard behind the desk I find dozens of magazines, a couple of beaten-up suitcases and another box labelled *Memoir, source material*.

The suitcases contain old clothes. I recognise several dresses as ones Vivienne wore when she was working in Hollywood. Vivienne's lucky dress – the one she bought when we first became roommates – is there. I slide the violet fabric between my fingers and a lump forms in my throat. How near yet distant those days seem.

I blink away sentimental tears. If I allow myself to be derailed by memories, this job will never be done. I toss the dress back in the suitcase and turn my attention to the archive box. There's a large scrapbook inside. I gently lift it out and open it.

On the first page there is a magazine article about Peggy from 1958. On the next page is some promotional material for *My Mermaid Wife*. I flip through the pages quickly. The book appears to be filled with milestones from all our lives. I pause briefly to look at a photo of Julia accepting her Best Director Oscar for *Stone River*. It seems Vivienne has clipped every skerrick of information about the three of us that has appeared in the press since she left us. It humbles me to think of her watching us from afar for all these years, and the now-familiar guilt roils in my stomach. Why didn't I try harder to find her? I force the thought from my mind and set the book aside, resolving to read it properly later.

I dig back into the box and discover a stack of notebooks. Vivienne's journals!

The tears return as I pick up each book and rediscover the familiar magazine cut-outs of Vivienne's idols – Marilyn Monroe, Vivien Leigh, Lucille Ball – that decorate the covers. The image of Vivienne sitting up in bed scribbling furiously in her journal each night is one of my most enduring memories from my time at the club. The first volume is emblazoned with the year *1950*. She'd started writing these when she was just a girl. The last notebook is labelled *1958* – the final year we all lived at the Studio Club.

Although I'm interested to read Vivienne's musings from before I knew her, I'm drawn to the volumes that record our time together. I pick up *1955* and flick through it, smiling at the memories elicited by the familiar handwriting and clippings. There's a photo of the two of us sitting on her bed. Vivienne has a cigarette in her hand and I'm laughing.

I remember Julia taking the photo. It was Peggy's birthday and we were planning a surprise for her – Vivienne and I had written a song for the three of us to perform and we were secretly practising it.

The book is filled with her thoughts, and photos of us and of Vivienne's idols. Vivienne seems so upbeat and happy. She fills the pages with her hopes for the future, her belief that success is just around the corner and her excitement at finally having made friends she can trust.

After I've thumbed through the familiar volumes, I pick up *1958*, the last notebook, and flip through the pages to get to her final entry.

One line jumps out at me and my breath catches in my throat.

Yesterday, I thought about leaving this world behind for good, but I couldn't do it.

She'd wanted to die! My goodness. Why didn't I try harder to help her back then?

I go back and read the rest of the entry, and as I read my heart begins to pound. If Vivienne is saying what I think she's saying . . . I can't bear it.

But I must. For all our sakes.

With my pulse thudding in my ears, I thumb back through the entries until I find what I'm looking for.

What I read next makes my blood run cold.

I can't sit in this knowledge alone. Without hesitation I pick up the phone and dial Peggy's number. Mercifully she picks up.

'Peg, I need you to get Julia and to come here right away. Please don't argue, just trust me. Come to Three Rivers as soon as you can. We need to talk.'

Chapter 30

Sadie

With tears streaming down her face, Sadie watched Vivienne load the last carton in the trunk. She'd held in her emotions until now, trying her best to be the rock that both her friends needed in the vain hope that, somehow, if she just kept a cool head, she'd be able to mend the rift between them. It was foolish of her. Peggy would never forgive Vivienne.

And just like that, the beautiful family of friends they had created was gone.

For her part, Vivienne offered remorse but no excuses.

At first Sadie couldn't believe it was true. The woman she'd shared a room with for the past few years wasn't capable of betraying her friend this way. Vivienne had never shied away from using her sexuality to further her career, but what did she have to gain by being intimate with Mike? It simply didn't make sense. Vivienne had always been a loyal and faithful friend. She wouldn't hurt Peggy on purpose. Sadie was sure there had to be some other explanation.

But then she'd seen Viv's journal. She hadn't meant to pry, but she'd accidentally knocked the diary from its place on the nightstand. It fell to the floor and opened to reveal an intricate illustration of a broken heart. The drawing caught Sadie's attention as she bent to retrieve the journal, and then she saw the entry beneath it.

How could I have been so stupid? I knew it was dangerous when I made the decision to go ahead and now everything is ruined. Everything!

Sadie's heart had lurched. Was Viv guilty after all? She'd read on quickly, hoping for some sort of explanation for this shocking incident.

Oh god, the look on Peggy's face. I'll never forget it as long as I live. I can't believe Julia told her. There was no need. Mike loves and respects Peggy. He'd never treat her badly. Why couldn't Julia just leave things be? All she's managed to do is hurt Peggy and break our little group apart.

I thought that maybe, after everything I've done for her and Charlie, she might have just a shred of sympathy for me in her heart. But no. It's all right for her – she's the anointed one who can do no wrong. If only there was a way to make her understand what it feels like to be shunned by the world. If she could feel the way I do, even just for a minute, she'd forgive me, I'm sure of it.

Sadie hadn't dared turn the page – Viv had gone for a shower and could return at any moment – but what she'd read was enough to convince her that her friend had indeed done what she was accused of.

Tears of dismay had pricked Sadie's eyes. How could the girl they'd shared so much with and trusted so deeply hurt one of their own in this way? Viv must have had her reasons, but Sadie couldn't fathom what they might be. Perhaps if she talked to Viv about it, gave her the opportunity to explain, she might be able to understand.

Over the next few days Sadie tried several approaches to get Viv to open up, but she wouldn't be drawn on the matter, saying only, 'It was my fault. I should have known better. I should never have let him in to my dressing-room.' She was clearly broken by the fallout of her actions and, despite everything, Sadie couldn't help but pity her.

Yesterday, Vivienne had told Sadie she was leaving the club. 'I've booked a room at the Hollywood Roosevelt for now. Maybe I'll even buy my own place in a month or two. We'll see. I should have left here ages ago. I stayed because . . . well, let's just say there's nothing keeping me here now.'

'Vivienne, you know you still have me, right? No matter what you've done, I still care about you.' It was true. No matter how disappointed she was in Vivienne's behaviour, Sadie found she couldn't turn off her feelings. Peggy and Julia swore they wanted nothing to do with her, but to Sadie it wasn't that simple. Viv was like family, and she wasn't about to turn her back on family.

Viv had smiled at her then. 'Sweet Sadie. Your friendship is the best thing that ever happened to me. If I stay here, you'll be forced to choose between me and Peggy. I'm not going to put you in that position.'

Sadie had tried to convince her otherwise, but in her heart she knew it was futile. And maybe Vivienne leaving was for the best. Even so, it didn't make saying goodbye any easier.

Vivienne closed the trunk. 'Don't cry, Sade. It's better this way. You know where I am. You can call or come see me anytime you like.'

Sadie hugged her tight. 'I will. I promise.'

Julia was already at Sal's Diner when Sadie arrived.

'Peggy's running a little late,' Julia said by way of greeting. 'She had some errands to do but she shouldn't be too much longer.'

Sadie nodded and took her seat. Julia didn't ask about Vivienne's departure and Sadie didn't mention it. Instead, the conversation went back to Peggy.

'Your bedroom must look like a florist's shop,' Sadie said as she picked up the menu and perused it.

'It does. Good thing I'm not allergic. Every surface in our room is covered with roses. Surely he'll give up soon.'

'You don't think she'll be swayed, do you?'

'No. I mean, I don't think so. What he did was unforgivable.' She shuddered. 'The man gives me the creeps. It's bad enough that Peggy will have to work with him every day. Poor thing.'

'But she's kept the flowers.'

'Yes, and that's not all. There's been several other deliveries too.'

'Like what?'

'A Tiffany pendant, for a start.'

Sadie's eyebrows shot up. 'Wow. She never mentioned that to me.'

Julia picked up her water glass and took a sip before answering. 'I'm not sure that she would have told me either, but I was with her when she received the delivery.' She placed the glass back on the table and sighed. 'I guess I've been trying to push this thought to the back of my mind because it's so incomprehensible, but . . . well, she has kept all the gifts. And while she has spoken to me at length about her anger and disappointment in Vivienne, she has barely mentioned Mike's involvement. I only hope—' Julia stopped mid-sentence; her gaze fixed on the entrance to the diner. Sadie turned her head to see Peggy waving as she walked towards them.

She slid into the booth next to Julia. 'I'm so glad to have you both here. I've just come from Mike's place and I have some very exciting news.'

Julia cast a worried glance Sadie's way but said nothing.

'We've settled on a date for the wedding!' She paused, possibly expecting a congratulatory response, but neither Sadie nor Julia said a word.

The waitress arrived then to take their order, putting a halt to the conversation for a moment. As soon as she was gone, Peggy continued, 'It's the second of June, which is soon, I know, but I've always wanted to be a June bride and that's the date that works best with the show's schedule. We'll be married a week after the first episode goes to air, which will be great publicity, don't you think?' She looked from one to the other. 'Well? Aren't either of you going to say anything?'

'Are you sure about this, Peg?' Sadie asked.

'Look, I know it'll be a rush to get the invitations out – let alone get my gown made – but I think it's doable. Especially if I can count on you girls to help me.'

'I don't think that's what Sadie meant,' Julia said carefully.

'Oh?' Peggy arched an eyebrow and looked at Sadie. 'What *did* you mean, then?'

Sadie shifted in her seat uncomfortably and searched for a polite way to say 'your fiancé is a two-timing creep'. 'I just meant, are you sure you'll be happy with Mike after . . . after what happened?'

Peggy pursed her lips and then exhaled audibly. 'Mike and I have discussed the matter and I have forgiven him. I've put it behind me now and I'd be grateful if you could do the same.'

'And Vivienne?' The question was out of her mouth before Sadie could stop it.

'What about her?'

'Have you forgiven her, too?'

'As long as there is breath in my body I will never forgive that woman. She threw herself at Mike. Granted, he should have resisted, but he is a red-blooded man, after all.'

Julia's mouth dropped open. 'In that case, how can you be sure he won't do it again?'

Peggy responded with a steely look and an even harder tone in her voice. 'Frankly, Julia, my relationship with my fiancé isn't your business. But seeing as you are so interested in my affairs, I am sure Mike won't stray again because he promised he wouldn't. And once we're married he'll have no need to look elsewhere.'

The waitress arrived with their food. Sadie was relieved to have something else to give her attention to. It seemed Peggy and Julia felt the same way, and there was silence for a few minutes while they all pretended to be occupied by their meals.

Peggy devoured her pancakes in record time, dabbed the corners of her mouth with her napkin and then reached for her purse.

Julia touched her arm. 'You're not going, are you?'

'I have a lot to get organised for the wedding. If you two aren't interested in helping me then I'd best make a start on my own.'

Sadie pressed her knee against Julia's under the table. 'No, Peg, stay. We're glad to help with the wedding. We just wanted to be sure that you are happy about it and not being pressured into it for the wrong reasons. We want whatever you want. Isn't that right, Jules?'

'Of course. What are bridesmaids for?'

The sparkle returned to Peggy's eyes. 'That's fantastic. There's so much to do. I thought we could make a list and divide up the jobs between us. If you're free later this afternoon, I'd like us to have a look at some magazines so we can get ideas for bridesmaids' dresses. I've already got a design in mind for my gown, I just need to find someone to make it for me.'

Sadie had planned on spending the afternoon writing. With Harry yet to comment on her screenplay, she figured it was time to start something new. Maybe even a novel this time. But if looking at bridesmaid gowns was what it was going to take to keep Peggy happy, the writing could wait until tomorrow. 'Sounds like fun. Don't you think, Jules?'

Julia nodded. 'I'm free all day.'

Poor Julia. This falling out with Vivienne was not only hurting her personally, it was also affecting her ability to see Charlie.

'Great! Darlings, I'm sorry, but I have to rush off. I'm off to Max Factor to have hair and make-up done for an interview. Queenie Watson is taking me out for lunch. Mike's organised to give her an exclusive on our engagement for *The Times*. I can't believe this is really happening!'

She took out her wallet, but Julia waved away her offer of payment.

'Breakfast is on me today. My way of saying congratulations. I hope you'll be very happy.'

Peggy blew them both kisses as she made her way to the exit.

Once she was safely out of earshot, Julia said, 'I just don't understand. How can she marry that *pig* of a man?'

'I don't know, but then again, what would I know? It's not like I've ever been in love. What if Charlie slept with someone else but was remorseful? Would that be the end of it for you?'

'Charlie wouldn't do that.'

'I expect Peggy thought the same thing about Mike.'

'I suppose she would have.' Julia was silent for a moment. 'I think if Charlie slept with one of my friends it would kill the relationship. I wouldn't be able to trust him anymore. Which is why I can't believe Peggy is so blasé about the whole thing, at least where Mike is concerned. She seems to have put the blame squarely at Vivienne's feet. I know Vivienne is in the wrong – I'm appalled at her behaviour – but Peggy must know that Mike bears some responsibility for this too?'

Sadie sipped her water and contemplated what could possibly be going through Peggy's mind. 'I guess denying his culpability is what allows her to stay in the relationship. In any case, she's an adult and she's made her decision. We've already lost Vivienne and I'm not prepared to lose Peggy as well. No matter what I think about Mike, or how misguided her decision is, we need to support her.'

'As much as it pains me to say this, I think you're right.' Julia lifted her water glass in a toast. 'Here's to being a perfect bridesmaid.'

Sadie raised her glass in response. 'To keeping our mouths shut.'

Chapter 31

Julia

A few days later, Julia and Peggy were having breakfast in the dining room when Babs interrupted them.

'Julia, Sadie is on the phone. She said it's urgent.'

Julia made a face at Peggy. 'Ooh, I wonder what that could be about? Secret bridesmaids' talk, perhaps?'

'Go on, then. You'd better not keep her waiting.'

'I'll keep you posted.'

Julia headed to reception to take the call. The girls on the desk were chattering away but went silent as she approached. Jeepers, was something actually wrong? Was Sadie ringing to give her bad news?

Janet pushed the desk phone towards her and pressed a button as she handed her the receiver. 'I have Sadie on the line,' she said.

Julia turned her back to the counter. 'Hey Sade, what's up?'

'Jules, have you seen today's paper?'

Her heart started to pound. 'Not yet. Why?'

There was a beat before Sadie answered. 'There's a story in *The Times* about you and Charlie. Mr Gold is on his way here and he's livid, Jules. I denied the story, of course, but he wasn't convinced. He told me to get you to come in right away.'

'How bad is it?' Julia lowered her voice, now acutely aware of all the listening ears around her. 'I mean, is it just gossip or . . .?'

'It's bad. There are details. The paper quotes a "source close to Miss Newman". It's going to be hard to deny.'

'Right. Can you get my driver to come now? He's not due to pick me up for another hour.'

'Already done. I'll see you soon.'

Julia had hoped to beat Harry to the office so she could get the lowdown from Sadie first, but upon her arrival at reception she could hear Harry bellowing. She couldn't exactly make out what he was saying but his tone was irate.

The receptionist looked sympathetic. 'You can go on through to Miss Shore's office and wait in there, Miss Newman.'

Sadie was nowhere to be seen or heard, but Julia assumed she was the person currently copping Harry's wrath. After a minute or so Harry's office door opened and the shouting became clearer. 'I will not tolerate this, do you hear me? Bring her in.'

Sadie appeared. 'I'm sorry, Jules, I've done my best but I can't calm him down. He's furious.' She squeezed Julia's clammy hand. 'I'll be right out here.'

Julia took a deep breath. She'd feared this moment from the first time she'd kissed Charlie. Now it was here, she felt a tangle of emotions. Her heart was hammering in her chest at the thought of facing Harry's ire, but beneath that was a sense of relief that the moment of reckoning had finally arrived. Now people would know. And no matter what Harry said, she would not give up Charlie. If it meant being sacked on the spot, so be it. She had money now and Charlie did too. They could leave Hollywood and go to Europe, just like they'd discussed. Charlie would get work there for sure. If she never worked again, fine. She'd happily spend her life supporting the man she loved.

She walked into Harry's office with her head held high.

The shouting began before she'd closed the door. 'What the hell is the meaning of this?' Harry brandished a newspaper in front of her.

'Good morning, Harry.' She kept her voice calm. 'Unfortunately, I have not seen a newspaper today, so I'm not sure what you are talking about.'

He threw the paper onto his desk, opened it to the offending page and slammed his hand down on it. 'This,' he said. 'Read it!'

Julia pulled the paper towards her and immediately saw the article in question.

Hollywood Golden Girl's Scandalous Affair! the headline screamed, and underneath sat three photos: one of Charlie on stage, one of her walking the red carpet at the premiere of her most recent film, and an enlarged version of the photo that had been previously published in the paper. She scanned the copy as quickly as she could.

Rumours relating to an affair between movie star Julia Newman and entertainer Charlie Hudson have been circulating Hollywood for some time. While both parties have previously denied any such relationship exists, this reporter can now confirm that the pair are definitely an item. A source close to Miss Newman confirmed that the couple have been secretly seeing each other at Mr Hudson's private bungalow at Chateau Marmont.

Miss Newman has been a resident of the Hollywood Studio Club since signing with Goldstar Studios. Sources close to the star claim this was so studio boss Harry Gold could keep tabs on her and prevent her from making inappropriate dating choices.

One can only imagine Gold's reaction to the current situation!

When she was done, she pushed the paper back across the desk and lifted her gaze to meet his.

'Well?' he demanded. 'What do you have to say for yourself?'

'What is it that you want me to say?'

Harry's face turned puce. 'I want you to deny it,' he said, his words dripping with anger. 'I want you to tell me that *of course* this isn't true, because you know how damaging it would be to your career if it were. I want you to say that *of course* you would never do such a thing, because you know how foolish it would make me look.'

'I'm sorry, Harry,' she said evenly, 'but I can't deny it. Nor do I want to. Charlie and I have tried to be discreet, but now that it's out in the open I refuse to be ashamed.'

Harry slammed his hand on the desk again. 'For Christ's sake, Julia. What the hell were you thinking? This will kill your career if we don't act fast. I cannot believe you would do this to me, after everything I have done for you!'

Julia's pulse quickened as her internal composure receded. 'I will not give Charlie up. I love him.'

'*Grow up!* This relationship can't work. You must know that or you wouldn't have hidden it. If you keep seeing each other, I will have no option but to terminate your contract.'

'That's just it, Harry. I don't care. Being with Charlie is more important to me than fame or money, or anything really.'

'Don't be a fool. It's not just your career that's at risk here. Charlie Hudson is a Black man sleeping with a white woman. A lot of people are not going to like that. Now, me? I don't really care what people do in the privacy of their own homes, but I have to think about what the average Joe cares about. And the average Joe doesn't want to think about the woman of his dreams going to bed with a Black man.'

Rage boiled her blood. 'Shut up, Harry! How dare you speak about the man I love with such contempt. The colour of his skin doesn't matter to me and it shouldn't matter to anyone else either.'

'What matters to you doesn't count one iota, little girl. You think you're being brave? Pushing the boundaries? Is that what turns you on? Well, you're playing in the big league now, missy, and you'd better understand the stakes. You're not the only one involved here. What about Charlie – have you thought about how this will affect him?'

'I don't have to listen to this. Besides, I need to get to wardrobe. We're shooting in just over an hour.'

'Oh no, you're not. I've already called off today's shoot. You're going home, and you are not to leave the Studio Club again until you get permission from me.'

'Why would I do that? I'm not a child and I won't be held prisoner by you.'

Harry huffed out an exasperated breath. 'Christ. You really don't get it, do you? This isn't a game, Julia. If we don't handle this situation carefully, there could be dire consequences. And not just for you. If you go on public record about being a couple, you could be in danger, and so could Charlie.'

'If you're asking me to deny it—'

'If you know what's good for you, what's good for *Charlie*, you'll do exactly as I say. Go home and keep your mouth shut while I get the head of publicity in here to work out how we are going to fix this. Don't talk to anyone. No reporters. And stay away from Hudson! I'm going to send Sadie home with you to keep you company, and we'll post a security guard outside the Studio Club.'

'A security guard? You can't be serious.'

'It's for your own good. I'm warning you, Julia, stay at the club. We can protect you there. If you leave, I can't guarantee your safety. Go wait in Sadie's office and tell her to come in here. I'll have your driver escort you home as soon as Sadie is ready to leave.'

Julia was seething by the time she and Sadie got in the car.

Sadie leant across the seat and took her by the hand. 'Are you okay?'

Hot, angry tears sprang from her eyes and she pulled her hand away. 'I'm being held prisoner. I can't believe you're going along with this, Sadie.'

'Honey, I'm on your side, I promise. And believe it or not, Mr Gold is too.'

'Harry? All Harry cares about is his investment. I'm just a possession to him, and he doesn't want his goods tainted.'

246

'I don't think that's true. Well, not entirely. Of course he's worried about your reputation and the effect any negative publicity will have on your career, but I honestly think he's concerned for your safety. That was why he sent me home with you. For extra security.'

'To spy on me, you mean?'

'Julia, I'm your friend. I would never betray you, and Mr Gold knows that.'

Julia swiped away her tears and turned her face to Sadie. 'Someone did, though. How the hell did *The Times* know about Chateau Marmont?'

'I don't know. Maybe you were seen there?'

'The article said "A source close to Miss Newman" . . . Oh my god.'

'What?'

'It's Vivienne. Vivienne spilt the beans.'

'Oh, Julia, she wouldn't.' Sadie shook her head vehemently. 'I can't believe she would do such a thing.'

It made perfect sense. 'Why? I mean, she slept with Peggy's boyfriend, so she clearly has no scruples. And I was the one who let the cat out of the bag. This is her way of paying me back for ratting her out to Peggy.'

Sadie looked unsure. 'Do you really think she'd stoop so low?'

'Clearly none of us knew Vivienne as well as we thought we did. And if it wasn't her, then who? You?'

'Of course not.'

'And as far as I'm aware, Peggy doesn't know specific details of our meetings. She asked me not to tell her and I didn't, unless . . .?'

'I haven't breathed a word. Not to anyone.'

'I wanted to believe that what happened between Mike and Vivienne was a one-time mistake – that he somehow caught her in a vulnerable moment, but now . . .' Her voice was shaky. 'Now, I realise the three of us were duped by her. I loved her, Sadie, and I was so grateful to her. But she was using us, the way she uses everyone. It suited her to have our friendship, but in the end she only cared about one person – herself.'

'Do you really think that's true? Viv loves us all. She's devastated about the falling out with Peggy. There's no way she'd want to make that worse.' Sadie's face drained of colour. 'Although . . .'

'Although what?' Julia demanded.

'It's just . . . well . . . I read something in her diary. I wasn't snooping, I promise. It fell off the nightstand and—'

'For god's sake, Sadie, I don't care why you saw it. What did it say?'

'It said . . .' Sadie bit her lip. 'Well, I can't remember the exact words, but she seemed angry at you for telling Peggy about what you saw and she said something about wishing you knew what it was like to feel public shame—'

'Oh my god! I knew it! See? It's exactly as I thought. Vivienne is our snake in the grass. The hide of her to blame me for her own terrible behaviour! But if she thinks this will break me, she's wrong. Charlie and I love each other. There's nothing anyone can do to tear us apart.'

Chapter 32

Sadie

When Sadie's alarm woke her from a restless night, her first thoughts were of Vivienne.

Sleeping with Mike was a terrible thing to do, but Sadie had thought perhaps Vivienne was too caught up in a moment of passion to think clearly. And she couldn't have known that they would be found out. She might have done the deed, but Sadie had been sure Vivienne hadn't deliberately set out to hurt Peggy. Now she really didn't know what to believe. Talking to the paper about Julia's relationship with Charlie was an act of pure spite, and the more Sadie thought about what she'd read in Viv's diary, the more convinced she was that Vivienne was responsible.

Even so, Vivienne would always have a piece of Sadie's heart. One day – if Viv had the courage to take responsibility for her actions and apologise for the pain she'd caused – maybe their friendship could be repaired. Right now, though, Sadie needed to focus on helping Julia through this crisis.

Not knowing if she was expected at the office or not, she decided to get ready just in case. Obviously, Harry would expect a report on Julia's state of mind, so she dressed quickly and made her way along the corridor to Julia's room and knocked gently on the door. When no answer came, she tried the doorknob but the door was locked.

She was probably still sleeping. Or maybe she'd gone down for breakfast. Please god, let that be the case. Harry would kill her if Julia had somehow managed to slip out of the club unnoticed. Although, Sadie guessed the security guard would have caught her if she'd tried to leave the building.

Sadie hurried downstairs to the dining area and was relieved when she spied Peggy at a table in the corner of the room. She raced over. 'How is she this morning?'

Peggy looked up from her breakfast. 'Still sleeping, and no wonder – she was up half the night crying.'

'Oh, thank goodness.'

'Thank goodness she was crying all night? I have to say that was no fun – for either of us.' Peggy frowned. 'I have huge bags under my eyes this morning and we're taping today.'

'I'm relieved she's still here, that's all. I was worried she'd try to sneak out after I left your room.'

'No, there was none of that. Although she did try to call Charlie twice last night – she bribed Trudie on reception to place the call, but he's not picking up.'

Sadie winced. 'That must be killing her.'

'I'd say he's been warned off. It breaks my heart to see her so distraught, but I did try to tell her. This is why being with Charlie wasn't a good idea, for either of them. She should have stopped it before it went too far.' Peggy sighed. 'Now they're in love with each other and I fear there's no future for them. Which is why, in this case, Harry Gold is right. They just need to keep away from one another so they don't end up with ruined careers as well as broken hearts.'

Sadie didn't think the issue was so cut and dried, but didn't want to argue with Peggy. She had more than enough drama to keep her busy at the moment. 'Peg, I hate to ask this, but can I borrow the key to your room while you're at work? I'm worried that she'll lock me out and I don't want her in there alone. I'm worried—'

'Say no more.' She pressed the key into Sadie's palm. 'Aren't you going to work today?'

'Actually, I don't know. Harry sent me home to keep an eye on Julia, but I'm not sure how long that is supposed to go on for. I'm going to call him soon to see what he wants me to do.'

'Right. Well, I have a show to tape. We were supposed to be having a bridesmaids' dinner tonight to discuss my wedding plans. I don't suppose that will happen now?'

Sadie's shoulders slumped. 'I don't think so. I mean, it seems a bit insensitive in light of the circumstances.'

'Far be it from me to take the limelight away from Queen Julia.'

'Oh, come on, Peg. She's heartbroken. I don't think it will kill you to refrain from talking about your wedding plans for a few days.'

Peggy's cheeks turned pink. 'I suppose you're right. It's just . . . well, I know this isn't strictly Julia's fault, and I feel childish even saying it, but . . .'

'What? Go on, spit it out.'

'I never seem to have a moment that's strictly about me. No matter what happens, either Julia or Vivienne ends up stealing my thunder somehow.'

Sadie stepped forward and took Peggy by the hand. 'Julia loves you and so do I. You will get your moment in the sun. In fact, it looks as if your time to truly shine has arrived. Julia is your friend, and she needs you to be there for her right now.'

Peggy nodded. 'You're right. I'm being a jerk. Sorry, I think I'm just tired. Of course I'll do my best to be understanding.'

'That's all I'm asking.'

Once Peggy left for work, Sadie made her way back to her room to place a call to Mr Gold. His wife answered their home phone and reported that he had left for the office an hour earlier – not a good sign. Sadie called Harry's direct line at the studio and he picked up almost immediately.

'What?' His tone was brusque.

'Mr Gold, it's Sadie. I'm just checking if you want me in the office today?'

'Sadie,' he said, his voice immediately softening. 'Thanks for calling. How is she?'

'She's sleeping right now. Her roommate reported that she cried all night, so I guess it might be some time before she wakes up.'

'Right. No need for her to come in today. In fact, she's not required for the rest of the week. I've told the director to focus on scenes where she's not needed. She can go back to work on Monday. In the meantime, if anyone asks, she's got a nasty head cold.'

'Okay. And me? Should I stay with her?'

Harry hesitated for a moment. 'I think that's best. But there are a few things I'd like you to work on from there if you can. I want you to look over some scripts for me and give me your notes on casting. There's also the costings for the sales conference to review. Perhaps you could come over and collect the documents while she's sleeping? We can talk more about the current situation when you get here. I don't want to say too much over the phone.'

Even though she was half an hour later than usual, Sadie arrived at the studio before the rest of the office staff. There was no one in reception and the typing pool was also empty, but as she opened her office door, she realised Mr Gold wasn't alone. The door to his office was slightly ajar and she could hear another male voice speaking. Sadie quietly slipped into the seat behind her desk and listened.

'In my experience these things don't just go away,' the voice said. 'It's best if we take action now. We need to make both of them see sense before this goes any further. Otherwise, you will be forced to sack her.'

Sadie's stomach clenched. Harry loved Julia. He would hate to have to let her go.

'Right,' Mr Gold said. 'So, you'll take care of him?'

'Yes, of course. I can speak to her too if you like?'

'No, let me deal with Julia. I'll leave the rest of it in your hands. Spare me the details.'

'Understood.'

Mr Gold's office door opened fully and the head of publicity, Walter Skinner, also known as The Fixer, stepped out, with Mr Gold behind him.

If Mr Skinner was surprised by Sadie's presence, he didn't show it. 'Good morning, Miss Shore.'

'Mr Skinner.' She nodded politely.

Mr Gold frowned. 'Sadie. How long have you been there?'

'I just got in,' she said.

'All right, good. Come into my office and I'll get you up to speed.' He turned to Walter Skinner once more. 'Thank you, Walter. I appreciate your help.'

'Of course, Harry. That's what I'm here for.'

Sadie followed her boss into his office, and he gestured for her to take a seat. 'Well, this is a damned mess, isn't it?'

'Is it? They love each other. Is that really so bad? I mean, why do people even care?'

Mr Gold scoffed. 'Truly, Sadie, you're not stupid. You know exactly why people care. Julia is a star. People love her. They think she's as pure as the driven snow. The thought of her cavorting with a Black man just isn't acceptable.'

A ball of frustration churned in Sadie's stomach. 'Charlie's a good man. A great man, in fact. He's kind and generous, extraordinarily talented and he makes Julia happy. Isn't that what counts?'

'Charlie Hudson might be all those things, but that's irrelevant. Julia is a star and the public won't stand for it. I don't make the rules, I'm just abiding by them. Now the press has got wind of it, I have no choice but to intervene. I'm trying to protect her – protect them both, in fact – from what could happen if we don't stamp out this speculation right away.'

'What are you going to do?'

'Let me worry about that. In the meantime, I want you to keep a close eye on her. She mustn't see him. Right now we still have plausible deniability, but god forbid that the press get a photo of them together now. If that happens we'll be screwed.'

'I can't physically stop her from leaving the building.'

'You can let me know if she tries to see him. You're her friend. She'll tell you her plans. You report back to me and I'll take care of the rest.'

'I'm not spying on my friend, Mr Gold.'

'For god's sake, Sadie, this isn't a game. You get that, right? Some people take this sort of thing to heart. There are crazy people out there who are all too happy to take matters into their own hands. Julia's life could be in danger. You're not spying on her; you're helping to keep her safe.'

Sadie didn't trust herself to answer. She wasn't sure that tattling on Julia was something she could do. Was Mr Gold overstating the situation to get his own way? She wasn't completely naive; she'd seen plenty of racially motivated acts of violence on the news. But those things happened in other places. California was different. People were open-minded here. There would be gossip, no doubt, but surely Julia and Charlie weren't in any real danger? Mr Gold must be trying to scare her.

At this point all she wanted to do was get the files she needed and get back to the club before Julia woke up, so she nodded her agreement. 'I'll just grab the documents and I'll be out of here. You can reach me at the club if necessary.'

'Wait a minute. There's something else I'd like you to do for me. You're friendly with that reporter fellow, Porter, aren't you?'

'Jack?' She hesitated for a moment. Where was he going with this? 'Sure – I mean, I guess. He dated one of my friends for a while.'

Harry scratched his chin. 'Maybe you could call him and get him to meet with you. See what he knows.'

'What do you mean, exactly? The story is already in the papers. What else is there to know?'

'Plenty. The source quoted in the paper is nameless. The photo of them together is an old one. I need to know if any of the reporters have more. If someone is sitting on a bomb and just biding their time until they light the fuse. That Porter boy seems to have his finger on the pulse. If there are more photos out there, or anything else incriminating, he's bound to know or be able to find out.'

'Even if he does know, what makes you think he'll disclose anything to me?'

He smirked. 'You're a pretty girl, Sadie. I'm sure you'll figure something out.'

Heat crept into her cheeks. She was used to sex being used as currency in this town, but Mr Gold had always behaved in such a gentlemanly way towards her that hearing him speak like this shocked her. Was this why he hadn't read her screenplay? Was she expected to offer some sort of *enticement* before he would do her the courtesy of taking a look? She pushed the thought from her mind. Now wasn't the time to be thinking about her own ambitions.

'I can't guarantee anything, but I'll give Jack a call and see what I can do.'

'That's my girl. I knew I could count on you.' He beamed. 'Now, I don't want you to worry about any of this. Julia will be fine as long as she does as she's told. This whole thing will blow over in a few days. Just you wait and see.'

'And Charlie? Will he be fine too?'

The smile disappeared from his face and was replaced with a steely expression. 'What happens to Charlie Hudson is not my responsibility.'

❧

Back at the Studio Club, Sadie dumped the scripts on her bed and kicked off her shoes. If she was working from home, she might as well be comfortable. She changed into capri pants and a short-sleeve sweater, before pulling her mop of curls up into a high ponytail. She was about to head down the hall to check on Julia when her telephone rang.

'Hello.'

'Is that you, Sadie?' Trudie's voice came through the receiver.

'It is.'

'I have Jack Porter on the phone for you.'

'Thanks, Trudie. You can put him through.'

Seconds later Jack's voice was on the line. 'Sadie.'

'Hi, Jack. Thanks for getting back to me so quickly.' She'd left a message with his office just before departing the studio and barely half an hour had passed since then.

'Of course. How can I help?'

This was definitely not something that could be spoken about over the phone. For all she knew Trudie could still be on the line, listening in. 'Jack, I need to speak to you in person if I can. Perhaps you could come here to the club for coffee.'

'Say no more. I'll be there in half an hour.'

Despite everything, she smiled at the thought of seeing him and then immediately chastised herself. Jack wasn't interested in her and she had to get over this silly infatuation. Still, knowing he was on his way helped her to feel a little less anxious.

Scooping up the documents, she made her way down the hall to check on Julia. She knocked softly on the door and when there was no answer, she used Peggy's key to let herself in.

Julia sat up and looked at her through red-rimmed eyes. 'What time is it?'

Sadie perched on the end of her bed. 'It's only just past nine. Don't worry. They're not expecting you at the studio. Mr Gold told the director you won't be back until next week.'

'Harry!' Julia spat. 'Don't talk to me about that bastard.'

Sadie rubbed her leg. 'I know you hate him right now, but he's only trying to protect you.'

'From what? From the love of my life?'

'You know what people can be like, Jules. It's not right, but there's still so much prejudice towards mixed-race relationships. Mr Gold doesn't want to see you get hurt.'

'People have no business making judgements about my private life. I will not be told who I can and cannot date. If Harry doesn't like that he can sack me. I don't care!'

Sadie exhaled slowly. There was no point arguing with Julia about this. She was right – people should mind their own business. But it seemed unlikely that anyone would.

256

'Has he called? Left messages for me?' Julia asked, her voice softer and more tentative now.

'Mr Gold?'

'Charlie, of course.'

'Not that I know of. But you should check with the girls on reception.'

'Yes. I will. He must have called by now. I left messages for him everywhere yesterday.'

'He's probably just trying to lie low for the moment. Maybe he doesn't want to risk bringing you any more negative attention. He'll find a way to get in touch when he can. I'm sure of it.'

'Yes, you're probably right.' Julia's forehead creased in confusion for a moment. 'If it's after nine, what are you still doing here? You usually leave for work at the crack of dawn.' Her eyes narrowed. 'Has Harry sent you to babysit me?'

'No, nothing like that. I was worried about you – Peg said you didn't sleep much last night, so I went in early and brought home some work I can do here.' The lie churned Sadie's stomach.

'Oh,' Julia said, accepting her explanation at face value. 'That was sweet of you, but you really shouldn't have bothered. I'm just going to check my messages and then go back to sleep if I can.'

'That's okay. I have things to do anyway. I'll be working downstairs in the living room if you need me. If I don't see you, I'll check on you around lunchtime.'

Julia lay back on her pillow, which Sadie took as her cue to leave.

She went downstairs to wait for Jack. The living area was completely empty. Most of the girls had already left the club to go to work, except for those such as Trudie, who were employed at the club itself. Meeting Jack somewhere more private, such as the writers' room off the library, would be preferable, but there was no way Miss McGovern would approve of that. She'd just have to be careful that she and Jack weren't overheard. With this in mind, she chose an armchair facing the entrance so she'd have a view of anyone coming into the room and settled in to look at the first script Harry had given her.

She'd barely read a page when Trudie showed Jack in.

'Sadie, how are you?' There was a concerned expression on his face. 'I came as soon as I could.'

As she stood to greet him, her traitorous stomach turned somersaults. *Stop it.* Jack was just being a good friend, nothing more. He took her hand and then leant in to awkwardly kiss her cheek. Trudie was still standing behind him and this display of affection caused her to raise an eyebrow. She winked at Sadie. 'I guess I'll leave you two to it.'

'Would you like a coffee, Jack? I can go into the dining room and make us one.'

'No, I'm fine, thanks. Just a little worried about you. You're not at work and your message said it was urgent we meet. What's going on, Sadie? Are you all right?'

She took her seat and beckoned for him to sit on the couch opposite. 'I'm fine, truly. It's Julia I'm worried about.'

A look of understanding settled on his face. 'Ah.'

'So you've seen the story?'

'I think everyone in Hollywood, if not the country, has seen it by now.'

Sadie sighed. 'Right. Well, Mr Gold wanted me to ask you if there's more.'

'What do you mean?'

'What does the press know? Are there more photos to come? More tell-alls from guests at Chateau Marmont?'

'Not that I'm aware of. I mean, there have been rumours of an affair for a while now, but nothing concrete. If anyone had any more than what was published yesterday, you can bet your bottom dollar they would have run it by now.'

'Well. Mr Gold will be pleased to hear that. He figures Julia can deny the story and, provided no new evidence comes to light, that it'll all die down pretty quickly.'

'Harry's probably right about that – so long as they're not seen together again.'

258

'Yes, well, that might be an issue.' Sadie paused. 'They're in love. Julia's prepared to throw away her career to be with Charlie.'

'And he feels the same way?'

'I guess. I don't really know. She hasn't heard from him since the story was published.'

'Sheesh. Although I can't say I blame the guy. Continuing the relationship carries a big risk for him.'

'Mr Gold said much the same thing . . .' A vision of Walter Skinner leaving Harry's office flashed before her eyes and a chill crept down her spine.

'Sadie? Are you okay? You look pale. Let me fetch you a glass of water.' Jack went to stand but she put out her hand to stop him.

'I'm fine. It's just . . . well, I'm worried about Charlie. This morning when I went into the studio, Mr Gold kept going on about what a dangerous situation this is for Julia. When I talked about Charlie, he was dismissive.'

'I suppose that's understandable. He's got a lot invested in Julia's success. Charlie's not important to him.'

'Yes. It's just that, well . . . this morning I overheard him talking to Walter Skinner.'

'Oh?' Jack looked at her intently. 'What were they saying?'

'He asked Mr Skinner if he would take care of Charlie. I thought he just meant speak to Charlie about the situation, but now . . .'

'Yeah, I see where you're going.'

A wave of nausea hit her. 'No . . . Mr Gold wouldn't suggest such a thing. Would he? I mean, he can be a bit of a grump at times, but underneath all his bluster he's a good man. I'm just over-dramatising.'

Jack reached across and squeezed her hand. 'Maybe. But I'll look into it. See what I can find out.'

'Oh, would you? That would make me feel a whole lot better.'

'I keep telling you, Sadie, I'll do anything for you.'

For a moment Sadie thought he was serious, but then he winked as he stood up to take his leave.

'Thanks, Jack. You're a good friend.'

Chapter 33

Julia

Two days had passed since the story had broken and there was still no word from Charlie. Julia couldn't stop crying. Where *was* he? Why wouldn't he take her calls? Today, just like yesterday, she'd barely moved from her bed. Sadie had tried to get her to come downstairs for a meal or even just a coffee, but she'd refused and Sadie, her kind face creased with worry, had resorted to bringing her meals up on a tray. Not that she'd eaten any of them. For the first time in years, Julia wasn't hungry.

Now Sadie had gone out for dinner with Jack, and Peggy had taken over trying to coax her out of bed. 'Jules, please. Get dressed and come downstairs for dinner. It's not healthy to be cooped up in here for hours on end. Sadie says you've barely moved since I left this morning.'

'I can't. What if Charlie calls? I need to be here to pick up the phone. If the girls have to put him on hold while they fetch me from the dining room he might hang up.'

Peggy gave her a pitying look. 'You can't spend the rest of your life in here waiting for him to call. What if he never does?'

Julia shuddered. The thought was too much to bear. 'Of course he will. Charlie loves me. He must be feeling just as terrible as I am.

There must be a reason he hasn't been in touch. Somebody is stopping him. But Charlie will find a way, I just know it.'

'Jules,' Peggy said, gently, 'it's been two days already. It might be time to face up to the fact that it's over. Nobody likes Charlie more than me, but if you recall, I did warn you that it wasn't a good idea to get involved with him. He's wonderful and so are you, but it's simply not feasible for the two of you to be a couple. The world doesn't work that way.'

'Well, maybe it should. It's the 1950s, for heaven's sake, not the 1800s. It's up to people like me and Charlie to change things. Go away, Peg. I just want to be alone.' Julia turned to face the wall and pulled the covers up under her chin.

She heard Peggy sigh as she left the room.

It was dark when she woke to Sadie calling her name. Why wouldn't they all just leave her be? At least when she was sleeping the pain disappeared for a while. She reluctantly sat up and rubbed the sleep from her eyes. 'What?'

'Wake up, Jules. I've got something for you.' Sadie reached for the bedside lamp and switched it on.

'Is it from Charlie? Did you see him? Is he here?'

'No, Jules, he's not here and I haven't seen him.' Sadie put her hand on Julia's leg. 'But he got this message to Jack, who passed it on to me.' Sadie handed her a sealed envelope.

Her heart lifted. She knew it! Charlie would never abandon her. He had promised her they would find a way to be together, no matter what, and she believed him.

With trembling hands, she tore open the envelope and pulled out a single folded page. Charlie's beautiful handwritten words danced before her and she scanned them quickly, eager to know his plan for their future.

My darling Julia,
I love you like I have never loved another. I love you more than I
love myself, so please believe me when I say I write this letter with
a broken heart.

I know I promised you we would always be together, but I realise now I was in no position to make such a claim.

What? How could he be saying this? It couldn't be true.

The promises I made were the wishful thoughts of a boy, not a man, and I had no right to make them. My remorse at causing you pain is endless. I'm so sorry that I could not keep my word, but I have come to understand that as beautiful as our love is, it's now time to let it go.

My darling, ours was a perfect union and I will treasure the memory of it always, but now it must end. There can be no going back. If there were any other way, I promise you I would find it, but for both our sakes this must be the end. I know it won't seem that way right now, but this is for the best. One day, I hope you will understand that I am making this choice because of my love for you. I can't bear to think of you living a life of shame.

Please don't try to contact me. I fear if I see you I'll break my resolve and in the end that will just cause you more grief. It will be easier on us both if this letter is our final goodbye.

I will love you always.
Your Charlie xx

The pain in her chest took her breath away and she began to pant, trying to suck in some much-needed air. This must be a nightmare, because there was no way Charlie would leave her. It just wasn't possible.

'Julia, honey, big breaths,' Sadie said. She rubbed Julia's back. 'Breathe with me. Come on: in, two, three, four. Out, two, three, four.'

Sadie's hypnotic voice somehow cut through Julia's whirring thoughts, and she began to comply. When she was calmer, Sadie asked, 'What is it? What did he say?'

Julia handed her the letter and watched her eyes scan the words, hoping that Sadie would explain that she was reading it wrong, or that Charlie was actually writing in code so his intentions wouldn't be discovered. When Sadie looked up at her with sorrowful eyes and said, 'Oh, Jules, I'm so sorry,' Julia's composure crumbled.

A wailing noise filled the room, and when Sadie took her in her arms and began to rock and shush her, Julia realised the howling was coming from deep inside her own body. It was the sound of her heart shattering.

What happened next was a blur. At some point Peggy arrived with a cup of tea and a glass of sherry, which she forced Julia to down. When the first glass was gone, Peggy poured her another. As the liquid burnt her throat and warmed her belly, she heard Peggy and Sadie talking, maybe even arguing, but she had no idea what they were saying. Nor did she care. There was nothing worth caring about now. Without Charlie, what was the point of anything? The alcohol was starting to make her feel fuzzy around the edges and even though she knew it wouldn't last, the pain in her chest loosened a little. She held out the empty glass for one of the others to fill. She needed to wipe herself out.

Peggy went to pour her another, but Sadie intervened. 'Whoa, hang on a minute, Peg, we don't want her getting drunk.'

'Why not?' Julia demanded. 'At least if I'm drunk I might forget about this ache in my heart. I don't want to feel anything.'

'Honey, you don't want to make yourself sick. You haven't eaten anything all day. The last thing you need is to wake up tomorrow with a hangover.'

'What I *need* is to speak to Charlie,' Julia wailed. 'Unless you can make that happen, pour me another drink.'

Sadie sat on the bed and put her arm around Julia's shoulders. 'Do you really think that's a good idea? I know it's hard, but maybe Charlie's right.'

'I don't believe he doesn't want me anymore. Someone made him write that letter. I won't believe otherwise until I hear it from his lips.'

'I don't blame you,' Peggy said, putting the bottle of sherry down on the nightstand. 'If he wants to end the relationship, he should at least have the gumption to tell you in person.'

'Peggy!' Sadie admonished. 'Why would you say such a thing?'

Defiance flared in Peggy's eyes. 'Because I know what it's like to have the rug pulled from under you. When Vivienne betrayed me the way she did, I thought I would die. I needed to hear from Mike's own lips what had happened and why. You both know I have never supported this relationship, and I'm not surprised to see it ending in tears. But that doesn't mean that I'm happy about it.' Her expression softened. 'Truly, I'm not. I hate to see you like this, Jules.' She shifted her gaze to Sadie then. 'At the very least, Charlie should pay Julia the courtesy of ending it in person.'

Sadie scowled at her. 'It's not quite as simple as that, though, is it? Right now, there's no way for them to see each other. Harry has a security guard parked outside.' She turned to face Julia. 'And it's not just Harry's people watching you, Jules. There's been a pack of reporters hanging around outside all day. Most of them seem to have given up, but who knows how many of them are stalking Charlie instead? If you go to Charlie's hotel you'll be caught for sure.'

'I don't care. How could being caught make things any worse than they are right now? If I can just see Charlie, maybe I can talk some sense into him.'

'I'll take you,' Peggy said.

Mike's engagement present to Peggy, and clearly part of his campaign to make amends, had come in the form of a convertible Ford Thunderbird. Julia had secretly vowed never to sit inside that car, hideous bribe that it was, but now, faced with the choice between upholding her principles and seeing Charlie, she felt she had no choice but to accept the offer.

'You're a true friend, Peg.'

'Peggy, please, this is madness. I know you think you're helping, but consider the consequences if the two of you are caught!'

'I guess we'll just have to make sure that doesn't happen.'

༄

It was a few minutes after midnight when Julia and Peggy slipped quietly out of the club's back entrance and into Peggy's new car. Once Sadie realised she wasn't going to change their minds, she'd insisted that Julia disguise herself to avoid any attention. Julia had complied to keep her happy.

'We won't get caught,' Peggy had vowed. 'No one will be expecting Julia to leave at that hour, and I still have my key so we won't have any problems getting back in. Nobody will know unless you tell, Sadie.'

'I won't. But I wouldn't be so sure about getting away with this.' Sadie had looked grim.

Julia had squeezed her friend's hand. 'I know you think this is crazy, but I have to do it. Maybe Charlie will look me in the eye and say it's over. But I can't accept it until I see him. You understand that, don't you?'

Sadie had nodded. 'Just be careful.'

'You're sure Charlie's still at Marmont?' Peggy asked.

'According to Jack he's holed up there, waiting for this to blow over,' Sadie said.

Peggy looked resolute. 'Good. Well, you should go about your business as usual and head off to bed early. That way you can deny knowing anything about this if we do get caught – which we won't!'

Now, as the bright lights of Sunset Boulevard flashed past, Peggy took her eyes off the road momentarily to look at Julia. 'Are you okay?'

Julia was anything but okay. What happened in the next few minutes would determine the rest of her life. Would everything be fine, just as Charlie had promised her the last time he'd held her in his arms? Or would he stand by the letter? Unable to trust herself to speak, she nodded.

'We're nearly there,' Peggy said. 'I think you should duck down so you can't easily be seen. Just in case.'

Julia nodded again and slid down in her seat right away.

A couple of minutes later, the car jerked to a stop – Peggy wasn't the greatest driver – and the engine was shut off. 'I don't think anyone has seen us,' Peggy said, 'but let me go to the door, just in case. Stay down until I let you know the coast is clear.'

Julia heard the knock at the door and the murmur of hushed voices. Charlie was here! She sat up in her seat and opened the car door as quickly as she could. Peggy turned towards her and seemed to be shaking her head. It was hard to be sure in the dark. Julia ran to the door, only to be confronted by Arthur, a member of Charlie's band.

'Julia, I'm sorry. He's not here.' Arthur's muscular frame filled the doorway, blocking her access to the bungalow.

'Let me in, Artie. I just want to talk to him.'

'I told you, he's not here.' Still, Arthur stepped aside and gestured for her to come inside. 'Be my guest,' he said.

Julia raced in and ran from room to room, calling Charlie's name. Arthur was telling the truth. She went back to the living room and found Arthur and Peggy standing there. 'Where is he?' she demanded.

'You can't see him, Julia. It's not safe – for you or for him. Charlie is just trying to protect you. You're his top priority. He keeps saying he will never forgive himself if something happens to you.'

Despite everything, Julia's heart lightened a little at Arthur's words. Charlie still loved her! There was hope.

'Maybe, Julia,' Arthur said, his voice gentle, 'you should think a little about Charlie.'

She stared at him, not comprehending. 'All I ever think about is Charlie.'

'He's worried about your safety, but really *he's* the one at risk here.'

'Charlie's the bravest man I know,' she said petulantly. 'He's not afraid of what people say.'

Arthur hesitated for a moment and then walked to the bedroom. 'Wait there,' he called over his shoulder.

She looked at Peggy, who simply shrugged.

'I didn't want to have to show you this,' Arthur said, holding up an envelope. 'Charlie would kill me if he knew. I took it while he was sleeping a couple of days ago. I knew he'd never agree to me snapping him looking like this, but I wanted evidence in case . . .'

'In case of what?' Julia asked.

'In case of worse to come.' He handed her the envelope.

Inside was a photograph. It took Julia a moment to grasp what she was seeing – Charlie, but not looking at all like himself. His beautiful face was all banged up. She gasped and clasped her hand to her mouth as the photo fluttered to the floor.

Peggy bent to retrieve it, and a shocked expression came over her face as she looked at the image. Arthur held out his hand and she handed the photo back to him. 'Who did this?'

'Thugs sent by people who stand to lose something if Charlie keeps dating a white woman.' Arthur stared into Julia's eyes. 'This was just a warning. Threats were made against Charlie's life, and yours. But not just that. They've threatened to hurt Charlie's family – his mom and dad, his sister and even her kids. These people mean business, Julia. If you truly love Charlie as much as you say you do, you'll leave him be.'

31 December 1999

Peggy's car pulls up in front of the house around lunchtime. Have I done the right thing by insisting that she and Julia come all this way? I think when they see Vivienne the way she is, and when they discover the truth of what happened to her, they'll find room in their hearts to forgive her. Tomorrow is the beginning of the new millennium, and I'm hoping we can leave all our past hurts behind in the old one.

I step outside onto the upstairs deck and wave, so they know they have the right place. Peggy toots the horn in response.

I go back inside and find Vivienne looking worried. 'It's okay. It's just our visitors – Peggy and Julia. They've arrived.'

She smiles but seems confused. 'Peggy and Julia,' she repeats slowly.

'They're here for lunch,' I say. 'Why don't you set the table for four people, and I'll go down and help them with their things. Is that okay?'

She nods. 'Of course! I can set the table. I love entertaining!'

I've prepared Vivienne as best I can for their arrival. Last night, we went through the diaries together, laughing at the photos of us as girls and reminiscing about the good times we had. As we talked about the club, Vivienne seemed to understand that I am the same Sadie as the girl in her photos. Of course, this morning she's forgotten again, but I'm optimistic that if the four of us sit down and go through the pages she wrote all those years ago, Vivienne might understand who we are – at least in the moment. But I need to explain everything to the others first.

I know now why George thought it was so important for Vivienne to tell her story. The world has done Vivienne a great injustice. And we, her so-called friends, were the worst offenders. Now it's time to make that right. I only hope Peggy and Julia will see things the same way I do.

I race down the outdoor stairs to the carport and beckon for Peggy to bring her car up behind mine. She parks and the two of them get out of the car, both visibly surprised by the chilly conditions.

Julia hugs herself and rubs her arms. 'Good god, it's freezing here. It was quite mild at home.'

I kiss her cheek. 'It's toasty inside. You'll warm up in no time.'

Julia eyes the house suspiciously. 'Is Vivienne here?'

I nod as Peggy comes over to hug me. 'She's setting the table for lunch.'

Peggy walks to the rear of the car and pops the trunk. 'I didn't know what you'd have here, but I brought some supplies.' She hands me a basket filled with bottles of champagne and wine, an assortment of cheese, bread and some condiments.

'You didn't have to do that. We have plenty of food.'

'If I'm going to be stuck here for the last New Year's Eve of the century, I need to have a few indulgences.'

'Thank you for coming. I promise you I wouldn't have asked if I didn't think it was important.'

'In the whole time I've known you, Sadie, I can't ever remember you asking me for anything. We've always said we would do anything for each other, and you've certainly been there for me when I've needed you,' Peggy says.

Julia nods. 'I have to be honest, Sadie, I didn't want to come. But I knew you wouldn't have asked us unless you truly believed it was important. I'm here for you, not *her*.' She lifts her eyes to the second storey. 'And I can't promise that I can even speak to that woman.'

'I understand, but you have to realise her memory has gone. She's quite fragile. You'll see what I mean in a moment. All I ask is that you try your best to be tolerant and patient. I have something to share with you that changes everything we thought we knew about Vivienne, but I can't show you when she's present. She's likely to have a nap this afternoon and then we can talk freely. Please try to be kind to her, at least until then.'

'I'll do my best.' Julia shivers. 'But honestly, I don't think there's anything you can say that will make me change my mind about Vivienne. I've had decades to think about what happened and the more I mull over it, the more convinced I am that Vivienne did not care one iota about me or any of us. She took her anger out on me without any thought to the real consequences her actions would have on me, or Charlie.'

'I don't think—'

'Let me finish. She had form. I knew she slept with Sam Hayden to get that part, but I excused her. That was the first sign of her ruthlessness. We should have known better.'

'There are things you don't know—' I begin, but Peggy cuts me off.

'Can we not do this out here?' she says. 'Let's go inside before I freeze to death.'

'Yes, of course,' I say. 'Grab your bags and follow me.'

❧

I'm not sure if Vivienne notices the tension in the air over lunch, but to me it's obvious. There are awkward silences in between snatches of small talk. Julia hasn't spoken a word since we sat down to eat, but Peggy is at least trying. She answers my questions about their journey here with as much enthusiasm as she can muster.

'It was a nice drive and reasonably quiet on the roads today, so we made good time. The scenery along the way was just breathtaking.' She looks at Vivienne. 'How long have you lived here?'

Vivienne turns to me for the answer, and I smile at her encouragingly. 'You came here a few years after you left the Studio Club, didn't you?'

'Yes, that's right.' She nods. 'In my van.'

'A van,' Peggy says. 'Were you travelling?'

Vivienne's brow creases. 'Yes. I went to a place at the beach for a while but people there bothered me. I wanted to disappear. I wanted to be me, not Hollywood Vivienne. I wanted that girl to be gone.' She balls her fists and then opens them quickly, as if to demonstrate herself disappearing. 'But people there took photos and always called out my name. So I bought the van and travelled all over the country. I got jobs here and there – waitressing, cleaning and even working as a farmhand for a while – until eventually I ended up in Three Rivers and George found me.'

'Your partner?' Peggy asks and Vivienne nods.

'Maybe you could find a photo of George for Peggy.'

Vivienne jumps up. 'Yes! There's one in my room.'

'This is George's house,' I say while Vivienne is out of the room. 'She left it to Viv in her will. But that's all there is. Vivienne hasn't worked properly since she left LA. She's had odd jobs here and there, but nothing substantial until she moved here and started working in the shelter. George was a vet, and she and Viv ran a sanctuary for injured and unwanted animals. The vet practice and the shelter were still in operation when George died.'

'And Vivienne couldn't manage it on her own?' Peggy asks.

'No,' I say. 'It seems her illness was quite advanced by the time her partner died. Which explains why April left Vivienne in our care.'

'*Your* care,' Julia says. 'You can't expect me to take responsibility for that woman. That's too much to ask.'

Vivienne comes back with a framed photo of George holding a baby goat and hands it to Peggy, who smiles warmly. 'She looks lovely.'

Vivienne returns Peggy's smile. 'She is. You'll see.' Her brow suddenly creases as she stares intently at Peggy. A look of recognition settles on her face and she suddenly begins to sing. '*Swish, swish, swish, you swam into my life. You're all I ever wanted, please say you'll be my Mermaid Wife...*'

Peggy's mouth drops open. 'You remembered!'

'You look like her. The Mermaid Wife. She was my friend, you know. Before she was famous. But I always knew she would be a star. She was so talented and so determined. I always knew. Always.'

Peggy's eyes shine, and the needy girl she once was makes an appearance. 'Vivienne,' she says softly, 'that means the world to me. Did you watch the show?'

Vivienne laughs. 'Of course! It's my favourite. I've seen every episode more than once. George laughs at me. She always says, "Why are you watching this? You know every word by heart!" and she's right, I do! But I just love it.'

Julia pushes her plate away and looks at me. 'Thank you for lunch. I might go for a walk.'

I glance at Peggy, willing her to follow my lead. 'I'll come with you, if Vivienne doesn't mind clearing up alone.'

'I can help Vivienne,' Peggy says, with a smile.

Good old Peg. She hasn't let me down yet. 'Did you bring a coat, Jules?'

Julia nods. 'Peggy said you'd told her we should pack warm clothes. I had to drag an old coat from the back of my closet. I haven't worn a winter coat in years.'

'I know what you mean. It didn't even occur to me to bring a weatherproof jacket.' I look at Vivienne. 'Can I borrow your coat? The one hanging in the laundry room?'

She nods. 'Of course.'

I beckon for Julia to follow me downstairs. In the laundry room I find the coat and some woollen gloves, which I offer to Julia before we head out.

We walk along the road, towards the town, which I figure is the safest route seeing as neither of us knows the area. We don't speak for a little while, both seemingly content to breathe in the crisp mountain air and enjoy the scenery.

After a few minutes, Julia breaks the silence. 'I don't think this is going to work. When we get back, I might get Peggy to drop me in town. There must be a motel I can stay at for the night.'

272

'What? No, Julia, please, I haven't had a chance to show you the diary. That's why I dragged you here. I have Vivienne's journal, and it explains what happened between her and Mike. And other things too. I really think you'll feel differently when you know the truth.'

Julia sighs. 'What possible excuse can she have for the things she did? I loved her once, but she betrayed Peggy and then me. I know you feel badly for her and I understand that. She's not the person she once was, but – and maybe this makes me a terrible human being – it doesn't change anything for me. I can't just forget what she did, how she hurt me. I shouldn't have come here. I'm sorry.'

'Julia, please. Just give me a couple of hours. Vivienne will most likely be asleep when we get back. I can show you what I mean. It will explain a lot of what happened and why she made the choices she did. And if you still feel the same way, I will drive you to a motel myself.'

'Okay, okay . . .' Julia rubs a gloved hand over her face. 'A couple of hours but no more. I'll read your "evidence" if I must. But that's it. You have to promise to let it go after that.'

'I will.' The wind has picked up and needles of fine rain sting my face. 'Should we go back now?'

'Might as well get it over with.' She laughs – a thin, high-pitched sound, unlike her usual warm, throaty expressions of mirth. 'My god, Sadie, I never thought anything could be worse than suffering through another one of Tony's interminably boring New Year's Eve parties, but I've got to hand it to you – you've trumped him this year.'

I sock her in the arm. 'Poor Tony. You really should be nicer to him. You're lucky to have him in your life.'

She stops smiling and looks thoughtful. 'Yeah, you're right. I take him for granted sometimes and I shouldn't. That man gave me everything I ever wanted. If not for him, Jeweltone Productions would never have been the success that it is. And we *were* happy for many years. Maybe we weren't "in love", but we really did care about each other. Still do.'

'Do you think he's happy now?'

'Oh, yes, he's head over heels in love with Maureen. It's beautiful to see. He deserves it.'

273

'What about you, Jules? Would you ever marry again?'

'There was only ever one man for me, and he's gone now.'

I put my arm around her shoulders and squeeze. Of course, she's talking about Charlie. He died two years ago of cancer. He called for her on his deathbed and she raced to his side. They managed to see each other one final time, but instead of bringing Julia peace, being with Charlie reignited her grief and anger at what they had both lost. No wonder she can't find it in her heart to forgive Vivienne.

Chapter 34

Sadie

After the headlines announced Charlie's secret marriage to Black singer Annette Davis on the first day of his European tour, Mr Gold told Sadie it was time for Julia to get back to work.

Julia had other ideas. 'I can't, Sadie. I just can't. I need more time. Make my excuses, will you?'

Sadie nodded. 'Of course.' Despite her concern that Julia was still struggling to get out of bed most days, in some ways it would be better if Julia wasn't on set today. Sadie had things she wanted to say to Mr Gold and it was probably best for Julia if she wasn't anywhere near the studio when Sadie took him to task.

Last week, after Julia and Peggy had returned from their late-night visit to Chateau Marmont, Peggy had crept down the passage to Sadie's room to let her know they were home. In urgent whispers, Peggy told her about the photo of Charlie and the threats that had accompanied it, and a wave of nausea washed through Sadie as she recalled Walter Skinner's words.

For the next few days she'd stewed over the snatches of conversation she'd overheard at the office, all the time trying to convince herself she was overthinking things and that of course Mr Gold, the boss she'd admired for so long, couldn't possibly have anything to do with the violence against Charlie. But last night Jack had come to visit her.

He'd waited downstairs in the reception room and insisted on taking her for dinner at Musso and Frank's – the very place where Sadie had first met Mr Gold. It could have been a pleasant evening, almost like a date, except that what Jack had to say wasn't pleasant at all.

'Charlie left the country a few days ago. He's been receiving death threats. He was told to put distance between himself and Julia, or else . . .' Jack said, between forkfuls of pasta.

'I know.' Sadie glanced around the restaurant, to see if there was anyone she recognised taking notice of them. She understood now why Jack had chosen this place for their meeting. The design of the booths made it hard to see or hear the other diners, a fact she was thankful for, not least of all because she wasn't really dressed to dine in such a fancy setting.

'How do you know that?'

She leant closer to Jack across the candlelit table and quietly recounted how Peggy and Julia had slipped out of the Studio Club in the middle of the night in the hope of seeing Charlie.

Jack raised his eyebrows.

'I know, I know. It was a stupid idea, but they went ahead anyway. Charlie wasn't there but his bandmate Arthur was. Arthur told them what was happening and showed them a photo. Charlie had been badly beaten.'

'Yeah, that's what I've heard too.'

'Who would do such a thing?'

A strange expression settled on Jack's face, a mix of pity and incredulity. 'Sadie, I think you know the answer to that already.'

'I really don't,' she said, hoping with all her heart that what she was imagining could not possibly be true.

'Every lead I followed led me back to Walter Skinner.'

Sadie pushed away her barely touched plate of spaghetti, her churning stomach unable to cope with another bite. She would have bet her life that Mr Gold, curmudgeonly though he was, would never truly harm another person. 'Really? Are you sure?'

'Please trust me, Sadie. I can't reveal my sources, but they're solid. In any case, it's not safe for me to tell you more. The less you know, the better.'

'I can't believe it.' As soon as the words left her mouth she knew they weren't true. Jack wasn't lying. She didn't *want* to believe it, but it was a fact. If she was honest with herself, the signs of Harry Gold's true character had been there all along, she'd simply chosen not to see them. His gentlemanly treatment of her and the other women who worked in his office had made him seem like a beacon of morality, especially when compared to the other executives who employed the casting couch openly and thought nothing of manhandling the women in the typing pool.

Of course, he had affairs; no one knew that better than Sadie. After all, she was the one entrusted with making covert hotel bookings and sending flowers and jewellery to his latest love interest. Sadie hadn't approved of this but comforted herself with the knowledge that Mr Gold was discreet – not to mention that if the rumours she heard were correct, Sylvia Gold had plenty of her own dalliances. She figured the Golds' marriage was their business, not hers. But Harry's ruthlessness in pursuing what he wanted – stars from other studios, scriptwriters or directors – should have tipped her off that there was more to him than just a man who was good at his job. She'd long admired his drive and ambition – his sheer bloody-mindedness had helped him achieve the impossible – but she should have realised that there were consequences of that behaviour.

And when she really thought about it, what sort of a man turned a blind eye to the appalling behaviour of his executives? Harry might not abuse the women who worked in his office, but he was no doubt aware of what was going on around him. Wasn't that just as bad? Because Harry had the power to stop it if he wanted. He was the boss. What he said was law at Goldstar.

Shame warmed Sadie's cheeks. She'd worked at Goldstar for years now, and apart from giving new employees a quiet word about which directors or executives to avoid being alone with, she hadn't done anything to change the work environment either. Sadie had been blinded by her own ambition. She'd so badly wanted Goldstar to produce her screenplay she'd allowed herself to excuse Harry Gold's abuse of power, pretending that it was simply the way Hollywood worked.

Not anymore.

After Jack escorted her home, she'd gone to the writers' room and thought carefully about her next move. What was she even doing working as a personal secretary? She'd come to Hollywood to be a writer, not to make coffee. Sure, she'd learnt a lot about the business by working at the studio, but how much more did she really need to know to write a good script? The job was so time consuming that her writing had suffered and she'd only managed to complete one project in the whole time she'd been out here. She'd originally hoped that working for Harry would help get her screenplay produced, but as far as she knew he hadn't even glanced at her script yet.

It didn't take her long to come to a decision.

Now, as she made her way to the studio, her resolve to do the right thing was strong. She wasn't foolish enough to think that her actions would change much, but she could no longer stand by and be a silent witness to the misdeeds this studio condoned.

Harry was already in his office when she arrived, which was hardly surprising seeing as she'd come in an hour and a half later than usual. Despite her tardiness, Harry beamed when he saw her. 'You're here at last! We've missed you, Sadie. Come in. We have a lot to discuss.'

Sadie didn't return his smile. 'Yes, we do.' She closed the door but declined to take a seat. 'Sorry, I'd rather not sit. I won't be staying.'

He frowned briefly. 'Look, I know you're probably keen to get started but I have a list of jobs I need to go through with you.'

'No need for that. As I said, I won't be staying. I've come to tender my resignation.'

Mr Gold looked amused. 'What's this about, then? Has your little break at home made you think I'm working you too hard? Perhaps you need a proper vacation, or another assistant. Would that help?' He sat on the corner of his desk, one foot touching the floor, the other swinging casually. He gave her a paternalistic smile. 'I just want you to be happy.'

Sadie shuddered as she thought about the many times he'd used this approach with her and how many times she'd been fooled by it. 'It's not about the workload, Harry. It's about . . . what happened to Charlie Hudson.'

Mr Gold stood up and moved behind his desk, settling himself into his plush chair. 'I hear he's married one of his backup singers. I'm sure Julia won't be happy about that, but it's for the best. She'll get over it.'

'That's not what I mean. Well, in a strange way I suppose it is. I'm talking about *why* Charlie married Miss Davis.'

Mr Gold looked nonplussed. 'I'm not sure what you want me to say to that. I can't be expected to know the inner workings of Charlie Hudson's mind.'

'I'm not a fool. Don't take me for one. I know Charlie's been roughed up and threatened.'

'That's terrible.' He had the audacity to feign shock. 'Although, I did warn Julia that there was a danger this could happen.'

'Yes, you did. I guess she didn't realise, and more to the point *I* didn't realise, that you were the source of that danger. How could you?'

'I'm sure I don't know what you mean.' He hesitated for a moment and then gestured to the empty chair in front of her. 'Please sit down. You don't seem yourself. I'll have one of the girls make you a cup of coffee, or would you prefer tea?'

'I don't want a hot drink. Stop patronising me. I finally see you for who you really are, Harry, and now that my eyes are open I can't believe I didn't see it before. I wanted to tell you that in person.'

He stood, his eyes flashing with anger as he placed his palms on the desk and leant forward. 'Who I am is a man who gave you a chance when no one else would. I've taught you about the business from the ground up. I'd hoped you'd follow in my footsteps. I saw you as executive material. You're smart and loyal – at least I thought you were. I've treated you like a member of my own family,' he seethed. 'Without me you'd be living in your daddy's house looking for a husband. You're not pretty enough to be an actress, not talented enough to be a screenwriter. I did you a favour by taking you on.'

His words slammed into Sadie like physical blows. She blinked back angry tears, not wanting to give Harry Gold the satisfaction of seeing her cry. 'I didn't ask for any favours, and as to my talent – you're entitled to your opinion. You're not the only producer in town.'

A thin, bitter laugh escaped his lips. 'Don't be a fool, Sadie. I've read your little screenplay. The writing's okay, I guess. Basic, but not terrible for a beginner. But no one wants to watch films about women eschewing marriage and motherhood for high-flying careers. You'll never find a producer for it. Especially if we're no longer friends. Mark my words, girlie, I can make it so you never work in this town again.'

Sadie's pulse thudded in her ears. He wasn't bluffing – she'd seen firsthand what happened to people who dared to displease the great Harry Gold. But no career was worth selling her soul for. She'd go back to New York and pursue an academic career if she had to. Maybe it wasn't her dream, but anything was better than spending another moment working for this creep.

Without another word she went back to her office and packed up her things.

Chapter 35

Julia

Julia was roused from her sleep by someone banging on her door. 'Go away!' she shouted.

'Julia, it's Trudie. You need to get up. Harry Gold is downstairs in Miss McGovern's office waiting to see you.'

Harry was here? Julia sat up in bed. She'd been refusing to take his calls for days now. How could she be expected to talk to the man after what Sadie had told her? He was the cause of Charlie's actions and her grief. She never wanted to see him again. 'I don't care.'

'He says he won't leave until he sees you,' Trudie called.

Julia got up and opened her door. 'Tell that snake hell will freeze over before I meet with him.'

Trudie shrugged. 'It's your funeral, I guess.'

Julia closed the door and slipped back into bed. A glance at the clock on her nightstand told her it was mid-morning, but she had nothing to get up for. She wasn't going to work and had no place else to be. Maybe she'd shower later, though. Peggy was determined to take her and Sadie out for dinner to discuss the wedding. As unappealing as

281

that idea was, she had agreed to be Peggy's bridesmaid and she didn't want to let her down.

The phone beside her started ringing. Reluctantly she picked up the receiver. 'Yes?'

'Julia, it's Trudie again—'

'I told you, I'm not coming down.'

'I know. I passed on the message, but now I have your agent on the line.'

Julia sighed. 'Put him through.'

'Julia, darling, thanks for taking my call,' Lester crooned down the line.

'I won't see him, Lester. That man is a monster.'

'Right. I see. So what's your plan?'

'What do you mean?'

'You have a contract with Goldstar. If you break it, you won't be able to work for any other studio. If you're not making movies anymore, what's your plan?'

'I . . . I don't know, really. I haven't thought that far ahead.'

'Darling, I know you're upset, and quite frankly I don't blame you, but I would think long and hard before walking away from this contract. If you do, it will make it hard to get another acting job.'

'You know what, Lester? I don't think I care.'

'You say that now, but I'm worried you don't realise just how significant the consequences will be. For starters, you won't be able to live at the Studio Club anymore.'

Julia bit her lip. She hadn't thought about that. But perhaps it was time to move on anyway. Peggy would be leaving soon. If Julia bought a house, maybe Sadie would agree to move in with her. 'I can afford to buy my own place.'

'That's true, you can. But the money won't last forever. All the things that you're used to – the clothes and jewellery, the hairdressing appointments, the lunches and dinners – these things cost money. If you want to keep living the way you do now, eventually you'll need to work.'

'I don't care about those things. Not really. I can live simply if I need to.'

'Well, that's good to know. And how will you be spending your time?'

In bed? Was that a valid answer? She couldn't see a future beyond today. Maybe tomorrow she'd think differently, but right now all she wanted to do was distract herself from the pain. The only time she couldn't feel the ache in her chest was when she was sleeping. 'I don't know, Lester, okay? But I don't see how I can go back to work for that man after what he did.'

'I understand.' Lester's voice was sympathetic. 'But for what it's worth, he's denying all knowledge of the assault on Charlie. He says Walter Skinner handles things his own way and that he certainly doesn't endorse violence of any type.'

'Humph! What garbage. I'm not swallowing that for a moment.'

'Julia, I'm only thinking of you. Right now, you're angry. I don't want you to make a hasty decision that you regret later. Is throwing away your career really what you want? What would Charlie want for you? He's already gone through so much; how do you think he will feel if you lose your career because of him?'

'It wouldn't be because of him. He's done nothing wrong.'

'You know what I mean.' Lester's tone gave away his growing impatience. 'I know he believed in you. I'm sure he'd be disappointed to see you throw away everything you've worked so hard for. Harry hates to lose, and he's invested good money in you, so right now he's keen for you to get back to work. If you go up against him, you'll be the one who comes off second best. There are hundreds of girls waiting in the wings to take your place. If you walk away, ultimately you'll be the loser, Julia, not Harry.'

Lester had a point. Was she really going to let Harry Gold take *everything* from her? His actions had led to the dissolution of her relationship and if she walked away from her contract, she had no doubt Harry would see to it that she couldn't work in Hollywood again. She didn't care about being an actress – that had never been her dream – but if she gave it up, what exactly would she do? She had no qualifications and no experience doing anything else. It was a no-win situation. If she went back to work like a 'good girl', Harry got what he wanted, but if she walked away she'd end up with no money, no career and at the beck and call of her father.

Goddammit! It seemed no matter what she did, her fate always depended on the approval of a man. It was infuriating. Right now, she wished she'd been born a man. That way she'd be able to take Harry on. She could get revenge by doing something outrageous – like forming her own production company and working her ass off to make it an enterprise so colossal it would eclipse Goldstar. The thought of the great Harry Gold being taken down by her – a mere woman – was immensely satisfying.

'Julia?'

'Give me a minute, Lester. I'm thinking.'

A spark of hope, a tiny flicker of ambition, burned inside her. What if there *was* a way to make that happen? For her to start her own production company? How would she even go about it?

Maybe Sadie would know.

She'd need money – as much as she could lay her hands on. She had some, but probably not enough for this type of bold venture. But . . . if she bided her time and saw out her contract with Goldstar, she'd be in a much stronger financial position. And while she was making movies she could quietly go about setting up her own company.

'Julia, I don't want to pressure you, but time is of the essence here.'

'All right, all right, I'll go downstairs and talk to him. I'm not making any promises, though.'

An audible sigh of relief came down the line. 'That's my girl.'

◦◦◦

Harry smiled at her when she entered Miss McGovern's office. He was clearly determined to be conciliatory, despite being kept waiting for over half an hour. Harry Gold waited for no one, so he was more than likely fuming inside.

'Julia, darling, how are you?' He got up from his chair, picked up a bouquet of flowers that was sitting on the desk and handed it to her. 'For you.'

She put them down on the chair in front of her without looking at them. 'What do you want, Harry?'

'I just wanted to see how you were and when you think you will be back at work. I know you've been under some pressure, and I wanted to give you time to rest. But we can't hold the movie up forever.'

'I don't know if I'll ever be ready to come back, Harry.' She looked him in the eye. 'Not after what Sadie told me.'

The smile disappeared from his face. 'Is that so? I wouldn't believe everything Miss Shore has to say. I had to tell her that we wouldn't be producing her screenplay and she didn't take the rejection very well, I fear.'

'So that's how you're spinning it? Don't treat me like a child. We both know the truth about what you did and why Sadie left Goldstar. She has more ethics in her little finger than you and Walter Skinner combined. In fact, I'm not sure you even know the meaning of the word.'

The veins in Harry's neck bulged. 'You don't want to be treated like a child? Then stop behaving like one. I warned you not to go out with Charlie. I told you there would be fallout. You were the one who put that man's life in danger and you should be ashamed of yourself.'

She folded her arms across her chest so he wouldn't see her shaking hands. She refused to be intimidated by this man. 'I will not be held accountable for the prejudice of others.' The pure love she felt for Charlie was no cause for shame.

'Is that so?' He moved towards her until there were mere inches between them, and dropped his voice so it was low and threatening. 'Well, girlie, here's something you are accountable for – the fact that there is a signed contract with your name on it sitting on my desk. Do you think you are irreplaceable? Let me assure you, there are plenty of beautiful young actresses willing to take your spot. In fact, I'm pretty sure Vivienne Lockhart will be looking for a new contract when her current movie is done. I bet she'd happily take your place.'

He was a clever bastard. Watching Vivienne inherit her place as Goldstar's golden girl really would be too much. She sighed. 'Okay, Harry, you're right. It's time to be grown-ups about this. I'll come back to work for you, but things are going to have to change.'

'What things?'

'I'm not a little girl anymore. I don't need to be watched over day and night. I'm moving out of the Studio Club and getting my own place. I don't want you keeping tabs on me. Don't worry, I have no intention of dating anyone for a very long time, but if I want to go out on a weeknight, I will. And I'm going to get a car, so I won't be needing a driver for much longer.'

Harry scratched his chin thoughtfully. 'Is that all?'

'I want you to respect me.'

'Oh, Julia, of course you have my respect. Let's not argue any more, all right? I'll see to it that your contract is amended to make the changes you want. But, in return, you'll be back on set tomorrow morning and you'll look happy about it. Do we have a deal?'

She nodded wordlessly. He thought he'd won. That was fine by her. She was done with being controlled by men. It might take time, but eventually she'd make Harry Gold pay for what he'd done.

Chapter 36

Peggy

Peggy waited patiently while Julia finished buttoning the back of her figure-hugging guipure lace dress.

Finally, Julia stepped back. 'There! Turn around, Peg, so we can see you.'

Peggy twirled as flamboyantly as the small space between the two single beds would allow, and the organza train attached at her shoulders billowed out behind her.

Sadie giggled but Julia's eyes glistened with tears. Maybe she was picturing herself as a bride, thinking of what might have been with Charlie. She'd been a brick, all things considered. During that first week of the break-up, when she'd cried constantly and refused to get out of bed, Peggy had wondered if it might be kinder to excuse her from her bridesmaid's duties. But just when it seemed as if Julia was heading for an interminable period of depression, she unexpectedly turned a corner and went back to work. From that moment on, she'd taken her role as maid of honour very seriously.

'Don't cry, Jules,' Peggy said in a mock-stern tone. 'We don't have time to redo your make-up now.'

Julia half-sniffed, half-laughed as Sadie handed her a tissue.

Where would they be without Sadie? Sadie's sudden resignation from her job had turned out to be beneficial as far as wedding planning was concerned. All that extra time she had on her hands had been spent on wedding preparations. She'd assured Peggy that she'd left no stone unturned to make sure that this would be the wedding of the year – if not the decade!

'Sorry for being so emotional,' Julia said. 'You look beautiful, Peg. I don't think I've ever seen a more radiant bride.'

Sadie glanced at her watch. 'We still have a little time left before the cars arrive to take us to the church. Should I go downstairs and fetch your mom, Peg?'

Peggy's parents had arrived the day before yesterday. None of her siblings had come – not even Joanie – but her parents had relented after much cajoling from Peggy. They'd refused her offer to pay for flights and had come on the bus, though, much to her annoyance. 'People will think I'm too cheap to pay for my own parents to attend my wedding,' she'd protested when her mother had outlined their plans over the phone.

'You worry far too much about other people's opinions,' her mother had said, her voice tight.

They had not been thrilled when Peggy called to tell them she was engaged. Mike's failure to ask her father's permission had been a setback, as was the fact that Peggy was marrying a 'Hollywood type'. That she planned to continue working didn't go down well either. Thankfully the promise of a big church wedding had met with their approval.

They'd been distant when they first arrived, but after dinner at Mike's house in the hills they'd thawed. Mike had been the perfect amount of charming. He'd flattered her mother in all the right ways – praising her for raising such a modest and virtuous daughter. When approaching her father he was respectful and apologetic – begging forgiveness for his rashness in asking Peggy without permission. He claimed his love for Peggy had made him momentarily foolish, and he hoped he could make it up to her parents by being a model son-in-law.

Nothing could ruin her day now. Well, not unless she was left standing at the altar. Perish the thought!

'Mom can wait a few minutes longer. This will be the last time all three of us are alone in this room and I want to take the time to cherish this moment.'

'Oh!' said Sadie. 'I hadn't thought about that.'

Julia's eyes were still glassy. 'I can't believe we're all moving on. We must make a pact not to lose touch.'

'We won't,' Sadie said brightly.

'But Peggy will be busy being a wife and TV star.' Julia's eyes met hers. 'You must promise not to be a stranger, Peg.'

'Of course I won't be. We'll still have our regular Saturday morning breakfast at Sal's. I'm not planning to change that.' She turned and reached into her near-empty nightstand drawer. All her belongings – with the exception of her wedding-day essentials – had already been packed up and moved to Mike's. She pulled out two wrapped boxes. 'These are for you,' she said, handing a box to each of her friends.

Sadie tore the paper from her gift eagerly, gasping when she saw the heart-shaped pendant contained in the box. 'Oh, Peggy, it's gorgeous! Thank you.'

Peggy smiled and looked at Julia. 'Yours is the same. I got one for each of us, so that even when we're apart we'll be reminded of each other.'

Julia leant in and squeezed her gloved hand. 'Friends forever.'

Peggy reached out to Sadie and pulled her in so they could all embrace. 'Friends forever.'

Chapter 37

Julia

Julia gritted her teeth and smiled as the best man twirled her around the dance floor.

Peggy's reception was the grandest Julia had ever attended. The bride had drawn on the wedding celebrations of Jackie Kennedy and Grace Kelly for inspiration, and as a result the ballroom at the Roosevelt Hotel was draped in garlands of tulle and the tables festooned with greenery and white roses. A sumptuous meal had been served, consisting of caviar blinis to start and duck à l'orange with green beans as the main course, followed by a dessert of fruit and cheese. And, of course, the champagne was free flowing. The five-tiered tower of wedding cake was yet to be cut; however, that moment couldn't be too far away. All this decadence seemed to be going over a treat with the guests. And despite Julia's very grave misgivings about the longevity of their marriage, the bride and groom both seemed ecstatic.

In some ways, enduring this wedding hadn't been as difficult as Julia had imagined. It wasn't the type of celebration she'd pictured for Charlie and herself. She'd imagined their nuptials as a simple affair, taking place in a registry office somewhere, followed by a blissful honeymoon in Paris.

Naturally, Peggy had chosen a church for her wedding. Standing beside Peggy at the altar as she vowed to 'love, honour and obey' a man who so clearly had no moral compass had been challenging for Julia, to say the least. It had taken all her resolve to fight back angry tears at the injustice of it all. Mike, a two-timing manipulator, was getting the prize of marriage to her beautiful friend. Meanwhile, Charlie had been forced into a marriage of convenience.

And she'd had to stand at the altar next to Peggy, as a bridesmaid. Alone.

But this marriage was what Peggy wanted, and she'd made it clear that she would be proceeding with or without her friends' approval. Their merry little gang had already lost one member and Julia was determined there would be no more disharmony in the group. As much as she hated to admit it, she missed Vivienne. She missed her infectious throaty laugh, her sharp wit and irreverence. Julia had always been braver with Vivienne by her side. But the qualities she'd most admired in Viv had ultimately torn their friendship apart. Vivienne's desire to please herself knew no boundaries and all of them had paid the price for that.

Julia simply couldn't lose Peg too. If that meant donning a pink gown and standing beside her while she hitched her wagon to a philanderer, so be it. Julia wouldn't complain. Maybe Peggy was right and Mike would settle down now they were married. If not, she'd be there to help Peggy pick up the pieces when the marriage fell apart.

As difficult as this wedding was to witness, one good thing had come out of it: Julia had discovered she was a good actress after all. Attending all the dress fittings, rehearsals, kitchen teas and other associated pre-wedding engagements had been incredibly distressing in her broken-hearted state. But she'd made up her mind not to inflict her pain on those around her, least of all the bride-to-be. Peggy had been through enough. So she'd played the part of the excited maid of honour, feigning delight over every aspect of the wedding preparations and spending the wedding day grinning like a Cheshire cat. It was an Oscar-worthy performance, even if she did say so herself. The thought made her chuckle. Just when she'd decided that acting wasn't part of her long-term plans, she'd finally discovered she had a little talent after all.

As the band brought the number to a close, Julia declined an offer to take another spin with the best man. 'Sorry, bridesmaid duty calls. I really need to be circulating among the guests.' She slipped out of his clutches and scurried away before he had time to protest.

Everywhere she looked there were people she'd rather not speak to – lecherous studio executives, handsy actors and gossipy actresses. Unfortunately, there didn't seem anywhere safe to escape to. Where was Sadie when she needed her? Moments ago she'd been dancing with Jack Porter, but now Julia's gaze searched the ballroom for her without luck. She did see one potential safe harbour, though. Tony Astor was sitting alone at a table, looking dejected as his eyes followed the bride around the room. Surely it was Julia's duty to keep the poor fellow company?

She slipped into the unoccupied seat next to him. 'Hello, Tony.'

He looked up, startled. 'Julia. Forgive me. I didn't notice you were there.'

She followed his gaze. 'Your attention was elsewhere, perhaps?'

His cheeks reddened. 'You're looking especially beautiful tonight. You make a lovely bridesmaid.'

'Always the bridesmaid,' she joked, but instead of laughing, a pained look settled on Tony's face.

He met her gaze. 'I heard about . . . well, your situation,' he said. 'I'm sorry, Julia. Tonight must be very hard for you.'

'Thank you. It hasn't been easy, but I guess things don't always work out the way we plan.'

'No, they don't,' he agreed. 'Maybe it's time for new plans, for both of us.'

She placed her hand over his and squeezed. 'You're a wise man, Tony.'

'I don't know about that, but I am a practical one. What say you and I make the best of this, eh? Shall we dance?'

Julia looked at Tony with new eyes. He was attractive enough, kind, perceptive and a true gentleman. Peggy didn't know what she was missing out on. 'I'd be honoured.'

Chapter 38

Sadie

Sadie moved around the crowded dance floor in a trance. Jack was a surprisingly good dancer. Why had she never noticed that before? He held her firmly and led in a way that freed Sadie's mind to wander.

The wedding had been a triumph of good organisation, which she could claim credit for, and oodles of money, which she couldn't. That was all courtesy of Mike and his trust fund. If Peggy was marrying him for his money, at least there was plenty of it. Apart from a small snag with the wedding cars arriving ten minutes late, everything had gone like clockwork. The ceremony was touching, the bride looked gorgeous, the venue was impeccable and the food delicious. There wasn't much left that could go wrong now. Cutting the cake was the only formality that remained. Once that was done, Sadie could relax. Of course, when the wedding was over she'd have to face up to the reality of her life.

Harry's words had hit home. The jibes about her looks had little impact but facing the truth about her writing had hurt. Harry was right. The chances of her making it as a screenwriter weren't great. Clearly, her 'original' idea about a future where women ran the world was original for a reason. Nobody was interested in producing such work.

And even if they could be convinced that the premise was a good one, now that she'd made an enemy of Harry Gold no one was likely to take a risk on working with her.

Her Hollywood dream was over.

She hadn't told the other girls yet, but she'd given her notice at the Studio Club and would be heading back to New York at the end of the month. She had no immediate plans, although she'd had thoughts of teaching or an academic career. Perhaps she could write in her spare time. She'd tried not to dwell on it too much, hoping that she'd think of some brilliant plan to stay right here, in the town she'd grown to love so much. But with the wedding almost over, it was time to face the fact that she'd been living in fantasy land.

Everything was changing here anyway. Julia was moving out, Peggy was married and Vivienne . . . well, it seemed she was lost to them forever. That's if the newspaper and magazine reports were true. And after her last phone call with Vivienne, Sadie suspected they were.

The reports in the press started filtering in not long after Vivienne left the club. At first it was just mentions in the gossip columns about late-night partying, but soon there were full articles in the movie magazines with headlines such as *Goodtime Girl* that talked about Vivienne's excessive drinking and hinted that she was entertaining many male friends in her hotel room.

According to the papers, Vivienne was still residing here, at the Roosevelt. Sadie had been nervous when Peggy booked the ballroom for the wedding reception and had tried to steer her elsewhere, but it had been impossible to get a booking at the Beverly Hills Hotel or Hotel Bel-Air on such short notice. They'd been lucky that the Roosevelt could squeeze them in, so there hadn't really been a choice. But Sadie worried that Vivienne might turn up uninvited, especially if she'd been drinking. It seemed that fear had been unfounded, which was a relief, because heaven only knew what Vivienne might do or say in that state.

When Sadie had accepted a phone call from her a couple of weeks back, she'd been barely coherent – laughing and singing and telling

Sadie to get out of the Studio Club while she was still young enough to enjoy herself. If that was Vivienne's idea of fun, Sadie wanted no part of it.

It wasn't just the papers talking about her, either. Rumours were flying around everywhere. Sadie had overheard snippets from other residents at the club – including a report that Vivienne had passed out in the ladies' room at Cocoanut Grove. Others told tales of bad behaviour on set. Sadie had no idea what was true and what wasn't, but it was obvious Vivienne was in trouble. Despite everything that had happened, Sadie couldn't bear the thought that her old friend was suffering. She would pay her a visit before she left for New York and let her know that, no matter what, she still cared about her.

'Penny for your thoughts,' Jack whispered in her ear. He was holding her awfully close. Perhaps she should put some space between them so he didn't get the wrong idea. But it felt good to be held this way. Jack's embrace made her feel both comforted and desired. It was an odd mix of emotions, but she found herself wanting to stay right where she was. 'Sorry. I've had a bit on my mind lately.'

'Anything you'd like to share? I'm a good listener.'

She pulled back from his embrace just enough to look him in the eye. 'I'm feeling a little sad, to be honest.'

'Sad? When you're dancing with me?' He took his hand from her waist and momentarily placed it over his heart. 'I'm wounded.'

'It's not you. In fact, you're a surprisingly good dancer.'

'Surprisingly?' He returned his hand to her waist. 'The compliments just keep on coming.'

'Sorry.' She giggled. 'It really isn't you. This is the most fun I've had all day – all week, in fact.'

'That's more like it. So, want to tell me what's on your mind?'

'I was just thinking how much I'm going to miss this place.'

Jack stopped dead, causing her to stumble slightly and him to tighten his embrace. 'What do you mean?'

'I'm moving back to New York at the end of the month.'

'What? Why?'

'I don't have a job, Jack, and I'm not going back to waiting tables. It's over for me here.'

He dropped his hold and clasped her hand. 'Let's go somewhere quieter where we can talk.'

She glanced at the still-uncut cake. 'I really shouldn't leave the room before the cake is cut.'

'Please. It won't take long, I promise. We'll just step out into the foyer for a moment.'

'A moment, Jack, that's all.'

He nodded and led her out of the room, not speaking again until they were seated side by side on a sofa in the hotel's opulent Spanish-style foyer. 'Sadie, I have something I've wanted to say to you for ages, and now I realise I might be running out of time to make my confession.'

'That sounds ominous.'

'I think I might be . . .' He winced. 'Actually, I *am* in love with you. Please don't go back to New York. Stay here, with me.'

Sadie stared at him. 'Are you drunk?'

'What? No! Why would you say that?'

'How can you say you love me? We've never been on a proper date. You've never even tried to kiss me.'

He placed his hand on her cheek. 'I can remedy that now, if you'll let me.'

This was ridiculous! It was Jack. Jack who liked to tease and torment her. How could she take him seriously? Jack who dated movie stars and sexpots like Vivienne. He'd made it clear that he saw Sadie as a pal. Was he being sincere or was this some sort of joke? 'I don't know what to say.'

'One kiss. That's all I'm asking.' He sounded deadly serious.

Her heart pounded. Why the hell not? She was leaving anyway. How could one kiss hurt? As she nodded her agreement, he leant in and brushed her lips gently with his own. Her heart raced at his touch. She responded, pressing her mouth to his. If only this moment didn't have to end. Eventually they drew apart and Jack said, 'Don't go.'

'I'm sorry.' She'd definitely felt a spark there and maybe, if things had been different, she and Jack would have made a great couple. But it was too late. 'I can't stay.'

'You can. We can find you another job. You can write. You have contacts. Maybe I could get you a job on the paper.'

'It's too late for any of that. I've already given my notice at the club.'

'I could—'

'Stop.' A wave of irritation washed over her. 'Why did you wait until now to tell me this? Maybe if I'd known earlier, if we'd been dating . . . maybe things would be different.'

Jack huffed. 'I asked you out dozens of times. You made it very clear that you weren't interested.'

'I thought you were messing around. Besides, you were always dating other women.'

'I've had a crush on you from the first time I saw you. When you resisted my charms, I tried to console myself with others, that's true, but it never worked. I made up my mind to play the long game. To show you what a good guy I am, to win you as a friend first. I hoped that eventually you'd develop the same feelings for me that I have for you. But now I've run out of time.'

'I'm sorry, Jack, it's too late. I need to get back inside.'

She walked away from him without allowing herself to look back.

Back in the ballroom, the party was in full swing. Peggy and Mike were on the dance floor, and was that Julia dancing cheek-to-cheek with *Tony*? This night was getting stranger and stranger. Sadie just wanted it to end. With no sign that the bride and groom were about to take a knife to the cake, she made a dash for the ladies' room. At least Jack wouldn't be able to follow her in there.

Inside the powder room, she took a seat in an armchair and rested her head in her hands. That kiss had been one in a million. Well, one in about a dozen – it wasn't as if she'd kissed hundreds of men before. Nevertheless, she'd never, ever felt like this. Her stomach fluttered as she recalled his lips on hers. The knowledge that it could never happen again almost made her weep. Damn Jack and his timing!

'Sadie, are you okay?' Julia's voice interrupted her thoughts. 'Peggy sent me to find you. They're almost ready to cut the cake.'

She lifted her head and a wayward tear rolled down her cheek.

Julia hitched up her pale pink bridesmaid dress and crouched down beside her. 'Hey, what's wrong?'

'I wasn't going to tell you until after the wedding, but I'm leaving, Jules. There's nothing here for me now. I have no job and Harry Gold has seen to it that I won't get any sort of traction in the industry. I have no choice but to go back to New York.'

'Oh, honey, of course you do. I can help you.'

'No, you can't. I need to be able to support myself. I can go back east and live with my parents while I start again. I'll be able to get teaching work.'

'But that's not your dream.'

'Who gets their dream? I was foolish to think I would be one of the lucky ones.'

'No, you weren't. I've read your work. You're immensely talented. You just need a break.'

'It's too late for that. I've made up my mind. I'm fine, really. It's only that Jack just kissed me and told me he loved me so I'm a bit out of sorts.'

Julia's mouth dropped open. 'Jack? Jack Porter?'

'The one and only,' Sadie said miserably.

'And how do you feel about this?'

'He's a fool! I mean, why tell me when it's all too late?'

'So you like him then?'

'Well, of course I like him. He's handsome, funny and smarter than he first appears. And he's been a good friend. But none of that matters now.'

'Sadie, I want you to listen to me very carefully. If you think this could be the real thing with Jack, you owe it to yourself to give it a shot. You don't have to go home. Next week I'm moving into a gigantic house all alone. I'd love nothing more for you to share it with me. You can stay rent-free until you're back on your feet.'

298

'I couldn't do that.'

'Of course you could. You lost your job because of me. This is the least I can do to make it up to you.'

'But that doesn't solve the work problem. What would I do?'

'Actually, this is something I was going to talk to you about after the wedding. I've got a business idea I'd like to pursue – something that I can really sink my teeth into once my contract with Goldstar is up. You know acting has never been my dream and . . . well, I think I've found something that could make me happy. There's no time to explain it all right now, but I'm going to need an assistant. With all your insider studio knowledge, I can't think of anyone better. Initially it will be research. I intend to go slowly and carefully at first, so the role would leave you with plenty of time to write.'

'This feels like charity.'

'It's anything but! I was going to employ someone anyway. And it won't be forever. You'll write something fabulous and it'll get picked up. Things change all the time in this town. Harry Gold won't always be on top, just you wait and see.'

'Well . . .'

'And you'll get a chance to see where things go with Jack. Please, Sadie, do this for me. After everything that's happened this year, I can't bear the thought of losing you too.'

The invisible cloud that had enveloped Sadie for weeks suddenly lifted.

'When you put it like that, how could I possibly refuse?'

31 December 1999

Julia and I trudge back to the house after less than twenty minutes walking. Peggy is wiping down the table when we arrive upstairs after dumping our outerwear in the laundry room.

'Vivienne has just retired to her room for a bit,' she informs us.

I don't want to waste any time. 'Should we have a coffee while we talk?'

'Is it too early for a wine?' Julia asks.

'That might not be a terrible idea.'

'I'll open a bottle. Where are the wineglasses, Sadie?' Peggy looks at the labelled cupboards. 'Oh, never mind, I can find them myself.'

'You pour. I'll be back in a minute.' I head into the office to get the journals, and when I return Julia is sitting on the couch. Peggy hands me a glass of wine and takes a seat next to Julia. I settle myself opposite them and hold up the *1958* journal. 'Recognise this?'

'I do!' Peggy replies. 'Wow, seeing that brings back some memories.'

'There are a few volumes. Lots of memories in there, but this one is from our last year at the Studio Club.'

Julia looks uncomfortable. 'Far be it from me to stick up for Vivienne, but should we be reading these? I mean, it's an invasion of her privacy.'

I've grappled with this myself but I can't think of another approach to deal with the information I've discovered. 'I understand your concern, but I honestly think it's the only way. April left all the source material for the memoir, including recordings of interviews with Vivienne made when her memory was stronger than it is now. Vivienne expressed a wish for her story to be told, and I think it's best if you hear it, or rather read it, in her own words.'

'Memoir?' Julia looks horrified. She turns to Peggy. 'You knew about this?'

'It was in the letter April left. Sadie read it to me over the phone.'

Julia's gaze flits to me. 'Why didn't one of you tell me? Dear god, a memoir—'

'We didn't want to upset you,' Peggy butts in. 'Especially as there was zero chance of it being finished seeing as April had left.'

Zero chance of being finished. Peggy's words sit uneasily with me. 'April has entrusted Vivienne to my care, and part of that is having her truth told. I'd like to see the memoir through, if I can.'

'What?' Julia says. 'You can't be serious, Sadie.'

'I'm not saying I would publish it, and I don't think that was ever the intent behind the project. But Vivienne deserves to have her story told. Even if it's just for us. I'd at least like to put all of April's notes together into one readable document and to flesh out any missing bits. I'm not sure it will be possible now that Vivienne's memory is so impaired, but I'd like to try because I know it's what she wants. I have heard the recordings of her telling April that she wants her story told before it's too late. I've been working through the tapes and the journals, and yesterday I came across something that affects us all. It's so earth-shattering that I couldn't know it and not share it with you.'

Peggy leans in, clearly keen to hear this new information, but Julia places her wineglass on the coffee table and folds her arms across her chest.

'Shall I read it to you?'

Peggy nods. 'We're all ears.'

16 April 1958

Today was the worst day of my life. Worse than when my mother died. Worse than when my foster father reached up under my skirt for the first time. Worse than when my foster mother dropped me off at the orphanage with the word 'slut' still ringing in my ears.

Yesterday I had a call from Peggy's Mike. He had a surprise gift for her and he wanted my opinion on it. Of course, I was happy to oblige. If I'm honest, I was chuffed that he thought enough of me to ask.

When he arrived on set, he asked if we could go to my dressing-room so he could show me the gift in private. I had no reason to be suspicious of him.

But once we were alone, he closed the door. He stepped towards me and touched my face. 'You're so beautiful, Vivienne,' he said.

He's supposed to be in love with Peggy! Why would he say something like that to me?!

He laughed then. 'Don't be shy. I know what sort of girl you are, what you like to do behind closed doors. Guys talk, Vivienne, and I know all about you.'

I look up to see how the others are receiving this news. Julia hasn't moved. Her mouth is set in a hard line. But Peggy's eyes are wide and her cheeks are flushed. 'Go on,' she says, with a hint of impatience in her voice.

'Have you been drinking?' I asked. It was the only explanation I could think of for his behaviour.

He shook his head. 'Not yet.' He moved towards me again and this time placed his hand on my breast.

I pushed him hard. Told him how upset his girlfriend will be when she hears about this.

He just laughed. 'Who's going to tell her?'

302

'Peggy's my friend,' I said. 'She needs to know what a slimeball she's dating.'

'Who's going to believe a whore like you?' He actually said that!! He called me a whore!!

He reached into his jacket pocket and then handed me an envelope. 'Open it.'

Inside were six black-and-white photos. One glance was all I needed. The nudes that I'd shot all those years ago.

'Pretty, aren't they?' He was laughing in my face. 'Go on, have a good look. That wig you had on wasn't much of a disguise.'

God, how could I have been so stupid? I should have known those photos would come back to haunt me one day.

'I'm sure the public would be very interested in these.' Mike sneered. 'And the studio heads, too. Isn't there a decency clause in your contract?'

He was right, of course. It would be the end of my career. This couldn't have come at a worse time – just when all my hard work has paid off and I'm finally being taken seriously as an actress.

I decided I had no option but to bargain with him. 'What do you want – money?'

'Money?' He scoffed at my offer. 'Little girl, I don't need your money.' He took the photos from me. 'I want a piece of this action.' He held up the dirtiest photo in the pack. The one that leaves nothing to the imagination. 'I want you to open your legs for me like this. What do you say? A fuck for the photos? Is that a fair deal?'

I shouldn't have been shocked but I was. 'You're Peggy's boyfriend!'

I started to feel afraid.

'Peggy's a good girl, not a slut like you. She won't give herself to me before marriage. I'm a man and I have needs. What difference does it make to you?'

'What if I say no?'

'I'll walk out of here and straight into the studio head's office.'

303

I wish I'd argued more. Tried harder to get him to take something else. But in the moment I felt I had no choice, so I let him have what he wanted. He's not the first man to treat me this way, although usually they buy me dinner or offer me a part in their movie before they tear my panties from me.

Peggy's gasp makes me look up. 'Are you okay?' I ask.

'That *bastard*! I wish I'd known. Why didn't she tell us?'

'She explains that soon. Do you need a break, though? I know this is a lot to digest. I was completely rattled when I read it yesterday.'

'No,' Peggy says. 'Keep going.'

Julia is stony faced and still hasn't spoken.

'Jules?'

She covers her face with her hands briefly, and then clasps her palms together. 'I don't know what to say. If this is true, I made the worst, most terrible mistake of my life.'

'I don't doubt it's the truth,' I say. 'I mean, she's kept it to herself all these years. I can't see why she would lie in her diary.'

Julia nods and the colour drains from her face.

'Read the rest,' Peggy says. 'I want to hear it all.'

Seconds later he pushed my hand away and thrust into me, pounding so hard that I cried out in pain. Not that my discomfort deterred him. In fact, my cries seemed to excite him further. He pulled my hair and slapped my face. 'Do you like that, whore? Girls like you like it rough.'

Just when I thought the whole ordeal was over, Julia opened the dressing-room door. She looked at me in horror and then ran from the room.

Now she thinks that I have seduced Peggy's boyfriend, and I don't know what to do!!!

Maybe I should tell the truth, but I'm not sure anyone will believe me. I have no proof he forced me. Peggy is IN LOVE with him. He's bound to convince her that the whole thing was my idea.

And he still has the photos.

If Julia tells Peggy what she saw, the girls will all hate me.

Julia probably already does.

Maybe I should warn Peg about Mike, but I can't believe he would ever treat her the way he treated me. Maybe he's right about me. Maybe I did deserve what I got. Peggy would never let anyone take dirty photos of her for money. She'd find another way. How can I break her heart by telling her the man she loves forced me to have sex with him? She doesn't deserve that.

I just have to hope that Julia doesn't spill the beans, and that Mike doesn't sell the photos.

But nothing will ever be the same again.

I only have myself to blame. I should never have posed for those photos, no matter how much money they earnt me.

In the end they will cost me dearly.

Julia, Peggy and Sadie are the only family I've ever known. I'm not sure I can survive without them.

Chapter 39

Sadie

Sadie stopped typing for a moment to look at the view from her office in Julia's new Beverly Hills mansion. The sight of the city she loved spread out in the distance beyond the treetops was immensely distracting. So much so, she was considering facing her desk away from the window.

As the sole employee of Jeweltone Productions, Sadie's days were varied and interesting. On paper she was Julia's personal assistant, because Jeweltone didn't officially exist yet. It was too tricky to set it up while Julia was still working at Goldstar, so they were keeping the whole thing quiet for the moment. With all the groundwork they were doing, the company should be ready to launch as soon as Julia was free from her contractual obligations. Tony Astor had recently come on board as a partner, and his financial acumen was proving to be a huge asset.

Together, Tony and Julia were a winning combination. Jules was brimming with ideas and enthusiasm whereas Tony was more reserved, focusing his energy on finding practical solutions to every issue they faced. The two of them complemented each other perfectly, and because of that, Sadie was optimistic that the company would succeed.

Initially, Julia had offered to make her a partner too. 'This is something we can do together, Sade. You have so many skills and I know I'll be relying on your expertise a lot to begin with.' But Sadie had refused. While she loved working with Julia and appreciated the opportunity to be involved in building her company, Sadie didn't have any money to invest in the project. Of course, Julia had said it didn't matter, but Sadie feared that the arrangement might one day cause issues between them, and she wasn't prepared to risk that.

Besides, being a partner would eventually mean her writing would have to take a back seat, and she'd never been more inspired to write. Currently, she was working on a new screenplay – a romantic comedy – and her mind was overflowing with ideas for TV shows and other projects. She'd even had the seed of an idea for a novel. Who knew being in love would be so good for her creative mind?

The sound of the office phone ringing jolted her from her thoughts. 'Sadie Shore speaking. How may I help you?'

'Sadie, it's me, Jack.'

Sadie's whole body reacted to the sound of his voice, and she smiled. They'd been seeing each other for over two months now, but her stomach still flipped each time he called. 'Couldn't wait until tonight, huh?'

'Honey, I'm sorry. I'm ringing with some not-so-pleasant news.'

'Oh! What is it? Are you okay?'

'I'm fine. But I heard on the grapevine that Vivienne collapsed on set. They're bringing her by ambulance to Mount Sinai Hospital, which is where I am now. Sade, I think it's pretty serious.'

Sadie didn't hesitate. 'I'm on my way.'

'How will you get here?'

After all this time in California, she still didn't have a driver's licence. 'I guess I'll call a cab.'

'How about I come get you? It'll be quicker.'

'Would you? Won't your boss be mad if you miss the story?'

'You're more important than that and so is Vivienne. I'm here because I want to make sure she's okay, not to get the scoop.'

'Thank you. I'll be ready when you arrive.'

Sadie contemplated calling Julia and Peggy to let them know, but in the end decided there was no point. They'd made it clear they wanted nothing to do with Vivienne, and besides, Sadie didn't have anything concrete to report.

She feared Vivienne had hit the booze again. After Peggy's wedding, she'd met Vivienne for lunch and tried her hardest to talk to her friend about her self-destructive behaviour, but Vivienne had waved her concerns away. 'I'm just having fun, Sadie. Making up for all that time I spent locked up at the club. I'm fine, really I am.' But the reports of her misadventures continued, each one worse than the last. Sadie strongly suspected it wasn't just alcohol Vivienne was abusing, but she was powerless to do anything about it.

About a month ago, the rumours ceased. Sadie asked Jack to dig around a little to see what he could find out, but it seemed that Vivienne was back to being a director's dream and working harder than ever. The sudden turnaround was a mystery to Sadie, but a happy one. The last time she'd seen Vivienne – just two weeks ago – she was her old self: laughing and joking and looking the picture of health. When Sadie had asked if there was someone special in her life, she'd looked coy. 'No one I want to talk about just yet, Sadie, but I promise when the time is right, you'll be the first to know.'

Something had gone dreadfully wrong since then. A broken heart perhaps? Whatever it was, it seemed Vivienne was back on the booze. Or perhaps . . . Oh god, she wouldn't have deliberately harmed herself, would she?

Jack arrived to collect her, giving her a quick hug before they headed to the hospital. She was quiet for most of the ride, consumed by worry and guilt.

'Are you okay?' Jack asked, momentarily taking his eyes off the road to glance at her.

'I should have spent more time with her. Checked on her more often.'

'Oh, honey, we don't even know what happened yet, but whatever it is, you mustn't blame yourself. I care about Vivienne too, but she's made a lot of mistakes. You're not responsible for the choices she's made.'

Sadie didn't answer.

They arrived at the hospital to find half-a-dozen reporters milling around outside. Any real-life drama on a movie set was newsworthy. Vivienne's starring role in *Agnes Grey* combined with her recent bad behaviour meant she was beginning to garner some attention from the press. Still, it wasn't as if she was a big star like Julia, so the fact that there were so many reporters here wasn't a good sign. Sadie's heart hammered in her chest. Were these journalists here because something terrible had happened? Was Vivienne already dead?

Jack squeezed her hand and told her to wait where she was while he found out what was happening. She watched as he worked the assembled group, backslapping and handing out cigarettes, obviously trying to loosen the tongue of anyone who might have information. Minutes later he was back.

'She's been admitted,' he said. 'Some are saying burst appendix, others saying drug overdose. Not sure whether either is true. In any case, there's no point trying to get in this way. There's security on all the doors. They're only letting patients and staff enter. It's protocol when any sort of celebrity or public figure is brought in.'

'I need to see her. Or at least speak to a doctor.'

'I don't know if I can help with those things, but I might be able to get you inside.'

'Really?'

'I know a nurse who works here. I can call the ward and see if she's on shift. If so, I might be able to convince her to let us in via the staff entrance.'

Sadie nodded, not daring to ask how Jack knew the nurse so well that she would be prepared to do them this favour. At the moment, all that mattered was seeing Vivienne.

Jack ran to the nearest phone box and returned five minutes later. 'We're in,' he said. 'Follow me.'

A pretty brunette met them at a small entrance on the other side of the hospital. She had the hide to greet Jack with a kiss on the cheek. She eyed Sadie appreciatively. 'So, you're the famous Sadie. I'm pleased to meet you at last.'

Sadie creased her brow in confusion and Jack sighed. 'Sadie, this is my sister, Angela. She's been dying to meet you.' Before Sadie could register her surprise, he looked at his sister. 'Ange, I meant what I said on the phone. This is an emergency. Sadie is a close friend of Vivienne Lockhart. We need to get her to wherever Vivienne is.'

Angela huffed. 'I know, Gianni. I wouldn't be risking my job for just anyone. I can get you to the ward, but after that you're on your own. I doubt they'll let you see her unless you're family, I'm afraid.'

Gianni? Sadie looked at Angela. 'What did you just call him?'

'Gianni. That's his name. Don't tell me he's still going by Jack with you?' Angela threw her brother an accusing look. 'I thought you were serious about this girl? Why haven't you told her the truth?'

Sadie looked at Jack with questioning eyes.

'I promise I'll explain later,' he said. 'Just take us to the ward, Ange.'

They followed Angela up a flight of stairs and along a long grey corridor that reeked of antiseptic, stopping outside the surgical ward. 'I believe she's gone to theatre, but that's all I know. They'll bring her back here when she's done.'

'Thanks, sis.'

'Yes, thank you so much,' Sadie said. 'I really appreciate your help.'

'You can thank me by coming for dinner at our mom's place one night.' Angela smiled. 'She's dying to meet you too. Gianni never stops talking about you at home.'

'For god's sake, Ange, put a sock in it.'

Sadie laughed. 'Deal.' She looked at Jack. 'But you have some explaining to do, mister.'

Angela looked at her watch. 'I'd better get back before someone notices I'm missing. I hope Miss Lockhart is okay. I loved her in *Agnes Grey* and Gianni tells us she's a nice person.'

Jack took Sadie by the hand. 'Come on. Let's see what we can find out.'

At the nurse's station the sister in charge was unsympathetic. 'I'm sorry, but we can only give out information to immediate family. I'm going to have to ask you to leave.'

'But I *am* family,' Sadie wailed. 'I'm all that Vivienne has.'

'I'm sorry, but rules are rules.'

Jack refused to move. 'Miss Shore is the closest thing to a family Miss Lockhart has. Surely that counts for something?'

The nurse looked up. 'Usually not,' she said. 'But did you say "Miss Shore"?'

'Yes,' Sadie replied. 'Sadie Shore. Vivienne and I were roommates at the Hollywood Studio Club.'

'Well, Miss Shore, you're in luck. We've been trying to reach you by phone. Miss Lockhart has nominated you as her next of kin.'

Sadie exhaled a long breath of relief. 'Does this mean I can see her?'

'I'm afraid not. She's in surgery. But you can wait over there,' she pointed to a row of hardbacked chairs, 'until there's some news.'

'Surgery? What for? What's wrong with her?'

The nurse glanced at Jack before returning her gaze to Sadie. 'Can we speak privately?'

Jack stepped back. 'I'll go take a seat.'

Once Jack was out of earshot, the nurse began to speak. 'This information is sensitive, but as the next of kin you are entitled to know. Were you aware that Miss Lockhart was pregnant?'

Pregnant? Oh, dear god. 'No. I had no idea.'

'As far as the doctors can tell she was around five months along.'

'Was?'

'Yes, I'm sorry. It's not as common to lose a baby this far along, but it sometimes happens. Miss Lockhart went into preterm labour earlier today and the baby was not developed enough to survive.'

'I don't understand. Why is she in surgery?'

'The doctors were unable to stop the bleeding, so they've taken her to surgery to try to remedy that.'

'But she'll be all right, won't she?'

'It's too early to say. She's lost a lot of blood. The doctors will let you know more when she's out of theatre.'

Sadie joined Jack at a row of chairs and they both sat, silently holding hands. Eventually, when it became obvious that they would be there for a while, Sadie said, 'So, Gianni, is it? Want to explain yourself?'

Jack's face coloured. 'I'm sorry, I should have told you earlier, but by the time we got together you'd known me as Jack for so long, and all our friends know me as Jack, I just never could find the right time to tell you.'

'Why call yourself Jack, though, if your name is Gianni? Why the deception in the first place?'

'I never meant to be deceptive. When I first got the job on the paper, the editor couldn't pronounce my name. "I'll just call you Jack, son," he said. It started there. Soon, I realised I'd get a lot further in Hollywood as Jack Porter than I would as Gianni Portelli. So I became Jack everywhere but at home. And it doesn't matter to me what you call me. Everyone else calls me Jack. Why not you?'

'Because, *Gianni*, I'm not everyone. I love you and it would be nice to know the name of the man I intend to spend the rest of my life with.'

Chapter 40

Sadie

Two days passed before Vivienne was strong enough to see her. Sadie and Gianni had waited hours for the news that the surgery had been successful, but the surgeon warned Sadie Vivienne wasn't out of the woods yet. There was nothing to be done but wait and see, he'd told them, advising Sadie to go home and get some rest. 'We'll call you when she's ready for visitors.'

Now, Sadie was shocked as she observed the frail woman propped up on pillows in the hospital bed. Vivienne looked small, childlike even. Her skin was pale and her blue eyes rimmed with red. Sadie held up the bouquet of sunny yellow roses she'd brought before placing them on the end of the bed. 'These are for you. I'll get the nurse to bring a vase in a minute.'

'Thank you,' Vivienne whispered. 'Thank you for coming.'

Sadie dragged the visitor's chair closer to the bed and took a seat. 'Of course I came,' Sadie said. 'Gian . . . Jack and I waited all day for you to come out of surgery. You gave us quite a scare.'

Vivienne attempted a smile. 'That Jack's a good guy, Sadie. You should stick with him.'

313

'Enough about me. How are you?'

'They tell me I'll survive.' She averted her gaze. 'So, you know . . .?'

'About the baby?' Sadie reached up and took her hand. 'Yes, I do. I'm so sorry, Vivienne.'

Vivienne sat up a little straighter and looked her in the eye. 'God, the papers must be having a field day.'

'The studio have put out a statement saying it was a burst appendix. No one here at the hospital will say differently. This won't hurt your career, Vivienne, the studio will make sure of that.'

A bitter laugh escaped her lips. 'My career? My career is the last thing I'm worried about. We're done filming *The House of Brides*. I only stayed on to finish it for the money. I wanted to give my baby the kind of childhood I never had.' A fat tear slid down her cheek.

'You'd planned on keeping the child?'

'Yes! I mean, I was shocked at first but then I got used to the idea. All I've ever wanted was a family. I thought I'd found that with you girls at the club, but . . . well, things got messed up, and then I discovered I was pregnant. I wanted this baby more than anything. It was my one chance at a proper family. At happiness.'

'Oh, Vivienne, I'm so sorry, but you'll recover. You still have your career and one day, when the time is right, you'll have another baby.'

'But that's just it. I won't.' Her voice rose, and there was a note of hysteria in it. 'To save my life they had to remove my womb.'

'Oh my goodness.' Sadie gasped. 'I had no idea. They told me about the surgery but I didn't understand. Not really. I can't imagine how you must be feeling.'

'It was my fault. I did so many things wrong.' Tears streamed down Vivienne's face now.

Sadie reached into her purse for a clean handkerchief, which she pressed into Vivienne's hand.

She wiped her eyes and continued. 'I didn't know, you see. After I left the Studio Club I was so lost, so ashamed about what happened that I spent all my free time trying to numb my feelings with alcohol, even pills sometimes, and I was swallowing diet pills like they

314

were candy. Then I realised I was pregnant. I swear I stopped all that as soon as I knew about the baby. But I think maybe the damage was already done.'

'And the father? Was it . . .?' Sadie left the question unfinished, too horrified to voice her concern. That knowledge would kill Peggy if she found out.

Vivienne's eyes flashed with anger. 'The baby was *mine*! Not his. We didn't need him or anyone else. My baby and I had each other, that was enough. Or, it would have been. But now . . . now I have nothing and it's all my own fault. I don't deserve to be a mother.'

Sadie rubbed her forearm in an attempt to comfort her. 'No one knows why you lost the baby, Vivienne. The doctors said it was just one of those things. You mustn't blame yourself. You need to focus on getting well. I know this must feel like the end of the world, but once you recover and get back to work, things will seem better.'

'You don't understand. I can't stay in this town. I'd already made up my mind that once this movie was done I was out of here. Don't you see, Sadie? This place has taken everything from me. I have nothing left – no family, no love, no self-respect. I fear if I stay any longer it will take my life. The movie caper is not all it's cracked up to be. Not for us girls, anyway. We have to give and give to get what we want. And even when we're rewarded for our sacrifices, it's a hollow victory. We're left with a version of ourselves we don't recognise anymore. I can't keep doing it.'

'Where will you go?'

'I've rented a little place up the coast near Monterey. I'd planned on raising my baby there, away from all this madness. I thought I could start again. Even though the baby's gone, as soon as I'm well enough I'm going to go there.'

'But what will you do?'

'Read, watch the sunset, maybe grow some vegetables. I have a little money now, so it's not like I need to rush out and get a job imme-diately. I can take a couple of months to decide what I want to do.'

Sadie couldn't see Vivienne in overalls tending a garden, but maybe she was wrong. If taking some time away from Hollywood was what she needed to heal, then who was Sadie to argue? 'That actually sounds quite lovely.'

'Sadie! You should come with me!' Her eyes sparked with hope. 'It would a perfect place for a writer. The house has three bedrooms, so there's plenty of room. Imagine how wonderful it would be, just the two of us.'

'As tempting as that sounds, I can't leave.'

'Why? You're not working for Harry anymore and you can write anywhere. If it's money you're worried about, please don't. I have enough to tide us over for a while.'

'That's so generous of you, but it's not the money. It's Jack – Gianni, in fact. His real name is Gianni; how about that?'

'An Italian boy, is he, our Jack? That explains why he's so dark and handsome.'

'I think it might be serious, Viv. In any case, I want to hang around for a bit and see.'

'I understand. I hope it works out for you both.'

A nurse bustled in to check Viv's temperature. 'Hmm, still a little high, Miss Lockhart, but it's coming down,' she said, after removing the thermometer. She glanced at the flowers on the end of the bed. 'Well, aren't these a little burst of sunshine? I'll go find a vase and bring them right back.' With that, she scuttled off, roses in hand.

'I probably should get going,' Sadie said.

'Not yet! Please stay a little longer.' Viv chewed her bottom lip for a minute. 'There's something I've been wanting to tell you for a while, but I need you to promise you won't say anything to the others. I don't want them to know about any of this. Please don't tell them about the baby, and not what I'm about to tell you either.'

'Of course. You can trust me to keep your secrets, I promise.'

'I . . . I want to tell you what happened with Mike.' Tears filled her eyes. 'I'm sorry I didn't tell you before. This is incredibly hard to say, but I've had time to think while I've been in hospital and I've decided I want to explain.'

'Oh, Viv, you don't have to do that right now. Maybe when you're feeling better.'

Heavy tears rolled down Vivienne's cheeks. 'It wasn't my fault, Sadie. I mean, it all happened so fast. I should have stopped—'

'What's all this, then?' the nurse said, as she returned with the flowers. 'We can't have you upsetting yourself, Miss Lockhart. You're already running a little fever and a crying fit won't help that.' She turned her attention to Sadie. 'I think you should go now. Miss Lockhart needs her rest.'

'Sadie, no!' Vivienne sobbed. 'I need to tell you now, before I chicken out.'

'Miss, I must insist.' The nurse's tone was stern. 'This distress is doing your friend no good.'

'Viv, shh now,' Sadie cajoled. 'I'll come back tomorrow, I promise. You can tell me then. Everything will be okay. You get some rest now.'

When Sadie returned the following afternoon, Vivienne had discharged herself.

Sadie tried everything she could think of to contact her but to no avail. She raced to the last place she'd visited Viv – a hotel in West Hollywood – but she'd checked out of there weeks ago and hadn't left a forwarding address. The phone number Sadie had for her was no longer in service. She tried her contacts at Paramount, but the studio was tight-lipped, saying that Miss Lockhart had fulfilled her contractual obligations and had intended to take a break. Even Gianni couldn't unearth any information about her.

'Sorry, Sade,' he said. 'Viv's simply not a big enough star for anyone to take too much notice.'

'But what about all those reporters who turned up at the hospital last week?'

'She collapsed on a movie set and was gravely ill. I know this is horrible, but there was a rumour that she'd overdosed and wouldn't live. When that didn't turn out to be the case, the papers lost interest. And there's really no story here as far as anyone else is concerned.

She left hospital and has gone away to recuperate – that's how it looks to anyone who doesn't know her.'

'She was in a terrible state when I left her. I'm really worried.'

'I know, honey, but there's nothing we can do. I'm sure she'll sort herself out and get in touch eventually.'

'I hope so.' The words felt hollow. Sadie had a sinking feeling that she might never see Vivienne again.

31 December 1999

After I've finished reading Vivienne's shattering diary entry, I place the journal down on the coffee table. Julia reaches for it and rereads the words she's just heard, shaking her head and sighing as she does so.

Peggy's face is ashen. 'I should have known. He was such a terrible man. Look at how he treated me.'

'But you weren't married to him when he did this. You didn't know about his violent streak,' I say.

'That's no excuse. Vivienne was my friend. I should have talked to her. Given her the chance to explain.' She drains the last mouthful of wine from her glass. 'I was just so angry at her.'

I understand how Peggy feels, but wallowing in guilt isn't the answer. 'She wouldn't have told you anything. I did try to talk to her back then. She blamed herself for everything. I just assumed that meant she'd made a mistake.'

Julia stands up and goes to the window. She sips her wine and stares out at the lake. 'If this is anyone's fault, it's mine. I was the one who told you what I saw, without bothering to ask Vivienne for her side of the story. She ran after me that day. I yelled at her and demanded that she tell me

319

what happened, and when she didn't immediately come up with a satisfactory explanation I assumed the worst. Dear god, she must have been
so traumatised. And I made that a million times worse. No wonder she
didn't think anyone would believe her.'

'I'm sure we all have regrets,' I say.

'I don't understand why she left Hollywood, though,' Peggy says.
'It's not like anyone ever saw the photos. If Mike still had them, he never
shared them with me and he certainly didn't give them to the studio.
There was no need for Vivienne to leave. It wasn't as if any of us were
talking about what happened with him. Her career was just starting to
take off, too.'

'Things got worse for her,' I say. 'It wasn't just the assault she was
dealing with. It's all there in the diary. But, basically, she got pregnant.
I believe it was from that encounter with Mike.'

'Oh, god!' Peggy says. 'I think I need another drink.' She heads to the
kitchen and grabs a bottle from the fridge.

Julia sits back on the couch and continues reading Vivienne's words
as Peggy refills our glasses.

'Vivienne planned on having the baby,' I say. 'She wanted to leave
Hollywood and give her child a normal family life. But then there was a
complication and she lost the baby. She haemorrhaged so badly that the
doctors had to perform a hysterectomy to save her life. I think that was
the final straw.'

Tears are now streaming down Julia's face as she reads. 'This
explains so much,' she says. 'No wonder she hated me. I knew she was
angry that I'd told Peggy about her and Mike, but I still couldn't believe
that she outed Charlie and me to the press. Now I understand why.
Mike raped her and I didn't support her. In fact, I made her feel worse.
She felt she'd been wronged, and she lashed out. It was a terrible
thing to do, but at least now I have some comprehension of why she
did it.'

'I'm not so sure it was her,' I say.

'What do you mean?' Julia looks aghast. 'You were the one who
confirmed it was her when you read her diary.'

'I know.' Guilt churns my stomach. 'What I read seemed so damning. But it was only one page and it was out of context. I thought she was confessing to having sex with Mike, but she was actually talking about the photos being a mistake. And now I've read the whole diary, I'm almost certain it wasn't her who outed you. She denies knowing anything about it. Why would she say that in her own journal? The excerpt I told you about – the one where I thought she was expressing a desire to get back at you – was just ranting on the page. Yes, she was angry at you, but she saved the worst of her contempt for herself. On the following page she does a complete turnaround and says that all of it is her fault and she doesn't deserve our love or friendship.'

'If it wasn't her, then who?' Julia looks unconvinced.

Peggy gulps her wine and looks stricken. 'It was me,' she says quietly. 'I was the one who told the press.'

'*What?*' Julia and I say in unison.

'It was an accident. I didn't deliberately out you. I would never, ever do anything to hurt you, Julia, not on purpose. You must know that.'

'It seems I don't know anything.' Julia's voice is flat and cold.

My head is spinning. It seems Vivienne is not the only one who's been keeping secrets all these years. 'Tell us how it happened,' I say softly.

'I was tricked by that gossip columnist who took me out to lunch to interview me about my wedding. She plied me with champagne – and you know I couldn't really hold my drink in those days. Anyway, she flattered and charmed me the whole time, behaving as if we were a pair of girlfriends having lunch. At the end she said something like, "Aren't you worried about your friend Julia having a relationship with Charlie Hudson?", so it seemed as if she already knew. I confessed that I *was* worried because I couldn't see how you could have a future together. I thought we were talking off the record, so I was utterly horrified when I saw the story in the paper.'

'I can't believe this. I never once suspected you. I mean, you didn't know any of the details of our affair, so how . . .' Julia trails off, seemingly bewildered by this information.

'I knew more than you thought. It wasn't that hard to figure out. Let's just say Charlie wasn't always careful about what he said around me. I guess he figured I already knew. But I didn't have to give Queenie any details – she already knew or at least suspected you were meeting at Chateau Marmont. I honestly don't know how. Someone must have seen you, Julia, or maybe some of Charlie's people talked. All I did was confirm the suspicions.'

'But you let Vivienne take the blame,' I say. 'How could you do such a thing?'

'I know, I know. It was reprehensible. Believe me, there's nothing you can say that I haven't said to myself. But it just sort of happened. I was so angry at Vivienne for sleeping with Mike. I had no desire to ever see her again. Then, when Julia assumed she was to blame for the story, I figured it was what she deserved. You know, God punishing her for what she'd done to me. I know that sounds a weak excuse, but I truly believed it at the time.'

'You sat there every day comforting me, when all along you knew you were the cause of my pain. How could you, Peggy?' Julia's voice is laced with rage.

'I'm sorry, Jules.' There's a wobble in Peggy's voice now and her eyes shine with tears. 'So sorry. But you must know that relationship was doomed. If it was meant to be, no amount of newspaper coverage could have destroyed it. I'm so sorry it was me who let the cat out of the bag, and I truly didn't mean for it to happen, but at the time I justified my mistake by telling myself you couldn't have kept seeing Charlie secretly forever. People were obviously talking. You were bound to get discovered eventually.'

'That's hardly the point, is it? He was the love of my life! You were my best friend. I trusted you and you let me down.'

Peggy hangs her head and presses her palms to her eyes. Eventually she looks up. 'I know that. I'm desperately ashamed of what happened. I wish I could go back in time and change everything. I wish I'd supported you and Charlie more. I thought you were making a mistake, but now I realise that I was wrong. I wish I'd never gone to that lunch. I wish I'd never met Mike—'

'You let me believe that Vivienne had betrayed me,' Julia says, cutting her off. 'For decades I've carried this grudge around. I hated Vivienne and you let me. I can't believe you deceived me like this, Peggy. What a fool I've been.'

Tears are streaming down Peggy's face now. 'Jules, I'm so sorry. So many times I've gone to tell you but couldn't. I was so afraid of losing you.' She pauses and looks at me. 'And you too, Sadie.' Her trembling hand reaches for her drink. She takes a sip and then wipes her eyes. 'After Harmony was born and things went pear-shaped with Mike, I had no one else. Remember? My parents wanted me to take him back. No matter that they'd seen my bruises. They told me I needed to go home and be a better wife to him. You girls got me through that time. I couldn't imagine my life without you.'

'Maybe if you'd told me in the beginning, I would have understood,' Julia says.

'Maybe,' Peggy says, her voice wobbling. 'But I couldn't take that risk.'

'But what about Vivienne?' I ask. 'You must have realised what an injustice you were doing her.'

Peggy exhales a long, slow breath. 'You have to understand how angry I was over what happened with Mike. I didn't know . . . what I know now. And then she was gone. I figured she wasn't part of our lives anymore, and so Julia's anger couldn't really hurt her.'

'How convenient for you.' Julia's voice drips with sarcasm.

'I know what I did was wrong. I've prayed every single day since then for God's forgiveness. And I've devoted my life to atoning for my sins. Every single charity I've formed has been a part of my attempt to redeem myself. All those library donations and the literacy charities I've founded, they're all in honour of Viv, because of her love of books . . .'

It seems both Julia and I are speechless, because neither of us responds.

'I don't know what else I can say,' Peggy finishes, wringing her hands. 'I hope that you can forgive me.'

'*Forgive* you? I can't even look at you.' Julia stands and walks to the window again.

This isn't how I pictured this afternoon unfolding. I'd hoped that when Julia and Peggy found out the truth about Vivienne, there could be some type of reconciliation between the four of us. That perhaps we could put the past behind us. 'I think we all need to take a breath,' I say. 'We can't change the past, and Vivienne needs us.'

'I'm Vivienne.' She walks into the room and takes a seat next to me. 'Who are you?'

There's silence as we all register her presence, but after a moment I recover enough to say, 'I'm Sadie, remember? I'm here to look after you. This is Peggy and Julia. They've come to spend New Year's Eve with us.'

Vivienne claps her hands together. 'Are we having a party? What fun! Will someone get me a drink?'

Peggy cocks an eyebrow at me and I nod. 'Consider it done,' she says.

Julia walks behind the sofa and places her hand on Vivienne's shoulder. 'Vivienne,' she says. 'It's so lovely to see you after all this time. I'm afraid I can't stay, though. I'm sorry to be a party pooper.'

I turn to look at her. 'Jules, please—'

'I'm going to need a lift into town,' she says. She squeezes Vivienne's shoulder and walks towards the stairs.

'Why is your friend leaving?' Vivienne asks.

'I'm not sure. You stay up here with Peggy and I'll go see if I can find out.' I pat her knee. 'Don't worry. We're going to have a great night tonight. Last night of the century!'

Peggy places a glass in front of Vivienne and then looks at me for reassurance. 'Sadie . . .'

I take her hand and squeeze it. We're too old to hold on to past hurts. We've all made mistakes. We've all let Vivienne down. What's important is what we do next. 'It'll be okay. Let me talk to her.'

I follow Julia downstairs to the spare bedroom, where I find her stuffing her coat into her suitcase. 'I'm going to call the motel in town. See if they have vacancy for tonight. Can you drive me there, please?'

'No.'

She swings around to look me in the eye, her expression indignant. 'Excuse me?'

'I will not drive you into town. For starters, I've been drinking. I'm not sure I'm fit to drive. But even if I am, running away from this is not the answer. Not talking about things is what got us where we are today. We dropped the ball with Vivienne. All of us. She was in trouble and we didn't reach out to help her. We didn't talk about what happened and that's led to a lifetime of hurt. I'm not going to make that same mistake again. She needs us *now*. I don't know what the future holds, but I know that I am not going to abandon her again.'

'What are you suggesting? That we just forget what happened? Let Peggy off scot-free? I'm not sure I can do that.'

'Not forget, but forgive. I'm saying we should put the past behind us and focus on making Vivienne happy. All she wants is a party. Please stay. At least for tonight. Don't you owe her that much?'

Julia sighs. 'I'm not sure I can move past this.'

'Of course you can, if you choose to. That's up to you. For heaven's sake, Julia, we're not getting any younger. What do we have in this life if we don't have each other? We're in our sixties and we're single. Peggy's the only one with a child, but I wouldn't bet on Harmony looking after her mother in her old age. We should be looking out for each other, not harbouring grudges about things that happened decades ago. We've already lost so much time, but we have an opportunity to make up for that. Tomorrow is the first day of the new millennium. I can't think of any better time for a fresh start. What do you say?'

She smiles. 'You and your words. You really should have gone into politics, you know.'

'So you'll stay?'

'I'll stay for tonight, for Vivienne's sake. You're right about one thing – I owe her that much. After that, well . . . let's just wait and see.'

⁓

It's 11 pm when I check my watch. There's a single hour left of this year, this decade, this century. I'm feeling optimistic about the new year. It's hard not to be when I'm sitting here with my three best friends in the world. For the first time since Gianni died, I'm not seeing in the new year alone.

Every year I lie about my plans so I don't have to go to Tony's New Year's Eve party. Not because it's dull (although, truly, it is) but because I feel Gianni's absence so intensely at this time of the year. These days my grief isn't at the forefront of my mind. When he first died I dragged his loss around like a boulder. It seemed almost impossible to get anything done. These days, it's more like a pebble in my shoe. Still noticeable, but I can keep moving forward, at least most of the time. But on New Year's Eve, the thought of the world turning without him for another year seems impossible for me to bear.

Gianni loved a celebration. He was always the life of the party, wherever we went. His charm and enthusiasm for life meant we were never short of invitations. It was ironic, really. Gianni was an acclaimed novelist. So many writers are sworn introverts and I count myself among that number. Despite having spent much of my working life in an extrovert's paradise, I would much rather stay home with a book than attend a party. It was Gianni, who loved people, dragging me, often against my will, out to socialise every chance he got. New Year's Eve was always the highlight of his social calendar.

In his absence, I have developed my own New Year's Eve ritual. I make lasagne – his favourite – and drink a couple of glasses of shiraz. I raise a glass to my love and tuck myself up in bed long before midnight.

But not this year.

By the time Julia and I make our way back upstairs, Peggy has turned the contents of the fridge and pantry into a veritable feast of finger food, which she's laid out on the dining room table. She and Vivienne have found an old Beatles record and are dancing to 'Twist and Shout'.

I look at Julia. 'Shall we?'

She only hesitates for a second before taking me by the hand and beginning to twist.

❧

We've spent the past few hours dancing, eating, drinking and laughing, but have now reached the point where our weary middle-aged bodies can tolerate no more. I put Joni Mitchell on the record player and turn the volume down as the others collapse onto the sofas. Vivienne, buoyed by the company and the activity, is still surprisingly alert. She doesn't recognise any of us, and I've come to realise she's probably never going to. But she's enjoying our company, accepting us as new friends, and that's something, at least.

I wish there was a way to make her understand that we all know the truth now. That she is redeemed in our eyes and that we are the ones who should feel shame for letting her down. Maybe if we all look at her old photo album and the scrapbook together, she might make the connection?

'More wine, anyone?' I ask. 'Or should I make coffee?'

'I'll take a coffee,' Julia says. 'I'm going to need it if I'm going to be awake to see in the new year.'

Peggy nods. 'I've had enough wine. I'll probably have a hangover tomorrow as it is.'

'I'll make a fresh pot,' I say.

While the coffee is brewing, I slip into the office to retrieve the photo album and scrapbook. When I return, Peggy's in the kitchen, putting coffee cups, cream, sugar and a bowl of chocolates on a tray. 'How are you doing?' I ask.

'I'm relieved to have told you after all these years. But Julia hasn't spoken to me directly since I confessed.' Her eyes glisten with unshed tears.

'She will,' I say, trying to convince myself that this is true. If I'm honest, I'm not sure how I feel about Peggy myself right now. I'm trying to keep my anger at bay for Vivienne's sake, but the depth of her deception has rocked me. I need more time to process my feelings about what she did. Even so, I know that in the end, I will forgive her. We've wasted enough of our lives holding grudges. I'm done with that.

I look Peggy in the eye. 'You two have been through too much together to throw your friendship away over something that happened when we were mere girls. Come on, let's take this in. I have a plan to get us all reminiscing.'

As Peggy pours the coffee, I show Vivienne the journals and scrap-book.

Her face lights up with recognition. 'My journals!'

I nod. 'Yes. I thought we could look at them together, if that's okay?'

'Yes, of course. I'd love you to see my photos.'

'Can we start with the scrapbook?' I say. 'I think Peggy and Julia would love to see that.'

Vivienne nods and she opens it up.

I beckon to the others. 'Come look at this, you two – it's amazing!' Somehow, we all manage to squish together on the one sofa, and I read the first article aloud.

Peggy's Perfect Role
Pretty Peggy Carmichael is the star of the hit new TV series My Mermaid Wife, *and it seems that after years of being a night-club singer, the talented actress has finally found her perfect role. Peggy, who plays a newlywed with a difference, says her recent marriage has prepared her for the role of Sirena. "As new brides, Sirena and I are going through a lot of the same things," she told* Sound and Screen Magazine . . .

The article is accompanied by two photos, one of Peggy on her wedding day and one of her wearing Sirena's fish-tail costume.

'Oh my goodness – look how gorgeous I was,' Peggy says, and we all laugh. Even Julia manages a little chortle.

Vivienne flips the pages, and our lives unfold before our eyes.

Peggy's marriage and her divorce feature, as does the birth of her daughter, and there are articles about her charities as well as her various TV roles.

When Vivienne gets to a piece about Julia's marriage to Tony, Julia puts her hand out and touches the image of her wedding. 'Poor Tony,' she says. 'He really got a dud deal.'

'Pfft,' says Peggy. 'He got a great deal if you ask me. He got to be the husband of Julia Newman, that in itself makes him lucky. But together you built something really special. All those hit TV shows Jeweltone produced in the beginning and then the movies. You were the brains behind all of that.'

'That's not exactly true.' Julia shakes her head. 'Yes, it was mostly me who found the talent and the scripts, but it was Tony who worked out how to make everything happen. He was responsible for the tedious things I didn't give a toss about, like budgets and taxes.' She laughs. 'And it was his idea to start with TV and work our way up to movies. That was a genius move. If it had been up to me, I would have started with big-budget movies and we would have been out of business before we'd got started.'

'That just shows what a great team you made,' Peggy insists. 'I'm sure Tony doesn't have any regrets.'

Vivienne turns the page again and Peggy says, 'Look. There's the announcement about Jeweltone Productions taking over Goldstar.'

Julia scans the article. 'That was Tony's final wedding anniversary gift to me. I guess it *was* a pretty good marriage, even if he only ever had eyes for you, Peg.'

Is this the first signs of forgiveness we're seeing? I hope so.

'It's a shame I didn't fall in love with him instead of that asshole I ended up marrying. It's just that—'

'He's Tony,' Vivienne says, and we all burst out laughing. I'm not sure Vivienne meant the joke or whether it was just a statement with fortunate timing, but who cares? We're together and we're laughing. That's what really counts.

We keep flipping the pages and the highlights of our lives, carefully curated by our friend, keep coming.

There are dozens of articles about Julia's movies and her directing debut. There are also pages devoted to Julia's work as the joint head of Jeweltone, and her activism to get equal opportunities for women directors.

My life has been less public, but nevertheless, Vivienne has found plenty to commemorate. There are clippings from some of the TV shows I've worked on. How Viv knew which shows I worked on is a mystery I'll probably never get to the bottom of. Also featured is an article from *TV Guide* where I'm mentioned as the writer of Peggy's next show after *My Mermaid Wife*. I wrote *And Baby Makes Two* – a series about a single mother after the loss of her husband – for Peggy in 1965, just after she left Mike. It was a tough time for her. Harmony was only two and Peggy was at her wits' end with both her marriage and her career in turmoil. Julia and I knew she needed stability in her life. We wanted her to know she didn't need Mike to be successful, so we worked together to make a show that would showcase Peggy's talents. It had a good run, too – three seasons with decent ratings, but then Peg was offered her own variety show at CBS and Julia and I both encouraged her to take up that opportunity.

The premiere of my one screenplay, *Before I Let You Go*, gets some page space too. The movie earnt some critical acclaim but was a flop at the box office. Not that you would know that by looking at Viv's scrapbook. As well as clipping a number of favourable reviews, she's illustrated the page border with balloons and streamers, and the glossy promotional material that's stuck in the middle actually looks quite impressive.

Of course, there are no marriages, births or divorces to record for me, but a lump forms in my throat when I see Gianni's obituary pasted on a page by itself. I press two fingers to my lips and then touch his photo. The now familiar regrets float into my mind before I can push them away.

Why didn't I marry him? Or give him a child?

Gianni never pushed me for anything, but he wanted the whole shebang. Wife and family, picket fence. He made that sacrifice for me. I was the selfish one. I wasn't prepared to give up my career and he accepted that. In the end, the joke was on me. He's gone and I have nothing of him. If we'd had a child, would I see Gianni in her eyes?

In her smile? There's no good answer to this question and I force myself to focus on the present.

Vivienne has moved on to the photo album now. She flips it open to the first page and gasps. 'Oh! Oh! This is the Hollywood Studio Club. I lived there when I was first starting out. So much fun! I'm a famous movie star, you know.'

'We know,' Julia says kindly. 'We've seen your movies.'

Vivienne beams. 'Well, aren't you sweet?' She turns the book to the next page. It's a photo of her with some actor whose name none of us can remember. 'I loved that dress,' she says, pointing at the black-and-white photo. 'It was the most gorgeous shade of violet and I felt so beautiful when I wore it. I bought it with the money I made on . . .' Her smile momentarily disappears, and she waves her hand dismissively. 'On a photo shoot for a magazine advertisement, I think. In any case, the dress was magnificent.'

'You still have that dress. It's packed away, but I promise I'll get it out soon and show you,' I say, making a mental note to make sure the dress comes back to LA with us and doesn't accidentally end up in storage.

The next photo is of the two of us sitting on Vivienne's bed, poking out our tongues at the camera. She laughs. 'Oh, this is Sadie. My roommate. My best friend.' Her face becomes more pensive. 'I miss her so much.'

'I'm Sadie,' I say gently. 'I'm here, Vivienne.'

She smiles. 'Yes, I know. You're Sadie and you're looking after me.'

I point at the cheeky girl in the photo. 'I'm *this* Sadie, Vivienne. We're the same person.' I take the album from her and flip until I find a photo of Julia and Peggy. I point to the image of Julia first. 'This is Julia.'

'I'm here too,' Julia says. 'I'm the Julia from the photo.'

Peggy points to the photo of herself. 'And I'm the same Peggy from all those years ago.'

'We're all here, Vivienne,' I say. 'And we love you!'

'Oh, oh!' she says, embracing us one by one. 'You're here, you're here! I thought I'd never see you again.'

It's a magical moment right on midnight. When the clock ticks over to twelve, we stand up, hold hands and sing 'Auld Lang Syne'.

I know that in the morning, Vivienne will have forgotten who we are, but we'll be here to remind her and, if nothing else, hopefully somewhere deep down the knowledge of our love will remain.

New Year's Day, 2000

Peggy and Julia are both up before me and I smell bacon frying when I come up the stairs. Julia and I shared the bed in the guestroom while Peggy made do with the couch. You'd never know, though. She looks fresh as a daisy and is busy cooking breakfast while Julia pours coffee. Neither of them is speaking, but I get the sense that the silence between them is an easy one. I hope I'm right.

Peggy waves a pair of tongs at me. 'Good morning! How's your head?'

'A little foggy, I've got to say. Unlike you two. What's your secret?'

Julia laughs and points to a champagne flute filled with orange juice. 'Peggy's famous hangover cure.'

'Oh? What's in it then?'

'Orange juice with hair of the dog. Do you want one?'

'Ugh. No thanks. I'll just grab an aspirin instead.'

They smile and exchange a glance. My heart lifts and with it some of the brain fog. Everything is going to be all right.

'Oh, come on,' Peggy says. 'You'll never know if it works unless you try it.' She leaves the bacon for a moment to pour me a glass.

I take a sip and wince at the bitterness, but don't say anything. 'I take it the world hasn't ended?'

'Not to our knowledge,' Peggy says. 'I put the TV on earlier to get the news and apparently Y2K has been a non-event.'

'Thank goodness for that.'

Julia laughs. 'I'm not sure it would have affected you too badly, Sadie. You'd be more than happy to go back to bashing on an old typewriter.'

'Speaking of which, there's something I want to ask you both. How would you feel about me writing Vivienne's story properly?'

'You mean writing the memoir?'

'Not quite, but fictionalising Vivienne's story. Turning it into a screenplay.'

Julia reaches out and takes my hand in hers. 'You're ready to write again?'

'I think I am.'

She pulls me in for a hug. 'That's great news as far as I'm concerned.'

Peggy nods enthusiastically as she takes the pan off the cooktop. 'That's fantastic, Sade. You should go for it! And Vivienne deserves to have her story told, one way or another.'

'I thought we could all be involved. It could be the project you're always on at me to write for you, Julia. Maybe you and Peg could even play yourselves – not your younger selves of course, but as you are now. Maybe Vivienne could do a cameo, if it doesn't stress her too much. Of course, we'd want you to direct too.'

'That's an amazing idea!' Julia says.

Peggy's eyes are shining with tears. 'We could call it *The Studio Girls*,' she says.

'That's not a bad idea. Let's run it by Vivienne when she gets up.'

Julia looks at the bacon in the pan Peggy's holding. 'Should we wake her for breakfast?'

I shake my head. 'She's a late sleeper and we kept her up way after bedtime last night, so best to leave her be, I think.'

Peggy plates up the breakfast and we head to the dining table to eat.

'Maybe this is a good chance for us to talk about Vivienne's future,' I say. 'Obviously we're all she has. It's clear that she can no longer take care of herself, so I think we have to work out what's possible.'

'I'd love to say she could live with me,' Julia says, 'but I'm still working. I just don't have the time to care for her properly. I guess I could employ a nurse to help out, but maybe she'd get better care in a specialist facility. Perhaps somewhere in Beverly Hills, then we'd all be able to visit regularly.'

I nod. As much as I hate the idea of putting her into care, I'm not sure any of us is equipped to manage her needs full time. 'I've been thinking similar things. I don't know that she has the money for a special-ist medical facility, though. She owns this house, but there's nothing in her bank account.'

'There's no need to worry about money,' Julia says. 'I can cover her costs no matter what they are.'

Peggy puts down her fork. 'Ladies, looking at those old photos of the Studio Club gave me an idea. I think maybe our former home could be the answer to our problem.'

Julia looks up from her plate. 'What do you mean?'

'The club's up for sale, right? We could buy it between us and renovate it into luxury apartments, but with a twist. One floor could have assisted care – an on-site nurse and maybe a staffed activities room. We could have some shared facilities, like a dining and living area, for residents to socialise in. Maybe even a beauty salon!' She was becoming more and more animated as she spoke.

'And Vivienne would live there?' I say.

'Yes. Vivienne could go into one of the assisted care apartments and I could live in one of the others. That way I'd be there for her when I'm not working but she'd be cared for properly when I'm away.'

I start do the sums in my head. 'It's a nice idea, Peg, truly. But it will cost a fortune.'

'Julia and I have got plenty of money. What else are we doing with it? Besides, it'll be a good investment. We could sell off the rest of the apartments to other single women nearing retirement age. Maybe we'll all end up living there together. How fun would that be? Just like when we were girls.'

'That sounds like a good solution, if we can pull it off,' Julia says. 'You have some building contacts through your work, don't you, Sadie?'

'Yeah, I do. I know quite a few builders who could advise us. You'd really live there, Peg?' I ask. 'What about your beautiful house?'

'It's way too big for me now. And maybe if I was in a smaller place Harmony would think twice about turning up uninvited and staying for months at a time. Honestly, it feels like the perfect solution. And in some small way, maybe it can help me to make up for all the heartache I've caused.'

Is this really something we can do? I can't contribute much financially, but I can definitely lend my expertise. Between them, Peggy and Julia easily have the money for such a project. Maybe we wouldn't even have to sell this place. We could keep it as a vacation home for Vivienne. That way she could maintain her connection to George. I nod slowly. 'You know what? Let's make this happen.' I raise my glass. 'Here's to bringing the Hollywood Studio Club back to life.'

The others raise their glasses, just as Vivienne walks into the kitchen. 'It seems I've walked in on a party,' she says. 'What are we toasting?'

'Old friends and new beginnings,' I say.

She smiles. 'I guess I'd better get myself a drink then.'

336

Author's note

Welcome to the Hollywood Studio Club: a boarding house for young women seeking a career in the movie industry that operated for a large part of the twentieth century.

I learned about the existence of the club when I was researching movie stars of the 1950s for my previous novel, *The One and Only Dolly Jamieson*. Much of the information I collected didn't end up being included in that book, but I found it so fascinating that I decided I would set my next novel in the club during its heyday.

The Studio Club began in the early 1900s after Mrs Eleanor Jones, a librarian at the Hollywood Public Library, noticed that a number of young women were staying at the library until closing time because they had nowhere else to go. Jones enlisted the help of several eminent Hollywood women to form a drama club at the library. After the YWCA became involved through providing classes in dance and other areas of interest to the women, the club quickly outgrew the library space and was soon relocated to the former home of the Hollywood Military Academy.

In 1916, the club officially opened its doors to residents and eighty young women – all with aspirations to work in the film industry – moved in. The residents had access to rehearsal spaces, classes, a gymnasium and many other facilities. Demand for accommodation at the club continued to grow, and after a decade in its original location it moved to a purpose-built home at 1215 Lodi Place, Hollywood. The club remained in this location until its closure in 1976.

Many of Hollywood's biggest names once called the Studio Club home. Barbara Britton, Ann B. Davis, Donna Douglas, Barbara Eden, Barbara Hale, Nancy Kwan, Marilyn Monroe, Rita Moreno, Kim Novak, Maureen O'Sullivan, Ayn Rand, Donna Reed and Sally Struthers all lived there at some point.

For the most part the club was a safe haven for its inhabitants, but there was a darker side to the supervised environment as well. Occasionally, studio heads who wanted to exert control over their female stars would make residency at the club compulsory.

Nevertheless, most former residents recall the club with fondness. Many of the women who lived there formed lifelong friendships with their housemates. These enduring relationships are the inspiration behind this book. I developed the idea after viewing an episode of *Visiting with Huell Howser* that was produced in the 1990s, which documented the friendship of five former residents who, at the time of filming, had been meeting weekly for five decades!

In this novel I drew on the stories of many former 'Studio Girls' – some famous, some not! – to construct my protagonists. Sadie, Vivienne, Julia and Peggy are entirely fictitious characters, but their experiences reflect the lives of many women who lived in Hollywood during the 1940s, 1950s and 1960s.

Book club discussion notes

1. April wasn't employed to care for Vivienne, but she took on that role after George died. Do you think she made the right decision to leave Vivienne at the Studio Club reunion? What other choices did she have?

2. When Vivienne comes back into the lives of the other women, it is clear she is vulnerable. Sadie feels compelled to help her, but the other women do not. Can you understand why Peggy and Julia are reluctant to get involved? What do you think you would you do in the same situation?

3. During the 'studio era', Hollywood studios exerted a great deal of control over their stars, particularly the female ones. Do you think the price of celebrity was worth it in that era? What about now?

4. Julia and Charlie are clearly in love. Why can't they make their relationship work? Do you think the problems they faced as an interracial couple are a thing of the past, or do couples today experience similar obstacles?

5. When Julia discovers Vivienne and Mike together, it is Vivienne who faces consequences; Mike comes out of the incident unscathed. In the 1950s, women often received the blame for men's bad behaviour. Do you think things have changed since then?

6. Why do you think Vivienne didn't try harder to explain what had happened with Mike?

7. What do you think of Peggy's behaviour? Can you understand why she let Vivienne take the blame for her mistake? Do you think she makes up for her betrayal by the end of the book?

8. This story is told through the eyes of Sadie, Julia and Peggy. Vivienne does not get her own point of view, except in occasional diary entries. Why do you think the author chose to tell the story this way?

9. The book was inspired by the real Hollywood Studio Club, which was established to keep young women in Hollywood safe. Do you think Peggy, Julia, Sadie and Vivienne benefited from their time living there? Why or why not?

10. The friendships in the book span a period of more than four decades. What makes some friendships last while others fade away?

Acknowledgements

This book was written on Gunaikurnai Country. I acknowledge and pay my respects to elders and storytellers past and present, and extend that respect to all First Nations people.

A huge thank you to all at Penguin Random House Australia – my amazing publisher, Beverley Cousins, editors Kathryn Knight and Vanessa Pellatt, cover designer Debra Billson and everyone who works hard in publicity, marketing and sales. I appreciate you all.

Thanks also to my spectacular agent, Anjanette Fennell, for her ongoing support and encouragement. Love our chats, Anj!

I count myself lucky to be part of a wonderfully supportive writing community. Thanks to all the authors, librarians, booksellers, reviewers and readers who are part of my writing world. I truly appreciate every one of you. I'd particularly like to mention: Ellie O'Neill and Kelly Rimmer for providing feedback on early drafts of this novel; booksellers Stacey Moore (Bookgrove), Natasha Hunt (Collins Booksellers Sale) and all at Collins Booksellers Orange for going above and beyond in promoting my books; and the staff of Wellington Shire Libraries for embracing me as one of their own! Also, a big shout-out to all the writers I mentor and those who join me for Write Along. Working with you energises me and reminds me of why I want to write.

I owe a huge debt of gratitude to my VA, Annie Bucknall, who works tirelessly to make me look good. Annie, I so appreciate everything you do for me.

This book is all about female friendship, and I'm happy to say I felt confident exploring this topic because I have the greatest friends in the world. (I'm mentally drawing up plans for our very own Studio Club for when we retire.) Thanks as always to Jane Cockram, Sally Hepworth and Kirsty Manning for being my crew, Kerryn Mayne for making me laugh on a daily basis, my Writers' Camp people – Amanda Knight, Emily Madden, Rebecca Heath and Rachael Johns – for sticking with me since the very beginning, and to Delwyn Jenkins and Kylie Ladd for always being there for me.

I'm grateful for the patience of my wonderful friends Jenelle and Fiona, who listen to far more talk about writing than any non-writer should have to.

Tess Woods has provided a sympathetic ear and wise counsel for many years now, as well as daily *Schitt's Creek* memes, which I think we can all agree makes her a gold medallist in the friend Olympics.

Kelly Rimmer is my daily sounding board, chief plot-untangler and unconditional ally in all things writing, politics and life. I wouldn't want to do this without you, Kelly.

To my local community: thank you so much for rolling out the welcome mat. I love living in this part of the world. Special shout-out to Badger and Hare for making me feel like a local and for having the best coffee anywhere in the state! Thanks to all the local writers I've connected with, especially my Reading Couch co-host, Renee Conoulty. To my new friends at The Joy Collective, thank you for including me. I'm so excited to see what comes from our creative collaboration.

As always, I want to express my love and gratitude for my wonderful family. Charlie, Will and Alex, you are the stars of the movie of my life, and David, you'll always be my leading man.

Finally, but most importantly, I want to thank my readers. Without you, there is no point in writing. Thank you so much for your support. It means the world to me.

After working for many years as a teacher (and a brief stint as a professional organiser – before Marie Kondo made it cool), Lisa Ireland is now a full-time writer.

Lisa lives with her husband in a small town in Gippsland, Victoria. When not writing, she spends her days mentoring aspiring authors, drinking coffee and playing minion to her incredibly spoiled dog, Lulu.

The Studio Girls is Lisa's eighth novel.

You can connect with Lisa at:
lisairelandbooks.com
Instagram: @lisairelandbooks
Facebook: facebook.com/lisairelandbooks
The Reading Couch: facebook.com/groups/149288140312440

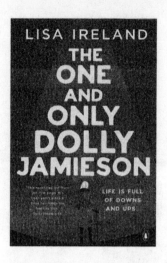

Life is full of downs and ups . . .

Dolly Jamieson is *not* homeless, she's merely between permanent abodes. The 78-year-old spends her days keeping warm at the local library, where she enjoys sparring with the officious head librarian and helping herself to the free morning tea. It's not so bad, really.

But it's certainly a far cry from the 1960s, when this humble girl from Geelong became an international star of the stage. As the acclaimed lead in the Broadway production of *The Rose of France*, all Dolly's dreams had come true.

So how, in her old age, did she end up here?

When Jane Leveson, a well-to-do newcomer to the library, shows an interest in Dolly, the pair strike up an unlikely friendship – and soon Jane is offering to help Dolly write her memoirs.

Yet Dolly can detect a deep sadness in the younger woman's eyes. Perhaps by working together to recount the glittering highs, devastating lows and tragic secrets of Dolly's life, both women can finally face their pasts and start to heal . . .

'From the glamour of Broadway in the 1960s to the realities of life for the unhoused today, this is a riveting and heartbreaking story of friendship, second chances and hope.' Kelly Rimmer

'This novel had me from the first page. It's been years since a book has made me feel like this.' Sally Hepworth

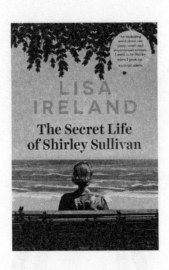

'Elderly. Is that how the world sees me? A helpless little old lady? If only they knew. I allow myself a small smirk.'

When Shirley Sullivan signs her 83-year-old husband, Frank, out of the Sunset Lodge Nursing Home, she has no intention of bringing him back.

For fifty-seven years the couple has shared love, happiness and heartbreak. And while Frank may not know who his wife is these days, he knows he wants to go home. Back to the beach where they met in the early 1960s.

So Shirley enacts an elaborate plan to evade the authorities – and their furious daughter, Fiona – to give Frank the holiday he'd always dreamt of.

And, in doing so, perhaps Shirley can make amends for a lifelong guilty secret . . .

'An endearing novel about one gutsy, smart and inspirational woman. I want to be Shirley when I grow up.'
Rachael Johns

'Beautiful, breathtaking and heart-wrenching.'
Australian Women's Weekly

Powered by Penguin

Looking for more great reads, exclusive content and book giveaways?
Subscribe to our weekly newsletter.

Scan the QR code or visit penguin.com.au/signup